Avon Books by Leland Frederick Cooley

CALIFORNIA	*15941*	*$1.75*
GOD'S HIGH TABLE	*17913*	*$1.50*

Where better paperbacks are sold, or directly from the publisher. Include 15¢ per copy for mailing; allow three weeks for delivery.

Avon Books, Mail Order Dept., 250 West 55th Street, New York, N. Y. 10019

THE RUN FOR HOME

LELAND FREDERICK COOLEY

AVON
PUBLISHERS OF BARD, CAMELOT, DISCUS, EQUINOX AND FLARE BOOKS

AVON BOOKS
A division of
The Hearst Corporation
959 Eighth Avenue
New York, New York 10019

Copyright © 1958 by Leland Frederick Cooley.
Published by arrangement with Doubleday & Company, Inc.
Library of Congress Catalog Card Number: 58-12034.

First Avon Printing, March, 1969
Third Printing

AVON TRADEMARK REG. U.S. PAT. OFF. AND
FOREIGN COUNTRIES, REGISTERED TRADEMARK—
MARCA REGISTRADA, HECHO EN CHICAGO, U.S.A.

Printed in Canada

FOREWORD

If this novel is ofttimes brutal and depraved . . . and sometimes, I hope, touched with gentleness and beauty, it is because brutality and depravity were the dominant forces affecting the lives of those of us who lived in the fo'c'sles of tramp steamers during the Merchant Service's lowest ebb in the mid-1920s. Gentleness and beauty were the infrequent solace, for those with eyes to behold it, that made bearable the endless months of tramping through the ports of Australia, New Zealand, the South Pacific Islands, the Straits Settlements and parts of the Orient.

The men and women depicted in these pages are fictitious. No character bears any specific resemblance, either physically or morally, to the shipmates or women with whom the author has sailed or consorted. They are, rather, typical elements in an impression of the people, the environment, the language, the actions and the reactions of their small and pathetic society.

The Run For Home recalls a way of life that has passed into historical limbo. The life of the brutish and perhaps adventurous Merchant sailor of that era deserves to be recorded in more detail than is found in the economic and sociological studies of the unions who mercifully ended it. The depiction is literal, the frequently loathsome language and detail are necessary, for they make painfully clear the depravity which destroyed incentive in most men and awakened open rebellion in others.

Seamen, such as Jack Hammer, Vic Warndahl, The Sheik and Spots . . . and officers, such as Third Mate Holst and the tragic Second Mate Lars Peterson, have been replaced by a new generation of American born seamen who have brought sailoring once again to the status of a respected profession.

As for the women . . . they will always be the same. In most instances this is a blessing!

Leland Frederick Cooley

New York City
April, 1958

To my wife, Lee, with all my love, for her unbelievable patience and constant encouragement.

To Toni, with deepest affection and gratitude, for believing and making it "happen."

And to my dear friends and shipmates, Ed Larson, Ralph Hutchinson and Dr. Murray Hoffstein, who directly or indirectly shared the years distilled between these covers.

— 1 — "Hey, kid!" Vic Warndahl, veteran able-bodied seaman of half a dozen merchant marines, addressed the frail, heaving back and shoulders of the new deck boy.

Slim was sick. Sicker than he had ever been in his eighteen years of life. His long, gangling body was limply propped against the chain rail on the starboard side of the after well deck. He had hoped he wouldn't be seen by the crew, who were busy securing the forward cargo booms for the trip up the coast from San Francisco to the lumber ports of the Northwest. But the big Swede had discovered him.

"Hey, kid!" he repeated.

Slim rolled his head slowly to one side. His mouth hung loosely open and a thin line of puke trailed off his chin.

Vic looked down at him for a moment, then laid a hand on Slim's scrawny behind. "You sick?"

The boy tried to nod his head before a new wave of nausea racked his body. He was at the most terrible stage of seasickness, the dry heaves.

"I'm gonna give ya some advice, kid. If ya feel something fuzzy in your throat, swallow hard—it's your ass hole!" He clouted Slim on the back with a big paint-stained hand and climbed the ladder to the midships deck. Even the wind couldn't wipe away the staccato bursts of ugly laughter that Slim would learn to hate in the months ahead. It was the laughter of a perverted humor that had made the Swede despised in a hundred fo'c'sles.

Slim clung to the stanchion and rested his weight on the slack chain rail. In between waves of retching he was aware that the cold salt mist, swirling up from the wash, felt good. The clean cold air, blowing toward the Golden Gate from out of the southwest reaches of the Pacific, filled his lungs and gave him some relief. But his eyeballs ached, and when he tried to move them from side to side across the horizon the sickness filled his whole body and the racking heaves squeezed involuntary groans from his throat. Too weak to prop himself against the rail any longer, the newest apprentice seaman on the tramp steamer *Tropic Trader* slipped to the deck and wearily rested his chin on the bony, white fist that clenched the bottom chain rail. He closed his eyes. He was tired, inside and out, from the strain of the horrible illness that overtakes most landlubbers on their first trip offshore.

Slim remembered some of the things his grandfather had told him. The old man had been an officer in the Royal Danish Navy. In the middle 1880s he had come to America with his French wife and retired to a big old house, overlooking the ocean at Pacific Grove on Monterey Bay. As the older of two grandsons, Slim had been his favorite. From the time he was five or six, he and his grandfather used to sit on the big rocks that punctuated the sandy little crescents of beach.

The old sailor would tie a length of cotton line around the young boy's middle and send him into the rough surf until he was chilled. Then he'd dress the shivering youngster and together they would explore the coves for shells and bits of floating treasure brought in on the previous tide. After a while they would rest in the lee of a rock and munch on chocolate bars. This was the time the boy liked best, for he knew it meant stories of wonderful adventures in the old square-riggers that plied the grain trade from the Baltic, around Cape Horn and across the south Pacific to Australia.

He urged his grandfather to tell him, over and over again, of the time he had fallen overboard in the North Sea and was picked up alive fourteen hours later by his own ship. It was a miracle that Danish seamen still recall in the taverns of Svendborg.

Slim remembered his grandfather telling him about his own first trip and how sick he got, and how in the midst of his misery the mate ordered him aloft. He remembered his grandfather's vivid description of climbing up the ratlines as the great ship rolled through sickening arcs, swinging him out over the water first on one side and then the other. A new wave of nausea shook Slim as his imagination easily re-created the old man's plight as a new cadet. He remembered how his grandfather used to laugh as he reminisced. It was a chuckle, gentle and quiet, that wrinkled the corners of his pale blue eyes and tipped up the ends of his great white Franz Joseph mustache.

One of the stories Slim remembered now was that of the young apprentice sailor who suffered from incurable seasickness. Finally one stormy day he could no longer take the agony and hurled himself over the side. Slim knew how a man could be driven to such an extreme. Suddenly the rusty tramp steamer that had seemed like a magic carpet to adventure had become an implacable enemy allied with the heaving sea for the purpose of destroying him. There was no fight-back left in the young deck boy. The ship and the sea had won. If he could survive until they made their first port, he would jump ship, suffer the trip home, and go on to medical school as his family had prayed he would.

His decision somehow seemed to make Slim feel better. He would just have to face being a quitter. But it was better to face that than weeks of vertigo and vomiting on this restless rusty hell. Finally Slim succumbed to an overpowering drowsiness. With eyes closed and with brain and body lead-heavy with fatigue, he was only vaguely aware of the pulsing of the ship's engine. The roar of the wind and the rushing swish of the wash below him blended and blotted out all other sounds.

Slim's body jolted heavily as the bosun shoved him in the middle of the back with his work shoe.

"Goddammit, get up off that deck and earn your money!"

The boy jerked his head up quickly and rapped the back of his skull on the top chain rail. A million needles stabbed his brain and subsided, leaving a cap of dull pain. He turned and looked up into the expressionless, flat Slavic face and ice-blue eyes of the bosun. He had heard about "Boats," as the crew called him. He was a Russian-Finn. He pretended to speak very little English. When he did speak it was in a deep growl, and the words were rolled in a heavy Russian accent. Ivan was well known in every fink hall on boath coasts. The company men liked to see his name on the ship's roster. It meant more work from the undermanned deck crews.

Strong unions, seamen's rights, decent working conditions, good food, and clean quarters were still some years in the future. Now the problem was a berth at the relatively good pay offered on American vessels. The Dutch and the squareheads were cleanest, the French and the Limeys were the dirtiest, with their Lascars and African crews. The Yankees were no bargain, but they paid best: twenty-five dollars per month for a deck boy, forty-seven fifty for an ordinary seaman, sixty-two fifty for an A.B., and seventy-five dollars a month for a bosun. On deck this was good pay, and the seamen would put up with a lot to pay off at the end of a long trip with what they could save, plus the half the captain held back in the ship's safe until the vessel made a home port.

Holding back half a man's pay was not done to insure his security on the beach but to make certain he wouldn't jump ship in some foreign port and leave it dangerously short-handed. Of the crew on the *Tropic Trader,* only five of the forty-five hands were American citizens. The rest were Germans, Swedes, Danes, English, Scots, Russian, Irish, French, and Filipinos. Given half a chance to jump ship in a homeland port, these men would disappear like wraiths, sea bag and all. Under Ivan's impersonal heavy-handed brutality many a seaman jumped ship and forfeited his held-back pay. The word had gotten around that Ivan was a "company man" and that the owners split the unclaimed pay with him and the captains. No one could ever prove it.

Slim struggled to his feet and braced himself shakily against the rail.

The bosun smirked at him. "Whadda hell's your name?"

The skinny young deck boy wiped his mouth and chin on his shoulder, brushed a forelock of straw-blond hair from his eyes, and looked embarrassed.

"Goddammit! I said what's your name?"

"They call me Slim."

"Who calls you 'Slim'—your mother and your fancy school friends? What's your *last* name?"

"Fredericks." The sound was followed by more sour, burning slaver as a new wave of nausea rocked him. The bosun looked on with disgust. Beads of cold sweat stood out on Slim's forehead and an involuntary shudder shook his thin frame.

The bosun grabbed him roughly by the shoulder and faced him toward the fore part of the ship. Pointing overhead, he said, "See that deck up there? That's the boat deck. On that boat deck are fifty sacks of galley coal. If you sweat on this ship, you gonna sweat from working. Get topside and dump that coal in the galley bunker. And be goddamn sure you don't get dust all over the deck!"

Slim looked up. From where he stood on the low after well deck it looked fifty feet to the boat deck. He could see the radio shack and sick bay, which occupied a boxlike structure on the after end of the deck. He could see the big buff-colored funnel with the insignia of the Asian-Australian Line painted in red, green, and black. And he could see the after lifeboats slung inboard on their davits and the thin cable guy wires that supported the galley stack. High overhead he could see the ship's antenna, with its thin lead wire coming down to a large porcelain insulator on the top of the radio shack. As he looked up he could see all these unfamiliar shapes go swinging madly across the mottled background of big white clouds and sky. He closed his eyes and fought off another wave of sickness. Uncertainly, he moved toward the ladder leading up the midship deck. A sudden lurch nearly sent him sprawling, but he caught the polished steel handrail and pulled himself up. Resting for a moment on the midship deck, he looked around for the ladder to the boat deck and saw it running athwartship up the after end of the midship deckhouse. Bracing himself against the railing, he reached the bottom of the ladder and made his way to the top deck. The bosun, satisfied that he was going to make it, muttered something about the "goddamn babies they send us for sailors," and walked forward through the midships shelter deck to lay out more work for the men securing gear on the forward well deck.

Slim stood uncertainly at the head of the ladder. He knew the bosun had said something about emptying coal into the galley bunker, but he didn't know *what* a bunker was, much less *where* it was. He started to move along the after end of the upper deckhouse, when a sudden pitch sent him sprawling against the radio shack door. Before he could steady himself, the door opened and Slim fell into the arms of Sparks, wireless operator of the S.S. *Tropic Trader*.

"And who shall I say dropped in?"

Slim managed a weak grin.

"Hey, you look a little pale in the gills! Come on in and sit a minute." Sparks helped him to the edge of the built-in bunk that served as bed and storage locker.

Slim sat down and turned his head slowly toward the pillow. He fought off a desire to lie down. Sparks poured something out of a small medicine bottle. He gave it a couple of quick stirs with a spoon and handed it to the young deck boy.

"Here, swallow this. It'll settle your stomach."

Slim drank it down and made a face. He didn't know what the medicine was, but it had a pleasant aftertaste of licorice.

"You'll feel better in a little while. I got sick like that the first time I shipped out. It's worse up here topside than it is down on the main deck. The higher you are, the more motion . . . but the better the view!" He chuckled at his small joke. "What's your name?"

"Lewis Fredericks. They call me 'Slim.' "

"You're one of the new deck boys, eh?"

Slim nodded his head.

"I've got a long, fancy name, too, but it's not important. Radio operators are always called 'Sparks.' I'm a radio operator, therefore I'm called 'Sparks,' Q.E.D."

Slim managed a wan smile and mopped the cold perspiration from his head. He kind of wished he could get out in the air again, but he didn't want to offend the first person on the ship who had seemed friendly.

Sparks looked at the deck boy closely. His eyes came to rest on a ring. "That's a pretty fancy ring you're wearing. What is it—a fraternity ring or something?"

Slim looked down at the large square gold ring on the third finger of his left hand. He was proud of the ring but now it embarrassed him.

"It was given to me—by my father."

"Oh, I get it. A graduation present."

Slim shook his head. "No, it's a family ring. The oldest son in each generation gets one. I got this a few months ago—on my eighteenth birthday."

Sparks came over and took the ring between his fingers. It was a beautiful piece of workmanship—a family crest delicately intaglioed into the square gold surface. He inspected the work closer and read the inscription: *Sempre sopra.* The radio operator thought a moment. "That's either Latin or Italian—or Spanish, maybe. I think it means something like 'Always upward.' Right?"

Slim was surprised that Sparks could read the inscription. Although anyone with elementary Latin could have figured it out, he had hardly expected to meet anyone on a tramp freighter interested or bright enough to try.

"Yeah, that's right. The family has always worn a ring like this for as long as anyone knows." Suddenly Slim felt embarrassed. He shouldn't have said anything.

Sparks smiled. "Don't worry, kid . . . a lot of us aristocrats get sidetracked for one reason or another. You may not believe it, but I was once an honor law student, and if you dig back in my family far enough you'll find two honest-to-God bishops!" He chuckled to himself. "I hope I

14

never meet them in the Hereafter—not after three years on this tub!"

Slim eased himself off the bunk and stood uncertainly. He was feeling a little better but he wanted to get out in the air. The stale cigarette smoke in the radio shack wasn't helping his squeamish stomach.

"How did you happen to sign on this paradise of rust and copra bugs?"

Slim moved slowly toward the open door. "I wanted to go to sea like my grandfather. I got the port captain to fix it up."

"He's no friend of yours for putting you on this tub!"

Slim managed another smile. "He said it would either make me or murder me."

"He wasn't kidding! What are you doing up here on the boat deck? Did the skipper or the mate send you up?"

"No. The bosun told me to do something with the galley coal, but I don't know what to do."

Sparks let out a mirthless laugh. "So you've met that charming son of a bitch, have you? Well, at first you'll only hate him, and then after a while it will ripen into a maniacal desire to kill the monster with your bare hands. But you won't—nobody does. He's got them all buffaloed! The miserable, inarticulate bastard!" Sparks was feeling the frustration everyone felt who tried to figure out the bosun.

"There's something about those Russians. They got the ephus on everybody. I don't know what it is. They cut and bleed and die just like anyone else, but they've got everybody believing they're tough as shark hide. You never know where you stand with them—except when they smile. Then, look out!" Sparks pulled a cigarette out of a pack on the small wooden desk that served as his office. He struck a match and puffed hard for a moment. "You want one of these?"

Slim shook his head. "No, thanks. I don't feel like one now." He stepped over the coaming that keeps deck water from running into the interior compartments of all ships and stood with his back to the after rail.

"Wait till I get a sweater and I'll show you where that bunker is." Sparks opened a long locker next to a maze of transmitting equipment that was the ship's wireless station. He pulled out a faded, heavy-ribbed cardigan school sweater on which Slim could make out the brighter outline of a long-since-removed insignia. In the sweater Sparks

15

seemed younger. Slim thought he was probably in his late twenties. He was of medium height—on the slender side —a studious-looking sandy sort of a man with a suggestion of a perpetual frown. The corners of his eyes had a built-in squint, as though pondering a problem. Actually the expression resulted from a mixture of mirth and myopia. He wore a pair of unobtrusive horn-rimmed glasses and a damp cigarette perpetually hung from the corner of his mouth. His shoulders seemed to slump under some invisible burden. Slim instinctively liked the radio operator. He knew he'd found a friend.

"Come on, Slim. I'll introduce you to the mysteries of a coal bunker. And you'd better work hard because it's in full view of the mates on the wing bridges!"

They rounded the corner of the radio shack and were buffeted by the full force of the fresh wind, made fresher still by the forward motion of the ship. Making their way through a maze of guy wires and ventilators, Sparks and Slim came to a small boxlike structure just aft of the big funnel. Sparks removed some wedges and battens that secured the canvas cover behind the coaming and pulled off a couple of small wooden hatch covers not unlike the heavy ones that covered the big ship's holds. Pointing to the opening and to a large stack of gunny sacks, Sparks said, "That's a bunker—and that's coal. Empty those sacks into it. Get it good and full, and maybe those black murderers who call themselves cooks will give you an extra piece of pie! This coal keeps their ranges going."

Slim nodded and gave a halfhearted tug on the hundred-pound sack. The effort made him dizzy.

"I'd give you a hand, but I'm not supposed to be doing deck work. You see, I'm a very important petty officer. That's why this generous bunch of bastards pay me less money than a good private secretary gets ashore. Come on in if you want another shot of Mother Sparks' Seasick Remedy. It'll make you dopey though. It's paregoric!"

Slim managed a smile as the wind pushed Sparks aft faster than he wanted to go. When he had ducked into the lee of the radio shack, Slim turned to tackle the coal sacks. He felt better. The medicine had calmed down his guts, but best of all the conversation with Sparks had taken his mind off his illness. The coal sacks were almost more than he could manage, but in a short time he had worked out a system for leaning them against the bunker, slitting the sack twine, and heaving the open end up over the edge of the

16

coaming. One deck below in the galley the two colored cooks and the Filipino scullery man heard the reassuring rattle of small coal falling into the overhead bunker bin as they prepared for the first evening meal at sea.

— 2 — By late afternoon the *Tropic Trader* had left behind some of the world's roughest waters: the Potato Patch, which lies between the Golden Gate and the Farallon Islands. Slim needn't have been embarrassed at his illness, for these waters have been known to turn inside out some of the toughest seagoing stomachs in the world. The old tramp headed out into them riding high in ballast, showing a good six feet of rusty-red boot topping. Deeply loaded, she would have made better weather of it; but, riding high as a cork, she pitched and rolled like something possessed until the course was altered northward for the Columbia River. Then she settled down to a monotonous roll as she worked up the coast in the trough of the prevailing beam sea.

The bosun and the crew had finished battening down the forward hatches and securing the long cargo booms in their nests and were now completing the same work on numbers four and five holds on the after well deck. Slim was still dumping galley coal into the gaping maw of the bunker. He was black with fine, powdery dust and so was the deck downwind of him, but he felt almost recovered from his seasickness and even just a little hungry. He hadn't eaten since breakfast. His middle was sore from retching, but the idea of a cup of coffee appealed to him. He wondered when supper was served aboard ship. From the sun he thought it must be after five.

As though his thoughts were being read, Sparks stuck his head around the corner of the radio shack and called, "You better knock off and go to the messroom. There's going to be nothing left!"

Slim nodded, beat the worst of the coal dust off his clothes, and started for the after ladder.

"Where de hell do you t'ink you're goin'?" The bosun was standing on the starboard side of the boat deck in the lee of the sick bay.

"I was going to get some dinner. Sparks told me that——"

"Sparks don't run de deck gang. I run de deck gang, understand?"

Slim nodded. "Yes, sir."

"Don't call me 'sir'! Dat's for de officers on de bridge!"

Slim stood and waited. The tightness at the base of his throat was not nausea now; it was anger. The deck boy had made up his mind that he would have to learn to get along with far different people than he'd experienced before. But he was not prepared for the crude sarcasm the Russian-Finn turned on him at every opportunity. He wondered if there was something about his own manner that asked for it, and then he remembered what Sparks had said about the bosun.

Motioning Slim to follow, the man moved forward toward the galley bunker. "What the goddamn—hell! Look at de deck!" He grabbed the front of Slim's blue denim jumper and pulled him close. "You know what you're gonna do? You're gonna swab dis deck clean. Looka dat! So you're gonna go eat and leave de hatch covers off de bunker too? If you're gonna be a sailor, de first thing you're gonna learn is to keep de hatches covered and battened when you're not working 'em! Understand?"

The stocky petty officer held the young deck boy face to face, and his beer-sweet hangover breath from the previous night's waterfront binge made Slim sick again. He wrenched himself free of the bosun's hold and steadied himself against a galley-stack guy wire.

"Okay, okay—I didn't know. But keep your hands off me. Just tell me—and I'll try to learn."

The bosun's ice-blue eyes narrowed. His mouth opened slowly in disbelief, then curled into a cruel line. "Keep my hands off of you? Keep my hands off of you? Why, you fuckin' skinny punk—— I'll teach you de way I want to teach you. I'll teach you like I learned! The first thing you're gonna learn is not talk back!" Slim backed off and tripped over the ring pad that secured the guy wire to the deck, and one leg buckled under him.

The bosun sneered. "Get up, you clumsy bastard!"

The heel of Slim's stiff work shoe slipped on the steel plate as he tried to force himself upright and he went ignominiously down on his rump. The bosun's laugh was mirthless. He hated these bright young deck boys the company signed on in the hope they would stay and become seamen and officers in America's dwindling merchant fleet.

19

They were a bunch of educated softies in his book and not worth the time it took to teach them the ship's work. Most of them would leave after a few weeks and go back to their families, glad to get away from the crudeness and filth of the fo'c'sles. They couldn't take it. None of them would have lasted one cruise on the old Russian or Scandinavian training ships. They would never be professional sailors—just a bunch of milk-sucking mama's boys looking for a few months of adventure.

"Get up off dat deck. Every time I see you, you're on your ass! Now get dose hatch covers back on—den get a bucket and wash down de dust. And when I tell you something, don't talk back or I'll split your mouth open!"

"And one of these days somebody's going to split *your* mouth open, Boats, and we're all going to stand around and laugh like hell!"

The bosun whirled around to face Sparks, who had walked up unobserved. He would gladly have broken the radio operator in half and thrown the pieces overboard. The two had hated each other for years. The bosun would always hate men like Sparks who he felt were superior to him in intellect and station. He particularly hated the radio operator, for he felt that technically their ranks were equal. He was jealous of Sparks' long leisure hours. He was only dimly aware of the fact that the radio man was actually on duty twenty-four hours a day at sea and that even his cat naps were not real rest, for his ears were constantly tuned to the strange hash of howls, squeals, dots and dashes that were the conversations of a dozen nations translated to the international gibberish of the Morse code.

Sparks stuck a hand under Slim's armpit and helped the deck boy to his feet.

The bosun glowered. "I don't give a fuck-all what you think! Mind your own business."

Sparks looked at the Russian-Finn archly. "My business right now is to wander around the boat deck. I consider this my private domain and I resent all the loud talk." His voice assumed the tone of one imparting a confidence. "I think the chief mate does too. He's been watching you, Boats."

The bosun whirled around and faced the bridge. Standing on the starboard wing bridge was Mr. Samson, first mate of the *Tropic Trader,* and for all practical purposes its executive officer. Like most of the officers, he had removed the grommet from the top of his khaki officer's cap, and the wind had blown it forward over the tarnished

20

gold company insignia as he leaned on the after rail of the bridge, facing the stern of the vessel. From his vantage point he could see over the entire starboard side of the vessel, and he had been regarding with some amusement Slim's clumsy attempts to load galley coal. His weather-ruddy face had broken into a broad grin when the tall, gangling deck boy had fallen over himself before the bosun's onslaught. He had watched the bosun bully many a young seaman, but the chief mate operated on the theory of the survival of the fittest. If the kid had anything he'd soon work out a way to live on the same ship with the big Russian-Finn.

Although the bosun had never received anything but the usual impersonal courtesies from the officers on the bridge, he stood in great awe of them. In their presence he was quiet and subservient. To the seamen who knew him for what he was, this abject politeness was revolting. If the bosun had guts enough to stand up to the officers, too, the men might have tolerated his bullying—or, as in the case of some tough bosuns, even borne him a certain begrudging admiration. Ivan, the Russian-Finn, had not one friend in any fo'c'sle in the years since he'd shipped out as a petty officer. Even his old shipmates who shared their cigarettes and women with him while he was still an A.B. found no sentiment when they signed on his ship, thinking he'd be an easy boss for his old companions. Instead, they got the dirtiest jobs and the worst watches.

As the bosun looked toward the wing bridge he felt a wave of fear and guilt. He wondered if the chief mate had seen him lay a hand on the young deck boy. Since the mate said nothing, and he could have made himself easily heard downwind from the wing bridge, the bosun assumed the incident had escaped unnoticed.

"Come on!" He motioned Slim to follow him. "Let's get dese hatches on!" Together they laid the heavy wooden hatch covers in place inside the coaming, spread the canvas tarpaulin over them and wedged the iron batten strips in place. When the hatch was secured the bosun tied the empty coal sacks into a bundle with a piece of rope yarn hanging from his belt.

Handing them to Slim he said, "Take dese up to de forepeak. Put 'em in the tool locker—and bring back a broom!"

Slim took the dirty bundle of gunny sacks in his arms.

"Go t'rough de shelter deck, so you don't foul up de

21

whole midships, and be careful you don't fall on your ass where de Old Man can see you!"

Slim made his way aft to the ladder leading down to the midship deck. Moving carefully so as not to sift coal dust around, he climbed down the steep starboard ladder to the after well deck, bracing his back against the rail. It was rapidly getting dark. Slim paused before the companionway that led forward past the icebox and scuttle butt, the ship's only supply of fresh water. There were no lights in this dark steel tunnel that connected the fore and aft well decks through the center of the midship section. Slim stepped through the watertight bulkhead door and picked his way forward. The deck felt gummy and it seemed littered with dunnage, the broken fragments of cheap pinewood that the stevedores use to level off the various layers of cargo so the top layers will have an even base. Picking his way carefully, Slim moved along the dark shelter deck, which inclined upward slightly toward the fore part of the vessel. The violent rolling made it hard work and it was all the deck boy could do to keep his footing. He got to the forward watertight door and stepped over the coaming. It was the first time he had been in the forward part of the *Tropic Trader*. Somewhere high up above his head the small ship's bell on the bridge sounded three times. Slim had to count from eight bells, four o'clock, to figure out that it was now five-thirty.

As he walked forward toward the fo'c'slehead, he looked over his shoulder at the high, white expanse of the bridge. Slim had never been on the bridge, but this was the magic land he longed to learn about—the brain and nerve center of the ship. This was "officers' country," where only the exalted were at home. This was the land of authority and decision, the land of punishment and reward. This was the land where supermen with mysterious instruments communed with the sun and stars twice every twenty-four hours and pinpointed the ship's position on great charts of the earth's far-off places. Suddenly it seemed foolish and hopeless for him ever to aspire to a place on the bridge. That was not a place for men with weak stomachs whose feelings got hurt at coarse language and inconsideration. That was not a place for a boy who was more artist than mathematician—to whom solid geometry was a fearsome and insoluble puzzle, and trigonometry an insurmountable road block that barred his way to college.

Slim walked forward, stepped through the watertight

22

bulkhead into the dark fo'c'slehead, dropped the sacks to the deck, and felt for a light switch. He found it without much trouble and turned it on. By its weak yellow glow he could make out a confusion of gear. Huge hawsers and cables were coiled down. Large blocks with tackle hanging limp were hooked on the forward side of the steel partition. The stale air was heavy with the sickening smell of paint and turpentine. Taking a long-handled fiber broom from the tool locker, Slim closed the door, snapped off the light, and made his way aft. As he walked the length of the forward well deck he moved slowly, his eyes taking in every detail of the bridge. No one was visible now, but high up in the wheelhouse he saw a faint light. One deck below he could make out simple curtains framing the three round portholes of the captain's quarters. Slim had no idea what they were like, but he had heard that the sitting room doubled as the ship's office and that the captain had a bedroom with a built-in berth and his own private stall shower. He even had his own private porch, the lower starboard wing bridge which led to his quarters. On the opposite side of the bridge, on the same deck level, was the chart room, where the navigating officers worked out their mysterious problems. Here was kept the ship's chronometer, the most prized and protected instrument on board, with the possible exception of the mates' sextants. In the neat pigeonholes of the flag locker were the various signals: blue peter, flown to indicate a sailing, yellow for quarantine and red and white for a pilot. Here, too, were the flags of fifty countries.

Slim had watched great liners and shabby tramps leave through the Golden Gate ever since he was a small boy, and he remembered the excitement he felt when his grandfather had told him how to tell a ship's destination by the colors she flew from the foremast. He instinctively looked up at the truck towering above his head, but the halyards lay flat against the ratlines, unused and tied off tightly. Slim guessed that they would not hoist a destination flag until they had cleared for their first foreign port of call. His bunkmate, an A.B. named Jack Hammer, said he heard their first call would be at Wauna or Westport on the Columbia River. If the rumor were true, it meant a deckload of huge pine timbers. Jack said that would be good. It would cut down on a lot of chipping, scraping, and painting, at least until the deck cargo was unloaded.

Slim picked his way back through the shelter deck and up the ladders to the boat deck. The bosun was shifting

23

some unemptied coal sacks so the stack wouldn't topple if the weather made up during the night.

"Take de goddamn broom and sweep dat dust over into de starboard scuppers. Den get some water in de bucket and wash it down!"

Slim took the big broom and began pushing the damp coal dust and small fragments to the scupper on the downwind side of the boat deck. There wasn't very much; most of it had been blown over the side or down into the well deck, and it seemed to him that the bosun was making a lot of trouble over nothing. Most of the dust was on his clothes, anyway, and he wondered how he'd ever get the denims clean. He'd been told the difference between a good seaman and a poor one was not only how well he knew the ship's work but how well he kept his own gear. He was proud of his new denims. He'd bought them in a seamen's outfitting store on the Embarcadero—a place called the Slopchest. Slopchest was sailors' lingo for the storeroom aboard ship where supplies were kept by the steward and sold to the crew. On long trips you could get gloves, socks, blue work shirts, dungarees, caps, and cigarettes. Some larger ships carried underwear and shoes and even luxury items like peacoats and watchcaps, mostly imitation Navy gear or rejects.

The bosun watched Slim for a moment. "I'm goin' below. When you finish, put da gear back where you got it and knock off."

It suddenly dawned on Slim that at last he'd reached the end of his first day as a deck boy, the lowest form of seagoing deck hand in the merchant marine. He acknowledged the bosun's orders and turned to his sweeping with renewed energy. He was hungry now and, except for a sore gut, recovered from the racking seasickness that would never again bother him during his months on the *Tropic Trader*.

— 3 — Slim replaced the scrubbing gear in the forward locker and walked aft to the crew's quarters. He wondered why they called it the forecastle when it was located under the poop deck at the extreme after end of the ship. He was glad that the crew didn't live up in the forepeak, where the heavy gear was stored, because the motion of the ship seemed to be exaggerated there, especially when she was rising and falling in a heavy sea.

Also there was much more room aft. The *Tropic Trader* was 800 feet long with 55 feet of beam, and she didn't taper down toward the stern but stayed full and wide right to the curve of her counter. This living space was divided fore and aft by a long passageway that led from the after well deck back to the steering engine room where a steam engine, obeying orders from the helmsman on the bridge, pushed the giant tiller bar from side to side. This, in turn, moved the great steel rudder that steered the ship.

Just inside the fo'c'sle another passageway ran athwartship. Off this were the living quarters and the messrooms for the deck gang and the engineering crew, known as the "black gang." The deck gang occupied the starboard half of the fo'c'sle and the black gang and crew's pantry occupied the port half. Most of the space was divided into two big common rooms fitted with double-decked pipe bunks. Normally twelve men would occupy each room. The ship's carpenter and chief water tender shared a two-bunk stateroom just forward of the deck gang's big room. The four Filipino mess boys were crowded into a small private stateroom next to the crew's pantry. Above their heads was the poop deck. Here was the capstan, the rope table, the big spoked emergency wheel, a spare propeller blade, and the potato box. Over this were the bare stanchions and supports of an awning, long since whipped to shreds and heaved overboard.

According to the custom of the fo'c'sle, a deck boy

25

rated one of the lower lockers and an upper bunk on the inside bulkhead, away from the portholes, which were the sole source of fresh air. Slim had taken the bunk directly above Jack Hammer when the A.B. had pointed out that it would be warmer there during the cold run up the coast. Some weeks later, down in the South Seas, this bunk, with the poorly insulated steam pipes running less than three feet overhead, would become unbearable, but for now Slim was happy. A wire had been rigged on which the men hung their bunk covers for curtains. There were no individual lights, just the one glaring globe in the center of the room, but even with the curtain drawn enough light spilled over the top to see by. Some previous occupant had rigged up a narrow shelf with a little raised molding around it to keep personal effects from sliding off. With his head aft, Slim found that the protruding locker shielded the light a bit and made the bunk quite snug.

When Slim walked into the fo'c'sle Hammer was sitting on the edge of his bunk rummaging through a canvas sea bag. "Hey, kid! How are ya?"

Slim smiled ruefully. "I'm okay now, but I didn't think I was going to make it a couple of hours ago."

Jack laughed. "You weren't the only one. That big Swede, Warndahl, had the first wheel watch. He said the Old Man was sick too. Came up on the bridge in his bathrobe and slippers lookin' like death warmed over. Soon as we cleared the lightship he went below again."

Slim squatted down and opened the door of his wooden locker. "If he feels like I felt, I feel sorry for him! Geez, I don't see how those guys can take it on those lightships!"

Jack inspected the soles of a pair of heavy work shoes he had pulled from his sea bag. "That's why I quit the fuckin' Coast Guard. They wanted me to sit out one of those bobbin' booby hatches and freeze my balls off all winter. Not for me, sez I. So I got a job as a streetcar conductor in Portland."

Slim sat down on a raised wooden channel that ran fore and aft along the deck. It was a necessary annoyance, because it housed the cables that controlled the steering engine. "How come you went back to sea?"

Jack winked at the deck boy. "I had a little trouble with the cops." He chuckled to himself. "I got out of town ahead of them with about a hundred bucks in small change."

Slim sat hunched on the deck and watched Hammer. He'd spent his last night ashore with the husky A.B. As a

26

result, Slim felt about him much as he felt about a dangerous dog that wagged its tail. Jack had helped him settle his
gear in the strange surroundings the evening before,
then suggested a couple of bottles of needled beer at a waterfront café on Howard Street. Slim felt uneasy but was glad
for the companionship. It was a long walk from Pier 47
on the north side of the Ferry Building at the foot of Market Street to Howard Street, south of Market. They
hitched a ride on one of the Belt Line railroad cars that
served the waterfront along the Embarcadero. Dropping
off at Pier 7, they walked the rest of the way. Jack had
remembered the beer joint from a previous trip, when he'd
shipped out on the Matson Line. They found it and looked
in through the steamed windows. The counter was lined
with stevedores and seamen hunched over thick-lipped
mugs of muddy coffee.

They opened the door and walked into the oppressive
air of the hole-in-the-wall joint. There were two empty
stools back near the filthy little kitchen. Jack and Slim
opened their coats and shoved their caps back. The Greek
counterman automatically set two cups of coffee before
them.

Jack looked at the man next to him, who was staring at
his cup and aimlessly stirring the coffee. "No coffee. You
got any beer?"

The Greek wiped the edge of the worn oilcloth counter
with a filthy damp rag. "Sure I got beer. What you want
—Eastside or Bevo?"

"I don't mean that stuff. I mean the stuff like I had last
time—the 'special' stuff." Jack waited.

The Greek wiped the side of his hand with the rag.
"You in the wrong place, pal." He turned to refill a customer's cup.

Jack stared at him for a moment. "To hell with it. Let's
get out of here!" The big A.B. slipped off the stool and
Slim followed him.

The Greek moved along the counter, watching Jack as
he walked to the door. "Hey!" The counterman leaned a
hand on the cash register. "What about the coffee?"

Jack reached for the door handle. "Keep it. We didn't
order it!"

"I pour it for you! You pay for it!"

"Give it to somebody else. I ordered beer!" Jack started
to open the door. The stevedore on the end stool looked
up from a paper he was studying. He was a square-built
man in his middle forties. A two days' growth of salt-and-

27

pepper beard covered his weather-lined face. A shiny cargo hook hung from under his faded Navy peacoat. He looked at Jack, then back to the Greek. The counterman waited until Jack had opened the door.

"Look, pal, I don' want no trouble. I just want ten cents —five cents each cups a-coffee."

There was a suggestion of a smile on Hammer's face, but Slim noticed his eyes for the first time. They were like pale blue glass and almost without expression. They looked lighter still against his weather-tanned face. The bridge of the nose seemed flattened and the area between the eyes and eyebrows had the pasty look of scar tissue. Women would find him handsome in a young bull-like way. Slim had seen faces like this on professional boxers—on rough club fighters whose stock in trade was their ability to take it as well as hand it out.

Jack spoke quietly. "Come on, kid, we'll try another place."

Slim tried to make his way down the narrow aisle, but, before he could move, the stevedore on the end stool stood up, blocking him with his broad back. He took a dime out of his pocket and threw it on the counter in payment for the coffee. Then he turned to Hammer.

"It must be pretty rough on this beach when you punks have to start hustlin' nickels!"

The dock worker never had a chance. A left hook and a right cross smashed into his grizzled face and snuffed out his consciousness, as though someone had clicked off a switch. The Greek stared in open-mouthed disbelief. The other customers turned as the stevedore's body fell with a dead-weight thud. None of them understood what had happened. "Come on! Let's go! Quick!"

Jack snatched the door open and hollered at the deck boy.

Standing behind the dock worker, Slim hadn't seen the blows. But when the big fellow went down, he nearly went down with him. Still not knowing exactly what had happened, Slim leaped over the heap of stevedore and jumped out into the darkness. Jack was already running down Howard Street toward the waterfront. Slim had to sprint to catch up with him.

"Whatya do to him?"

"Save your breath—I'll tell ya later!"

The A.B. turned the corner and headed north along the Embarcadero. They ran on a few hundred feet and ducked into a darkened doorway. Jack was puffing. It was hard work, running over the uneven stones of the waterfront in heavy work shoes and thick woolen sea jackets.

"I'm outta shape. I shoulda kept up with the road work!"

They stood puffing for a moment. In the chill night air their breathing made quick little clouds of vapor. Jack peered carefully around the doorway, looking south in the direction of Howard Street. Everything was quiet. The cold, clammy fingers of fog that clutched the tops of San Francisco's sun-browned hills in the late afternoon had slid in from the sea and laid a moist, muffling blanket over the entire city. Through the mist the bright lights of the Ferry Building looked like clusters of luminous yellow thistles.

Slim could hear the insistent trolley bells and the sustained squeal of wheels against steel rails as the cars swung around the loop in front of the terminal. But the sounds seemed far off and unreal.

"I thought those bastards would come after me." Jack reached inside his heavy twill jacket and pulled out a cigarette. "You want one?"

Slim shook his head. "I got one, thanks."

Jack held the light for him and they both took deep drags. After a moment they stepped out of the doorway and walked quickly along the waterfront until they came to the main artery of San Francisco, the foot of Market Street. Streaming in and out of its famous Ferry Building were endless lines of people who commuted across the bay from Oakland, Berkeley, Alameda, and the other well-tended suburbs of the residential East Bay district.

Jack stepped into a corner cigar store and Slim waited outside. He looked into the brightly lighted entrance of the Ferry Building. He could make out the ticket window and the ornamental iron fences that funneled passengers to the proper slips. He imagined he could hear the hollow tattoo of many hurrying feet half running down the wide gangplanks that rested on the blunt sterns of the S.P. and Key Route Boats. He imagined he could hear the wooden squeak of the rub rails chaffing against the diagonal planking of the slips and the agonized straining of the great hemp hawsers secured to the pilings. He could hear the metallic clatter of chains over winch sprockets as the guard cranked up the gangplank. It took no imagination to hear the short, shattering blast of the departure whistle as the great diamond-shaped walking beam started to rock up and down, and he could hear the rush of water as the giant side-wheelers churned up a millrace in the slip.

Slim felt a touch of lonesomeness gnawing at the base of his throat. Across the bay he knew he'd be able to see the twinkling lights of Berkeley. He knew that if he looked up the hills and to his left he could pick out the necklace of street lights along Arlington Avenue. One of those twinkling pinpoints at the top would be the family house on Santa Barbara Road. He fought to keep his imagination from wandering to that comfortable and loving home so carefully furnished in early American. It would be a long time before he could safely let his thoughts off the leash and revisit in memory the warm, glowing house that looked down over the silver-gray eucalyptus and dark green oak that half concealed irregular rectangles of roof laced together with flower-lined walks and bordered streets. He agreed with his father that Thousand Oaks was one of the most beautiful places in the world to live.

As they stood before the great picture window in the new home they had dreamed and planned for so long, Slim's parents saw only the neat blocks in the lower reaches of Berkeley running down to the tidal margin that separated the town from the silty, beige-gray waters of the bay. They saw Yerba Buena Island. On beyond was Alcatraz and, silhouetted against the setting sun, the fabulous headlands that are the pillars of the Golden Gate. And these things were the symbols of a peaceful dream come true.

But Slim's gaze had stopped short at the distant Ferry Building, then searched right and left along the Embarcadero for the irregular outlines of great ships nosed into berths between the towering dock sheds, like live things feeding from a giant trough.

Slim was a part of the peaceful dream his family had struggled to make a reality—an important part. He and his younger brother were the reason for the dream—in fact they *were* the dream—the long-cherished family that his mother and father had planned for. The two sons were the living receptacles into which these parents would painstakingly place the related data of learning, together with a mixture of pride, prejudice, ambition, and responsibility.

Slim's mother was the custodian of the familial yardstick, and her determination to apply it to her boys was simply another expression of the built-in sense of responsibility common to each generation of this family. That there could ever be any serious objection to being measured and molded never entered her head. But there was objection. Born in the secret recesses of invisible genes, it grew as Slim grew, and it began to take the form of rebellion when it was decided that he would be a doctor. The last time Slim had stood before the big window and probed the distant San Francisco waterfront with a pair of ancient binoculars his grandfather had used in the Danish Navy, he knew that his unstated objection to the career chosen for him would soon flare into the open.

This would be no petty petulance—no adolescent disagreement with authority—but a fundamental stand for independence from the past. Slim hated the whole idea of the medical profession. The smell of illness made him shudder and the thought of scalpels slicing into the waxyellow fat of stinking cadavers was completely revolting, even when his father likened the process to that of dismantling a complicated machine to see how it ran. The human engine and the mechanical engine were things that Slim was ready to take for granted. He had no desire to become an expert in the repair of either. And still, such was his destiny that his survival would ultimately depend upon his ability to improvise with both!

Slim lost some time in school which he had worked hard to make up. Graduation would come in a few months. Then a summer of camping in the Tuolumne Meadows with the family and the breath-taking sport of exploring the upper reaches of roaring trout streams born in the high-mounted sapphire lakes of the Sierra Nevada. Then would come the day of decision—the hour of rebellion. Slim had brooded for over a year and at last his mind was made up. The decision weighed all the more heavily because of the guilt it engendered. He knew that his mother's heartbreak and father's uncomplaining disappointment would be the price for taking his choice in open family forum. He knew that a discussion now would spoil all the spring and summer months ahead and would involve not only the immediate family but his beloved grandmother and great-aunt as well. In the face of their pleading logic he might relent for a time and, by doing so, prolong the agony for everyone.

So he quietly made up his mind to turn to the sea for a career as his grandfather had done and, having taken the decision, would keep it secret until it was too late to take any other course.

But the day of decision and the day of action came much closer together than Slim had anticipated. Through

31

a school friend whose father was a member of the Port Captain's Office for the harbor of San Francisco, he learned that the Asian-Australian Line had openings for several deck boys. Slim knew he could not qualify for cadet officer without first entering the University of California, since most of the lines preferred college boys who would train in the summers. Even so, most of the cadet's jobs were reserved for boys whose families had influence with executives of the steamship companies.

It was clear that, if he was going to make the move, the timing would be dictated by opportunity and not by a schedule of convenience. So at four o'clock one Saturday morning, armed with papers secured from the port captain, Slim eased himself out of bed, lowered a laundry bag filled with clothes and rain gear to the front lawn, quietly walked down to Arlington Avenue, and boarded the first streetcar of the new day. In an hour he was on the ferry bound from Berkeley to San Francisco, and in another hour he was walking in the foggy gray dawn, picking his way north along the Embarcadero in search of Pier 47 and the steamer *Tropic Trader*.

Jack gave Slim a fresh pack of Chesterfields, and the pair walked up Market Street to the Palace Hotel and crossed to the north side at New Montgomery. Turning west again, they made their way toward Steve's Bar. Before prohibition this had been one of the most famous bars in a city long famous for its drinking places. But things were quieter now. It had become a repository of recollections, and its comfortable, dim-lit interior was filled with the haze of leisurely smokers whose voices droned in endless narrative.

The A.B. and the young deck boy straddled two tall stools and sipped excellent hot coffee.

Slim offered Jack a cigarette and laid the pack on the counter. "What happened in that joint? Why did you hit him?"

Jack rubbed his knuckles. His right hand was swelling a bit. He looked at it and grunted out a short laugh. "I'm going to have to pee left-handed for a couple of days." He massaged his knuckles thoughtfully. "I clipped the son-of-a-bitch because he accused me of walking out on a check."

Slim looked at the A.B. His feeling for Jack was a mixture of uneasiness and admiration. "Where did you learn to punch like that?"

"I used to fight pro in Bellingham, Tacoma, and around there. I never made it into the big clubs, but I did fight light-heavy main events. I was getting pretty good, but I wasn't gettin' any younger, so I quit." Jack opened his heavy coat and slipped it off. "Want another coffee?"

Slim shook his head. "No, thanks, this is enough."

The A.B. drained his cup. "Here I'm sittin' on my ass drinkin' coffee and what I really want is a shot of booze." The remark was intended for no one. He looked down the bar and motioned to the barrel-bellied bartender, who was obviously one of the original furnishings of the place. Jack indicated he wanted to speak quietly and the bartender did his best to lean closer.

"I know you don't have it here, but can you tell us where we can get a bottle?"

The bartender's expressionless face didn't change. "Sorry, Mac, I'm not in that business." He lumbered up the bar to refill a glass with pale prohibition brew.

"The hell he ain't in that business! He can't keep that pork belly of his going on the thin piss they serve in here!" Jack snorted in disgust and Slim saw the glass-cold look in his china blue eyes—a look that in months to come he would see many times, usually preceding a disaster for someone.

Slim had not been aware of the man sitting on the next stool until he heard a low voice addressing him. "What are you guys looking for?"

Slim started to answer, but Jack gave him a sharp jab with his right elbow. "What's it to ya?"

The weasel-faced little fellow shrugged his shoulders and twisted the corners of his mouth down. "It's nuthin' to me. I thought ya was strangers. I hop bells up the street. I know the town."

Jack pushed Slim back a little so he could talk across him. "We *are* strangers. We're shipping out in the morning and we want a bottle."

The bellhop looked at Hammer intently for a moment, then reached in the pocket of his cheap overcoat. Taking out a card, he wrote a name on it and handed it to Slim.

Jack took the card from the deck boy. It read: "Birch Hotel." There was an address in one corner on Van Ness Avenue, and in pencil across the face one word: "Tony." Jack looked at the card again, then pointed it at the bellhop. "You work in *this* joint?"

The man shook his head. "No. A friend of mine owns the place."

33

Jack put the card in his shirt pocket. "What do we do, ask for Tony?"

"I'm Tony. You don't ask for nobody. When they see the card they'll let you in."

Slim slid off the stool and got out a few coins to pay for the coffee, but the stranger pointed to a silver dollar lying on the bar in front of him. "It's okay—it's on me."

Jack looked at the fellow closely. "Okay," he said slowly, "we'll see ya."

They left the bar, hopped a Market Street car, and dropped off at Van Ness. They walked north for several blocks, until they came to a small four-story residential hotel that seemed almost crowded off the corner by a new automobile showroom. The hotel was marked with an unlit sign that hung from a bracket on the corner of the building. Jack and Slim looked at the front of the place. It seemed like dozens of other such buildings in San Francisco. Built after the earthquake and fire in 1906, they stood shoulder to shoulder in monotonous rows on twenty-five-foot lots. Most of them were gone from Van Ness Avenue now, crowded out by the buildings of the growing automotive industry which had chosen the street for its "automobile row." Precariously perched as it was, the little hotel still looked well-tended and prosperous.

Jack and Slim climbed the short flight of stairs that led to the small, buff-painted porch and stood, for a moment, trying to peer in through the thick, beveled glass in the front door. A coarse lace curtain was carefully pulled across it, screening the interior from view. The overhead porch light was unlit. Jack felt along the lower panel of the door until he came to the handle of the mechanical bell. He gave it a strong turn and waited.

After several moments someone switched on a light in the lower hall, and they could hear the padded thud of feet on the second-story staircase. Suddenly they were flooded with a yellow glow. They caught a fleeting glimpse of a face peering at them through the curtain. Then the light snapped off again and they heard someone fumbling with a lock. Slim felt a creeping excitement and tried not to show it. The front door opened a few inches and snubbed to a stop against a chain.

"What do you want?" It was a woman's voice.

Jack took the card from his pocket and handed it through the crack. Unseen fingers took it from him and the door closed again, leaving them in the shadows. Slim thought for a moment that they were being refused, but

34

before he could say anything the door reopened, this time to admit them.

They stepped into the hall and the door closed behind them. The woman's face showed neither curiosity nor concern. She appeared to be in her middle to late forties, and she had a look of old-fashioned respectability about her. To Slim, she seemed familiar. She was dressed much as the women in his own family had dressed when he was a boy. She wore a tan pongee shirtwaist and a long dark green corduroy skirt that came down to her shoe tops. The clothes were well kept and the woman was well groomed. Her graying dark hair was brushed up softly and pinned in a flat bun on the top. It reminded Slim of the hair-dos in the drawings he admired so much by Charles Dana Gibson.

The woman motioned the two of them to follow her. Turning left, she led them up a carpeted stairway to the second floor and directed them into a front sitting room. She indicated chairs. "Sit down and have a smoke. I'll be back in a minute." She returned to the head of the stairs, doused the first floor light with a turnswitch and disappeared down the half-lit hall.

Jack pulled out a cigarette and tossed the pack across to Slim. He fumbled the match and hoped that his companion hadn't noticed the nervous shake. They sat in silence, waiting. Slim thought he heard a girl's muffled laughter from behind one of the doors down the long hall. A toilet flushed somewhere in the back of the building.

Jack rolled to one side of his buttocks and broke wind. "Son of a bitch! Is she makin' the stuff? I gotta eat pretty soon. My stomach thinks my throat's cut!" He mashed out the cigarette in a glass candy dish that served as an ash tray, and looked at Slim. "You hungry?"

The deck boy nodded his head. "Yeah, I could eat." Slim was over the first excitement of the speak-easy and was growing restless with the waiting. He found the second-floor sitting room depressing. He didn't like the musty smell of old green carpet and the ferns that grew in damp, spongy baskets in each corner, or the cheap, spiral-twisted, opalescent glass cornucopia, half filled with stale water and trailing sickly green tendrils of wandering Jew. He was depressed by the red plush divan, with its back to the front windows, its antimacassars matching the coarse lace curtains; the grained-oak end tables with their ornately lathed legs, and the heavy, mottled green-and-yellow leaded-glass lampshades supported by a pair of dead-eyed pewter cupids. Slim heaved an impatient sigh, got up and put out his smoke. He'd tasted prohibition booze before and it gave him no particular pleasure. Even the best of the stuff tasted like poison. And now here he was with a guy he'd known all of two hours waiting for a bottle as if it were the most important thing in the world. He shook his head and sat down again.

The big A.B. got to his feet, rubbed his bruised knuckles absently, and walked to the entrance of the sitting room. He looked down the hall, saw nothing, then turned his attention to a gray-green eucalyptus-ball portiere that hung across the opening. He fingered one of the odd-looking top-shaped beads absently. "This fuckin' thing looks like it's been here a hundred years." Jack let the beaded ornament drop. It swung down and rattled loudly against the wooden casement. He peered again into the gloom of the long hall. Suddenly his body tensed and he leaned forward. "For Chris' sake!" Hammer motioned urgently and Slim jumped across the room to his side.

"What's the matter? What didja see?"

The A.B. didn't answer for a moment. Squinting, he tried to make out something in the darkened hallway, then turned his head slowly and looked more past the deck boy than at him. He spoke as though to himself. "I'll be a blind bastard if I didn't see a dame cross that hall just now —without a goddamn stitch of clothes on!"

A door opened, the light inside the room sliced across the hall floor and up the wall. The figure of the woman who met them was silhouetted for an instant, then the light snapped off and the door closed from the inside.

Slim felt a little embarrassed at being caught peering. Jack had no such qualms. He stood waiting until the woman walked into the sitting room. He smiled broadly at her. "I thought you'd sneaked out the back way." He chuckled at the attempted joke.

The woman gave no indication that she had heard. She walked over to Slim. Deliberately she took in every detail of his person. "How old are you, boy?"

Before he could answer, Jack broke in. "He's old enough to be an able-bodied seaman—and he's old enough to drink."

The woman turned to Jack. "All right—since you do the talking—he'd better be! How much money do you have?"

The cold look came back in Jack's eyes, but he smiled

36

and patted his pocket. "Enough to buy all of the stuff we can drink!"

The woman returned the A.B.'s cold look, then her face seemed to relax a little. There was even a suggestion of a smile as she spoke. "Sorry I kept you boys waiting. But I had to make sure where you got that card. Did Tony tell you what kind of a place I run?"

Jack's eyes narrowed. "He said a friend of his ran it—and that we could buy a bottle here."

The woman smiled. "Did he say you could find 'friends' here to drink with?"

Hammer looked at her curiously. "No. Why?"

Slim began to feel uneasy. He remembered the girl's muffled laughter down the hall.

The woman seemed relieved. "Sit down, boys."

Jack sat on the sofa with her, and Slim sat on one of the stiff oak chairs to the side. They both waited for her answer.

"We don't sell bottles to take out. We prefer to entertain our guests here in the hotel. Gin and bourbon are five dollars a fifth."

The smile left Jack's face. Suspicion replaced it. He'd been waiting for the hook he felt sure would come in a joint like this.

The woman continued: "The 'friends' will entertain you for three dollars." She turned slowly from one to the other.

Jack relaxed slowly and the cold smile returned. He leaned over to Slim. "How much money you got?"

The boy felt a sudden panic. He had ten dollars and change in his pocket, and it was all the money he had in the world. It would be a month before he collected any from the ship, and then half of it might be held back if they were in a foreign port. In that case he'd have only twelve dollars and fifty cents coming—to last another whole month. Slim reached in his pocket and pretended to feel. He pulled out a few rumpled bills and counted out six of them.

Jack watched him closely. "Okay, kid, we'll split a bottle and you take care of your own girl." He turned to the woman. "What do you recommend—the gin or the bourbon?"

"Take the gin. We got a good batch this time." She stood up, moved toward the hallway and paused. "I'll send the kids in. Pick the ones you want and they'll show you to the rooms." She nodded to Jack. "I'll see you get the bottle. Take it easy—we don't like guys who can't hold their liquor. You can pour some in the pitcher for your pal here." She indicated Slim with an over-the-shoulder thumb and disappeared down the hall.

Slim waited until she was out of earshot. "Jeez, Jack, I'm gonna end up broke."

Jack laughed at the deck boy. "Look, kid, we fell into something! This is great! We shove off tomorrow on that stinkin' tub. At least we get laid."

Slim looked away. He was torn three ways. He'd never been in a whorehouse before. Up to now his experiments with sex had been with neighborhood girls. There was one girl he'd met in sketching class at the Arts and Crafts School, where he'd taken some part-time instruction, who had taught him most. She was several years older than Slim—a small, intense, dark-haired girl with a real talent for drawing and an irrepressible enthusiasm for men. There was something almost clinical about her approach to sex. She had been the aggressor almost without Slim being aware of it. And he had enjoyed being with her. There was no self-consciousness. She made him feel grown-up and effective. But the idea of going to bed with a professional prostitute frightened him even more than it excited him. And then there was the money. He couldn't afford to squander money on gin that he really didn't want in the first place. And he certainly didn't want a three-dollar girl and the possibility of disease that went with her. But he did need Jack's companionship. He thought it odd that Jack seemed to need him.

The husky A.B. looked at the deck boy closely and the smile disappeared from his face. "Listen, you're not goin' to chicken out on me, are you?"

Slim shook his head. "Hell, no, Jack. I'm just worried about the dough. When this is gone, that's it—and it's a long time before we draw any pay."

Jack brushed aside the argument. "Oh, fer Chris' sake! Quit worryin'! If you start figgurin' out what's gonna happen tomorrow, you'll wind up missin' today! Ferget the dough. I'll lend ya some if ye're short. You'll be all right. I got a couple of angles, too, once we shove off. We could be partners. But not if ye're yellow!"

Slim swallowed hard. He felt ashamed that he'd even let Jack see his reluctance. He knew that his life would be hell on the ship if the word got around that he had no guts. He'd seen what happened to guys who weren't regular, even in the comparatively tame society of his high

38

school classes. He fumbled for a cigarette and managed a twisted smile. "Le's go—what the hell!"

Hammer pushed a slow-motion punch at his shoulder and winked. "Okay, kid. Stand by to hoist your boom! Here come the playmates!"

Slim looked down the hall. He hadn't seen the girls coming. Now they were there, five of them, moving slowly into the room. Slim's heart started to pound and their faces seemed to blur. They weren't the tired old harlots he'd always imagined worked in such places. These girls seemed young and fresh. They looked surprisingly like the girls he and Eddie Lang dated on weekends. They were no different from the older high school and younger college girls. They looked the same.

He stood rooted to the floor, looking, trying to separate them into individuals. He was only vaguely aware of Jack, who had walked over and was inspecting them like merchandise. As Slim's eyes traveled from one to the other, a sharp spasm hit the pit of his stomach and his legs felt weak as he discovered that the girls were wearing only the flimsiest lace kimonos. He could see the flesh of their breasts and the smooth skin of their stomachs and groins. He felt as though his racing heart would suffocate him and his head would burst from the blood coursing through it. His mouth was dry and he could feel the frozen, stupid smile on his face, but was powerless to do anything about it.

Jack looked the girls over with a casual, appraising eye and finally settled on a buxom redhead. He inclined his head toward the door. "Come on, honey, I've got something I want you to try on!"

The redhead moved out with a pleased expression and disappeared down the hall. Jack followed, sliding out of his coat as he walked. Slim was alone with the four remaining girls, who watched him with amused smiles. One of them sat down on the arm of a chair near the portiere. Her robe slid open, revealing her legs, and Slim saw a blur of pubic hair against gleaming white flesh as she slowly crossed her knees and took a package of cigarettes from a pouch in the kimono sleeve. She seemed a little older than the rest.

She looked at the young deck boy with the pat smile of a practiced salesgirl. "What do you like, honey—blondes, brunettes, or redheads?"

Slim laughed nervously and shrugged his shoulders. He

39

felt like a fool, like a complete and utter idiot, but he was powerless to do anything about it.

"Blondes, I guess——" His tongue was thick and his mouth dry, but he managed to get it out in a barely audible voice that verged on cracking.

"Well, honey, the only real blonde in this place is Boots." She looked at a girl standing near the door. She seemed younger than the others. She was trying to look disinterested and bored.

"Boots, ya got a customer. Take the young gentleman to your room. And good luck—I think you're going to do the driving!"

The girls laughed. Slim felt the blood rush to his face. He fought off a desire to bolt for the stairs and get out of the place. He felt like running through the night until he was out of the city—out into the country—away from anything that would remind him of these past few minutes. But he stood stock-still—rooted to the spot.

The other girls sauntered out and Slim was left alone with the young prostitute. They looked at each other awkwardly for a moment. Slowly the girl turned to move down the hall. Slim stood still. She stopped, half turned, and looked over her shoulder. He forced his feet free of the carpet and moved after her, but his legs were like lead. Halfway down the hall she paused before a door on the right side, opened it, and motioned him in. She followed and closed the door behind them.

Before they had time to speak, there was a knock. Slim's heart jumped. The young girl turned to answer it. It was the woman again. She handed a jacket to Boots. "Give this to the kid. He left it outside. And here's your share of the bottle."

The girl took the glass water pitcher. It was about a fourth filled with clear liquid.

"Have fun—but keep it quiet."

The door closed from the outside. Boots laid the jacket on a chair and placed the pitcher on a night stand beside the bed.

Slim had a chance to look around. The overhead lights revealed a cheap hotel room. The furnishings were meager, and in the uninspired taste of the period between Victorian and early Grand Rapids. There was a closet but no private bathroom. Slim guessed that was down the hall. But there was a familiar-looking marble-topped washstand against the inside wall next to the hall door. On it was a large white basin containing a matching pitcher. Both were old and covered with a fine tracery of gray cracks. A worn hotel hand towel was folded on the corner of the stand.

The bedstead was wrought-iron rod with brass rosettes connecting the points where the vinelike designs touched one another. It had been painted many times. Under the chipped places, in its most recent coat of blobby white enamel, he could make out earlier layers of pink and blue. The brass rosettes had been splattered but spared. Drab green roller shades were pulled down tightly against the sills and coarse lace curtains, stiff, ungraceful, and graying with age, were pulled across them. To Slim it was a room in which only evil things could happen.

"You want me to leave the light on?" The girl spoke in a flat voice. She was standing with the kimono pulled tightly closed in front, holding it together with her folded arms.

Slim glanced at her, then up at the light. "Yeah, let's leave it on." He hesitated. "For a while, anyway——"

Boots walked over to the night stand and pulled two glasses to the edge. Taking the pitcher of gin, she poured about an inch in the bottom of each. "We don't have any ice. You want water with it?"

Slim shook his head "I'll take mine that way, thanks." He crossed to the girl and took the glass. He smelled it. It wasn't too bad, he thought. At least there was enough oil of juniper in it to cut the taste of the grain alcohol. He tasted it. It was raw and burned his lips, but it seemed no different from stuff he'd drunk before.

He held up the glass. "Well, here's luck." He took a swallow and made an involuntary face.

Boots was still holding her drink. Her head was down and she seemed to look at the glass without seeing it.

"Don't you like it?" He was feeling a little easier now.

She looked up with a slight start. "I s'pose I'll get used to it." She raised the glass to her lips and took a small sip. Her expression didn't change, but it was obvious she was forcing herself.

"Why do you take the stuff? You don't have to drink with me if you don't want to. To tell you the truth, I don't like it either."

Boots directed a mirthless smile at the glass and inclined her head quickly toward the door. "She wants us to drink with all you—you customers. She sells more booze that way."

For the first time since he'd seen the girls, Slim felt something besides his own uneasiness. He had been able to get a fair look at her during the brief exchange. She was pretty, he thought. A real blonde with a peaches-and-cream complexion and a good body that still was more girl than woman. Her hair wasn't bobbed and shingled, like most of the females who followed Hollywood's latest edict. It was soft and feminine. She wore it pulled back and tied with a small ribbon. Slim thought it was becoming, the way it fell down the back of her neck. But it was her eyes that arrested Slim's attention and excited him. They were very blue and lined with long drooping lashes. Downcast, they lent a pathetic quality to the young prostitute, and something inside Slim stirred, replacing the excitement that swelled restlessly beneath the fear and embarrassment. Slim took the glass from her. He placed it on the night stand.

"We'll pay for it—but we don't have to drink it." He reached in his shirt pocket and took out a dime pack of Chesterfields. "Want a cigarette?"

She took one and Slim held the match for her; it shook a little. They took a couple of drags in silence. Slim took another short swig of the raw gin, then sat down on the edge of the bed. Boots stood for a moment longer, then walked over and leaned against the foot of the iron bedstead. She looked at Slim with a forced boldness. "You want me to take off your clothes?" Her voice sounded loud, and the question came like a bolt and struck him in the pit of the stomach. For a moment he'd almost forgotten what the girl was there for. Again his pulse started to pound as fear, desire, and pity fought it out in his tormented middle. The girl stared at him, waiting.

A cold sweat broke out on the young deck boy's body. He lifted his hand to his collar, and the cigarette ashes dropped in his lap. Startled, he jumped to his feet and brushed away the sparks. He looked around for an ash tray, found one on the corner of the dressing table, and rubbed out the butt. The girl's question was still ringing in his head and he was close to panic. He turned to look at her, not knowing how to answer. But no answer was necessary. She was there in front of him. Taking the glass from his hand, she put it beside hers on the night stand, then reached for the towel and patted his glistening forehead.

"The booze makes you warm, honey." She replaced the towel and lifted her arms to undo Slim's shirt buttons. As she did, the kimono slipped open and perfume, diffused by the warmth of her body, enveloped the boy and melted away the fear and the pity. In their place came a pulsing ache that pounded in his ears and blurred his vision. He was aware of the girl's body close to him and he wanted to tear off the confining clothes, but his fingers belonged to a stranger.

Her voice sounded almost gentle as she pushed his fumbling hands aside. "Sit down, honey, I'll do it for you——"

It could have been a moment—or a month. Slim couldn't tell how long he'd been in this strange world. He felt the pillow against his cheek and the rumpled sheet beneath him. He felt the warm body next to his withdraw slowly and leave the bed. He heard the splash of water in the basin and the drip of a wrung-out towel, and then the sudden shock of cold, wet cloth against his perspiring flesh. He groped for the towel and held it. His legs slid slowly over the edge of the bed and he pushed himself upright. The girl stood with her back to him. She had slipped back into the kimono and was lighting a cigarette. Slim reached for it and put the moist end in his mouth. He could taste the raspberry-sweet lipstick and the smoke felt good as he pulled it into his lungs. The girl held the kimono tight around her, crossed the room and slipped out into the hall. Slim sat for a moment, his middle caved in, then slowly rose from the bed and dressed himself. Again the distant sound of a toilet flushing.

In a few moments the girl came back. Closing the door gently behind her, she crossed to the cabinet and tossed the damp towel inside. Slim finished tying a shoe. He felt he should say something, but the words that came didn't seem to make sense.

The girl rescued him. "Your friend's still busy. Finish your drink here if you want."

Slim took the glass and drained the rest of the gin. It didn't seem to bother him now. It felt almost good as it seared its way down his throat and spread warmth through his middle. He picked up the lipstick-smeared cigarette from the edge of the marble top, but the end was dead. He took out a fresh one and offered it to Boots.

"No, thanks. My mouth feels like a chimney."

Slim lit the cigarette for himself. He was glad the girl had spoken. "Are you from San Francisco?"

She shook her head. "No."

"Where were you born?" For the first time Slim saw something other than indifference on her face. It was cold and defiant.

"Look, Junior, I don't want to know your life story. Don't ask about mine!" The girl turned away and walked to the dressing table. Picking up a lipstick, she daubed at her mouth for a moment.

Slim felt embarrassed and angry. He hadn't meant to pry into her life. He thought she would understand that all he wanted was a little small talk to help them over an awkward moment. He reached in his pocket and slipped out three paper dollars. He folded them as unobtrusively as possible and held them out to her. Their eyes met in the mirror for an instant. Then she saw the money. Her body stiffened and her hand clenched the kimono until the knuckles whitened. She closed her eyes tightly and pressed her mouth into a thin, red line.

"Jesus, Mary, and Joseph, kid. Put the damn money on the washstand and get out of here!" Her hands dropped to the top of the dresser and she lowered her head.

Slim wanted to say something but caught the words before they came. Turning, he placed the bills beside the porcelain basin, picked his coat and cap off the chair by the door, and stepped out into the darkened hall. He closed the door quickly, and the unexpected slam startled him. He fought off a desire to run downstairs and out onto the street. Instead, he walked to the sitting room. It was deserted. He looked out the window down onto Van Ness Avenue and could hardly wait to get out into the air. Suddenly he felt dirty, drained, and miserable. Fear came creeping back. He looked around at the beaded portiere, the humid ferns, and the sickly wandering Jew rooted in filthy water and slowly wasting away, as though from some insidious disease. He wanted to get back to the ship and wash—scrub himself clean of the last few minutes—but he knew that nothing would help now. He'd done it—and he'd have to live with himself until time and work had worn away the sharp edges of memory.

It seemed like a long time before Jack came down the hall. He was smiling, but he looked pale and his faded blue eyes were gin-bleary. "Okay, mate, let's shove!"

They loped down the long stairs and let themselves out onto the street. Once on Van Ness Avenue, they turned left and retraced their steps to Market and took a downtown car. Getting off at Powell Street, Jack led Slim to a drugstore where they bought two Doughboy prophylactics. They walked down Market to the Ferry Building and went into the coffee shop. Over mugs of hot coffee and pie Jack mumbled instructions to the young deck boy on how to use the patented precaution. Some of the worry left him. Later, aboard ship, he felt ridiculous as he secured himself in the Bull Durham-like cloth bag that would keep the medication from oozing out into his underclothing.

Slim slept hard the first night on the *Tropic Trader*. The bunk was snug and secure. During the night he was half aware that several new men had come in and stowed their gear in lockers. He guessed part of the crew was coming aboard. In a few hours he would begin the big adventure —his first day at sea.

— 4 — Jack looked at the young deck boy sitting on the fo'c'sle deck. He held up the work shoes. "Soon as we get to port, get yourself a pair like this. They'll last ya the whole trip. You can get 'em in St. Johns or Westport—any store where they sell loggers."

Slim reached over and took one of the shoes. He inspected it, felt the inside with his hand, then set it on the deck beside Jack's sea bag. "I'll bet they cost a lot, don't they?"

Jack dismissed the question with a shrug. "Seven bucks." The big able-bodied seaman continued to rummage in the bag. He took out a deck of cards and a little leather case with four red celluloid dice. He looked at them lovingly, patted them, and put them on the shelf beside his bunk. "Those are my best friends, kid. My little money makers. When we get set on a long run, I'll break these out and we'll get a game going in the messroom. I'm goin' to watch you, kid. If you look smart enough you'll do all right too!" He looked at Slim closely.

The smile on his face seemed friendly, but the boy could never look at him for long. The pale glass-blue eyes had no expression. Not even the night before in the whorehouse, when he'd had his woman and his gin, did the eyes change. They just got a little bleary-looking, but the cold, impersonal watchfulness never left them. Slim thought that Zane Grey would have described them as the "steel blue eyes of a killer."

Jack got up from the edge of the bunk and stripped off his blue denim work shirt. Reaching into the sea bag, he took out a blue knitted Navy watch sweater and pulled it on over his skivvy shirt.

"I've got the eight-to-twelve watch tonight. That bastard of a second will probably make me stand two hours in the forepeak, running coastwise like this."

Slim wasn't sure what Jack meant exactly, but he

thought he knew that the second meant the second mate, Mr. Peterson, and that the two hours in the forepeak meant breaking the four-hour watch into two hours on the wheel, steering, and two hours on lookout. He wondered how long it would be before he would get a chance to stand a watch on the bridge. He got the shivers thinking about the moment when he would first be asked to take the helm and hold the big ship on its course. This was a man's work! A fraction of a turn to the port or starboard, and he could command thousands of tons of steel and machinery to do his slightest bidding! He felt impatient and was about to ask Jack how long it might be. But the A.B. had a sudden thought.

"Hey, kid, I forgot to show you somethin'." He peeled the blue wool sweater up to his ribs and slid his right arm out of the sleeve. Slim noticed the hand was still swollen, but Jack seemed to have forgotten about it.

"Take a look at this shoulder."

Slim got up from the deck and bent over to get a close look. There were red marks on it—several of them—teeth marks, and in some places they had broken the flesh.

"How d'ya like that?" Jack smiled at the deck boy and waited for his comment.

"Looks like somebody bit you."

The A.B. laughed. "You goddamn right somebody bit me. It was that redheaded cunt at the hotel last night." Jack's tone was boastful. "Kid, when you can make a whore holler for help, you done your work well!" He chuckled to himself. "Boy, she *loved* it!" He pushed his arm into the sleeve and pulled the sweater down into place.

Slim thought of his own experience with Boots and he felt like a half-baked amateur.

The A.B. looked at him for a moment. "What dame did you take?"

"She was a blonde. They called her 'Boots.' "

Jack nodded his head. "Yeah. I remember her—she looked like somebody's kid sister. I don't like babies. I want a pro who knows what to do." He took a pack of cigarettes off the bunk shelf and handed one to Slim. "How'd you make out? I was kinda fogged up last night. I didn't ask ya, I guess."

The boy shrugged his shoulders. "I made out okay."

Jack nodded his head at Slim's middle. "You can take your joint outta that bag tonight. The medicine killed everything by now." Slim had almost forgotten about the

47

Doughboy. He was glad that Jack had told him about the prophylactic, but he'd be glad to get rid of it too.

"Hey, did you get any food?" The A.B. suddenly remembered he hadn't seen the kid at the mess table.

"No, not yet. I guess I didn't want anything but coffee until now."

"Go stick yer head in the pantry. There's some plain cake there. It tastes like cornbread but it's filling."

The idea appealed to Slim. "Thanks. You want some?"

"Naw, kid. I'm full. I'll get some when I come off watch at midnight."

Slim went to the pantry and stepped inside over the low coaming. It faced forward out on the well deck and was ventilated by one porthole. The opening was secured by the heavy round glass plate, and the dogs that locked it tightly were caked with paint, as though they hadn't been opened for years. He lifted the lid of a breadbox-like container and discovered the cake. It had been cut into four-inch squares. The boy took two of them and closed the cover. Next he took one of the coffee mugs and pulled a cupful from the urn. It had a strange, stale smell, totally unlike the smell of good coffee ashore. Slim spooned sugar into the brew, added some condensed milk, and took the food back to the fo'c'sle.

Jack had gone into the head. There was no safe place to put the cup in his bunk, so the deck boy went forward to the messroom and slid onto one of the two long benches that flanked the oilcloth-covered table. The table ran athwartship and the outboard open porthole. Not much wind was coming in because it was on the lee side, facing toward the coast line. Slim could feel the steady throb of the propeller and hear the intermittent rattle of the steering engine as it answered the commands from the wheel. Above all he could hear the rush of water as it slid along the rusty steel sides of the tramp steamer and entered the churning maelstrom of the wake. It was a good sound. Slim began to enjoy the monotonous roll of the vessel and reveled in the realization that it no longer bothered him.

The boy was finishing the last of his cake when he heard the hollow ring of footsteps on the deck outside. In a moment the bosun was standing in the doorway, smirking at him. For some reason he felt guilty, being discovered in the messroom alone.

"So you feelin' better now, eh?"

Slim nodded. "Yeah, I'm okay——"

"Sure you okay!" The bosun stepped closer and leaned

both hands on the end of the table. His face was a foot from Slim's. "Sure you okay. Just like all the rest of dem. You don't eat nothin' for the first day, den after dat you eat t'ree times more than you worth!" He grunted in disgust, stood upright, looked at Slim for a moment, then went into the fo'c'sle to turn out the watch.

Slim fought down his anger. He saw Jack go out, bundled up in a sweater and peacoat, with an old Navy white-top stuck on the back of his head. The bosun followed him, and after that came one other seaman whom Slim hadn't seen before. The fellow had been asleep behind the curtain of his bunk ever since he'd been relieved.

Slim knew there were several other seamen aboard but he hadn't met them yet, except Warndahl, whose crude joke earlier in the afternoon had added to the torture of his seasickness.

He finished his coffee and took the cup back to the pantry. Pulling his jacket tightly closed, he buttoned it up high around his throat. From its pocket he pulled a blue knit watchcap and put it on, rolling the edges to make it look as salty as possible. He stepped out onto the well deck and climbed the aft ladder to the poop deck directly above the fo'c'sle. He made his way through the confusion of gear to the rope table.

The great stern hawsers were carefully coiled down on the big circular platform that was perforated like a giant waffle to permit the wet lines to dry more quickly when they were made up for sea. Slim climbed up on the table and curled himself inside the huge coil. It reminded him of the snug sand forts he and his grandfather used to scoop out along the shore. He grinned to himself as he turned from side to side to settle himself comfortably. The action reminded him of his beloved Irish terrier, Tommy Tucker, who, following an ageless instinct, used to try to make a burrow for himself in the shallow nap of the carpet beside the family fireplace.

Scrunching down with his back to the wind, Slim was sheltered and alone in a strange and wonderful new world. The sounds of the wind and the sea and ship blended into the muted background that would underscore the deck boy's adventures for the next year. He wished his grandfather had lived. He wished he could write to him every detail of this new life; and he wished that he'd brought along some of the precious letters that his grandfather had written to him. After his grandmother had died suddenly, the grieving man would hold back the rising flood of loneli-

49

ness for a few hours at a time by writing dozens of beautifully penned pages of advice, experiences and bits of information picked up during the eighty years he lived. And then one day the tide of loneliness rose too high to stem. The old man sat in his easy chair overlooking the Pacific and Monterey Bay. The neighbors saw the milk bottles collecting, and wondered. They found him with his hands folded on the evening paper, looking out to sea. The serene old sailor had gone to live in Fiddler's Green.

Slim pried his hand between the buttons of his jacket and fumbled for a cigarette in his shirt pocket. He had trouble lighting it. He had to learn how to do it with the first match if he was going to earn the right to be called a professional seaman. After a few frustrating attempts, he managed to get one corner glowing and nursed it into a full light. The sulphurous match fumes spoiled the taste but the smoke felt good and relaxing, and he snuggled his neck against the soft warmth of his sheepskin collar and gave himself over to the ship and the cold, starry night.

Off to the northeast he could make out the sweeping flash of a lighthouse. He tried to estimate how far up the coast they might be. They had sailed on the tide at six o'clock that morning, nearly fourteen hours before. At nine knots they would be approximately one hundred and twenty-six miles north now—except that they had traveled westward through the Golden Gate and out to the Farallones before making the turn. Also, Slim had heard Jack say that the *Tropic Trader* would be a "slippery piece of steel" if she could make nine knots! He guessed they were about ninety miles up the coast by now. The light might be on Point Arena. He'd been up there once with his dad and brother—a bleak, beautiful surf-pounded point of land adjacent to one of California's Indian reservations.

As Slim stared into the night, trying to make out the dark silhouette of the shore line, he noticed the masthead lights of another vessel inshore of the *Tropic Trader*. He raised up to get a better look. Soon he could make out the green riding light and in a few more minutes the vessel was abeam. She seemed very small from her lights and appeared to be working her way down the coast very close inshore. Slim guessed she must be one of the stream schooners that hauled lumber from the Pacific Northwest down to San Francisco and Los Angeles.

He had heard about the sailors on these small, rugged ships. Steam schoonermen were the best paid of the lot, because in addition to doing the ship's work at the going

50

pay scale they also worked the ship's cargo loading and unloading. It was not unusual for a man to pay off with as much as two hundred dollars a month—huge pay for an able-bodied seaman in those days. And the steam schooners fed well, too. But it took a real man to stand up under the constant grind.

Slim remembered his grandfather's amusing story of the "barking-dog navigators." The old man had borne a begrudging admiration for the skippers of those dingy little vessels, but he used to say they wouldn't last a week in the North Sea. They were not really navigators. They picked their way up and down the coast line in good weather by running landfalls by day and shore lights by night. When the coast fogged in, they coasted dangerously close in, with their ears turned to the sound of the surf and the shore. They earned the name "barking-dog navigators" because it was said they could determine their exact position by the sound of a particular bark. The skipper might listen for a moment and then say to the helmsmen, "That's the O'Leary dog—we're off Point Cabrillo!" This kind of canine-assisted dead reckoning cost the lumber industry plenty of schooners in the early years of the trade. And many a snug house was built by farmers along the coast from the pine timbers and planks that washed ashore, foretelling another disaster at sea.

The little vessel disappeared astern and Slim suddenly felt the chill seeping through his heavy clothing. He shivered and pulled himself into a tighter ball, but the cold was in his flesh now and so he reluctantly left his hempen nest and made his way down the ladder to the well deck. H looked up forward to see if there was anyone on the wing bridge. There were no lights except the two masthead lights high overhead and the wire-covered lights that lit the midships deck by the galley and the bosun's quarters. A dim glow came from the companionway that led into the fiddley and down into the fire-room in the bowels of the ship. He looked up at the radio shack and saw a light glowing behind the curtains. He thought for a moment that he might go up and visit Sparks to show him how well he'd recovered from the seasickness, but decided against it when he heard the wheelhouse bell strike four times. Ten o'clock—time to crawl into the bunk. Tomorrow he'd be turned out at seven to do another full day of deck work. He'd better get his rest.

At six-thirty the next morning Chico, the Filipino mess boy, stuck his head into the fo'c'sle and announced breakfast. Chico was a fixture man on the *Tropic Trader*. A bright, smiling little miniature of a man from Mindanao, he had learned Spanish and English in a Catholic orphan home, which he'd left a few years before to go to sea. He shared quarters next to the pantry with three other brown little messmen, all from the Philippines. Chico was the most respected and oldest in point of service with the shipping line.

No day of his life ever passed without offering prayers to the Virgin Mary and the Savior before the little shrine he'd constructed on the bulkhead by his bunk. Chico enjoyed a relationship with officers and men alike that was unique in his profession. He had become the mascot of the *Tropic Trader*.

He delighted in turning out the first watch each morning by coming into the fo'c'sle with the top of a pot, banging it loudly and hollering the traditional mustering call: "Let go your cock and grab a sock!" But when Chico called, his soft Filipino-Spanish accent and inflection took the crudeness from the words and substituted humor.

Slim kicked off the bankets, slid open the bedspread that served as a curtain and dropped his legs over the side of his bunk. Jack hadn't stirred below him, so he felt cautiously with his foot for the edge of the A.B.'s bunk and lowered himself to the deck. He had slept in his underwear because of the chill in the steel-plated fo'c'sle.

Pulling on his soiled corduroy work pants, the deck boy went to the head and relieved himself in one of the filthy open hoppers that drained over the side of the stern. There was no fresh water in the fo'c'sle, but Slim had learned from Jack to save some in his personal bucket brought from the scuttle butt the night before. He pulled the galvanized pail from under Jack's bunk. Returning to the head, he set it on the deck and placed the end of a small steam pipe in the water. Turning a valve, Slim let the live steam bubble in until it was too hot to touch. Washing the sleep away, he dried his face and hands on the threadbare ship's towel that was issued fresh once a week, finished dressing, made up his bunk, and went to the mess-room for breakfast.

Two crew members were already seated. Slim silently slipped into place opposite them and helped himself to a bowl of oatmeal from the white enamel pot. Mixing in a generous spoon of sugar, he covered the mush with condensed milk cut half and half with water. With enough sugar it was edible. Chico brought a big pot of coffee from the urn and Slim poured the mug half full so it wouldn't slop over from the steady rolling of the ship. Every few seconds an unusually big swell would start to slide the table setting and automatically hands would restrain them. This constant awareness of dishes, glasses, pitchers, and so on, became a conditioned reflex to a seaman, who could rescue a catsup bottle without missing a mouthful.

Slim ate in silence, except for acknowledging Chico's small joke when he placed a stack of hot cakes before the boy. The little messman had never forgotten the name an ex-Navy seaman had given the cakes—"collision mats"— and from that day on Chico served them as such. They fitted the description. Thick, overcooked, tough, and tasteless, they had just one virtue: they'd fill a working belly and keep it satisfied for a whole watch. The syrup pitcher was a sticky, heavy glass affair set in a saucer and glued to the same by the dried accumulation of its own drippings. The syrup itself was the cheapest available blackstrap that still carried a lingering reminder of the heavy chemicals used to render it. To Slim the combination was revolting but, like the others, he learned to eat—or go hungry.

The man opposite Slim stifled a belch and lit a cigarette. He looked at the deck boy for a moment and smiled. "I didn't see ya in here yesterday. Lose yer appetite?"

Slim wiped his mouth on his handkerchief and grinned ruefully. "Yeah. But it's okay now. I don't suppose it ever gets much rougher than that, does it?"

The boy's hopeful tone made the seaman smile. "Kid, let me tell ya somethin'. That Potato Patch is a pool table compared to some of the water we'll be sailin'. Even on a flat day, the Tasman Sea is twice as bad!"

The second man beside him looked up from his food for the first time and glanced at the sailor, then across at Slim. He was a short, stocky fellow, sort of all squares. Even the gray mustache seemed squared up to conform to the shape of his head and shoulders. His look was one of mild, impersonal curiosity, and the expression on his face betrayed no opinion he might have of his companion's statement.

The big fellow continued, "I remember one time crossin' from Hobart to Adelaide, we hit seas that put green water clear up to the wheelhouse. The spray goddamn near doused the boilers, so much of it was goin' down the stack." He paused to take a sip of coffee. "You'll be all right, though. If you're the type that gets sick easy, you'd still be throwing your guts up today."

Slim's tone was fervent; "I hope so——" He pushed his empty plate back and reached for a cigarette. "I guess I ought to introduce myself. I'm Slim Fredericks, the new deck boy."

The man stuck his hand across the table. It was a big capable hand, callused but as clean as caustic soap could scrub it. "Call me 'Chips'—I'm Hansen, the ship's carpenter." Indicating his companion with a nod of his head, he introduced him merely as "John." The square little seaman nodded jerkily without looking up and continued his slow, stubborn attack on the "collision mats."

The conversation lagged for a few moments and Slim had a chance to study the big man, who seemed preoccupied with something inside his coffee mug. He liked the carpenter. He liked the clean, unironed blue denim work shirt and the clean white skivvy shirt that cut across the base of his neck beneath the open collar. Even the blue denim dungarees were clean—old, but faded-clean from frequent scrubbings. The carpenter looked like a man who was happy with his profession and proud of the work that came from his hands. He might well be, for the ship's carpenter, along with the sailmaker of olden times, was one of the most responsible and respected members of the fo'c-'sle.

Slim couldn't tell exactly what nationality Chips was, but from his name and the sandy blond hair he assumed he was probably Scandinavian, perhaps Swedish. One thing the boy was certain of—he liked the carpenter. Without conscious effort he was quietly analyzing the members of this new society in order to find his place in it. Of the men he'd met so far, Hammer and Warndahl were undisciplined and dangerous. Sparks, the radio operator, and Chips, the ship's carpenter, were disciplined and dependable. The bosun was inscrutable and brutal. John was probably cut from the same stock as the carpenter, only not so gregarious. Slim felt sure he was equally capable. Chico—well, Chico was the catalyst that blended tension and humor into a less dangerous atmosphere as the tedium of ship-board life increased.

As for the others—the men in the black gang, so named from the early days of steam, when the entire engineering department was continually coated with coal dust—the officers on the bridge, and the stewards' department under Mr. Pugh, Slim knew nothing. He'd not even met all the members of his own fo'c'sle, much less the black gang in their adjacent quarters. The ship's complement would not be filled until after their return to San Francisco or San Pedro. In the meantime the *Tropic Trader* would make out with the minimum hands on the deck until she'd taken the cargo consigned to her in the Northwest.

Slim spent his second day aboard the *Tropic Trader* learning to mix soojee. Using one of the galvanized buckets from the paint locker, he poured into hot water half of a small box of Turco, a very strong commercial cleaner. Into this the bosun begrudgingly showed him how to shave half a bar of strong salt-water soap. When the solution was felt between the fingers, it had the consistency of light oil. The young deck boy was given the port side of the midship deckhouse to wash down, directly exposed to the full blast of the wind coming out of the west.

Slim's unaccustomed hands became soft and shriveled at the fingertips within the first few minutes, and the area around the fingernails began to burn from the harsh solution. But he kept wiping away at the white paint on the bulkheads and rinsing the cleaned area with clear water from a second bucket. After a time he began to enjoy the work and took pride in the gleaming expanse that slowly lengthened behind him as he worked his way forward. By lunch time—or "dinnertime" as it was called by the crewmen—he had finished half of the area assigned to him.

Down in the messroom Chico had a bigger job. When Slim washed up and took his place on the bench there were more crew members present than he'd seen at one time before, including a couple of new faces. No one bothered to introduce him, but during the course of the meal he identified the two new men. The tall redheaded fellow with the bleached-looking eyebrows and eyelashes was a fellow called "Rusty." He was an able-bodied seaman in his late twenties. His watch companion was about the same age—a compact, medium-built German named Otto. Neither of the men joined in the conversation to any great extent. Most of the talking was done by Chips, who addressed his remarks to no one in particular, unless he asked for confirmation on some point. Slim listened as the conversation ranged from the food on previous ships to experiences with officers who were remembered with respect for their treatment of the men. The bosun came in for some passing comment, none of it flattering. The ship's carpenter, who had sailed with him before, summed up his advice succinctly: "Do the work he lays out and keep the hell out of his way!"

During a lull in the conversation Slim sought to fill in

his knowledge of the Northwest. "When they load lumber, do they take big ships like this right up the Columbia River?"

Jack answered the question for him. "They take a lot bigger than this tub up the river—*if* they can get 'em across the bar!"

Slim was puzzled. "What bar?"

"The Columbia River bar. It's one of the worst anywhere in the world—if the skipper don't catch it just right."

The carpenter nodded in agreement and his eyes crinkled at the corners as he recalled an earlier adventure in the big inlet.

"I remember one time comin' across on flood tide in a Luckenback ship. There was a bad set to the port when we come between the outside markers. We were in ballast just like this tub and the wind hauled around into the southeast. First thing the pilot knew we were aground on the edge of Sand Island. He used his head, though, and hauled her off tail first with the screws." The carpenter continued, "I remember another time. We came down the river late one night, headin' out for Seattle and Tokyo, and the goddamn ferry from Astoria rammed us. Nobody got hurt, but we had to run for the Union Iron Works in Oakland to get repaired. When we crossed the bar the next morning, you couldn't get a bet that we'd make it without trouble. That was the kind of luck we were havin'."

Slim waited to see if Chips would finish the story, but the carpenter took another mouthful of pork and fried potatoes.

"What happened, Chips, did you make it?"

The carpenter struggled to swallow the great wad of food. "Hell, no, kid—we all drowned!" He laughed and the other seamen joined in as Slim flushed with embarrassment. The carpenter washed the remainder of the food down with a swallow of coffee and looked at the deck boy. "We got over all right, Slim." His tone was gentle, as though he regretted the joke at the youngster's expense. "But I'll tell you one thing. If a pilot don't know his business he can bust a ship right in half on that bar. You'll see why when we go over in ballast—though it won't be so bad goin' in as comin' out."

In Slim's mind the Columbia River bar was assuming the proportions of a gigantic maelstrom and deadly obstacle course that taxed the cunning and resources of every pilot and shipmaster who dared to cross it. For some reason he half remembered the words of an old hymn he'd

56

heard at Sunday services in the little schoolhouse up on the northern California ranch. He could see again the Moses-like visage of bearded Farmer Goodheart as he led the little congregation in the hymn, accompanied at the pedal organ by his spinster daughter. Slim remembered the gilt-edged hymnal resting in the huge, knobby, workman hands of the lay preacher and he could still hear the clarion voice, devoid of melody but filled with fervor. bellowing above all the others Tennyson's immortal words:

Twilight and evening bell, And after that the dark.
And may there be no sadness of farewell, When I embark.
For though from out our bourne of time and place,
The flood may bear me far,
I hope to see my Pilot face to face
When I have crossed the bar.

— 5 — The *Tropic Trader* arrived off the mouth of the Columbia River late in the afternoon of the third day. The weather was cold and crystal clear. All that day Slim had been excited by the coast line that was clearly visible off the starboard side of the vessel. He had often heard his aunt Josephine and uncle Otis talk of the beautiful scenery along the pine-clad coast line. Ever since the first automobile roads had opened up the country along the Pacific coast line, they had packed the little pickup truck to the groaning point with camping equipment, prospecting tools, and fishing gear. Each summer they would wander at will after the crops were in, sight-seeing, sniping for gold in the bedrock crevasses along the roaring streams that tumbled into the ocean from the snow-fed lakes of the Coast Range, and fishing in the surf. To mountain and valley people the Pacific shore line was the edge of a huge piscatorial grab bag from which one could pull priceless delicacies for the big iron frying pan.

From the midship deck of the freighter he could see in panorama what his aunt and uncle had seen and explored in detail, and he hoped that one day he could share such an adventure with them too. But for now a greater adventure lay ahead.

He felt the throbbing of the propeller shaft slow down to half speed in answer to a command from the bridge. He and Jack leaned on the midship cap rail, each with a foot hooked over the lower pipe. The A.B. smoked thoughtfully and let his eyes rove along the stretch of water between the *Tropic Trader* and the coast line. "We oughta be pickin' up that pilot boat pretty quick."

Slim had forgotten that part of his new adventure would be watching the hazardous business of taking aboard the skilled bar and harbor pilots from their cockleshell craft bobbing alongside the towering black steel plates of the freighter. He could well imagine the problem—even in a fairly calm sea, such as the one they were easing through at the moment.

Jack flipped the glowing butt over the side and the wind gave it an erratic ride to oblivion. "Pickin' up the pilot's not so bad as *dropping* him. In a choppy sea it takes a good hand on the helm of the pilot boat to keep him from bashing the sides in—and one mistake in timing when the Old Man drops off the ladder can put him in the hospital —or maybe the morgue. They earn their dough—those guys."

Slim thought they had dropped a pilot outside the Golden Gate the morning they left San Francisco, but he had been too sick to care. Now he wished he'd seen the delicate maneuver.

Jack looked at his cheap wrist watch. "I got the wheel in ten minuges. I'm going to get some java." He straightened up and buttoned his pea jacket at the throat.

"Jack, will you be on the wheel when we pick up the pilot?" Slim wished with all his heart that there was some way he could be on the bridge to watch the whole operation.

"Yeah—but there's nothin' to it. Just do what the Old Man tells ya—*when* he tells ya—and ya got no problems. Most of the bar pilots are quiet guys. It's an old story to them."

"Boy, do I wish I could be up on that bridge!"

Jack looked at Slim and laughed. "You gotta get some more whiskers in this man's outfit, kid! You're smart— you'll get up there soon enough. Relax!" He pulled the soiled white hat securely down over one eyebrow and headed aft to the pantry.

Slim picked up the soojee bucket and moved along the starboard bulkhead to begin anew the endless job of cleaning. He was busy at work when Jack returned on his way to relieve the wheel.

"That's Tillamook Head off the quarter, kid. Another forty-five minutes and we should see the pilot boat. You oughta be off watch by then. We'll pick him up on this side. You'll see the whole show." The A.B. continued forward and climbed the ladder to the upper wing bridge. The ship's bell struck eight times just as Jack disappeared into the wheelhouse.

Slim wrung out a worn soojee rag and walked to the rail. He decided to work on the stanchions amidships so he wouldn't miss anything. He had just got started when the bosun came out of his stateroom a few feet farther

59

forward. Slim didn't know he was there until he heard the familiar guttural growl.

"What the hell you doin'?"

The deck boy was standing on the lower pipe of the ship's rail, clinging to one of the stanchions that supported the boatdeck overhead. Reaching up, he was wiping the top of the support. When he heard the bosun's question he stepped down quickly, but before he could answer, the Russian-Finn fired another question.

"Why you soojee da stanchions? What's da matter wid da bulkhead? You finished with it?" He turned and looked at the half-washed paint. "You goddamn punks! Don't you speak English? Don't you hear me tell you to soojee da starboard side like you do de portside? You t'ink I'm kiddin'?"

Slim felt guilty. He knew the bosun was right and he was angry with himself for being so stupid. He couldn't think of any excuse for leaving the work on the bulkhead half finished, so he decided to take the abuse in silence. He bent over to pick up the bucket of dirty gray solution, but the bosun caught his arm and straightened him up again. This was the second time the Russian-Finn had laid a hand on him. Slim felt the cold fury start in his middle and run through his limbs. The color drained from his face and his mouth pulled to a hard, straight line.

The bosun let his grip relax and laughed. "So you don't like to take orders, is dat it?"

Slim's face felt numb. His jaw locked shut, but he knew the bosun could see the anger in his eyes. This time it was not the hurt surprise that followed the encounter on the boatdeck when he was stowing galley coal. He had been right then. He'd done nothing more than follow a suggestion given him by Sparks. Technically the radio operator had no business interfering with deck work ordered by the bosun, but common decency dictated enough consideration of the new deck boy to permit him a much-needed meal. Common decency and the bosun were total strangers. But this time Slim was wrong and the bosun was right. Slim knew he had to stand and take the stream of guttural abuse he felt sure was coming. But to take physical abuse without striking back was something else.

"Answer me, you goddamn young bastard! You don't like to take orders and you don't like people to touch you. You don't want no dirty hands on your nice clean upper-class skin, is dat it? Answer me, you fuckin' punk!"

Slim felt a roaring rage building up in his throat. His

60

arms ached with the desire to hit. His eyes focused like two burning glasses on the bosun's ugly mouth. His ears heard none of the filthy challenge, just the roar of blood pounding in his head and a voiceless command that said, over and over again, "Smash that mouth shut—rip it to a bloody pulp—do anything to turn off that smirking stream of abuse. Never mind what will happen to you. Anything will be better than more of this. Go on, hit him! Hit him! *Hit him!*"

"All right! All right! What's going on here, Boats?"

The bosun's mouth opened in surprise as he turned to face Third Mate Holst. Fourth in command, including the captain, the mate was not too well known on the Pacific Coast in recent years, but his reputation was a legend. He was one of the few officers in the Merchant Marine whom the bosun respected completely. He had never sailed with him, but he'd heard Holst's incredible story recounted a hundred times by as many admiring seamen who had sailed aboard ships on which the mate had served in every capacity, including master.

The bosun forced a smile to hide his surprise. He indicated Slim with a jerk of his thumb. "The kid don't understand English too good. I'm just gettin' him squared away."

Holst glanced at the deck boy and back at the bosun. "You don't speak English too good yourself, Boats. Maybe he doesn't understand *you.*"

If anyone else had questioned his facility with the language, the bosun would have been outraged, but he chose to feel there was nothing personal in the third mate's observation.

"He understands okay." The bosun leveled a cold look at Slim, then turned back to Holst. "He understands plenty. He just don't like orders!"

As the bosun spoke, Holst inspected the young apprentice seaman from head to toe. His eyes came to rest on Slim's face and he saw that some of the anger had subsided. "Is that right, son?"

The deck boy shook his head. "No, sir. I know how to take orders, sir. I just don't like to be jerked around."

The bosun's mouth tightened into a thin-lipped smile, and a suggestion of a smile crinkled the corners of the mate's gray-green eyes.

"Most of us don't. What happened?"

The bosun opened his mouth to start an explanation,

61

even though the question had been directed at the deck boy.

Holst cut him off. "Let the boy talk. What happened?"

Slim compressed his lips and looked at the deck for a moment. His mouth felt dry and he could feel his heart laboring under the load of repressed anger. The mate stood silently, the short, ever-present butt of a cigarette wedged firmly into the corner of his partly opened mouth.

Slim managed to control his voice. "It was my fault, sir. I was told to soojee the bulkhead here but I wanted to see the pilot boat, so I went to work on the rail and stanchions."

The bosun smirked. "He t'inks he's on a sight-seein' cruise!"

"Never mind, Boats!" Holst removed the butt from his mouth and tossed it overboard. "Have you ever seen a pilot boat?"

"No, sir. Not that I know of."

"How long have you been going to sea?"

Slim's face broke into a trace of an embarrassed smile. "Three days, sir."

"How long does it seem like?"

The embarrassment was taking the sharp edge off his anger. Slim smiled and rubbed his ear. "Three days, sir."

"Not three years, eh? Well, that's a good sign." The third mate reached into the pocket of his peacoat and pulled out a single cigarette. The bosun began fumbling for a light, but before he could get one Holst snapped a large parlor match on his thick thumbnail, fired the cigarette, and flipped the flaming stick overboard in one sleight-of-hand motion. "Where's your home?"

"Berkeley, sir."

"Why did you ship out?"

The deck boy hesitated for a moment, then decided to answer, even though he felt the truth would probably sound pretentious. "My grandfather was a captain in the Royal Danish Navy, sir. I would like to be a merchant marine officer someday if I can." Slim could see the scorn in the bosun's eyes without looking at him. But in the third mate's eyes he found a look of real interest.

"Have you any idea what you'll have to go through to get your third mate's ticket?"

Slim hesitated for an instant before he answered. "I think so, sir. My grandfather used to tell me some of the things."

"Did he think you had guts enough to make it?" The

third mate's sea-gray eyes crinkled a little more at the corners as he waited for the deck boy to answer.

The answer came without hesitation. "Yes, sir!" Slim looked directly at the officer. He found understanding in the face and a trace of humor—and something that he hoped might be friendliness too.

The bosun snorted in disgust. "He's got guts enough, all right! What dese kids don't have is brains!"

Holst turned and regarded the bosun for a moment, and the look was neither friendly nor belligerent. "Do you think *you* could be an officer, Boats?"

The bosun snorted again and dropped his eyes. "I like the job I have! You can't run a ship without good bosuns!"

"You didn't answer my question, Boats. Do you think *you* can be an officer?"

The bosun shuffled his feet and began fumbling in his shirt pocket for a smoke. Though his impassive face betrayed little of it, he was growing extremely uncomfortable. No officer had ever before put him on the spot in the presence of a crew member, much less a gangling, brand-new deck boy who didn't know his ass from a wind scoop about ship's work! He found a match and lit the cigarette. He took a drag and exhaled the smoke impatiently.

When he spoke Slim was shocked at the undertone of whining defensiveness. "How could I be an officer? In my country we had to work from ten years—even younger— to stay alive. You gotta have money to go to school to be an officer. I never had no money, except what I earn to eat. I shipped out when I was twelve years and I work ever since. Who knows—mebbe if I gotta break den, when I was a kid, I could be an officer." The petty officer's eyes lifted and looked at the mate. In his anxiety to defend his position he momentarily lost enough fear of authority to be belligerent.

"But I tell you one t'ing. I get to be a goddamn good bosun! I get dat way from learnin' how to take orders! I learn because if I don't take orders on the windjammers dey punch my head in. I learn quick! Dat's de way all punk kids gotta learn!"

Holst thought a moment, then inclined his head toward Slim. "Is that the way you're going to teach this young fella?"

The bosun looked at Slim with thinly veiled hatred gleaming in his ice-blue eyes. "If he don't do what he's told, he should get it—just like we all learned!" He jerked

63

his thumb in Slim's direction. "Mebbe it could even make a *man* out of him!"

"I'll tell you something, Boats." The mate's eyes lost the trace of humor now, and the bosun's assurance sank back behind the resentment and fear of authority that masqueraded as respect. "It takes a *man* to admit he's wrong like the kid just did. Now you say you've learned how to take orders. I'm going to give you one now. Get off the kid's back! Give him a chance to learn ship's work. Don't teach him with your fists. Talk to him—he's green. Teach him the names of things and how they work. Whenever a young kid wants to make a career in this lousy, stinking merchant marine, encourage him. Maybe someday these bright young 'punks,' as you call them, will make things a lot better for the likes of you and me! Do you understand me?" The mate watched the bosun's face, but it betrayed no sign.

"I'll do the best I can wid him, sir."

"Okay. And if he shapes up, assign him to my watch when we leave for the Pacific run."

"Yes, sir."

"All right, Boats, get back to your work." The mate turned to Slim and regarded him for a moment. "Kid, if you're as smart as I think you are, what I'm going to say won't be necessary. But if you take advantage of what I just told the bosun and use it as an excuse to get hunk with him, *I'll* break your head before he has a chance to. Now get back to the bulkhead and finish off your work!"

Slim wanted to assure the third mate that he would never take advantage of his protection and he wanted to thank him, too, but somehow it seemed wrong to try to say anything. He started to say the usual "Yes, sir," but before he could open his mouth to speak the mate had stepped back into the alleyway and disappeared into the officers' head.

The deck boy picked up the soojee bucket and moved across to the forward end of the midship bulkhead. Once again he began the tedious task of wiping the paint clean with the burning caustic solution. Through the wide open door of the fiddley he heard the distant clang of the engine-room telegraph and felt the old tramp suddenly cease her throbbing. Up forward on the starboard side of the well deck he could see the bosun and two men rigging a Jacob's ladder for the pilot. It was being set at the lowest point to shorten the difficult climb. The men had barely finished when the pilot boat hove into view. She seemed to

64

be making a big circle inshore of the freighter, a few hundred yards ahead.

Slim swabbed the bulkhead automatically, without watching his work. He saw the pilot boat turn slowly and run parallel to their own course; then he heard the telegraph again and felt the *Tropic Trader* shudder as the big screw turned in reverse and checked her headway. He could hear the boiling backwater washing against the plates and then die down as the telegraph ordered the engine to a dead stop.

Looking quickly to see if he was being watched, Slim moved across the narrow deck to the rail and leaned over. The short, sturdy, black-hulled pilot boat, her sides protected by massive woven rope fenders, eased to within inches of the tramp's rusty plates. The pilot, dressed in an unseamanly gray topcoat and fedora, stood poised in an opening in the stout chain rail. Timing his move with the precision of a trapeze artist, he waited until the little craft rose to the zenith of the long ground swell, then grasped the flat wooden rung and stepped across. Immediately the little boat fell away as the swell receded. With a dexterity born of two decades of practice in the roughest of waters, the pilot climbed the swinging ladder and gained the deck. No one made a move to assist him. No one ever would.

A sudden fan of white foam spread under the stern of the pilot boat and it moved forward quickly and veered away from under the looming, rust-streaked topsides of the old freighter. As Slim watched, the pilot moved aft to the ladder leading to the bridge. The bosun turned and looked up toward the pilothouse. As he did, the deck boy felt certain he'd been seen. He pulled back quickly and crossed to the bulkhead. A feeling of guilt caught him in the middle, and he cursed his curiosity as he wrung out the rag and turned to the work again.

He had been at it just a few moments when the telegraph signaled the engine room to proceed half speed ahead and the *Tropic Trader* moved easily forward. Up on the fo'c'slehead the chief mate, Mr. Samson, stood with the forward deck gang, ready to let go the great anchors in case of emergency. The pilot stood on the wing bridge with the second mate. The big freighter rounded the tall, flashing buoy that marked the entrance of the channel across the bar and headed in along a line of smaller markers. The big ground swells were sliding squarely under her high stern now, and Slim felt her lift and then squat as the rollers moved under her and raced on ahead to break in boiling foam on the shoulders of the bar. From his position on the midship deck he couldn't make out the relatively calm center of the breaker line that marked the deep-water channel. To Slim it looked as if the pilot was heading the old tramp straight into a line of boiling coamers. To the left of the channel he saw something that made shivers of excitement and apprehension run through his slender frame. It was the stark, rotting ribs of a wreck. They appeared to have belonged to an old sailing ship long since dismasted and reduced to a skeleton.

Slim tried to picture what had transpired aboard the little vessel on the day she met her fate. He wondered if any of the crew had survived, and he wondered what he'd do if the *Tropic Trader* suddenly ground up on that bar and turned broadside to the smashing force of the sea. It took very little imagination for the boy to picture the Columbia River bar in a storm. Slim imagined Jack at the wheel, repeating the pilot's orders and executing them with a sure hand. He longed for the day when the great vessel would be under his hand and he could repeat crisply the orders from the wing bridge, "Starboard five, sir! Steady as she goes, sir!" And then the boy succumbed to a fantasy in which suddenly all the officers on the bridge were stricken and he alone was left in command. He could feel the power of authority and the pride of brave decision and, after the crisis had been met, the reward of warm gratitude and high praise from the men whose lives and business he'd saved.

The sound of heavy feet on the midship ladder busted Slim from exalted hero back to lowly deck boy, and he quickly began wiping the paint with the dirty gray rag. It was the bosun. Slim knew that even before his ugly head and belligerent shoulders appeared above the deck level. He paused at the top of the ladder and looked at the boy, then looked up at the bridge. Walking aft, he paused at the door of his quarters a few feet forward of the spot Slim was cleaning. He looked carefully at the bulkhead and rubbed a dirty forefinger along it. Inspecting the end of the finger for a moment he looked up. "You make dat soojee too strong! You takin' da paint off too! Don't be so lazy. Use more elbow grease—not so much soap!"

Slim nodded and began rubbing harder. The bosun watched him for a moment. He forced a cheap watch from the small pocket in the front of his dungarees and glanced at it. "Finish up down to dat door and knock off at five o'clock!"

Slim looked aft to the door. There was a good ten feet of dirty bulkhead remaining. He knew it must be close to two bells already and he'd have to hustle to finish, but he nodded his understanding to the bosun and speeded up still more.

"An' don't leave no holidays—or you'll do da whole side over! Ya hear?"

Slim looked straight ahead at his work and nodded again. The bosun waited a moment longer, then stepped over the weather coaming into his stateroom and closed the door. Slim knew that the bosun had deliberately given him more to finish than was possible to do carefully in the time allotted. He understood also that the bosun would be waiting for an excuse to make him do the entire side over if he could find any places that were not done properly. Slim felt anger and frustration rising again, but he set his jaw and went on with the work. It took about ten minutes longer to finish up to the door. Slim was just cleaning the last of the drippings from the sill and the deck when the bosun came out of his quarters. He walked a few steps toward the deck boy and stood looking at him with a disgusted smirk.

"It's ten after five. What de hell are ya doin' out here now? Tryin' to show de bridge dat you work hard?" He laughed at his own crude joke. "I told ya to knock off at two bells, didn't I?"

Slim straightened out and shook out the worn soojee rag. "It took longer to finish up to the door."

The bosun snorted. "If ya wasn't so fuckin' lazy ya'd do de whole side by now! Okay, so ya finish up tomorrow in port instead of goin' ashore! Now stow dat gear and go below!" The bosun stared at the boy for a moment longer, then turned and re-entered his stateroom.

Slim carried the bucket to the after well deck, threw the gray slop over the lee side of the ship, and moved aft to the fo'c'sle to wash up for chow. He had already decided that he'd eat quickly so he could go topside to the poop deck and watch the countryside along the Columbia River.

All hands who were not on watch were crowded into the messroom. Slim stuck his head in the pantry door and asked Chico for some bread and butter.

"What's'matter? You estomach ees seek some more?" The Filipino mess boy looked at Slim with genuine concern.

The deck boy smiled. "Naw, I feel fine, thanks. I just don't want to miss anything!"

67

Chico smiled with understanding. *"Muy bueno.* Is good!" He knew these deck boys on their first voyages. He'd seen many. He liked them. Most of them were courteous, even bashful; easy to get along with, asking for no special consideration. It was the grumpy old pros, the chronic complainers and the rule breakers—that gave Chico and the other mess boys their real trouble—not these green deck boys. Chico liked Slim and, as the voyage stretched out into monotonous weeks and the food grew steadily worse, he found quiet little ways of seeing that the deck boy got his share of the best there was.

When Slim went up on deck again, it was nearly dark. On both sides he could make out the dark outline of the fir-clad hills. He judged the river must be nearly a mile wide and quite strong, because he could feel the vibration of the great triple-expansion steam engine and the thump of the turning shaft as the vessel forced its way upstream toward Astoria. Up ahead he could make out the glow of lights in the night sky, and in a short time the town came into view around a low point of land. As he looked southeast with the evening sky behind him, the lights glistened brightly and their images shimmered on the dark mirror of the river. He could make out the black outlines of buildings and the shapes of vessels and small boats tied up along the waterfront. The air was chill and clean, scented with a heady mixture of salt, balsam, and a trace of burning pitchwood.

Slim flipped his cigarette over the side and filled his lungs to the bursting point. When he exhaled he felt dizzy, but he repeated the process until he tingled all over. He felt good—alive—and for the first time he felt the stirrings of a strange new happiness. The feeling would grow as Slim grew, but it would be some weeks before he recognized it as the happiness of freedom—the happiness that comes with the awareness that one is no longer dependent upon family for security, but upon one's own courage and resourcefulness. Slim snuggled into the coil of hawser on the big rope table and gave himself over to the indigo and crystal night. Up forward he could make out the shapes of several men on the bridge—probably the pilot and the mates.

Suddenly the throbbing of the engines stopped. Slim sat upright to see better. The *Tropic Trader* was directly opposite the town now, and out of the darkness he could make out a small launch heading toward the freighter. In a minute or so it was alongside and Slim understood then that the bar pilot would drop off here and the vessel would proceed up the river on her own. He went to the poop rail and leaned over. Up forward he could see the dark shape of the pilot outlined against the glow of the worklight. He paused for a moment at the head of the Jacob's ladder, then disappeared against the black sides. With a short toot of its air horn the pilot launch veered away and headed toward the waterfront lights. Down in the bowels of the ship the vibration resumed and Slim heard the rush of the wake as the screw churned up the river and fought to force the freighter upstream against the current.

The deck boy spent another half hour out in the night, then went below to sleep.

— **6** — It seemed to Slim that he'd just fallen asleep when he was awakened by the booming voice of Mr. Peterson, the second mate. "Aw right, you men—come on! Come on now—hit the deck!"

Slim heard the footsteps retreat along the passageway and climb the companion ladder to the poop deck. He swung his feet over the pipe rail of his bunk and lowered himself slowly to the deck. Other men were stirring too. Someone reached up and turned the weak little bulb in its socket and a sickly yellow light filled the quarters. Slim had been assigned to the after gang during arrivals and departures, so he knew his place would be on deck with the second. He tied his shoes with the special sailors' bowknot his grandfather had taught him, pulled on his sheepskin jacket and pea cap and went topside.

It was still very dark, but up ahead of the ship to the east Slim could make out the first pale trace of the new day. The air was cold and sharp and still perfumed with fir, only now the pungent smell of freshly sawn timber was heavier. The men of the after gang were silent, bulky silhouettes as they sat bundled against the pre-dawn chill, waiting for the freighter to come alongside. A match flared and the deck boy could make out Chips, the carpenter, and his shipmate, John. Mr. Peterson leaned against the extreme after rail and dragged on a cigarette with the mechanical precision of a smoking machine.

There was no sound but the steady throb of the engine and the slosh and swish of the wash along the ship's sides. Several hundred yards off to the right, on a road paralleling the banks of the Columbia, the lights of a vehicle blinked intermittently between the trees, and the raucous squawk of a Klaxon horn echoed across the water.

Slim got up off the edge of the rope table and moved closer to the second mate. He spoke to the officer in a low voice. "Sir, what's the name of the port we're going to?"

70

The rhythmic puffing continued for a long moment. Then suddenly a miniature comet tail arced through the night sky and disappeared below the decks.

"Who the hell said it was a port?" The mate didn't expect an answer. "The name of the infinitesimal and unnecessary appendix to the large intestine of the sovereign state of Oregon is Wauna. It was undoubtedly named after some sick Indian maiden who did a one-and-a-half off the high board into the local waterfall to appease the god of fertility." The second mate spoke with the exaggerated clarity of a Thomas Cook travel guide.

Slim felt like a fool for asking the question that unleashed the stream of quiet sarcasm. He thought it was intended for him personally. But Mr. Peterson was never personal. After a few weeks Slim would learn that the second mate welcomed any question that would give him an excuse to exercise his considerable and picturesque vocabulary. He preferred to direct it toward the destruction of a host of trivial and unchangeable things which he seemed to feel had been placed in his path to torment him.

The lumber ports of the Columbia River were among these, for it was part of his duty to see that the dangerous deckloads of timbers were stowed properly for the long trip across the Pacific. He could look forward to a week of twenty-hour days as the *Tropic Trader*'s fore and aft well decks were piled ten feet high with pungent fir timbers a foot square by twenty feet long. The dour second mate was made doubly dour by the prospect. His answer to Slim was born of built-in annoyance for having fallen so short of his mark as to be a merchant marine officer instead of the warlike naval officer he had been briefly during the "war to make the world safe for democracy." Only it never occurred to him that he'd fallen short. The Navy had fallen short in not recognizing his superior talent and insisting he stay, even though he lacked the advantage of being an "Academy man." He'd been the navigating officer aboard a four-stacker in the Atlantic. He'd been a good one. Every skipper he'd served under had told him so, but never once was he given a commendation. These only went, he was convinced, to men with the proper background, like the fuzzy-faced ensigns with their textbook manners and their stuffy attitudes toward tradition. He told himself that he pitied them. To envy them was unthinkable.

To make life bearable the second mate had, insulated himself with an elaborate defense of rationalization that

71

explained away satisfactorily every unrealized ambition. There was, however, one shortcoming that was unavoidable. He met it every time he looked in a mirror. The second mate was ugly. Not grotesque or deformed—just ugly. Well over six feet, he was Ichabodish, lanky and stooped. His arms were overlong and his hands outsized. The long, prehensile fingers were knobby and workworn —not the fine hands of the skilled mathematician who could pin-point the position of the dirty tramp steamer on the face of the earth within an impossible half mile in half the time it took his fellow officers.

From the sunburned collar line up, his face had the look of flesh barely recovered from a second-degree burn. The features were fairly regular. No single part of his visage vied for attention with any other. His nose was only slightly bulbous; his eyes were squinty and blue. His mouth mirrored deep discontent but was not misshapen. His teeth were long and yellowed from the constant stream of cigarette smoke that poured over them. His hair was stick-straight and straw-colored and his eyebrows and eyelashes were bleached white by years of sun.

It was mostly his skin that made Mr. Peterson ugly. Ever since boyhood he'd suffered from an unnatural sensitivity to the sun. During adolescence a ghastly case of acne had pocked his face. In later life the deep pits had become unsightly blackheads. In his futile attempts to keep them controlled he squeezed them and treated them with a dozen ointments. In spite of meticulous scrubbings they often became infected and broke out in boil-like bumps. In time these healed and left irregular patches of dead-white scar tissue. The result was undeniably repulsive.

The second mate cared little for the opinion of his fellow officers and not at all for that of the crew. But he knew that women found him unattractive. They always had. Even in the Navy he had shunned the social activity of the Officers' Club and had avoided facing his plight by studying longer and harder than anyone else. To his fellow officers he became a "queer duck." They didn't accept him, but neither did they laugh at him. They were forced to give Lieutenant Lars Peterson begrudgingly admiration and respect for his remarkable professional ability. They even gave him a calculated sort of companionship in return for assistance. Peterson needed and enjoyed their company and tried with enthusiasm to instruct them in navigation, until it slowly dawned on him that he was the short-ender. Hurt, he found excuses to turn down their casual invitations and kept more and more to himself. He began to read the classics and all the current books he could get his hands on, and in time found a world into which he could escape. But it didn't satisfy him for long.

At the war's end, when he was passed by and returned to civilian life while others, less qualified professionally, were kept on because of their skill at shore-side politics, Peterson relinquished the last vestige of his dream. For a time he wandered around New York. Later, in San Francisco, he found a berth on a freighter running out to the Hawaiian Islands. He signed on as a replacement third officer. His ability soon earned him the berth of regular third and Lars Peterson's die was cast. That he had proceeded no farther than second officer he blamed on the times, and he was partially right. The postwar shipping boom had tapered off. Foreign bottoms were carrying cargoes as quickly and much cheaper than American vessels, and only old-time officers with long company seniority occupied the top posts. And so because he was unable, often for reasons beyond his control, to shape his own destiny, destiny shaped Mr. Peterson. The result was a bright but bitter man who stood by the side of life and hurled caustic-tipped barbs at its passing parade.

Mr. Peterson, finding an unexpected audience in Slim, had no intention of leaving the subject of Wauna with a mere thumbnail gouge. "Boy, I'll tell you something else, as long as you've expressed an interest in this trivial township. It has a permanent population of three hundred, an itinerant population of approximately the same who do seasonal work in the mills, no whorehouses and two of the worst restaurants in the Western Hemisphere."

Slim felt he should say something. "It doesn't sound like much of a place to live in, sir."

The second mate unhooked his heel from the lower pipe rail and walked a step toward the starboard side of the poop deck. He peered into the night gloom that lay low along the water, made deeper still by the brightening edge of dawn. The new day set off in sharp silhouette the pointed lace of pine that trimmed the rim of the darkened hills. Whatever he saw—or didn't see—apparently satisfied him for the moment. He returned to the rail and lounged against it. "If you don't mind walking around up to your scrotum in mud all winter and sawdust all summer, it's paradise!"

From up forward on the front of the pilothouse came

the faint sound of two bells—five o'clock. Mr. Peterson slipped a flashlight from his back pocket and played its bright beam over the big hawsers coiled down on the rope table. "Okay. Let's get these lines ready. We'll be laying starboard-side-to. Gotta heavin' line, Chips?"

"Yes, sir." The big carpenter stepped over to the dome-like top of the steam capstan and removed a coil of light line. On one end of it was secured a weight captured in a braided rope ball.

Under the second mate's direction Slim and Chips and John secured it; then they led the great eye splices that would be dropped over the dockside bollards out through the starboard stern chocks and doubled them back over the lower stern rail to keep them from hanging down over the side. Two lines were rigged and ready: the stern line and the forward quarter spring line. Slim was beginning to know the names of the various hawsers and their uses. He felt a warm glow of pride when the second mate asked for the spring line and he had jumped to pull it off the rope table and lead it to its proper chock.

Chips grabbed the line just behind him and made note of the boy's progress. "You're catchin' on quick, kid. Good goin'!"

Once the lines were made ready, the little after gang had another moment of leisure. It was getting quite light now and Slim could make out the flat land on either side of the great river. There were some open fields that had been cleared of timber, but each house seemed to be set in its own little stand of native evergreens. Off in the distance a rooster crowed . . . and then another and another. The hollow barking of a dog drifted across the open water. Here and there a light shone dimly behind a half-shaded window. A sharp pang of home-sickness stabbed the base of Slim's throat and was gone as quickly as it came.

The river made a gentle turn a bit south of east and the freighter passed a low, timber-clad point of land. Directly ahead lay the town of Wauna—one of the principal lumber ports of the Northwest. From the deck Slim could make out a collection of sheet-metal sheds, tall stacks, a large conical burner, hallmark of lumber mills all over the West, and several long piers jutting out into the stream. On these were piled millions of feet of lumber, ready for shipments to ports all over the world. A part of it was consigned to the *Tropic Trader*.

It took better than an hour for the vessel to work its way upstream to the dock. Captain Jensen issued orders to

Third Mate Holst, who relayed them to the A.B. at the wheel or down to the engine room via the shiny brass telegraph device whose opposite number was located near the throttle control of the big steam engine. Slowly, foot by foot, the *Tropic Trader* eased her four hundred and eighty feet in close. Suddenly a heaving line snaked through the pale morning light and a stevedore ran to it, stomped a heavy logger boot on it, then picked it up and signaled to the first mate to pay out the headline. Across the water Slim could see the thick outline of the hawser moving toward shore. It was an eerie sight in the half light which made nearly invisible the thin heaving line that connected it with the shore. It looked like a horizontal version of the Indian rope trick.

In another half hour the breast and spring lines were set and trimmed to the strong river current and the crews were knocked off for breakfast. Slim ate a big meal and drank several cups of the chicory-tainted coffee from the big pantry urn. The men didn't talk much. They knew that a day's work lay ahead of them, rigging the ship's booms for loading and preparing the big cabin lashings and turnbuckles that would eventually secure the rickety deckload to the big pad eyes riveted to the topsides on either side of the well decks.

It seemed to Slim that they'd been below only a few minutes when the bosun stuck his head into the messroom and turned the crew out on deck. In port no watches were stood. Instead the men worked a straight eight-hour day, with an hour off for lunch and two fifteen-minute "smoko" breaks—one in midmorning and one in midafternoon. Slim was sent back to finish up the soojee job on the starboard midship deck.

Jack came by on his way to the fo'c'slehead for some gear. "What the hell has he got you soojee-ing in port for? The work'll get fouled up from loading as fast as you clean it!"

Slim grinned at Jack. "He gave me more than I could do yesterday, so I have to clean up today."

Jack looked aft, where the bosun was directing the men as they topped the booms and got the winches ready for loading, scheduled to begin at 8 A.M. "I'm gonna give that son-of-a-bitch more than he can handle someday if he don't take it easy on this ship!"

It was the first time Slim had heard the ex-fighter threaten physical harm to anyone. It seemed to him that

Hammer just slugged when he felt the need to, without any preamble.

"I hope I'm around when you do it, Jack. That guy's a pain in the neck."

"That ain't where he bothers me!" The A.B. looked aft over his shoulder once more, then ambled forward and disappeared down the ladder to the well deck. Slim finished his work in a few minutes and was mopping up the dripping when Mr. Holst stepped out of his quarters onto the midship deck. He had a towel thrown over his shoulder and the fresh look of a man just out of a shower.

Slim looked up and smiled at him. "Good morning, sir."

"Morning, Fredericks. How you makin' out?"

Slim stood up and folded the dirty soojee rag. "Fine, thank you, sir."

"Did you learn anything this morning?"

"Yes, sir. I believe so, sir."

"Good! Learn a couple of things every day and you'll soon get the hang of it. It's not too hard and it doesn't take too many brains. If it did, most of us wouldn't be here."

Slim wanted to grin at the third mate's grim joke, but he kept a straight face and waited for the mate to speak again.

"Did the bosun tell you to clean up here this morning?"

"Yes, he did, sir. I didn't quite finish last night."

"Okay. Then finish up—and keep your eyes open."

The last little piece of advice was delivered over his shoulder as Mr. Holst made his way forward to his stateroom on the deck level of the bridge. He tossed the towel inside the open door and ran easily down the ladder to the forward well deck. Slim looked at the bucket of fresh soojee, still warm from the live steam he'd turned into it back in the fo'c'sle. He wondered whether he should start on a new section of bulkhead or follow the bosun's orders implicitly and stop with the area bounded by the doorway. The decision was made for him by the bosun himself, who suddenly appeared up the well-deck ladder and walked aft to where Slim was standing. Apparently he had gone forward through the shelter deck below the midship deck. Slim was surprised. He had expected he'd come from aft if he showed up at all.

"Did you finish dat bulkhead?"

Slim nodded.

The bosun walked close to him and examined it carefully. "Okay. Knock off now and get aft and give us a hand." He turned and moved toward the after well deck.

Slim crossed to the portside and emptied the dirty water over the chain rail. It made a murky gray cloud in the river and moved slowly away on the current. He stowed the bucket under his bunk in the fo'c'sle, picked up a pair of work gloves, and came out on deck. The deck gang was gathered around number four hatch at the forward end of the well deck. Steam was hissing from loose connections on the deck winch that served the two number four booms that sloped steeply upward from the great steel main mast.

Although Slim knew the function of the machinery, he'd never seen it working, and the tangled maze of cable and rope that rove through the big blocks on the booms looked like an insoluble mess spilled over the deck from which no order could ever come. He felt useless and a little foolish standing around with his brand-new work gloves on. He slipped them off unobtrusively and put them in the back pocket of his dungarees.

The deck boy watched and listened and what he heard was a strange jargon—the curious "slanguage" of the seaman working with the familiar tools of his profession. One piece of rope was a "topping lift" while another identical piece that seemed to go to the same place was a "guide." Pulley wheels were "shivs" and cable grease was "crabfat." I-beams were "strong-backs," and so it went. Slim tried to keep track of each item and learn its use, but the work was being done too quickly and the monotonous, half-spoken orders of the bosun were almost impossible for the uninitiated to understand. The boy was glad when they knocked off for dinner at noon. It would give him time to ask a few questions and get things straight—at least some of them.

But Slim didn't eat with the crew. He was washing in his bucket when one of the A.B.'s, a fellow he was introduced to before, named Otto, told him to report to the bridge.

"The bridge?" Slim was startled. "I wonder what they want?"

Otto grinned at him. "Maybe you done something wrong and they're gonna give you piss and punk for thirty days!"

Slim looked puzzled. He'd never heard the expression before. "What's that?"

The seaman adopted the air of one imparting a secret.

77

"That's bread and water in the brig for thirty days." He laughed and moved off, leaving the deck boy filled with uncertainty and a couple of salty new words for his fast-growing vocabulary.

— 7 —

Ever since he had dreamed of going to sea Slim had thought of the day when he would be ordered to the bridge. And now the day had arrived. But the reason for the order—as a matter of fact, who issued the order—was a disturbing mystery to him. He took a comb and ran it quickly through his hair, pausing to put a part along the right side. He glanced quickly at his clothing to check its condition and then started forward. Crossing the well deck, he climbed the midship ladder and walked past the officers' washroom, the bosun's stateroom, and the open fiddley door. He crossed the small deck between the midship deckhouse and the bridge beneath, which were the deep tanks and the small number three hold. At the foot of the bridge ladder he paused, half expecting the third mate to appear.

High up on the starboard wing bridge he saw the first mate, Mr. Samson. He was leaning on the cap rail, watching the men at work below.

When he saw the deck boy he called down to him. "Come up here, boy. I want to talk to you!"

Slim climbed the ladder quickly. He had that same curious feeling of guilt that he used to get when he was inexplicably called to the principal's office. But most of all he felt excitement at being asked to enter the sacrosanct precincts of the bridge.

The first mate didn't wait for the deck boy to climb to the pilot bridge. Instead he met him on the captain's deck and motioned him to come around aft of the structure to the portside doorway that led to his quarters. He opened the screen door, stepped through and held it open for Slim. "Come in here. I want you to do something for me."

Slim stepped into the stateroom. It was very simply furnished. There was a built-in bunk with drawers beneath, a desk that served as the mate's office, a small sink in one corner, with a mirror and chest above it, and a couple of businesslike-looking chairs.

Mr. Samson walked to the desk and picked up an envelope. "Captain Jensen is sick this morning and I can't leave the ship. I want you to take this envelope to the office of the lumber company and give it to this man." He indicated a name printed by hand on the envelope. "He'll have some papers for me. When they're ready, bring them back and deliver them to me. Get it? To me *personally*—here on the bridge."

Slim took the envelope and looked at the name. "I'll give it directly to him, sir, and wait for the other envelope—and I'll give that to you personally—here on the bridge."

"That's right. Did you have any chow?"

"No, sir, not yet."

The first mate reached into his pocket and took out a single dollar bill. "The other papers may not be ready. Eat in one of the greasy spoons, but don't waste any time. I've got a lot of work to do on those manifests before we finish loading."

Slim moved toward the door. "I won't stop for lunch if the papers are ready, sir."

The mate smiled slightly. "Take time to eat—and be careful how you spend the dollar. That's more than a day's day for a deck boy, isn't it?"

Slim grinned at the officer. "Yes, sir."

"Okay, boy. Shove off."

Slim stepped over the coaming and out on the deck. He made his way to the temporary gangplank that had been set across from the starboard side of the forward well deck to the lumber-stacked dock. He rattled over it and headed toward shore. It was the first time he'd been on solid ground for three days. He felt like the world's smallest midget as he passed beneath the great overhanging flare of the bow. High above him hung an anchor, its stock hauled up into the hawsepipe. It was so large, it looked unreal. As Slim passed the cutwater, he saw the draft numbers painted in rust-stained white. The *Tropic Trader* was drawing only six feet of water forward, but the numbers ran up to thirty feet. Slim wondered if she was ever loaded that deep. She was, as he was soon to find out . . . and *when* she was, the sea was disconcertingly close to the low well decks.

The deck boy came to the end of the dock and walked through a high wire gate which let out onto what appeared to be the main street of the town. He looked around and easily located the office of the lumber company. It was housed in a neat white building about a half a block away. He followed the walk along the high wire fence and stepped into the tiny reception office. It was divided from the working area by a small counter and a low swinging gate. Nobody appeared to be around. Slim guessed they might be out to lunch. He thought it was strange they'd leave the place unlocked.

He stood for a moment, wondering whether to wait or go out into the yard and see if the man he wanted might be there. He decided to knock on the counter. His knuckles had no sooner struck the linoleum top than a girl came out of a big vault in the back of the room carrying a small card file.

She looked at Slim in surprise, then smiled. "Oh, hi! I didn't hear you come in!" She was quite pretty, Slim thought.

"I'm sorry. I didn't mean to scare you. I was just about to go out back and look——"

The girl put the file down on a desk and walked over to the counter. "I'll bet you're from the *Tropic Trader* and you want to see Mr. Slater about the lumber list for the manifest."

Slim smiled and nodded.

"I'll bet the chief mate, Mr. Samson, sent you, too. Do I win?"

"Yep, you win. Pick up the money!" Slim laughed with the girl. He liked her. She had an easy friendliness that made the deck boy feel he'd known her for a long time.

"Pick up the money? The only thing I pick up here is splinters!" Then the mock injury left her face and a puzzled look appeared. She wrinkled her brow and compressed her lips for a moment. "You know something . . . I wonder why it is that your chief mate never comes ashore. He always sends someone for the papers. I'll bet he thinks we have the bubonic plague here in Wauna. All the other chief mates check the papers themselves. Funny!" She dismissed the puzzle with a small shrug. "Oh well, sailors are strange ducks, anyway." She shot a startled look at Slim. "Oh-my-gosh! I'll never own the lumber company if I keep doing that!"

They both laughed. Then the girl's manner became businesslike. "Look . . . uh . . . Mr. Slater's out to lunch He oughta be back in half an hour. If he isn't, I'll starve! Do you want to wait for him . . . or come back later?"

Slim didn't have to make the decision. The office door

opened and the girl looked past him at a man who was entering.

"Here he is now. He's back early!"

Slater was a middle-sized man in his middle years. He wore a plaid woodsman's cap and a mackinaw to match. His trousers were tucked into the tops of mud-spattered loggers. He was a serious-looking person who seemed less weather-beaten than most men around the yard.

"Mr. Slater, this man is from the *Tropic Trader*. Mr. Samson sent him for the bill of lading."

Slater looked at the deck boy briefly, then reached over and pressed an inside lock and let himself through the gate into the office. "They won't be ready for an hour. Better come back then."

Slim looked at the big clock on the wall at the back of the office. It was half-past twelve. He could go back to the ship, but most of the chow would be gone by now. Besides, he was anxious to look around the town a little. It was the first time he'd ever been out of California. He decided to wander for an hour, get a sandwich and then come back. "I'll be back at one-thirty, sir."

Slater seated himself at a desk, unlocked the shallow center drawer and pulled out a small pile of papers. "Okay. If I'm not here Edith will give 'em to you. See that Samson gets them personally. Y'understand that?"

Slim nodded. "I got my orders from the mate, sir." Slim turned to the door.

"If you're going up into town, I'll walk with you." The girl was pulling on a bright green woman's version of a logging coat. "You might get lost in this big city!"

Slim made a clumsy attempt to help her with the jacket but he was too late. When he tried to hold the door for her, he was on the wrong side and got fouled up again. She ducked under his arm and stepped outside. Slim followed with an embarrassed grin.

"There's not much to see here in Wauna . . . unless you like lumber. We've got plenty of that!"

"I like it okay. . . . I like the smell of it." They were walking along a moist, hard-packed path that paralleled the road in front of the piers. "You may get tired of smelling it before you get down to New Zealand!"

Slim stopped dead in his tracks. "New Zealand? Is that where we're going?"

She looked up at him with an amused smile. "Do you mean to tell me you don't know where you're going?"

The deck boy felt a little embarrassed. "I guess they

don't bother to tell deck boys very much on the *Tropic Trader*. Some of the men said we'd probably be on a Pacific run, but this is the first thing I've heard for sure."

The girl tried to fall into step with Slim as they walked on toward the main business district a couple of blocks ahead. Suddenly she stopped and shook her head sadly. "You know something, sailor—you've got the longest legs in the world!"

Slim looked at her and laughed. "I'm sorry. I guess I have! Up on my grandmother's ranch the hired men used to say that I traded legs with a shied-poke and got cheated out of my——." He broke off the sentence in confusion when he realized that the bucolic witticism was out of place.

The girl shot him a puzzled look.

Slim smiled ruefully. "Sorry."

They walked a step or two in silence.

"I'll never own the shipping company if I keep doing that!" Slim shortened his gait and she was walking easily beside him now.

"If you *did* own the ship, what would you do with it?"

The deck boy frowned. "Well, I haven't thought much about it, but the first thing I'd do would be to clean up and paint it. Then I'd make myself the skipper, and every trip I'd come back here and load lumber—if *you* owned the lumber company!"

They both laughed at the nonsense. He'd known her all of ten minutes but Slim liked this girl. She made him feel like smiling. He didn't get much of a chance to look at her, but from the quick sidelong glances as they talked, he knew she was even more attractive than he'd thought. Her hair was more red than brown and it looked pretty against the collar of the big green coat. She wore a plaid wool skirt with the same green in it and a pair of short, heavy wool socks over her stockings. Her shoes looked like some sort of woman's moccasins with a fancy beaded buckle where the strings usually tied.

"Well, young man, I guess if I want to sell you lumber, I'd better 'git crackin'!" She pretended to moisten her palms and rubbed them together, then she added, "On fifteen dollars a week it may take me a little while——"

Slim looked at her reprovingly. "That's a fortune, woman!"

The girl's tone was defensive. "Not compared to what sailors make!"

Slim stopped and faced her. "Who told you sailors make a lot of money?"

"Nobody. I just guessed the way they spend it in town, they must make a lot."

"Well, for your own personal information, Miss . . . uh . . . Edith——"

When he spoke her name the girl looked startled, then grinned and wrinkled her nose at him.

"For your information, you make more in one month than an able-bodied seaman. And almost as much in one week as I make in a whole month."

The girl looked at him in frank disbelief.

"I'm not kidding. You know what they pay me? Twenty-five dollars a month—eighty-three and a third cents a day—and all the rotten food I can eat!" Slim was surprised that he'd added the comment about the food. It just came out, probably because for almost a week he'd heard the crewmen voicing their traditional complaints. Actually the food hadn't been too bad so far. The cooks didn't help it any but it was fresh, at least. Slim waited for the import of his statement to sink in, but the girl just blinked in amazement and started walking slowly.

"Holy smoke!" It was almost a whisper. "How do they expect you to live on that?"

A soundless laugh heaved Slim's shoulders. "I'll let you know when I collect my first month's pay."

They walked in silence for a few yards, then the girl stopped him again. "Listen . . . I hope you won't get mad at what I'm going to say, but I was going to let you take me to lunch."

Slim frowned at her and started to say something, but she interrupted him. "Now wait a minute! Don't get your manly feelings all boiled up. I'm not going to offer to buy *you* lunch, but I'll tell you what we could do. We could go Dutch." She waited for Slim to consider the proposition.

He inspected the back of his own hand for a moment, then looked up at the girl. "Okay. But only on one condition——"

"What's that?"

"Only until I own the ship——"

The girl looked at him with mock earnestness. "All right, kind sir. I accept your terms!" She stuck out her hand and he gave it a strong, exaggerated shake. She didn't withdraw it immediately and Slim felt a little tingling thrill run through him. Her hand was warm and soft and seemed very small in his.

"Now then, sailor, since the deal's made, let's find a place to eat."

Slim liked the way she called him "sailor." "Mr. Peterson, our second mate, didn't have very good things to say about your restaurants, this morning."

"Nobody does! But if you know what to order, it's fine. We'll go to that place across the street. A woman does the cooking. That automatically makes it good!"

Slim let the chance go by. They waited for a heavily loaded lumber truck to pass, with its rumbling exhaust, its clanking chain drive, and the loud rattling and slapping of overhanging planks bouncing against one another. She led him across the packed dirt street to a small shedlike frame building. On either side of the door were two large windows. The lower halves were covered with checkered café curtains and in one corner of the glass was a small handmade sign reading: "Home Cookery." Slim opened the screen and pushed the heavy storm door.

Before he could open it, the girl stopped him. "One little detail, sir. I don't know your name."

"Gee, I'm sorry. I should have told you. It's Fredericks. Lewis Fredericks."

She pursed her pretty lips and nodded in approval. "That's a good name. Mine, as you seem to know, is Edith —Edith Morrison. They call me 'Edye' around these here diggin's, pardner." She attempted the deep voice and slow drawl of the typical western gun-toting hero. Dropping the character, she looked at Slim. "Pretty bad, huh?"

Slim nodded in agreement and opened the door. Inside, the place was warm and clean. There was no counter, but there were half a dozen tables covered with oilcloth. It was a workingman's lunch room—sort of family style. The center table was occupied by four men. When Slim and the girl entered they looked up.

One of the men smiled. "Hi there, Edye! Kinda early today, ain't ya?"

She waved her fingers. "Hi, Uncle Ed. Gotta break. The boss took a short lunch."

The man nodded and returned to his conversation.

"That's my mother's brother. He's the mill foreman."

Slim chose a table in the corner of the little room and held the chair for the girl. "Is this all right?"

She gathered her skirt under her and sat down. "Sure. It's the best table in the house!" Slim helped her slip the big green coat off her shoulders and draped it over the back of the chair. He could see the girl's uncle watching them with interest. He said something to the other men but Slim couldn't make it out. The three looked around and smiled at what appeared to be a private little joke.

The girl rearranged the sugar bowl, the shakers, and the catsup bottle to her liking and folded her hands in her lap. "There's one thing I ought to tell you, Lewis———"

Slim looked startled, then began to laugh.

Her eyes opened in mild surprise. "For pity's sake! What's come over you?"

The deck boy forced his face into an expression of exaggerated sternness. "Around these here diggin's, ma'am, they call me 'Slim.'"

She thought it over for a moment, then a slightly stubborn set came to her mouth and chin. "I prefer Lewis!"

Slim made a wry face. "Every time somebody calls me that I feel like I've done something wrong."

"Well, you haven't *yet,* but you're a man, so you probably will! Now then, what do you want to eat?"

The deck boy looked at her and chuckled. He'd never met such a girl. He couldn't get over the feeling that he'd known her all his life and that this was a happy reunion. He enjoyed her humor and her directness, and as he sat across the table from her he realized that she was extremely pretty. She reminded him of the outdoor girls that McClelland Barclay painted for magazine covers. He had often tried to copy them in pencil. The sound of her voice jolted Slim.

"Lewis! I asked you what you wanted for lunch! What on earth were you thinking about?"

Slim felt embarrassed. He looked around the walls for a clock.

"We have plenty of time. Here . . . take this menu."

They ordered a good meal from the motherly woman who owned the place. The food was simple and well cooked, and only a sprinkling of conversation passed between them. When Slim pushed his plate back the girl watched him with an amused smile.

"If you keep eating like that, they won't be calling you 'Slim' much longer!"

The deck boy looked at her, then down at the empty plate. "Don't worry. The bosun'll work it off of me in no time!"

"Tell me something, Lewis. Are all bosuns tough characters?"

Slim finished the last of the coffee. "This one is."

The girl looked at him closely for a moment. "You

86

know something? I've wondered what makes a fellow want to go to sea." She waited a long moment for the boy to answer, then she tried again. "Well, let's put it this way. Why did *you* decide to work on the boats?"

Slim began slowly and in the next few minutes told her about his boyhood with his grandfather and his longing for a career as an officer in the merchant service. He also told her the considerable difference between a boat and a ship.

She listened quietly until he finished. "Well, I guess that it makes sense. I can understand a boy wanting to travel and see the world. Gosh, I've hardly been out of the state. But it must be a terrible life if you ever feel you want to have a home and kids and things. You never know if you're going—or how long you'll be gone. Sometimes you're gone for over a year. I mean for over a year before you ever get to see your folks—or your friends. Don't you think you might get lonesome?"

A curious thing happened inside Slim as he watched the girl and listened to her. He'd felt a pang or two of homesickness in the last few days, but they went away as quickly as they came. Now, here he was, sitting with someone he'd known less than an hour and all of a sudden the prospect of sailing away from her made him feel vaguely sad. He didn't know how to answer and she didn't press him.

"You know something, sailor? I think we'd better get back or old man Slater will dock me half a day's pay—and you'll get in trouble with the mate and just never get a chance to wear gold braid and impress the native girls in Wauna!" She pushed her chair back and got up while Slim went to the back of the room to pay the check.

Before he could take care of it she was at his side. "Don't forget our deal—fifty-fifty!"

Slim started to protest, but she cut him off. "I hate people who don't keep their promises!" She slipped some change out of a pocket and made Slim take it.

He looked at it uncertainly, then added his money to it and paid the woman. As they walked toward the door Slim hesitated. He didn't want the woman to hear him. "Am I supposed to leave her a tip?"

The girl looked at him with mock severity. "If you do she'll have you run out of town! We have our pride here, you know!"

When they got back to the office Slim stopped outside the door. He wanted to ask the girl if he could see her again, but he was ashamed of being so broke. He was sure she had a regular friend among the local boys; still, she'd been so friendly to him. It seemed to Slim that she felt pretty much the way he did—about feeling as though they'd known each other before. He finally decided to try anyway.

"Look, Edye . . . uh . . . the ship's going to be here for a couple of days . . . and I was wondering if I could see you again?"

She looked at him for a long moment. "You know something? I think it might be arranged."

The deck boy felt an electric shock of happy anticipation go through him. The words came tumbling out. "In port I get off at five o'clock and I don't have to be back until eight in the morning."

The girl's face broke into a broad smile. "Well, now, I don't think I'll be able to spend *all* that time with you. But why don't you come to dinner? I know the folks will be happy to have you. I'll meet you here at the office at five-thirty." She turned and walked up the short steps. "Come on, you'd better pick up those papers and get them back to the ship!"

Slim followed her inside and took the envelope. He barely remembered the walk back to the dock, and even the excitement of climbing up the bridge ladder to the first mate's quarters was lost in the larger emotion he felt at the prospect of seeing Edith again. He knew the bosun would badger him about being gone, but even that didn't matter. What did matter was that the afternoon would be far longer than usual.

— 8 —

The deck boy took great care not to do a single thing to irritate the unpredictable bosun during the balance of the afternoon of deck work. Strangely enough, the bosun didn't ride him for being late, but seemed to ignore the fact that Slim hadn't appeared until well after the noon meal was over. Slim wondered if he expected his absence. He remembered the chance observation Edye had made in the office, and he remembered Slater's rather matter-of-fact acceptance of his presence and his willingness to entrust the bill of lading to a green hand.

At five o'clock the crew was knocked off, and after stowing some loose gear in the fo'c'slehead lockers Slim went aft and got washed and into clean clothing. He looked in the mottled mirror secured to the bulkhead in the washroom and was fairly well satisfied with what he saw. His hair still didn't need cutting, and it behaved well after being held down all day under the knitted watchcap. He wished his shirt were ironed better; the collar was wrinkled, but it would have to do. Checking on his comb, a clean handkerchief, and what small money he had, he left the ship and arrived at the lumber company office promptly at five-thirty.

Edye was waiting for him. She checked the big office safe, left a paper on Mr. Slater's desk, and locked the outside door behind her. She led Slim along the waterfront, past the little café where they had shared their Dutch-treat lunch, and then turned up a small side street lined with modest homes of families who worked in the mill.

Slim listened to the babbling brook of her voice, happily giving him what she called "the chamber of commerce guided tour of Wauna." He could not remember ever being more comfortable and at ease with a girl. He liked the gentle pressure of her hand resting in the crook of his elbow, and when he looked at her walking beside him he felt a curious possessiveness. There was a rightness about her being there. He felt proud of her and proud of himself for being with her.

Near the end of the little street she steered him into a gravel driveway that led a hundred feet or so to a neat frame house. The front yard was set in lawn, just beginning to emerge from its dormant winter brown. Several trim blue spruce trees, set in spaded loam circles, screened the front of the house from the street. From the driveway a narrow red brick walk led to a small glassed-in front porch.

The screen door had no sooner closed behind them than the front door opened, framing a smiling woman who was unmistakably Edith's mother.

The girl laid her hand lightly on the deck boy's upper arm. "Mom, this is Lewis Fredericks—only he doesn't like to be called 'Lewis.' He prefers 'Slim.' "

The woman smiled and held out her hand. Her gray-green eyes twinkled like her daughter's as she quickly inventoried the boy from head to toe. When she spoke her voice carried the same indefinable undertone of humor. "I think 'Slim' is perfectly appropriate. I think you invited the young man to a good home-cooked dinner just in time! They must be very stingy with their food on those frightful old boats."

Edith gasped in surprise. Then a bell-like tinkle of laughter filled the porch for an instant. "Oh, you poor boy. I forgot to tell you about Mom! She can't help calling a spade a spade. I think she's been a grade-school teacher too long! Don't be surprised if she asks if you've washed behind your ears before you eat!"

Mrs. Morrison led the way into the small sitting room while Edith was talking. "Don't you worry, Slim! I can tell a man who washes behind his ears, first crack out of the box! Now then, Papa isn't home yet, so come out in the kitchen. We'll get acquainted there a lot quicker and dinner'll get ready sooner too!"

The girl took Slim's jacket and hung it on one of several hooks along the short hall that led from the small dining room into a large open kitchen. The room was warm and cheerful. It reminded Slim of the kitchen at the ranch. It was smaller, but all the familiar things were there.

While Mrs. Morrison and Edith tended to the details of fixing the meal, Slim sat at the big kitchen table. The three of them talked, and the conversation was easy. Before he knew it, the deck boy found himself telling the girl's mother many of the things he'd told Edith earlier at lunch.

He was hardly aware of the friendly questions that elicited his forthright answers. The gentle ebb and flow of conversation was interrupted by the strident ring of the telephone. Mrs. Morrison left the kitchen after a hurried peek in the oven and disappeared into the hall. There was a brief exchange of muffled conversation and she was back.

"That was Papa. He'll be home as soon as he drops some papers with your uncle." Mrs. Morrison lifted the cover from a large boiling pot, peeped into the cloud of steam, and carried it cautiously to the sink board.

"I'll just drain these potatoes and get them ready for mashing. Slim, why don't you help Edye set the table?"

Slim pushed back his chair and rose, glad to be able to help with something. "I'm an expert at setting tables. It was one of my chores at home. I used to get stuck with drying dishes too!"

Mrs. Morrison was half hidden by the warm cloud rising from the sink.

"Well, Slim, I'll promise you one thing. That won't happen to you here. Men don't do dishes in the Morrison house. It just isn't allowed!"

Suddenly Slim felt embarrassed. He hadn't intended the remark the way it must have sounded. "Oh, I didn't mean it like that! I'd be glad to *wash* them, even!"

Both the girl and her mother laughed at the boy's confusion. "Now just you relax. You'll have enough dirty work to do in the months ahead! Tonight your only duty will be to eat!"

Before Slim could make any further apology Edith handed him a fistful of silverware and, with a hand in the middle of his back, steered him into the little dining room. He put the settings on the sideboard and helped the girl spread a clean white pad over the oval table. Next came the good linen tablecloth, reserved for special occasions, and finally the napkins and silver. For a moment Slim felt a tinge of homesickness. The muted tinkle of silverware being arranged had the familiar sound of secure surroundings so recently left behind. But as he worked beside the pretty young girl a stronger emotion welled up and displaced the loneliness. It was a curious new feeling. For a moment this was his home . . . and the girl was his . . . and together they were performing their first exciting domestic duties. Slim felt a sudden possessiveness as he looked at Edith, and her loveliness made a pleasing pain in his middle. He wasn't aware that he'd stopped working until she turned and looked at him for a long moment.

Her face broke into a puzzled smile. "Where on earth did you go? I just had a feeling you'd gone off some-where——"

Startled out of his brief reverie, Slim hastily began arranging things on the table.

The girl reached across his outstretched arms and took the napkin he'd just put down. "Emily Post says it goes on the right side. But I don't suppose I should expect an old salt to know that!" Then she grew serious. "Slim, what were you thinking about just now?"

The boy looked down at the table. He could barely explain his emotion to himself, let alone to the serious little face looking up at him in real concern.

She took his arm gently and turned him to face her. "Slim, answer me honest injun. Were you feeling sad about something?"

"Oh, gosh no, Edye! How could a guy be sad here with you . . . with you folks?" He shook his head. "No. I was just thinking, I guess. I don't know how to say it. . . . It sounds sorta silly, but I was just enjoying being here. That's all. Honest injun!"

The girl looked at him closely an instant longer, and then her face relaxed into a gentle smile that made Slim's heart flip. "You know something, sailor? That's the prettiest speech you've made to me in all the years I've known you."

"In all the years you've known me? Why we just met this——"

She put a small hand over his mouth and shut off the rest of the words. "Shsssh. Don't go talking. You'll spoil it!"

A sudden ache seized the base of Slim's throat again, and he struggled against a desire to reach out and take the girl in his arms. He wanted to hold her close to him, feel her soft, lovely little head snuggled under his chin and smell the sweet perfume of her hair. As she stood there, making no effort to move away, Slim felt his vision blur as the ache in his throat robbed him of his voice and spread through his whole being. He wanted to reach out and somehow he sensed that she wouldn't move away, but his arms felt like lead. What had happened? Who was this girl? Why did he feel this way? Why had she suddenly become so dear?

The screen door slammed out front and booted feet thumped heavily on the wooden porch. An electric shock of guilt jarred Slim, and the girl brushed quickly past him toward the front room.

He heard the front door open and heard her happy greeting: "Hi, Pop! It's about time you got home. We have company tonight!"

Slim tried to find something useful to do at the table, but everything was in its place so he moved a knife and fork unnecessarily and waited uncomfortably for Mr. Morrison to enter the room. He could hear Edith speaking softly and he could hear her father's voice making low, rumbling replies as she helped him out of his heavy coat. And then she was in the doorway with him.

"Dad, this is Lewis Fredericks. Slim, this is my dad."

The boy moved toward them and reached out to shake hands. Mr. Morrison was a big man with a big, coarse hand that encased Slim's like a vise.

"Glad to know you, Lewis. Edye tells me you're off the *Tropic Trader*."

Slim tried to match the older man's grip. "Thank you, sir. We came in this morning from San Francisco."

"Gonna cart off some of our good Oregon timber, eh?"

"Yes, sir, I think we're going to start loading in the morning."

The big man smiled at the deck boy and released his grip. "Well, now, you take all you want. We've got plenty to go around!" He looked past Slim toward the kitchen. "Something smells awful good out there. What have you girls been up to?"

Edith gave him an affectionate hug. "Why don't you come on out and see?"

They moved through the little hall to the kitchen. Mrs. Morrison blotted her brow on the end of her apron. She had to stretch up to give her husband an affectionate peck on the cheek.

"I'm glad you weren't late tonight, Harry. Everything's ready." She turned to the stove and lifted the potato pot over to the sink board. "Do you think you have enough strength left to mash the potatoes for me?"

He laid a big arm gently across his wife's shoulders. "Honey, I'll mash 'em flat! Just give me the tools!"

Edith handed him a heavy wire potato whipper and Mrs. Morrison went to the icebox for a pitcher of rich yellow country cream. She set it on the sink beside the big pot. "Why don't you kids go in and sit down? I'll have everything on in a jiffy."

The girl motioned Slim to follow and they went back

into the dining room. "Pop sits there, and Mom sits there, near the kitchen." She motioned to the two chairs at either end of the table. "Since you're the guest of honor tonight, we'll put you on Pop's right. By the way, if you're interested, I learned my etiquette in the Backwoods School for Forward Girls—very exclusive! Aren't you impressed?" She waited expectantly for Slim's answer.

He grinned at her and the strange, new feeling was still there in his middle. "I'm very impressed—with everything in Wauna!"

Mr. Morrison came into the room with a large china serving dish resting in the palm of his hand and placed it on one of the small mats to the side of the main serving area.

" 'Scuse me." He gave his daughter a sheepish look. "I got heck from your ma for not washing my grimy mitts."

Edith laughed as her father disappeared through a door in the short hall. Mrs. Morrison came in with a huge platter of golden-brown spareribs and returned a moment later with a bowl of gravy and a vegetable dish.

Slim couldn't remember when food tasted better. All his uneasiness at meeting the family disappeared in a matter of moments. The conversation with the father was as easy as it had been with Edith and her mother. To Slim these people felt like his own. He tried to avoid talking about himself any more, but Edith kept prompting him until Mr. Morrison had also heard about his ambition to be an officer in the Merchant Marine.

The deck boy was genuinely interested in the lumber business and Mr. Morrison was more than willing to talk about it. Slim found out that he was a forester with the company—in fact, most of the family had worked in the woods or in the mill for two generations. Before the meal was over, Slim had received an elementary education in the economics of the lumber business. He had been told how each operation worked, from cutting and hauling to sawing, planing, and grading. He found out that the *Tropic Trader* would probably load a million board feet of timbers on deck for heavy construction in Australia and New Zealand. Part of the timbers would be recut and sold for finished lumber down there because of cheaper labor and less chance of damage in transit.

As Edith's father talked, a new awareness of the importance of those ugly, deeply laden tramps came over him. He began to realize their critical role in the development of the growing countries "down under" and their importance to the people of the Northwest, whose livelihood depended upon the far-flung markets so laboriously reached by the slow, work-horse freighters of the American Merchant Marine. He felt proud to be a part of it, and what he learned at the dinner table with the Morrisons firmed his determination to become a responsible officer in whose charge some of these precious cargoes would be placed.

It seemed to Slim that they had been at the table only a few minutes when Mr. Morrison pushed his chair back. "Do you smoke, son?"

Slim nodded.

"Care for one of these?" He proffered a pack of Chesterfields.

"I have some right here, thank you." The boy reached into his pocket and took out a crumpled pack. He hadn't smoked since he'd been in Edith's home and she hadn't suggested that he do so. The cigarette tasted good, and the conversation turned from the lumber business and ships to little fragments of personal conversation in the family. The kitchen clock struck nine times.

Edith listened to it. "Nine bells—and all's well."

Slim looked at her and smiled. "You mean two bells and all's well."

She frowned across the table at him. "You better jiggle your receiver, sailor. The bell rang nine times."

Slim looked at Mrs. Morrison with mock concern. "I don't know what they teach young girls in school these days!"

Edith's mother raised her eyebrows. "Well, now, I never could make sense out of these silly ship's bells, either!"

Mr. Morrison looked from his wife to his daughter and then down the table at Slim. "Young man, I think you'd better set the womenfolk straight about those bells, don't you?"

Slim nodded seriously. "I'll be glad to, sir!" He started to speak and was seized by a quick little panic when it occurred to him that there was no easy way to explain the complicated system of bells that tolled off the four-hour segments of a ship's watch. "Well, you see, first of all . . . uh . . . well . . ." He straightened up in his chair and leaned forward.

Edith watched him with a suggestion of a twinkle in her eyes. It made Slim nervous. He started again. "A watch is four hours long. So every half-hour—starting at four o'clock, eight o'clock, and twelve o'clock—they ring a bell on the bridge. They ring it once for every half hour. So at

95

eight o'clock they ring it eight times and at eight-thirty they ring it once. At nine o'clock they ring it twice—at nine-thirty, three times—and so on, until they get to eight bells again at twelve o'clock—only they ring the bells in two's, so they're easier to count. So if they ring eight bells, they ring, 'ding-ding, ding-ding, ding-ding, ding-ding.'" Slim paused and looked at the three of them.

Mr. Morrison nodded in approval. "That's all there is to it. Simple as can be!"

Mrs. Morrison sniffled. "Simple? It seems to me they went out of their way to make it complicated. I'll never understand it and I never want to! I'll just stick to Big Ben out there!"

Edith was mulling over the problem and counting to herself. She looked up. "Ding-ding, ding. What time is that?"

Slim had to do a little quick mental arithmetic. "That's nine-thirty—or one-thirty—or five-thirty!"

The girl compressed her brows in concentration for a moment. "Well, it's almost ding-ding, ding—and that means it's time to get up from this table." She pushed her chair back. "Isn't that ridiculous? 'It's almost ding-ding, ding!' I still think it's a real goofy way to tell time!"

Slim knew from the tone of her voice that no amount of persuasion would change her opinion of ship's bells, so he let the matter rest. As a matter of fact, he halfway agreed that the system was bothersome, but it was part of the tradition of the sea and as such it was worth learning.

"Pop's going to help me clear the table. You two kids go in the front room and visit awhile, and then I'm going to send the sailor back to his ship!"

Mrs. Morrison smiled at Slim and the boy understood that their hours were necessarily quite different from his. He and Edith wandered into the next room and collapsed on the overstuffed sofa. He had eaten too much, he was actually ashamed of himself, but the food had been so good. Now he was beginning to feel drowsy. He stayed until the girl's mother and father came out of the kitchen. They made no effort to sit and the boy knew it was time to leave.

Edith got his coat from the hall and, after genuine thanks and "good nights," he and the girl stepped out into the darkness of the front yard. The night was crystal clear and very cold. Slim pulled his coat closed and fastened the buttons. Edith shivered and folded her arms about her. They stood facing each other for a moment. There were important things to say—desperately important things like when could he see her again—but the deck boy didn't know how to begin.

"I had a wonderful time, Edye . . . and I like your folks . . . very much."

The soft light coming from the living-room lamp half lit her face, and Slim could see her smile.

"They liked you too, Slim. I'm glad you had a good time."

There was something about the way she said it that brought that disturbing feeling back to Slim's middle. He knew he had to leave and he knew that he couldn't without asking to see the girl again. "Edye, do you think maybe we could . . . uh . . ."

She interrupted him. "Do I think maybe we could kiss good night?" She paused an instant. "Well, now, if you're sure you're up to it?" Before he knew what was happening, she moved close to Slim, took his face in both her hands, pulled it down, and kissed him lightly on the lips. "There, now! Scoot back to your ship, sailor . . . and call me at the office if you get a chance!" She turned and disappeared inside.

The door closed with a gentle click and the front-room light snapped off. Slim was left standing alone on the dark porch. Like one in a daze, he turned and left the house, walked down the drive to the street, and headed back to the ship. Suddenly he felt like laughing, like singing, like shouting, like running, suddenly he felt happier than he'd ever been in his whole life. And then it dawned on him: for the first time he was in love. He'd known a lot of girls at home and kissed a lot of them. But none of them had ever made him feel like this!

Slim hardly remembered getting back to the ship. He picked his way into the darkened fo'c'sle, scarcely hearing the snores of the sleeping men. He folded his clothes, put them in the locker, gingerly stepped on the edge of Hammer's bunk, and lifted himself up into his own. He snuggled down into the blankets, buried his face in the pillow, and gave himself over to a wonderful half-real dream of a wonderful girl named "Edye."

— 9 — The day watch was turned out at six-thirty the next morning. After break-fast the bosun, with Mr. Peterson and Mr. Holst, directed the crew in preparing the well decks to receive the great stacks of rough timbers that the steve-dores were getting ready to load.

As interested as Slim was in everything that happened and as hard as he worked carrying dunnage to make a foundation for the first big timbers to lie on, his thoughts kept turning to Edith and the unexpected climax of their first evening. The longing to see her was an insistent dull pain that filled his entire being. Whenever his work took him to the dockside rail of the ship, he looked toward the street in the hope of catching a glimpse of her. He won-dered if she was feeling the same loneliness and if she might find an excuse to leave the office on an outside er-rand on the chance she might see him. He dismissed the thought as silly. Once he thought he caught a glimpse of her in the lumberyard, but the figure disappeared behind a miniature city of stacked lumber.

Slim raced through the noon meal and took no part in the messroom conversation. With thirty minutes of free time before the afternoon's work began, he walked rapidly up to the dock gate and turned along the street to the lum-ber-company office. His heart was racing from the excite-ment and exertion of walking on the bolted lunch. He paused at the front of the office, almost afraid to climb the stairs. When he stepped up to the door his heart sank. Sla-ter was alone in the room. Edye was not to be seen. Slim moved quietly away so he'd not have to explain his pres-ence to the man. He wandered aimlessly along the path they'd taken the day before. Near the main part of town he decided that Edye had probably gone home for lunch. He retraced his steps slowly, still hoping against hope that the girl might appear. With only five minutes to get back aboard, Slim relinquished the last forlorn shred of hope, climbed the gangplank and joined the crew, gathering around number four hatch.

Several times during the afternoon the deck boy was surprised to discover his longing for the girl had been overshadowed by the excitement of watching the towering booms tremble under the strain of great loads of timbers. He watched the dockworkers tie thin cable slings around four timbers at a time, watching the boss stevedore signal the winchman that the load was ready for hoisting aboard and he was filled with wonder and apprehension as the wheezy old steam winches, faltering under the task, gained momentum with an erratic thumping clatter, until they held the load suspended thirty feet in the air. Then he held his breath while the lumber was lowered gently into position on the deck.

The afternoon wore on and the deckload began to grow noticeably. As the heavy bottom timbers piled higher and higher, the stevedores began stacking lighter lumber on the top. Four by fours and two by fours were added, until by late afternoon the after well deck was stacked deep with fragrant, freshly cut pine. All day long the deck gang had been carrying heavy sections of chain lashing from the fo'c'slehead and stretching them out on the canvas hatch covers. When the load was as high as it could safely be, these great chains would be pulled across the top at six-foot intervals and shackled to pad eyes riveted to the top-sides of the freighter. The inboard ends of the chains would be secured to great turnbuckles that the sailors would tighten, until the huge deckload was packed as tightly as a well done package.

After the crew had been knocked off, Slim went to the fo'c'sle and began cleaning up.

Hammer watched him closely for a few minutes. "What the hell are you rushin' around for? You act like you got a heavy date or something."

Slim concealed a guilty little shock. He wondered if the A.B. had just taken a lucky guess or whether someone had seen him and passed the word. "Naw, I just want to go into town. We'll be cooped up long enough. I'm gonna stretch my legs while I can." He tried to sound casual but he wasn't sure he was getting away with it. A sudden thought turned him cold. Suppose Jack asked to come ashore with him . . . like San Francisco? He could never introduce Jack to Edye. Jack put all girls in one category. The only difference between them, according to him, was

99

the length of time it took them to succumb to his earthy charm. The thought of Jack with the girl filled him with revulsion and a tinge of fear. He knew the big A.B.'s cocksure manner with women and he felt a touch of envy, too. He remembered Jack's assurance in the San Francisco brothel . . . and his own ineptness. The remembering made him afraid.

"I'll tell ya what, kid, if you *really* want to stretch your legs, let's walk up the tracks to Westport. It's got more doin' than this sawdust pile!"

The deck boy slipped on his jacket and put a pack of cigarettes in his breast pocket. He needed time to think. "How far is it?"

"Just a couple of miles."

Slim was about to decline when the A.B. named Otto came in from the messroom. "Hey, Hammer, come here a minute. I want to show ya something."

Jack looked around slowly and without interest. He'd barely spoken a dozen words to Otto since leaving San Francisco. "What is it?"

"Come on out here. I got something to show ya——"

There was an urgency about the sailor's manner that interested Slim. Jack looked at the seaman closely, then rose slowly from his bunk and walked to the passageway. Otto showed him something concealed under his coat. Jack took the object, looked at it carefully, glanced over his shoulder at Slim, then disappeared out on deck.

Slim seized the opportunity to get off the ship without unwanted company. Once on the dock, he hurried toward the little office building where he hoped Edith would still be working. It was nearly quarter of six and he felt close to panic that he'd taken so long.

He restrained an urge to run as he turned the corner onto the waterfront street. He could see a light burning in the side window. He wondered if Slater would be working. The early winter dark had not quite given way to the longer days of the north-coming sun. There was no hesitancy in Slim now. He took the short front steps two at a time and entered the warm little office. Slater was sitting at his desk, and Edith was there, too, standing at a corner table and running a long tape on the adding machine. She turned as the door opened. Slater glanced up briefly.

A great wave of relief passed through Slim, as Edith smiled and motioned for him to wait. She turned back to a pile of colored business forms and flipped them over with her thumb as she punched the necessary keys on the little machine. Slim felt self-conscious standing in the small outer office. There were no chairs, so he leaned against the little counter and reached for a cigarette. Before he could put a match to it Slater looked up.

"There's no smokin' in here, kid!" His voice was rough and unfriendly.

Edith paused for an instant and looked at the man sharply, then shot a sympathetic glance at the deck boy. Slim felt a flush of embarrassment as he put the cigarette back in the pack and returned it to his pocket. He was just about to tell Edye that he'd wait outside, when she pulled the handle on the machine quickly a couple of times and tore off the long ribbon of paper. Picking up the work, she carried it over to the counter.

She looked at Slim sternly. "There's one thing you've got to learn, young man——"

Slim shrugged his shoulders sheepishly. "I didn't know you couldn't smoke around here. Why don't you put up a sign?" He spoke softly, so Slater wouldn't hear.

Edye shook her head. "I'm not talking about that. You've got to learn not to keep ladies waiting!"

Slim looked puzzled.

She let him wonder for a moment, then laughed softly. "Last night when you left, I asked you to call me if you got a chance. I've been waiting all day. In fact, I stayed late tonight, hoping I'd hear." Her pretty face assumed a hurt expression. "Do you know what it's like to be kept waiting?"

Slim didn't answer. He couldn't. He wanted to tell her how well he knew—how he'd looked up toward the end of the dock a hundred times that day in hope of seeing her. He wanted to tell her that he'd run all the way to the office at noon; that he'd been hopelessly impatient all day for another few precious hours with her.

"Edye, they've worked the tail off us all day, with the loading. I did come by about twelve-thirty, but you weren't here."

Edith looked disturbed, then nodded toward the man in the back of the office. "He was here. I told him if you came in to say I'd gone home for lunch but I'd be back before one."

"I know—I saw him but I didn't want to come in. He looked like he was busy."

"Well, never mind. Wait'll I put these away and we'll go. Mom said if you have nothing better to do you're to come and have potluck with us again tonight."

Slim looked at the girl and blinked with confusion. "Look, Edye, I thought maybe tonight I could take *you* out . . . maybe to a movie or something——"

She brushed aside the suggestion with a shake of her dark red hair. "Not a chance, sailor. The closest movie worth going to is on the other side of the river—in Longview. You're coming home with me!"

Before Slim could protest further she left the counter and crossed to the big safe in the back of the room. Stepping inside, she placed the papers and tape in a correspondence box and then stepped out to the heavy steel door.

"Mr. Slater, have you got anything to go in here before I lock up?"

The man continued looking at the papers he was examining and shook his head. "No. Go ahead and shut up for the night."

Edith swung the heavy door slowly into place and gave the combination dial a short whirl, then tried the handle to make certain the lock had taken hold. Lifting her big green coat off the rack, she crossed to Slim and let herself out into the little reception area.

"Good night, Mr. Slater, see you in the morning."

Slater's reply sounded like the grunt of a disturbed animal. Edith made a little grimace at Slim and the two of them stepped out into the street.

"He's a grumpy old coot, isn't he?" Slim indicated the man inside.

"Oh, he's all right after you know him. He's kind of a sourpuss these days because he didn't get the job of general superintendent for the company. They brought in some bright young college man from Seattle who's been with Weyerhaeuser for a few years."

Slim had a sudden disturbing thought. "Is he . . . good?"

The girl inclined her head in thought for a moment. "I think so. He's done a lot of good reorganizing. I don't know him too well, but I know his wife. She's wonderful. She's only in her middle twenties and she's got two awful cute babies already."

Slim's spirits soared up from the edge of despair. He took Edye's arm and linked it through his and they walked in silence toward her home.

This time they dined in the kitchen. Edith's father hadn't come home. It was lodge night and he'd gone into Westport with some of his friends. The three of them sat around the big kitchen table and talked. The conversation ranged from the lumber business to some of the personal problems of the Morrison household. Edith's disarming candor extended to the matter of family finances and the need for her to work. She had wanted to go to the University of Oregon as her mother had, but there had been no chance. Her father loved his work, but foresters made little money, and schoolteachers did no better.

Slim found himself telling of the trials his family had gone through, and the parallels were obvious. The conversation sounded like any one of a hundred he'd overheard or participated in with the family, before his grandfather's estate had been divided and the tidy fortune had brought welcome relief to their stringent economy. He found himself wondering at the ease with which he'd fitted into the Morrison home. Their ready acceptance of him was put in words by Mrs. Morrison herself.

"It's a funny thing, Lewis, but I think it's going to be a bit lonely around here when your boat sails."

Edith looked threateningly at her mother. "Mom! For Pete's sake, watch it! Of course, *I* don't care—but if you want him to come back, never call his ship a boat! He lectured me for ten minutes on the difference!"

Mrs. Morrison made a little gesture of despair. "You'll just have to take us with all our imperfections, Lewis. I'll never ever know the difference between a boat and a ship —and I'll *never* be able to tell time by those silly little bells!"

Slim compressed his lips and glowered at Edith. "Listen, you little redheaded vixen with the silly nose. I didn't lecture you! I told you a boat is a small vessel that can be hoisted aboard a larger one, which is usually called a ship!"

The girl giggled. "Oh, Slim, what a pity! We're having our first quarrel! Mother dear, why didn't you tell me men were so cruel?"

Slim wadded up his napkin and threatened to fire it at Edith.

The girl gave him a warning look. "Don't you dare, you young roughneck!"

"All right you two, use up some of that precious young energy clearing the table!" Mrs. Morrison put on a half apron and went to the sink. She took a large graniteware dishpan from the cabinet below and began to fill it with hot water.

Edith carried her plate to the sink board. Reaching behind her mother, she undid the apron and tied it around herself. "Skeedaddle, sweetie! I'm going to make the sailor earn his keep tonight."

Mrs. Morrison started to protest but gave in to her daughter with a little gesture of surrender when she caught Edith's fleeting wink. "Well, all right, if you two think you can get along without me for a little while." She dried her hands on the corner of a tea towel and left the room.

Edith looked at Slim. "I'd put an apron on you, too, but I'm sure you'd strangle me with it!"

Slim nodded in agreement. "I would! Except I'd hate to muss up your pretty kisser!"

The girl shooed him with the skirt of her apron. "Flattery'll get you nowhere!" She handed him a wet plate. "Here, dry the dishes!"

They worked side by side and again Slim had the warm, possessive feeling he'd felt the night before when they had set the table together. Even up to her elbows in dishes she was the prettiest girl he'd ever seen.

She worked in silence for a few moments and her face grew serious. Holding a suds-covered plate, she turned slowly to face the boy. "Slim, do you know when you're sailing?"

He thought for a moment, then shook his head uncertainly. "I'm not sure. I heard the mate say something about half a million feet of lumber here at Wauna, but I don't know how long that'll take. Why?"

She turned back to the sink and slowly rinsed the plate. "Because *I* know. You're sailing at noon tomorrow. You're going to Vancouver, B.C., for more lumber—then you go south."

A sinking feeling hit his middle. "How do you know?"

"I heard Slater talking to someone on the phone this morning. Another boa—ship is coming in your place tomorrow at four."

She put the dish in the drain rack and in silence they finished the rest of the job. When they had straightened up the kitchen they walked into the front parlor. Mrs. Morrison was busy running a sewing machine in the front bedroom.

"Slim——"

"Yeah?"

"If we go now, I can walk back to the dock with you."

Slim looked at his watch. It was a little after eight. "Are you sure it's all right for you to be out alone?"

She smiled at him indulgently. "Of course, silly. I'm

104

free, white, and darn near eighteen! If I have to work I sometimes come home alone a lot later."

Slim looked down at her and pinched her nose gently between the insides of two crooked fingers. "If you were my girl, I'd never let you out of my sight!"

She took his hand gently from her nose. "That would be very nice."

They looked at each other for a long moment, then she turned toward the door. "Get the coats. Let's go."

Slim brought the two coats from the wall hooks in the little hall and helped Edith into hers. He was slipping into his when Mrs. Morrison came out of the bedroom. "You two going out?"

"I'm going to walk Slim back to the dock, Mom."

"All right—don't be too long." The woman held out a hand to the boy. "Lewis, we've enjoyed having you with us. I hope if your ship, or whatever you call it, gets back here, that you'll come and see us again."

Slim was genuinely grateful to the Morrisons. He expressed his gratitude as best he could and left the little house. Even though the girl walked beside him in the night, he felt a gnawing loneliness and the prospect of going back aboard the bleak old freighter appealed less and less to him. His hand brushed against the girl's and their fingers linked very gently. They walked in silence to the waterfront street, each enjoying the nearness of the other.

When they reached the little office of the lumber company they stopped. Inside, the night light glowed dimly. Further along a floodlight bathed the entrance to the dock in a pale yellow glow. The high pipe-and-wire fence suddenly looked like a prison compound to the young sailor. He knew that once he went through the gate and headed out along the dock he'd be leaving behind one of the most important things in his life—this lovely girl whom he'd known for exactly two days but whom he felt he'd known since the beginning of time.

Edith shivered slightly and pulled Slim gently over to the low steps. They sat and she snuggled close to him. He took her hand in both of his, and she rested her head on his shoulder. He inclined his head toward her until his cheek brushed lightly against her soft, sweet hair. They sat for a time, not talking, just feeling. Then, very slowly, the girl turned her face up toward him and their lips met in a kiss that moved from tenderness to the edge of passion. After a time she pulled away and stood up.

When she spoke her voice sounded close to tears. "Oh, for Pete's sake! What the heck am I doing, anyway?" She turned to face Slim. "I ought to hate you, you know! You came along and bollixed up all my fine plans for little old me!" She turned away and lowered her head, but Slim turned her back toward him very gently. "You fouled up my plans too, Edye—only for some reason I don't seem to mind it!"

She looked up at him and managed an uncertain little smile. "I know. I don't really mind it, either. All I mind is that you're going away. It may sound silly, Slim, but I feel like I've always known you. Mom said the same thing. She's never said that about anybody else—even the kids I've grown up with. The darn trouble is that the little town is going to get lonesome now!"

Slim inclined his head toward the dock. "So's that old tub out there!"

She nodded in understanding. They stood facing each other a moment longer, then started slowly for the dock gate.

"Slim, will you write me a letter once in a while?"

The boy laughed gently. "I was about to ask you the same thing."

She brightened a bit. "I can find out where the *Tropic Trader* is going to be through the office. I mean *where* in New Zealand. Then I can write you in care of the American Consul. That's where we address any letters to the captains and mates if we have to write a ship about anything."

They stopped in the shadow of a lumbershed just before they reached the dock gate.

"Do I need a street address here in Wauna to reach you?"

She shook her head. "Just 'Wauna, Oregon,' that's all. I'll get it when I go to the post office for the company mail."

Slim looked around suddenly. He thought he had heard voices but he could see no one. He squinted to see his watch in the shadows. It was almost nine o'clock. "You better be getting back, Edye. I'll watch you until you get up the street—just to make sure."

The girl moved close to him and put her palms flat against the front of his coat. She spoke very softly. "I want to shove you right out of my life, and I want to hold onto you, too! What am I going to do? What *am* I going to do?"

106

Slim took her hands in his and slid her arms around his neck. His long arms wound around her slender waist and firm little shoulders and pulled her tightly to him. She stretched her lovely body up along his lanky frame to reach his lips and they kissed—a long kiss—a kiss that would last for as long as they both could remember. When his arms relaxed, she drew away, looked at him closely for an instant, then turned and walked quickly back along the waterfront street, past the office and on toward her home. Slim turned slowly toward the dock gate.

Suddenly a voice from the shadows startled him. "Pretty goddamn good, kid! Pretty good! In town two nights and you knock off the prettiest squaw on the reservation! He's pretty cute, ain't he, Otto?" As he spoke, Hammer moved out into the pool of light under the floodlamp.

Slim felt sick. The last person in the world he would have shared that precious moment with was Hammer.

He greeted the men flatly. "Hi! I didn't see you guys."

The A.B.'s laugh was smug and salacious. "We didn't want you to, kid. We thought you might try to give her a quick one up against the shed." They laughed and moved over to Slim.

Otto gave him a knowing clout on the arm. "Yeah. We figured if we couldn't find any of our own you might share with us. You know . . . shipmates. We don't mind a wet deck once in a while, do we, Jack?"

Hammer twisted the corners of his sensuous mouth down and shook his head. "Naw! Not if they ain't *too* wet!"

Slim felt a cold rage welling up inside of him. Suddenly the two men were the personification of all the filth he'd been brought up to despise. He wanted to strike at them but he knew it would not only be futile but would make his life unbearable for the rest of the trip. Besides, Jack's attitude shouldn't surprise him and Otto's attitude seemed to be typical of most of the men in the fo'c'sle.

"Look, fellas, you're wrong. She's a friend of mine. So's her family."

Jack looked at the deck boy suspiciously. "I thought you said you'd never been up here before?"

Slim started with fear. He'd forgotten about that. He fumbled for words a moment and then he told a deliberate lie. "That's right. But I had a letter to her family from friends in Berkeley. Her mother went to school with a neighbor of ours."

Jack looked at Slim and slowly smiled in open disbelief.

107

"I think that's a crock of shit, kid, but it's okay. I can see I'm going to have to keep an eye on you when the dames are around. You're a sneaky bastard for a long drink of water!" He winked at Otto and they both laughed. "Come on. Let's go get a cup of 'jamoke.' I wish to Christ we had something to spike it with."

The three of them started the long walk down the dock. In the bright glow of the cluster light, at the head of the gangplank, they saw Warndahl sitting out his gangway watch on the small bunker hatch.

As they came aboard he tugged at his crotch and rose to greet them. "You guys get yer nuts rattled?" He wet his ugly lips in eager anticipation.

Hammer made a gesture of disgust. "Hell, no. Not in this Godforsaken dump." He nodded his head toward the deck boy. "I think the kid made it, though!"

Warndahl looked at Slim with interest. "No kiddin'? Tell us about it, kid."

Slim fought back a new wave of anger and disgust that brought him close to tears. He started to say something, then clamped his jaw shut on the words and hastily walked aft to the fo'c'sle. Once inside, he undressed quickly, climbed up into his bunk, and pulled the worn-thin bed-spread screen across the wire. Lying quietly on his back, he stared at the ragged asbestos covering on the steam pipes and fought his outrage at the three men.

After a time the memory of Edye took the edge from his anger and in its place came a sad-sweet longing for the girl. Drowsily he turned his cheek to the shabby pillow and felt once again the warmth of the girl pressed against him and the magic softness of her lips against his. He heard Hammer and Otto go to the pantry for coffee and a little later he could hear fragments of their rough conversation as they sat in the adjoining messroom. After a time he heard nothing except Edye's gentle voice chiding him for coming into her life.

— 10 —

Wet, gray fog wrapped the old freighter in flowing folds and muffled the work sounds of stevedores completing the loading and of the seamen getting her ready for the trip down the river. Edye had been right. The *Tropic Trader* would sail at noon for Vancouver, British Columbia, to complete the lumber load. Already half a million board feet of it was piled eight feet deep on the after well deck. More was destined for the foreward deck and some for the holds.

By eleven o'clock the booms had been topped, the turnbuckles tightened fiddle-taut and the men summoned to their stations. Slim joined Chips, Square John and the old Russian on the poop deck and, under the second mate's orders, prepared to bring aboard the hawsers that held the after end vessel to the pier.

Slim's mind was a battleground. Anxiety, indecision, fear and loneliness for the girl sent simultaneous and painful messages through him. He only half heard Peterson's orders and Chips looked at him strangely several times, when he seemed confused. During a lull in the preparations the boy went over to the rail and leaned far out to see if he could get a farewell glimpse of Edye.

Peterson joined him and studied the lines, then something in the deck boy's manner attracted his attention. He looked at him closely for a moment. "What's the matter with you, kid?"

Slim turned in surprise. He'd been aware that someone was beside him, but he didn't know it was the second mate.

Peterson looked at the wan face and woebegone expression. Suddenly he chuckled. "I'll be unbuckled and buggered!" He turned to the others. "I've seen a lot of things, but this is the first time I've ever seen a deck boy get seasick *before* the ship was untied!"

109

The men glanced at Slim. Chips laughed gently, but the others ignored the joke completely.

Slim managed a small embarrassed grin. "I'm okay, sir. I guess I didn't get much sleep last night."

Peterson looked at him in mock surprise. "Now don't tell me that you got caught like a moth in the flaming night life of this water-logged metropolis?"

"No, sir. I turned in early. I just couldn't get to sleep."

The second mate spat a speck of tobacco from the tip of his tongue. "Musta been something you ate. You're too young to have a guilty conscience!" He returned to his inspection of the lines for a moment more, then turned away and looked forward.

From the bridge, scarcely visible through the swirling mist, they could see the captain. He was leaning far out over the end of the wing, megaphone in hand. Slim could not understand the hollow-voiced bellow, but the mate and the others seemed to. It was the order to cast off. Peterson immediately bent over the rail and shouted orders to the men on the dock. Willing hands heaved the great eyesplice off the iron cleat, and strained to keep it from dropping into the water between the sides of the ship and the pilings. On deck they worked feverishly to bring the lines aboard, and as soon as they were clear the second mate cupped his hands and shouted toward the bridge, "All clear aft, sir!"

In a moment the stern trembled beneath their feet as the giant screw began turning. Now the river current that had made the docking so difficult three days before made the departure easy.

Slim stood at the rail, straining for a glimpse of Edye. He felt that if she could possibly make it she would be on the dock to wave good-by. He strained his eyes to see through the fog. The heavy-coated dockhands became dark blobs against the lighter gray of the pier shed. He looked forward to the head of the pier and the lumber office. For a fleeting moment he thought he saw a lone figure standing beside the little building, but now nothing was visible but the rectangular stacks of damp lumber. The ship moved out a few more yards and the last precious chance to see the girl was denied the boy as the docks of Wauna disappeared behind the curtain of mist.

The men set about coiling down the hawsers on the rope table. As usual, Chips did most of the effective work, and most of the talking. "Sir, what the hell are they takin' her out on the river for in weather like this?"

110

The mate shook his head sadly and raised his eyes in a gesture that was at once hopeless and reverent. "My good man, who are we to question the infinite wisdom of the owners? If we don't get to Vancouver and pick up that load, some ubiquitous Limey will!"

Chips pondered the explanation for a moment, then spoke with patient resignation. "Well, I always wanted a chicken farm in Oregon." He jerked his thumb toward the bridge. "If they make any mistakes up there, I'll be able to step off this scow—right onto it!"

Even as he knew it would, Chip's triumphant arrival on his chicken farm would have to wait, for the *Tropic Trader* eased northwesterly along the channel for only a short time before the sun began to burn through the mist and visibility increased, until both sides of the river could be seen.

The mate knocked the men off for the noon meal. By the time Slim finished washing, the messroom was packed. When he finally got a seat the best of the hot food was gone, so he filled his stomach with bread and coffee and some coarse yellow cake which he pried loose from its scorched bottom crust. As he ate without relish, he took no part in the conversation but listened to fragments of rumor and information. He still couldn't separate fact from fancy but listening dulled the edge of his loneliness for Edye.

After the dinner hour all hands were turned out to prepare the forward well deck for its load. Slim felt a small excitement, as he watched the north shore of the river moving by and realized that the ship was actually running directly along the imaginary line that divided the states of Oregon and Washington.

By late afternoon the river had widened and they were opposite the town of Altoona. At dusk the ship slowed down, pulled out of the main channel, came about, and stopped. He heard Mr. Samson's shouted order, followed by the roaring rattle of heavy chain in the hawsepipes. A geyser of water shot up as the huge anchor dived under the surface and buried itself in the river bottom. Later, in the messroom when Slim asked Chips why they had anchored, he was told they never crossed the Columbia River bar at night.

When Slim awakened the next morning the *Tropic Trader* was under way. The bar was not so rough as it had been three days earlier, and the pilot, who had come aboard very early, was dropped without incident near the lightship.

The old tramp coasted north along the timber-topped headlands of the Washington coast. When night fell Slim saw only an occasional light on shore and by the next morning the ship was off Cape Johnson. Sometime during the next night the vessel turned a little south of east and entered the Strait of Juan de Fuca. By late the next afternoon they were tied alongside, close to the center of Vancouver's waterfront. On Monday they finished loading lumber on the forward well deck and sailed for San Pedro.

The trip down the coast was uncomfortable. The weather was blustery and cold, and because of the additional deckload forward and the lack of any appreciable amount of cargo in the depths of the holds, the *Tropic Trader* rolled like the top-heavy tub she was. Slim had difficulty in understanding why they'd loaded the decks first and then filled the holds. The process seemed backward to him until Chips explained that on tramps the owners take cargo where they can get it. In this case the timbers, first to be loaded, would be the first of the cargo to be unloaded, hence they could not be stowed below decks. Also the sheltered holds would be needed for more perishable cargo, if and when it could be found. From this and other fragments of information about the uncertain life of a tramp, Slim began to get some idea of the problems that confronted these particular ship's officers—especially those confronting the taciturn second mate.

A new deck boy had been taken on in Vancouver. He was an American—a boy from Iowa—who had set out to see the country and lately had decided to extend his excursion to the rest of the world. He was a husky, open-faced lad who gave his name as Horatius Edwards and was promptly nicknamed "Ioway." Accepted in the fo'c'sle in much the same manner the crew had accepted Chico as a mascot, he reminded Slim of an overgrown setter pup. He had a tail-wagging sort of personality that was impossible to dislike and he willingly became the butt of many mess-hall jokes, including some especially vile ones calculated to make him lose interest in eating. Slim had been warned about this trick. Deck boys were deliberately made ill and the older men divided up the uneaten portions. For some reason the tactics had not been used on him.

The first night out of Vancouver, Ioway had listened to the worst they could throw at him and had smiled.

"Shucks, the fellows are always tellin' stories like that durin' harvest time back home in Marshalltown!"

It was some time before the men gave up trying, however. If the unspeakable obscenities failed to turn the new boy's stomach, Slim thought nothing would. Several times he had been on the verge of leaving the table himself. But Ioway blithely bolted down the food, then retired to the bunk with his harmonica. Somehow it seemed right that the farm boy should play the mouth organ. Ioway did indeed play it, with near professional skill. The special instrument was capable of reproducing several octaves of the chromatic scale. After the first supper aboard he had stretched out in his bunk and started to play softly. Before many minutes the conversations ceased and the men just listened and smoked. Even Russian John opened the curtained bunk a trifle and Chips sauntered in from his own quarters forward of the messroom. When after half an hour the boy stopped, he was urged to a second concert and was immediately adopted as an indispensable member of the tight little fo'c'sle society.

The second day out the bosun set the two deck boys to cleaning up number five hold. Both of them finished large breakfasts; then, armed with wire brushes and factory brooms, they helped the bosun pull back the tarpaulins and remove a few covers from the hatch. Down into its dim recesses they climbed to clean from behind the horizontal wooden slats that lined the steel plates, remnants of rotten copra that had remained there from a previous cargo. Down in the tomb-like gloom the air was heavy with the putrid odor of rotting vegetable matter. It lay sticky and moldy green behind each batten and each blob of the rotten stuff harbored hundreds of tiny black copra bugs. The only light came from a squared shaft of sun that speared down through the overhead opening.

It took them two sickening days to finish the job. The hard, black little bugs were indestructible and seemed to multiply as they watched them. Soon they had occupied every nook and cranny of the after end of the ship, joining the cockroaches in the pantry and messhalls. When the crew complained, they were told the ship would be fumigated in Wilmington. But in that port, when the last of the cargo was loaded, there was still no sign of the fumigators; nor would there be for many months, until the tramp returned to the States and the precaution became a legal mandate.

Early one morning the freighter moved to San Pedro

and began loading a cargo that soon attracted the attention not only of the crew, who watched it come aboard with misgivings, but of the dock-workers, seamen from nearby ships, and a group of serious-faced business executives. The cargo that created this unusual interest was gasoline or "case oil," as it was called by the officers. Each wooden case contained two imperial five-gallon cans of gasoline, consigned to the city of Auckland, chief port of New Zealand. It was rumored in the fo'c'sle to be the largest such shipment of inflammable material ever sent across the Pacific. And then, to make the incendiary nightmare complete, twelve steel drums of a new type of jellied high explosive were carefully loaded into the 'tween deck of number five hold.

Hammer and Otto were assigned the task of posting large "No Smoking" signs at conspicuous points around the ship. They were permanently bolted to the stanchions midship and were painted directly onto the bulkheads by the crew's quarters. The signs were hardly necessary, for the ever-present smell of gas fumes was a constant reminder. Even using what for them was extreme caution, the stevedores punctured some of the cases with their sharp cargo hooks, and raw gasoline soaked adjoining cases, some of it finding its way down into the bilge.

All three mates supervised the loading. Second Mate Peterson seemed to be everywhere at once. Frequently he'd call Third Mate Holst to size up a specific problem, and the two men would climb down into a hold and check the work of stowing, making changes here and there, insisting that air space be left between the cases of gasoline to make circulation possible in the dead heat of the tropics. The work proceeded night and day, until the freighter was loaded deep below her red-boot topping.

From the fink hall in San Pedro came the rest of the ship's company. The night before they sailed, Slim had a bad time with himself. Four hundred miles to the north was San Francisco and across the bay, Berkeley—and home. When they were opposite the Golden Gate on the way south, the boy had felt a tugging homesickness that pulled harder at his innards than the loneliness at leaving Edye in Wauna. But the bosun's continual pressure and the necessity for showing Ioway the ropes soon turned his mind away. The feeling didn't come back until the departure from San Pedro to the other side of the world was an imminent reality. Slim knew it would be his last chance to decide. He tossed and turned most of the night and once he nearly got out of his bunk and packed his seabag.

Hammer, in the bunk below, put a foot up and kicked the bottom of his mattress springs. "Fer Chris' sake, what are you doin' up there—screwin' a ghost?"

Slim didn't answer. He curbed the nightmarish thoughts compounded of his own indecision and the crew's talk of the dangerous cargo. After a time he fell asleep.

— 11 —

As the first week at sea went by and the weather became warmer, Slim began to feel a growing excitement. The ship was taking him into a strange and beautiful world; a world of emerald and sapphire seas whose crests were fire-frosted with dancing diamonds; a world of new blue skies above the tumbled tops of sun-tinted clouds that seemed always to stay a horizon away; a warm world that embraced his thin body and charged it with energy and a feeling of inner strength. In place of the loneliness for his family and the girl with whom he'd fallen in love came a deeper longing to be a part of—and to move freely in—this larger world that belonged to the men who dared to challenge it.

Suddenly the boy felt ashamed of his misgivings about himself. He felt at once the rightness of his decision to be free—the rightness to challenge the problem of being a man after his own liking and the growing certainty that he was equal to the test. These did not come to Slim as separate and distinct revelations, but rather as a new feeling of sureness. Over the months it would separate into crystal-clear convictions that would alter in detail but not in content. The immediate result was a new enthusiasm, noticeable even to the bosun. The second mate marked it, too, and spoke of it to the third who remembered his earlier order. And so Slim was assigned to Holst's twelve-to-four watch.

The bosun broke the news to him. "Hey! Report to de bridge at eight bells!" He looked at the deck boy with open scorn but Slim was oblivious to anything but the excitement at finally being summoned to that exalted world.

The morning passed slowly. At eleven o'clock the bosun sent word for him to knock off and get some food. Slim went below and changed into fresh dungarees and a skivvy shirt, standard uniform for seamen on the bridge. He was

116

ready to report to the third mate a good fifteen minutes before the watch was to change.

Timing himself to be at the foot of the bridge ladder a minute before the bells struck, Slim made his way from the fo'c'sle up through the companionway to the poop, and then across the lumber that completely blocked the passageway leading out onto the after well deck. He picked his way carefully across the irregular top of the deckload, avoiding the big chains that strapped the timbers in place, walked quickly along the length of the midship deck, and paused at the foot of the bridge ladder. His heart was pounding and for a moment he felt the old uncertainty. As his foot reached slowly for the first step, the wheelhouse bell struck eight times. Slim glanced at his watch. It was a minute slow. He scrambled up the ladders to the pilot bridge, walked to the wheelhouse door, and peered inside.

Coming from the brilliant sunlight, his eyes took a little while to accommodate to the dim-lit interior. Then objects began to take shape in the gloom. The first person the deck boy saw was one of the new seamen, the fellow called "the Shiek," standing at the wheel. The room seemed smaller than Slim thought it would be. The deck sloped gently up to the center of the wheelhouse, then away to the opposite side. The Shiek, whom Slim knew had signed on as the "ordinary," was standing on a small wooden grating, slouched over the spoked wheel that was a part of the binnacle assembly: the compass, the binnacle top, with its two small oil lights now converted to electricity, and the two compensating magnetic balls which kept the compass corrected. The place seemed surprisingly bare. To either side of the binnacle stood the engine room telegraphs, with their shiny brass handles pushed forward and their pointers reading "full ahead." Beneath the forward windows was a tachometer that counted each revolution of the big propeller. Along the back of the wheelhouse was a workshelf and, underneath that, some lockers and drawers. In the corner was a speaking tube to the engine room. On the bulkhead next to Slim's left shoulder was a small blackboard and upon it in chalk was written the compass course for the helmsman to steer.

Slim was debating whether or not to step inside, when he felt a large hand squeeze his buttocks. "All right, sweetheart, clear the way and let the professionals take over!"

It was Warndahl, the A.B. he had met during the depths of his first seasickness—Warndahl, whose penchant for putting his hands on posteriors, annoyed and embarrassed the boy. He stepped quickly inside and let the A.B. pass. The Shiek mumbled the course to the Swede, stepped off the grating, brushed past Slim, and disappeared down the ladder to the main deck.

The older man looked at the deck boy after he had satisfied himself that the freighter was on course. "Whatta they got you doin' up here—helpin' the skipper run the ship?"

The joke didn't amuse Slim. He shook his head. "I was told to report to the bridge—that's all I know."

Warndahl rotated the wheel a couple of spokes to the left, then steadied it back right again. "On this lousy tub they'll probably teach you punks to do all the soft steerin' so the old hands can do the hard work on deck!" He glanced over at Slim. "Ever do any steerin'?"

"Nope."

"Look, kid, if you wanta be real good friends, I can help you catch on quick." The A.B. leered at the boy and waited for an answer.

Slim controlled a shudder. There was something so evil and repulsive about the man that it made him both angry and fearful. He had felt it that first day and each time he'd seen him since. He still remembered the look on the Swede's face when he had asked Slim for the details of his supposed conquest of the girl in Wauna. There was something dirty, inside and out, about Warndahl that repelled not only Slim but to a lesser degree the rest of the crew. He felt a disheartening disappointment that he'd be on the same watch.

"What's the matter, kid? Don't you want to be ass-hole buddies?"

Slim was spared the necessity of an answer when Peterson and Holst stepped into the wheelhouse from the port wing bridge, where they had been taking a noon sun sight. Warndahl turned back to the wheel and concentrated on his quartermaster duties.

Holst looked at the deck boy. "Don't stand there. Come over and watch him." He indicated the A.B. with a quick tilt of his head and turned back to a notebook that he'd opened on the workshelf.

Slim moved close enough to Warndahl to see down into the compass. The gloomy interior of the shiny brass binnacle was dimly lit by a small shielded bulb that illuminated the big compass card. He had seen many compass cards before, but none so large and complicated as this one.

Around its outside edge were numerals dividing the circumference into three hundred and sixty degrees. Inside this ring of numbers was a complex design of elongated diamond-shaped points, which Slim knew divided the card into the old quarter-point system that his grandfather had tried so hard to make him learn.

After a while Slim began to feel more confident. He liked the atmosphere of the bridge and the commanding feeling it gave him to be in the highest part of the ship. From the wheelhouse windows he could look forward and down across the forward deckload to the fo'c'sle deck, with its confusion of windlass gear, fair-leads, anchor chains, secured by huge devil's claws that clutched the links in steel fingers to keep them from running loose to the bottom, and on to the breastplate and very eyes of the ship.

He watched Warndahl's sure hand on the helm and after a time he began to grow impatient. The two mates were comparing some intricate calculations from the readings they had taken from their stop watches and sextants. Slim wanted to turn and watch them as they filled their notebook pages with confidently scrawled figures and symbols that would add up to the exact number of degrees, minutes, and seconds of latitude the vessel was situated on at that precise moment. Out of the corner of his eye he sneaked a glance at the two officers. Presently he heard Peterson put down his pencil and light up a cigarette.

Holst was still laboring over the calculations. In a moment he, too, looked up. "Take a look at these, Pete, and see if I'm gaining on ya!"

Peterson took the notebook and compared the end figure with his own quicker calculation. "That checks close enough." He walked to the little blackboard, erased the old course scrawled there and carefully put down a new one.

Warndahl looked at the board, read the figure "232 degrees," and immediately altered the course until the big compass pointed to the same heading.

Peterson waited until the ship steadied up, then turned to the third mate. "She's all yours. It must be downhill—she's making nine knots!"

Holst smiled at the joke. "You gotta watch her. She's a slippery piece of steel!"

Slim knew the two officers were joking about the old tramp. He'd heard the second mate talking with Chips some days before at Wauna. Peterson was convinced that the fastest time she'd ever made was when she slid down the ways of the Los Angeles Shipbuilding and Drydock Corporation in 1918, one of the last of hundreds of such vessels built to meet the World War I need for American bottoms. To him they were painfully slow ships. Designed to average ten knots, they seldom were able to make it, unless wind and currents were favorable. The vessels were well built, though roughly constructed with an absolute minimum of comforts for officers and crew. They were picked up for a few cents on the dollar by private owners, and very little was added to them to make them more livable. The *Tropic Trader* was no exception.

The second mate left the wheelhouse and went below to relax on his watch off. This meant taking a tour of the ship to inspect the deckload and chain lashings, to see that the big hornlike ventilators were properly turned into the wind and to stop by the radio shack to pick up the latest gossip from Sparks.

The third mate turned back to his notebook and looked over the figures for a few moments. Slim heard him close the book, put it away in one of the drawers and curse softly. "I'll be a sonuvabitch——"

Warndahl reached up over his head and gave the short cord hanging there a sharp tug. Outside, on the forward end of the wheelhouse, Slim heard the ship's bell strike one time—twelve-thirty. He'd been on the bridge half an hour and it had seemed like half a minute.

Holst leaned against the sill of the open window and the wind flattened the top of his faded khaki officer's cap. He stared out ahead for a long time, apparently lost in thought, then turned slowly, fished a cigarette from his shirt pocket, lit it with his characteristic sleight-of-hand trick and put the burned match in a metal can on the work shelf. He walked slowly over to the deck boy and leaned on the starboard engine-room telegraph. "Ever see a compass before?"

Slim was startled by the loud sound of the voice in the deep quiet of the wheelhouse. "Yes, sir, I have——"

"Know what it means to 'box' a compass?"

Slim nodded, glad to be able to answer. "Yes, sir, I do——"

"Okay. Can you do it?"

The deck boy hesitated a moment. "Not very well. I used to be able——"

The third mate interrupted him: "Tomorrow, when you come up for your wheel watch, know how to do it. Warndahl, when you're off watch, give the boy the main points so he can learn them."

Warndahl shot a worried look at the mate. "I will if I can remember 'em myself!"

Holst looked at the A.B. closely. "You either know 'em or you don't!"

He walked to the back of the wheelhouse and took a paper from one of the drawers. With a pencil he carefully wrote down the thirty-two points, reading clockwise from north around to east, south, west and north again. He handed them to the deck boy. "Here!" Nodding toward the A.B., he looked at Slim and winked. "Most of these guys know their poker cards better than their compass cards. He'd probably give it to you all ass-backwards!" He handed the paper to Slim, who folded it carefully and put it in his pocket.

"Thank you, sir. I'll try to know it by tomorrow."

Holst looked at the boy, as though trying to make up his mind about something. He exhaled a long drag, pinched the hot end off into the can and rolled the dead butt between his fingers. "All right—I'll tell you what I'll do. You come up tomorrow and box that compass right the first time, and we'll break you in on steering."

Slim felt a tingle of excitement run through him. "I'll sure try to have it down, sir!"

"Okay, but get it down good, 'cause I may ask you to box it around the other way, too, from north to west!"

A small worry wave replaced the excitement, but he made up his mind he'd know how to box the compass upside down and backward if he had to work all night. He'd get Ioway to help him and maybe he'd manage it all right.

The rest of the four-hour watch passed slowly for Slim. At two o'clock the seaman called Rusty came up to relieve Warndahl at the wheel. Holst put the deck boy to work shining the brass binnacle top which he removed from around the compass. Slim sat out on the wing bridge, the warm sun on his back, doing his best to get the creamy white liquid polish into all the intricate corners.

When Rusty pulled the cord and struck the bell eight times to indicate four o'clock and the end of the watch, Slim was just putting the final touches on the brass cover. It gleamed in the sun and, were it not for the many little dents denoting long usage, it would have passed for factory-new.

Slim saw Jack come up on the starboard side of the bridge and enter the wheelhouse. He knew that the ex-fighter was taking over from Rusty. Mr. Samson, the first mate, had been on the bridge for some minutes talking with Holst. The deck boy blew the dried polish from the cracks in the binnacle top and entered the wheelhouse. He wasn't sure whether or not to replace it until Holst took it from him and carefully put it back in place.

"Good job, kid."

When he heard the third mate speak, Samson turned around. He saw the gleaming brass dome and stepped closer. For a moment he studied it with interest. "Who did *that* job?"

Holst inclined his head toward the deck boy as he put the brass securing pins in place. "The kid here."

The first mate looked at Slim and grunted.

As the two mates turned their backs to the wheel and began the routine of changing the watch, Hammer caught Slim's eye. He spoke just above a whisper. "You keep on doin' work like that and you'll wind up being a brass monkey on the bridge!"

Slim didn't know exactly what the A.B. meant, but he sensed there was something wrong with the status of brass monkey from Jack's tone and warning look.

"You better shove off now before the mate finds something else for you!"

Slim nodded and turned to go. As he reached the wheelhouse door, Mr. Samson called to him. "Fredericks! Take this to the radio shack." He held out a folded piece of paper.

Slim stepped back into the wheelhouse and took the message. "Yes, sir." Stuffing it in his dungaree pocket, he descended the ladder to the main deck, made his way aft and climbed the ladder to the boatdeck where he had first met Sparks. The heavy outside weather door was opened and secured to the bulkhead with a large bronze hook. Slim peered through the screen and saw the radio operator hunched over the receiving unit, headphones clamped tightly over his ears.

He didn't hear the boy open the door and was startled to find he had company. He turned a knob until it clicked and took off the listening device. "Well, what the hell happened to you?"

Slim smiled at the slender, studious-looking radio operator, who looked almost scrawny in the oversized skivvy shirt that hung loosely on his thin frame. "I looked for you a couple of times in port, but you were never in."

Sparks removed his glasses and blew on the lenses.

"Sounds like you've been on the go yourself. According to the most reliable scuttle butt I can get, you were pretty busy with the ladies in Wauna!"

Slim frowned. "Who told you that?"

Sparks shrugged and replaced his spectacles. "Nobody ever starts a rumor aboard ship. They just get around by mental telepathy."

Slim felt a little flattered that he should be the subject of fo'c'sle conversation, particularly concerning his prowess with the ladies, but at the same time he felt a growing resentment that Edye had become the subject of gossip. It didn't take any imagination on his part to reproduce the dialogue that must have gone on behind his back. It suddenly became important to tell the truth to Sparks. He was one of the few on the ship who would understand and believe him. It was not important to defend himself but to make certain that they understood that the girl was no waterfront pickup.

When Slim finished Sparks smiled indulgently. "My young friend, I want to tell you something. If the girl had been the Virgin Mary, those filthy wolves would still have accused you of making a pitch. Forget 'em. It's a lot better to let them think you've got five balls than to let 'em think you're a 'queer-o.' You're going to find out that, before we hit another port, most of these guys'll be ready to screw anything on two feet, including each other. Feedin' and fuckin' are the only two things they'll have on their minds. Three weeks out they won't even think about food!"

Sparks took two cigarettes out of a pack on the table and offered one to Slim. "I'll tell you something else, too. You're going to be expected to tell some tall tales about the dames you've laid—and you're going to have to listen to some horrible shit those guys will dream up as their pricks get stiffer. Just be ready, boy, 'cause it's due to start any day now."

Slim fished the paper out of his pocket and handed it to the radio operator. "The first mate asked me to bring this to you."

Sparks took the paper and looked at it for a moment. "Position report for the owners—1896 miles out of Pedro at noon." He looked at the message again and stuck one edge of it under a loaded ash tray. "How you makin' out on the bridge?"

Slim sat on the edge of the built-in bunk and puffed on the cigarette. "Okay, I guess. So far I've just watched— and shined the brass."

"I hear you're on Holst's watch."

Slim nodded. "Yeah. He asked for me."

"That's a break for you, son. He's the best all-around officer on the ship. Do you know anything about him?"

"Not much. I've heard the guys talking a little, but they haven't said anything I believe."

Sparks slumped into his desk chair and poked the glowing butt into the heaping ash tray. "You can believe almost anything they tell you about him. The guy's life reads like a book. Someday when you get tired of these tubs dig out the newspapers from five years back and find out who you were sailing with!"

The boy reflected for a moment, remembering the things he'd heard in the messroom—stories that Holst had been one of the toughest rumrunners in the business, that he'd been in service and had been court-martialed, that he'd been a skipper on the Yangtze River tankers, but somehow the man didn't look like a swashbuckling adventurer. Slim *did* believe that the man had been in the Imperial German Navy at one time, because he'd heard the third mate refer to the Kaiser's elite service and the benefits of its unswerving discipline. Holst kept bemoaning the lack of responsibility in most of the officers and men of the merchant service. But there was something kindly about the stocky, gray-bristled officer. There was no suggestion of the cruelty and brutality usually associated with the career adventurer—the ruthlessness that is prerequisite to survival in a world in which no quarter is asked or given.

Slim was not sure whether he should report back on deck to the bosun for more day work or whether he was finished now that his watch was over. But Sparks seemed in the mood to talk and the boy's curiosity about Holst had long since been whetted by the fragments of fo'c'sle gossip, and so he listened as the radio operator rambled on and pieced together the fabulous truth of the third mate's life—truth that Sparks had long since verified to his own satisfaction.

Holst had earned the right to his legend some years earlier, when as an officer in charge of a revenue cutter out of San Francisco, he had deplored the effects of rot-gut bootleg on the youth of his adopted country. Being a man of action, he conceived and effected a handy arrangement with a gang of runners who had been bringing good scotch and gin ashore at a lonely landing on California's north coast line.

To provide the officer with the incentive to be elsewhere with his armed vessel, the runners supplied him with a thousand dollars a week in cash. Everything went fine. Holst met his commitments and sailed the other way on the nights the stuff was being run ashore. In due time he'd rendezvous, pick up his money, and split it with the crew. But the day came, as it always does with rackets, when someone thought the pay-off was too high, that Holst was taking from others—competitors. So the pay-off was stopped in order to bring about a better understanding.

Holst knew only one thing—the original deal was the only deal. He was actually having no contact with other runners. He warned the boys to get back in line but the warning was ignored. A second warning was ignored, and then came the day of judgment. As the boats were bringing the stuff through the surf at Barks Landing, the cutter appeared and opened fire. All the runners were killed by machine-gunning. One of the runners lived long enough to point the finger at Holst, and the day of judgment came for him too.

After a quick court-martial he was given a stiff sentence in the naval prison and dishonorably busted out of the service. He was released after two years for exemplary good behavior. Deprived of his rank and his papers, he went to the Orient and became skipper on a small American tanker operating on the Yangtze River. His service was so exceptional and his personality so ingratiating that he prevailed upon some officials to get his licenses reinstated in the States. In due time Holst and his wife returned to San Francisco. Aboard the *Tropic Trader* as the new third mate, he was beginning the first chapter of a new life.

It was obvious to Slim that the radio operator shared the admiration and respect for Holst felt by the rest of the crew. Slim had listened to Sparks' long biography without interrupting. It had been a fascinating tale to the deck boy, but he had trouble relating what he had heard of the man to what he had seen of the man. Why, for instance, would Holst be interested in the welfare of a lowly deck boy on one of the most miserable tramps in the Pacific? Slim had sensed something almost paternalistic in the third mate's attitude toward him. There was nothing about him that he feared, on the contrary, Slim had experienced an outgoing feeling which he had checked, for he instinctively felt that any manifestation of it would be rebuffed. Slim listened but said nothing to Sparks about his own meager impressions of the third mate, beyond commenting on the incident with the bosun and Holst's just and direct manner of handling the affair.

Sparks looked at the chronograph on the bulkhead over his desk and reached for the paper Slim had given him. "I've been batting the breeze long enough. I better bat this bug awhile!" He swung around in his chair, flipped a couple of switches and began sending a long code message that crackled through a small spark gap in a series of mechanically precise dots and dashes.

Slim watched him for a moment, then quietly let himself out the screen door onto the boatdeck. On his way to the ladder he peered through one of the square portholes of the sick bay, which occupied one half of the same deckhouse that contained the wireless room and Sparks' quarters.

Inside he could make out two pipe bunks, one above the other. Two thinly filled bags of ticking passed for mattresses. In one corner was a small built-in basin with a tap above it and against the bulkhead, directly beneath the porthole, Slim could see a large wooden chest with a red cross painted on it. Upside down he could read the legend: "Medical Supplies." The whole interior was tongue-and-groove wood, like the wainscoting he remembered in the kitchen of the ranch house. The floor was smooth blood-red cement. The deck boy wondered how long it had been since anyone had been confined to the sick bay. He knew that it was the steward's responsibility to administer to the sick and that he was also the sole custodian of the keys to the place.

Pugh, the steward, was a sour-faced individual who insisted upon wearing a shiny blue serge uniform he'd worn as second steward for a defunct passenger line. Slim saw him several times in port supervising the loading of ship's stores. The man was an important factor in the complicated relationships and economy that make a vessel a "good" ship or a "bad" one. Slim joined the crew in an instinctive dislike of the man from the very first. The feeling was generally shared by the officers too. Pugh's quarters were on the portside of the midship maindeck, next to the ship's storeroom and the petty officers' mess. This was his domain and he seldom left it, except to confer with Mr. Samson, the first mate.

Slim descended the ladder to the main deck and walked aft over the deckload. In the fo'c'sle again, he took a ruled pad to the messroom and began a letter to Edye. He had heard that when they got to Auckland there would be mail from the States aboard the *Tahiti* or the *Maunganui*, two of the crack Union Line ships that made contact with the Northern Hemisphere. He hoped there would be word from the girl.

— 12 —

After the evening meal Slim went up to the poopdeck, where a canopy had been rigged to keep the sun from heating the steel deck-plates unbearably and prevent the fo'c'sle from becoming more of an oven than it already was. Even the wind scoops in the portholes brought in almost no fresh outside air, because the following breeze moved at nearly the same speed as the ship. Up on deck after sundown it was bearable and, unless a rain squall drove them below, little pinpoints of glowing cigarettes positioned each man in his favorite corner.

Slim found a place atop the large slatted, wire-lined potato box. He had folded an old tarpaulin into a cushion and back rest which he leaned up against the athwartship's rail. Curled up, he could look over the entire deck and directly aft down along the florescence of the ship's wake. A bright moon silvered the smooth surface of the sea and outlined the crest of each long swell that rolled beneath the rising stern. Occasionally a flipped cigarette traced a dull red arc through the night as it disappeared below the topsides. The only sound was the rhythmic beat of the shaft and propeller as each submerged blade bit into its allotted volume of sea water and pushed it back into the rushing malestrom of the wake. The men talked softly. The conversation was general and lingered on no particular topic for very long.

The Shiek and John were on the bridge, standing their four-hour watch with the second mate. Jack and Otto were below in the mess-room poker game with Mike, the fireman, Squirt, the oiler, and Brill, the water tender. Sharing the luminous moon shadows beneath the awning were Chips, Rusty, Warndahl, Ioway, Stokes, the third-watch fireman, an A.B. known as Spots, and Slim.

As usual, the ship's carpenter both started and steered the conversation. Lounging on the rope table, the ac-

128

knowledged seat of the seniors, he leaned his back against a coil of thick hawser and supplied new topics as each discussion lagged and ended. "There's a hell of a lot of things wrong with this tub, but there's one thing she has got, and that's the three-watch system. I remember when we used to hafta stand two watches—four on—four off. On a long trip you sure could get beat down. At least with this deal you can get eight hours in the bunk if you've a mind to!"

The men mumbled in agreement and someone offered the carpenter a cigarette. He scorned it for one of the brown-paper Picayunes that he preferred.

Using the still flaming match as a pointer, he wagged it at the proffered pack. "Them white paper smokes'll kill ya. That's the trouble with that sick Russian down below!"

Though no one replied, Chips had made his point. At one time or another they had all wondered about the strange old fellow called "Russian John." He had an A.B.'s ticket, but no one could figure out how he managed to get it, much less pass his lifeboat test. He spoke almost no English but appeared to speak both French and Spanish fluently. The bosun spoke to him in his native tongue.

No man on the ship was more out of character as a sailor, unless it was Stokes, the renegade Oxfordian who hid in the bowels of the fireroom and contentedly worked in a world that never challenged him, populated by people he could subdue with one withering and perfectly constructed sentence.

The bosun assigned the Russian to the second mate's watch, twelve to four. When the watch was turned out at quarter to midnight, the men were nearly always awakened by the peculiar hacking cough that wracked the old man. Each day he went through the same ordeal—five minutes or more of fighting to free something that seemed to fill the top of his lungs and throat. Slim could hear him expectorate behind the privacy of the curtain. He wondered how the sailor got rid of the massive amounts of phlegm that seemed to well up from inside the frail, bony chest. There was no porthole to spit through. Quite by accident, one morning, Slim found out the answer. The Russian dropped a shoebox from the shelf by his bunk. Among the contents was a collection of cast-off Copenhagen snuff cans that he used for cuspidors, then heaved them over the side. None of the men in the fo'c'sle liked the sound of the cough. On more than one occasion Jack predicted that the old man would spit his lungs out some night and wind up in a weighted canvas bag.

129

As the men talked on deck they knew that the strange old Russian would be propped up on a pillow behind his curtain, reading from one of several books he kept safely under lock and key in his locker. Slim had managed to get a glimpse of them once, they appeared to be classics in French and in Russian. The books were old and very expensive.

Warndahl, thinking of the ailing old man, spat over the side. "He's a filthy old bastard. He oughta be offa ship!"

Chips echoed the thought that crossed Slim's mind. "Filthy's not the word for him, Warndahl! He's cleaner than most of us. He's sick, like I said, from smokin' too many of them fancy white-paper cigarettes. Them Russian cigarettes with all that gold printin' can't be no good goin' up in smoke down yer lungs! It just figures!"

Warndahl snorted in the darkness. "Cigarettes my achin' ass! No cigarette never hurt nobody! He's got the bug— and the first goddamn thing ya know *we'll* all have it too! Why do ya suppose they got them places in the mountains where they keep all the lung cases? So they won't spread the germs, that's why! An' here we are cooped up with the guy. I just as soon be sleepin' with a leper!"

"Ya probably would, Warndahl, if the leper put out."

There was a pause before the A.B. replied. When he did, he spoke softly. "Watch it, Chips. Don't go pullin' a dog's tail if you don't want to get bit."

Slim could feel the carpenter's broad smile. The spectacle of Warndahl trying to do any bodily harm to the big carpenter without sneaking up on him in the dark was ludicrous to everyone. Several of the men laughed softly at the idea. Warndahl got up from his place and walked to the companionway that led down into the fo'c'sle. For an instant he stood silhouetted against the dim light from below, then his shadow retreated down the buff-painted plating and disappeared. The men sat in silence for a moment. A match flared nearby and Slim made out Spots.

Like Ioway, the new deck boy, everyone liked Spots. He was a round young man somewhere in his early thirties. His moon face beamed with a built-in friendliness. He spoke with animation and always managed to see the humor in a situation. There was, however, one exception. Spots found no humor in the problem he had with liquor.

It seemed to be his only problem and his shipmates had run headlong into it the night he came aboard the *Tropic Trader* in San Pedro. Spots was a compulsive boozer who took no joy in his weakness. He had been drunk the night he came aboard and had been in rough condition for two days afterward.

The A.B. took his nickname not from freckles, as one might suppose, but from an oil spot on the seat of his pants that appeared at regular intervals when he was on the bottle. The spot was caused by massive doses of mineral oil that the fat fellow took to "spike his liver" when he could no longer keep his vows and fell off the wagon.

Sober, Spots was the soul of friendliness, drunk, he was the persistent and prodigal bestower of everything he had, including the clothes on his back. There was no refusing him and the inevitable end of each binge was a chubby, stark-naked cherub sprawled in his bunk, blissfully snoring at one end and oozing mineral oil at the other. Spots was just recovering from a twenty-four-hour binge that had used up the last of the gin he'd smuggled aboard when Slim had signed on.

Chips broke the silence. "How ya feelin', Spots?"

The fat A.B.'s tone was reassuring. "Oh, I'm fine now. I feel a hundred per cent better."

Chips laughed. "If you only feel a hundred per cent better, you're still in bad shape!"

Spots heaved a long sigh. "Man, I know! But it'll be okay now. I'm off the stuff for good!"

Rusty spoke and there was more than a little sarcasm in his voice. "Tell us about it, Spots. How *did* ya lick ole demon rum?"

The fat seaman ignored the taunt and answered simply. "I took the vows in Pedro. I went to church and confessed and I took a vow before the father."

A mirthless laugh came from Rusty. "Works like a charm, don't it, Spots? So how come you tied one on two nights later?"

Spots sat in silence for a moment. When he spoke, there was a trace of embarrassment in his voice. "To tell you the truth, when I took the vow, I held out on that one bottle because it was good stuff and I had a terrible time gettin' it. I sure didn't want to waste it!"

A ripple of laughter came from the men.

Chips offered the fat A.B. an alternative in case he ever found himself in such an embarrassment again. "Next time, mate, just let us know about your problem and we'll see if we can't figure a way to take it off yer hands!"

There was a general murmur of agreement and a brief moment of silence. Then from the shadows came the beautifully modulated voice of Stokes. Making one of his rare appearances on deck, the English fireman had been sitting silently during the conversation, puffing on one of his carefully guarded English cigarettes.

After listening, he felt constrained to comment. "At the risk of offending, my dear Spots, I must say that you are hardly a person upon whom good gin should be wasted. As a matter of fact, I dare say that none of you chaps have palates sensitive enough to properly appreciate its delicate bouquet."

There was another moment of silence before Chips could find words. "What the hell are you talkin' about, Stokes?"

The fireman obliged with an immediate answer. "I merely said I don't think *any* of you deserve a drink of good gin."

Rusty picked up the challenge. "I appreciate a good drink of gin, you can bet your ass!"

"My dear chap, I'm not in the habit of wagering parts of my anatomy. I hope you'll forgive my presumptuousness, but there's a vast difference between a good drink of gin and a drink of *good* gin. As a matter of fact, to cite a case in point, had our friend Spots here taken a drink of 'good' gin, he would have gone forthwith to his church to give thanks to God for the subtle art of the distiller. Whereas on a 'good drink of gin' he went to church to swindle the Almighty and wound up cheating himself!"

"Oh, fer Christ sake, Stokes, why don't you knock off with that high-sounding crap?" Rusty got up and walked aft, undid the front of his dungarees, and relieved himself over the stern.

Stokes glanced at him. "Makes you feel rather small, doesn't it, old boy?"

The men laughed and Rusty grunted his disgust. Spots sat quietly for a moment, pondering Stokes' commentary. He shifted his position on the deck and gingerly pulled the oily seat of his pants free of his behind. Rolling over on one buttock, he braced himself on the bias against the rail.

"I don't see how I cheated myself, Stokes. I got an extra bottle, didn't I?"

The fireman ignored the question.

"I admit I cheated the father when I took the vow, but I don't see how I cheated myself."

Rusty returned to his place. "Why don't you drop it, Spots? He's tryin' to get yer goat!"

"Indeed, I am not trying to 'get his goat' or, for that matter, am I trying to save his soul. I have no doubt that

Spots will save his own soul by the simple expedient of going to confession—both before he buys his next bottle and after his next binge."

Stokes mused for a moment, then spoke softly, as though to himself. "I have long since acknowledged the futility of trying to save souls by failing so miserably to rescue my own. Each of us does penance in his own way. You, Spots, with your seared gut and soggy seat, and I, my friend, in mortal struggle with fear and reason."

There was no self-pity in the Englishman's voice, but Slim felt curiously sorry for the unkempt little man who wasn't really a little man but who somehow managed to give that impression. Stokes sat in silence for a few minutes then quietly rose and disappeared down the companionway to the black gang's fo'c'sle.

It was Rusty who broke the silence. "What the hell's eatin' that guy?"

Chips cleared his throat. "He's harmless. I've sailed with him before. He likes the sound of his own music, but it ain't very often he talks. I heard some fellows say once that he was a college guy—from Oxford or one of those places. He's got somethin' on his mind but he's okay!"

Spots spoke up from his uncomfortable position against the rail. "He was wrong about that gin. It was good stuff —real grain alcohol and juniper oil. I know the druggist who made it. It cost five bucks!"

Chips laughed. "Kid, if you need a drink, *any* gin is good! The boys are just a little put out at ya for not passin' the bottle around. Next time remember yer friends!"

The sound of heavy boots echoed on the companion ladder, and Mike, the big fireman from the first watch, came out on deck. He leaned against the rail and shook his head. "Jesus but that Hammer is a lucky son-of-a-bitch! I'm cleaned. The guy took six hands in a row—and I was bettin' some good cards too. Since when ain't three aces good in a five-card-draw game?"

Chips looked interested. "What'd he beat ya with?"

"A full house—threes and sevens——"

The carpenter shrugged. "That's the way it runs sometimes. I'll tell ya one thing, though. When ya play with the same guys all the time, the money just keeps goin' the rounds. The only lucky guy is the guy who wins the last night out!"

Rusty confirmed the obvious truth. "That's the game that counts!" He got up slowly and moved toward the companionway. "I think I'll go take him on for a few hands." He stepped over the coaming and disappeared down the companionway.

Slim wondered what time it was. He turned his head toward the bridge to listen for the ship's bell. As he peered forward into the moonlight gloom he saw a shadowy figure moving quickly aft along the portside of the deckload. It was the Shiek hurrying toward the fo'c'sle. He walked rapidly over the lumber and stepped onto the poop, ignored the men entirely, and ducked quickly down the companionway after Rusty.

Chips rose from his place on the rope table and walked to the rail. "Wonder what he's doin' off the bridge?" He stood looking out along the wake for a moment or two, then stretched out a big yawn. "Think I'm going to turn in. Wish to God I could get some air in that place of mine. They got that deckload piled so high the port's covered. I used to get a little breeze off the well deck." He paused at the head of the companionway. "See ya in the morning."

Slim, Ioway, and Spots all murmured their "good nights," as he went slowly below. They liked Chips. He was a good shipmate—a fair and dependable man who bore no grudges and who generally saw the best side of everything.

Slim slid down from atop the potato box and took over the carpenter's place on the rope table. Ioway came over and moved in alongside.

Spots stayed seated on the rusty steel deck, his arms hooked through the lower rail and around one of the dirty white stanchions. "Geez, man, I don't know why I drink that stuff. I sure feel horrible!"

Slim looked over his left shoulder at the blob of a shadow. "Why don't you go down to the pantry and get some coffee?"

Spots shuddered. "I can't drink that stuff black."

Slim looked at the fat A.B. again. "Put some milk in it. There's an open can in the pantry."

Spots struggled to his feet, and leaned weakly against the rail. "Have you used that milk lately?"

Slim shook his head. "Nope. Why?"

"It's fulla dead copra bugs. The stuff's the color of tobacco juice!" Spots shuddered at the thought.

"Why don't you look for another can?"

Ioway volunteered the discouraging answer. "Bolo says we don't get another can till Sunday!"

Spots pushed away from the rail and steadied himself upright. "To hell with it. I'm goin' to turn in. G'nite, fellas——"

The two deck boys murmured their replies and the fat, hangover-ridden sailor waddled to the companionway and slowly negotiated the steep ladder below to the fo'c'sle.

Slim and Ioway sat in silence for a while. The moon had slipped behind a dark cloud bank. They heard the faint ring of the wheel-house bell, borne aft on a vagrant breeze. It sounded like four bells. Slim yawned and leaned comfortably back against the coiled hawser. The little air that stirred felt pleasantly cool and dry. It moved around his thin body and flapped the loose folds of his skivvy shirt against the tight skin of his belly. He stared out into the new darkness and tried to make out an horizon lost in the Stygian band that invisibly bound the sea to the sky.

– 13 –

At breakfast the next morning the messroom talk ran up and down the table with more animation than usual. There was an undertone of tension when Slim took his place at the end of the long wooden bench. Chips, Rusty, Warndahl, Ioway, Jack, Otto, and a vastly improved Spots were eating before starting their deck work or wheel watches.

When Slim slid quietly into the vacant place at the end of the bench, Rusty was finishing an appraisal of the Shiek. "And not only that, but the sonuvabitch came aft in the middle of his watch last night and didn't get back to the bridge for half an hour. Boy, we got some wild ones on this tub!"

Chips shook his head. "John told me that Peterson chewed his ass off for it, but the guy said he was sick and had to get some medicine."

Warndahl snorted and slurped his coffee. "It don't take much figgerin' to tell what kinda medicine that guy takes!"

Rusty looked up with interest. "What do ya mean by that crack?"

Warndahl looked up and down the table to make sure the men were listening. "I'll tell ya what I think—I think he's a snow bird!" Warndahl speared a piece of dry fried egg without looking and raised it to his mouth.

Chips thought a bit. "He could be a cokey, too. He's got glassy eyes, all right. I've sailed with some guys who were on the stuff and they all look alike. Unhealthy-lookin' skin —queer ducks—they stay to themselves."

Ioway, whose face bore the concentration of a kid watching the final scene in a Pearl White serial, looked at the carpenter. "Do you mean that he takes dope—that he's a real dope fiend?"

Chips looked at him with exaggerated concern. "That's right." Then, with the air of one imparting a choice bit of *sub rosa* information, he leaned toward the new deck boy.

"There's somethin' else ya oughta know. We're *all* dope fiends on this ship—every one of us! Ya gotta be dopey to go to sea in the first place!"

The carpenter waited a moment for his joke to sink in, then leaned back and laughed and the others joined in. Ioway looked embarrassed and returned to his food with downcast eyes and a grin.

Spots looked thoughtful. Chips' obvious joke hadn't amused him. "Poor guy. If he's hooked on that stuff, there's nothing you can do for him."

The carpenter looked at the fat A.B. "Don't worry about 'poor' him. Worry about 'poor' us, if the guy runs out of whatever he's takin'. That's when it gets rough—on everybody!"

The men avoided looking at the fat A.B., so securely "hooked" himself. Slim thought he could understand why Spots took no pleasure in the plight of the Shiek. The aura of mystery that surrounded the patent-leather-looking ordinary seaman grew more ominous with each mess-hall conjecture.

Warndahl kept the conversation going with fresh anecdotes about dope addicts he'd sailed with. He was right in the middle of a particularly lurid tale of an opium den in Macao, the Portuguese colony off the southeast coast of China, when the Shiek appeared quietly in the doorway. An embarrassed silence fell over the table. The pallid, glassy-eyed sailor surveyed the messroom with an unfocused sweep and leaned against the steel doorframe. There were no seats and nobody moved to make a place for him.

Ioway fidgeted nervously, wiped his mouth on his handkerchief, and began hauling his legs out from beneath the long table. "You can sit here if you like. I'm through."

The Shiek's expression changed to an insolent smirk, as he watched the nervous deck boy extricate himself from the bench and edge toward the door along the narrow space behind the backs of the quiet seamen. Ioway hesitated a moment when the ordinary seaman showed no signs of letting him by.

Chips leaned on his elbows, holding his coffee cup in both hands. He looked closely at the Shiek for a moment, then spoke quietly. "The kid made a place for ya. Let him by, what do ya say?"

The Shiek ignored Ioway completely, moved slightly to one side to let him squeeze out of the cramped messroom, then resumed his slouch again. "I'll tell you what I say." His voice was low and edged with the insolence that

137

twisted his thin, bloodless mouth. "I say you guys talk too much. That's what I say." A series of low, monodic sounds heaved his flat chest and escaped from his lips.

It was unlike any laughter Slim had ever heard. The look and sound of the man made his scalp creep and the sinister quality held each seaman speechless during the long moment that the Shiek looked at them. Then he turned and disappeared into the passageway.

Hammer was the first to come out of the mood. "Why, that miserable sonuvabitch! Who the fuck-all does he think he is?" He set his jaw and started to rise from the table.

"Cool off, Hammer. He musta heard the chatter!" Chips' voice was friendly but it carried a subtle edge of command.

The younger A.B. held his half-upright position for an instant, then sank slowly back into place at the table. Chico came in with a pot of fresh coffee. Slim took it and handed it down the line.

The little Filipino had a puzzled smile on his face. "Deed thot crazy fallow come een here?"

Chips grinned at the messboy. "Yeah, Chico, but he didn't stay. He wasn't in a very good mood!"

The messman nodded his head in emphatic agreement. "There ees som'theeng bod about thees mon!" He shook his head sadly. *Loco—muy loco!* Picking up a handful of empty dishes, he left the messroom and returned to the pantry.

Hammer scowled. "Jesus, what a collection of weirdos! A Russian stiff who spits up his lungs all night and a hophead who thinks he's Rudolph Valentino!" He fished a cigarette out of his blue workshirt pocket and lit it.

To Slim, Hammer's reference to "Valentino" seemed strangely apt. The Shiek, so called behind his back, did bear a curious resemblance to the Hollywood movie idol. Most of the time he wore a black leather cap cocked rakishly over one side, obscuring the ear but revealing the tip of his long, carefully pointed sideburns. His skin was pale parchment, even after hours of exposure on deck. Except for the times when he was needed on deck to man the lines, he worked by himself: chipping, scraping, painting, content to do the minimum necessary to get by. Even the insensate bosun seemed happy to let him alone, much as one would avoid a strange creature that might possibly have a poisonous bite.

The conversation lagged after the Shiek's brief appearance. Each of the men seemed lost in his own thoughts. Warndahl tried to revive the discussion by telling of a rumor he'd heard that the Shiek had been kept by a woman in San Pedro after he'd jumped ship from one of the Luckenback freighters running through the canal to the East Coast. If the scuttle butt interested the men, they gave no sign.

At eight bells the bosun turned the watch out on deck to resume the tedious and endless task of cleaning, and fighting the salty corrosion and rust that slowly consumes even the best tended vessels.

To Slim it was a special day. Long after he had turned in the night before, he had gone over the points of the compass time and time again, drilling into his head the complicated quarter-point system that he must know if he was to earn his chance at the wheel. He left the deck at eleven-thirty, when the bosun knocked him off for the noon meal with his usual brand of heavy-handed sarcasm.

"Okay, 'Admiral,' go fill yer belly. You gotta eat good if you're going to show de captain how to run de ship!"

Slim went aft to the messroom to eat and study. At eight bells he reported to the bridge. As before, the Shiek was relieved by Warndahl while Peterson and Holst figured the noon sight, and as usual the second mate completed his calculations first and the third mate differed with him by several miles on their position. And as usual, after Peterson left the bridge, Holst quietly went over his figures again and shook his head in annoyance.

Without waiting for instructions Slim took the brass polish from the locker and began to clean up the handles and trim of the engine-room telegraphs. Warndahl made no effort to talk and concentrated on holding the *Tropic Trader* on her new course, a few degrees farther south than the day before. The wheelhouse was hot, but even so it was the coolest place on the ship. The front windows had been dropped down into the slots in their casements, their leather pull straps barely showing above the sills. A gentle breeze moved through the small enclosure and out the two side doors. It barely stirred the papers on the workshelf. The thermometer read ninety-six. The *Tropic Trader* was moving along with the north equatorial current and the accompanying northeast trade winds.

As the perspiring third mate said, "It's a Mexican standoff! No breeze southbound—and too much northbound!"

Slim's skivvy shirt was soaked with perspiration as he

cleaned and polished the brass and waited for some indication from Holst that would tell him whether or not this was to be the big day in his life—the first time he would be permitted to take the helm. As he shined away he went over the points until, by closing his eyes, he could summon up a vision of the compass rose, just as his grandfather had told him he could.

The first hour of the watch passed and the third mate gave no indication that he even remembered the conversation of the previous afternoon. Slim finished the engine-room telegraphs, the brass case of the tachometer and the pipes and mouthpieces of the speaking tubes.

He was beginning to feel more at home on the bridge. The mysterious upper world was taking on meaning for him, as his understanding of the entire ship grew with each day. He wanted very much to take a peek into the chart room and to get a close look at the tools of the navigator's trade, but he knew that the chance was unlikely; he'd have to be content to pick up as much as he could from watching and listening.

Warndahl reached for the cord above the wheel to ring three bells. Holst, his flattened officer's cap shoved back on his grizzled head, was gently scratching his back and shoulders on the edge of the wheelhouse door. The third mate looked like a shaggy gray bear. From the base of his throat to his ankles and wrists his body was covered with inch-long hair. The perspiration matted it and made it itch, with the result that Holst was continually scratching himself like an amiable animal against anything that was handy. The man was clean, immaculately so, but no amount of salt-water showering could keep the copious perspiration from taking over and soaking through his clothing. In fact, Holst cursed the salt-water showers and swore they did more to irritate his skin than the sweat itself.

As the bells rang the third mate stopped scratching suddenly, as though he'd remembered something. Giving his back one last rub, he stepped back into the wheelhouse and moved close to Slim, who was putting the final polish on the long speaking tube.

"What point comes after east?"

The deck boy rose from his kneeling position on the deck and fought back a flash panic. He closed his eyes hard and summoned up the picture of the compass rose.

"Uh . . . uh . . ." He hesitated for another moment,

then suddenly the answer came rushing out like a kid reciting in school. "East by south, sir!"

Holst looked at him for a long moment, and Slim got a worried feeling that he'd given the wrong answer. He mentally started around the card from the north to check his answer, but before he could get to east the third mate spoke.

"Can you take it all the way around from the top?"

"I believe so, sir." The boy's heart was beginning to pound. He wanted very much to box the compass perfectly for Holst. His respect for the third mate had grown each day—respect without fear. Slim was as anxious to please him as he had been to please his grandfather, and the feeling carried in it the ripening seeds of affection.

"All right, son, give it a try, and face the bulkhead here, away from the compass. You kids have sharp eyes!"

Slim turned his back to the compass and began. The words came in gasps. His heart was pumping hard, making it difficult to breathe. Holst glanced at him, then turned his eyes forward along the ship's course. Slim couldn't see him fighting to stifle a smile. The boy got around to south without a mistake.

"All right, take it around to north now—without stopping!" He barked the order, and Warndahl glanced apprehensively over his shoulder at the pair standing behind him.

Slim began slowly. "South . . . south by west . . . south-southwest southwest . . . west by south . . . west. West by north . . . west-northwest . . . northwest by west . . . northwest." He paused for another breath and completed the task. An involuntary sigh heaved his broad, bony shoulders and he looked quizzically at the third mate.

Holst seemed to be mulling over something. He turned to the lanky youth, looked at him closely, fished a cigarette from his pocket and set it in the corner of his mouth. Again came the sleight-of-hand flare of the match. Holst exhaled a cloud of smoke, and as he spoke two thin plumes continued to stream from his nostrils. "That was pretty good for a deck boy. But remember one thing—tomorrow you'll forget it all unless you keep working at it. Remember that."

"Yes, sir, I will!"

Holst walked across the wheelhouse and leaned in the open forward window. Without turning his head he addressed the quartermaster. "All right, Warndahl, clear the wheel. Let's see if the boy can keep this ship walkin' a straight line."

Warndahl looked up from the compass in surprise, then turned and looked at Slim in disbelief. Uncertainly he stepped off the grating and stood to one side. Slim's feet seemed rooted to the spot. Now that the longed-for moment was upon him, he seemed to have lost his power to act. The *Tropic Trader* plowed along for a few seconds with no one at the helm. Holst turned slowly and saw Warndahl standing helplessly, waiting for the boy to move. The boy stood stock-still, a frightened look frozen on his face, and made no move to take over.

"Fer Christ's sake, get on that grating and take the wheel. Do you expect it to come to you?"

The mate's sharp order jarred Slim from his daze. He stepped quickly forward to the raised grating and took the helm gingerly in his hands. He made no effort to turn the wheel. The compass remained steady on course, the floating card tipping only slightly, as the gimbals leveled the instrument against the gentle lift and roll of the sea.

"Steer two hunnerd 'n' forty degrees . . . like it says on the board." Warndahl issued the order in a low, growling, disdainful voice. "She don't run on rails, ya gotta keep 'er there!"

Slim glanced over his right shoulder at the small blackboard and saw that the course had been altered since the day before. He looked down into the dimly lit interior of the binnacle cover that shielded the compass itself and saw the white poles of the lubber line. Lined up directly between them was the two-hundred-and-forty-degree mark on the compass. He kept his eyes fixed on the figures. They remained still. He glanced up at the third mate, who was staring straight ahead, out over the bow of the freighter. He squinted hard at the card again and was shocked to find that the course mark had moved out from between the two poles of the lubber line and had shifted to the starboard. The figures were beginning to move past the line. Two hundred and thirty-eight . . . two hundred and thirty-five degrees— Slim felt the heavy pressure of panic begin to rise in his chest.

The mate turned in the open window and looked at the boy. "What's your course read now?"

Slim peered into the binnacle and read off the numbers, going slowly past the line. "Two hundred and thirty degrees, sir."

"What course are you supposed to steer?"

"Two hundred and forty degrees."

"Well, then turn the goddamn wheel and put her back on!"

Slim started to turn the wheel to the port and saw Warndahl make an involuntary move to check him.

Holst straightened up and turned away from the window. "Warndahl, I think you're making him nervous. Take the broom and sweep down the wing bridges."

The A.B. shrugged helplessly, went out on the wing, and disappeared below to get a broom. The third mate came over and stood beside the grating. He peered at the compass a moment, took the wheel, and steadied the ship back on its course. It looked so easy to Slim when Holst and Warndahl did it.

"All right, let's try it again. Loosen up! You look like you've got an oar up your ass! Relax a little! We all had to learn, you know. Now look up. Get your head out of that binnacle!"

Dancing daggers of sunlight stabbed Slim's eyes as he lifted his gaze from the compass to the open windows of the wheelhouse. He blinked and looked back into a blind void that filled the binnacle.

Once again the ship began to swing around toward the port and once again the boy tried to check it. He turned the wheel timidly to the starboard. Holst watched him for a few moments, then turned and walked out on the starboard wing bridge. He stood facing aft and Slim could see him looking at the ship's wake and scratching his back against the heavily varnished caprail.

The boy barely breathed as he watched the bow start its inevitable swing to the port again. He couldn't understand why the ship wouldn't stay on the course once she was put there. The wind was dead astern—such as it was—and it certainly wasn't strong enough to blow an eight thousand ton freighter off course, even if it had been hitting on the quarter. Slowly he turned the wheel to the starboard to check the swing. This time it went a little better, but once again the correction had been too much, too late, and the lubber lines swung past the two hundred-and-forty-degree mark and climbed toward the west. Again Slim put the correction in, gently at first, until the bow began swinging back to port.

He glanced out on the starboard wing bridge and saw Holst still staring aft and rubbing his shaggy back gently and rhythmically against the scabrous varnish of the caprail. He looked for a moment out to the port and saw

143

Warndahl sweeping something into the scupper. The ship's clock caught his eye. It was two minutes past two—time for someone to ring four bells. He tried to catch the A.B.'s eye but didn't dare look away from the compass for long. The mate was still occupied with the wake. After a brief moment of indecision Slim reached above his head and pulled the ship's bell four times in two groups of two rings each. The clear, high-pitched ring shocked him. Warndahl looked in the wheelhouse door in surprise. Holst continued scratching.

The third mate finally stepped back inside, walked over, checked the compass, then resumed his earlier station in the open window. "Make sure you ring those bells on time."

Slim looked at him in surprise, then a little smile of relief teased the corners of his mouth. "Yes, sir."

The boy fought to keep the course tighter and found that, as time passed, he could anticipate the ship's swing and, by so doing, was able to use less helm. His back and shoulders ached with the strain of standing at the wheel and his legs felt like lead. At two-thirty promptly he rang five bells. He pulled a bit too hard on the last single ring and the clapper smeared the tone.

"Don't pull it out by the roots, kid!" The mate didn't bother to turn, but if he had, Slim would have seen again the suggestion of a twinkle in his sea-gray eyes. When he did turn, his face was stern, but his voice betrayed a new gentleness.

"All right, son, you've had enough for today. I'll tell you one thing—you may not be a very good helmsman, but you can hold your breath longer than any kid in the world!" Shaking his head in disbelief, Holst walked to the portside wheelhouse door. "All right, Warndahl, take over!"

– 14 –

A fresh breeze ran wrinkled fingers over the smooth young face of the morning sea and the *Tropic Trader* doggedly shoved her plumb bow through the indigo deep of the serene Pacific. The course had been more southerly for the past few days and the chart that the men kept on the fo'c'sle bulkhead showed them to be 3,467 miles southwest of San Pedro, with 2,219 miles left between them and Auckland, New Zealand. They had been out fifteen days and boredom was beginning to lie heavily on the men. There was a little flurry of excitement when it had been rumored that the ship would put into Honolulu, but the rumor died when Slim checked it with Sparks who had become his good friend and chief source of accurate information. Five days had gone by since the unfulfilled promise of women in the islands and the conversation clearly indicated the crew's growing preoccupation.

At breakfast the men got into an argument about which women were the best: the mixed bloods of Hawaii or the pure blood of Polynesia. The expert opinion was about equally divided. Both Slim and Ioway abstained from comment. They listened as the men described the nuances of the various techniques employed by the two groups under discussion. Warndahl managed, as usual, to top the best story—this time with a tale about a girl he'd met in the bar of the Raffles Hotel in Singapore the trip before. According to Warndahl, she had refined her art to a point where, when practiced on him for the better part of one night, she had rendered him unable to walk for a week.

Chips listened patiently until the A.B. had finished. "I don't know what *she* was smokin', sailor, but I think you've been coppin' junk from the Shiek!" He snorted in disgust and went out on deck.

Slim was standing regular wheel watches and the third mate had even complimented him tersely on the way he'd

145

"caught on." The routine of ship's work was familiar now and the boy had begun to change. He'd filled out, even on the poor food that grew worse each day as the ship's cooks, Mr. Jones and Mr. Bones, tried their best to camouflage it with quantities of spices and condiments. There was a new hardness in the boy's face and a new line to his muscles. His hands had changed from the soft hands of a shore-side schoolboy to the hard, capable hands of a seaman. He was seldom thought of as a deck boy. Ioway had taken over that position, in spirit and in fact, by continuing to be as amiable, inept and underfoot as a cocker spaniel. Peterson, the second mate, had given him a chance to steer some days before, but gave up in disgust after an hour.

A number of low, palm-fringed atolls passed astern. The news that there were natives on them sparked long debates in the messroom and another collection of minutely described affairs with the local ladies of a dozen copra islands in the vicinity. Ioway believed every story right down to the last lurid detail. Slim listened, too, but got little of the vicarious pleasure that the deck boy seemed to find. As often as he could, he would find excuses to leave the conversations and get out on deck. The evening was his favorite time and one of the most pleasant places on the ship was the boatdeck, just to the portside of the radio shack. He could see the light shining in Sparks' quarters, as he made his way forward over the deckload and climbed the ladder at the after end of the main deck.

Sparks was leaning back against his workdesk, talking to Stokes, the English fireman who had taken to coming topside for a little intellectual exercise with the radio operator. Both chairs were occupied, so Slim stood in the open door. He had arrived at what appeared to be the end of an argument in which Sparks had been defending the legal philosophy of Sir William Blackstone, father of English law, and the fireman had taken the part of Blackstone's chief critic, Jeremy Bentham, founder of utilitarianism.

Stokes was speaking with mock seriousness. "Now look, old boy, I don't think we're going to settle the issue here tonight. But I suggest that if you really wish to pursue this cerebral cricket match you arm yourself with a few facts instead of a lot of silly generalizations!"

Sparks' mouth gaped open and he rose slowly from his chair. "So it's facts you want, is it? Well, I'll tell you a fact. You act like the fucking Prince of Wales!"

Stokes considered the idea for a moment, then cocked

146

his head uncertainly. "If you're referring to the present one, old chap, I question your choice of adjectives."

Sparks looked at the smiling deck boy and spread his hands in a gesture of defeat. "Let this toothless clown out of here. His presence offends me!"

Slim moved from the doorway.

The little fireman looked pleased. "I must say there's one thing I detest, and that's a person who outstays his welcome. Since I should hate having that happen to me, I'll run along now. Cheerio!" Stokes stepped over the coaming, winked broadly at Slim, and walked across the starboard end of the boatdeck to the main-deck ladder. He disappeared below into the night.

Sparks was preoccupied with his own thoughts for a time before he spoke to the deck boy. "I don't know why I let that little bastard get my goat. He's such a cool, cock-sure sonuvabitch! But I've got to admit he's got a head on those bony shoulders! What a horrible waste!" The radio operator walked over to the locker and got a fresh pack of smokes. He tore the tinfoil off one corner and rolled it in a ball between his thumb and index finger. Holding it in the crook of his finger like a marble, he flipped it past Slim, out the open door.

Slim took the proffered cigarette and draped himself loosely in the still warm chair. Sparks was rankled. He puffed grimly on his smoke and stared through the door, down over the after well deck. Both he and Slim could see the occasional flare of a match as the off-watch members of the black gang talked or mused in the deep shadow-dark of the awning.

Slim watched his friend a moment and could almost hear the rebuttals that he knew the radio operator was framing for his next encounter with the little fireman. He decided to change the subject. "What's the latest poop on the party line?" The young seaman nodded toward the wireless receiver and the headphones hanging on the bulk-head hook.

Sparks stirred himself from his fury fantasy. "The only earth-shaking news I've had today is that the Dollar Line is buying a couple of new *President* ships. As soon as I can get clear of this stinking tub I'm going to try for a berth on one of them—and live like a gold-braid gentle-man again!" He shook his head vehemently. "I don't want to have happen to me what's happened to Stokes!"

Slim thought a moment. "He seems happy."

"Happy? He's out of breath from running away from

himself all the time!" Sparks ground out his cigarette and reached for a fresh one. "And do you want to know something, my skinny young friend?" The radio operator wagged a tobacco-yellowed forefinger at the deck boy. "It's a goddamn tragic waste of brain power. That Stokes either ducked out on something or gave up. But it doesn't make any difference now—he's stayed away too long. He can never go back. It's too late!"

In the silence that followed, Slim wondered about Sparks and what he might be running away from; and he thought of himself and the things he'd run from, except that he told himself he was really running *toward* something—something he wanted very much. Slim knew from previous conversations that the radio operator had become interested in radio as a child back in the early days of the World War and that his amateur hobby had finally won him a professional license. Sparks was equipped for two professions: the law, which he'd indicated he'd studied for quite a time, and telegraphy. What had caused him to leave, Slim didn't know. He did know that most of the men on the *Tropic Trader* had run from something. The two sat for a time, immersed in their thoughts. From the headphones swinging gently on the bulkhead came the faint sound of high-pitched Morse code being sent with mechanical precision. Sparks would stare vacantly toward the phones, occasionally half listening to the messages, then resume his introspection.

"Sparks, do you mind if I ask you something?"

The serious-faced, sandy-haired young man looked over his glasses at the deck boy. "I don't know. Go ahead and we'll see!"

"Well, you told me that first day I met you that you'd been an honor student in law school. Is that right?"

Sparks nodded his head. "That's right."

"Were you close to getting a degree?"

The radio operator rubbed his forehead with the flat of his palm. "I was ready for the bar exams. Why?"

Slim hesitated for a moment to find words that felt right. "Well, it's kind of hard to say, but when we were talking about Stokes wasting his life, it kinda seemed to me that you might be wasting yours, too, out here on these ships. Where can a radio operator go, except to another ship? At least a sailor can study to be an officer."

Sparks stirred uncomfortably and the frown pushed the horn-rimmed glasses down on the bridge of his nose. He pushed them back with a gesture of annoyance.

Slim hastily added an afterthought. "Unless, of course, that's all you want to be—a professional radio man. I mean it's okay if you like the sea better." Slim wished he hadn't started the conversation. He didn't want to offend Sparks and he hoped his friend understood that the question was prompted by genuine concern.

Sparks made no effort to answer and the long silence was painful for the deck boy. Finally the radio operator spoke. His voice was low, matter-of-fact. "I don't know whether or not you're going to understand what I'm talking about, Junior, but one of the reasons I get so peed off at Stokes is that in him I see a lot of myself. I look at that wreck of a human being and I'm repulsed—and then he opens that mouth of his and out of it comes some of the most beautifully chosen language I've ever heard. We talk nonsense a good part of the time, and I let myself get boiled over when he puts his intellectual hooks into me. But what's really happening is that I'm getting frightened. Maybe Stokes did something wrong or maybe he didn't think he was good enough to compete in whatever profession he trained for—and maybe he wasn't. Somewhere along the line the same thing happened to me. I studied to be an attorney—a criminal lawyer, because they make more money, or so I was told. But in all my life I've never won an argument—not even from the time my older sister and I first began to argue. I studied to be a lawyer because it was easier to do that than argue with my mother about being something else. I didn't have a father. He died when I was three. When I got out of high school I thought maybe I wanted to be a newspaperman—or an electrical engineer. I had a chance to go to work for the telephone company as an installation and maintenance man, but I couldn't get excited about it. Finally, to shut off the everlasting discussion about my friggin' future, I went to law school. It was easy but tedious. A friend of mine—a kid who was a wireless 'ham' too—knew a guy who worked on a ship. We went to visit him. I got the bug and I've been here ever since—three years now."

Sparks looked out into the night. Slim followed his gaze. As they sat watching the stars swing in a gentle arc across the velvet black outside the door, Slim had a feeling that Sparks had probably said more than he'd intended. The boy thought it might make him more comfortable if he knew he had company. "It's pretty tough to argue with women. I know! My family wanted me to be a doctor."

149

Sparks glanced over the shaft of his spectacles. "What did *you* do about it?"

Slim shrugged and smiled ruefully. "I'm here too, aren't I? But I'll tell you something—it's different with me, Sparks. I didn't spend a lot of time studying. I'm not wasting anything. I've always wanted to be an officer in the merchant marine."

A soundless laugh heaved Sparks' shoulders and exploded in a soft snort. "You've been reading too many 'Cappy Ricks' stories. You think the sea is romantic—and that all sailors are either heroes or villains!"

Slim grinned at the radio operator and shook his head. "I think the sea is beautiful, but I think most of the guys I've met, with a couple of exceptions, are a crummy, evil-minded bunch who figure all there is to life is drinking and dames!"

Sparks challenged the boy. "And what makes you think the officers are any different?"

Slim hesitated for a moment. "Well, they're a higher type of person——"

Sparks smiled sadly. "Sonny, you've got a few things to learn. Let's just take this ship for instance. The captain—how many times have you seen him on the bridge?"

Slim thought a moment. "Only a couple of times. He looked to me like he was wearing a bathrobe or something."

"That's right. He was! The poor bastard is a still-drinker. Half the time he's gassed up and can't perform the work, and the other half he's recovering from the ulcers he got from worry and booze. The chief mate runs the ship. The skipper had two ships shot out from under him by U-boats and he's never gotten over it. He hides in the bottle!"

The radio operator shifted himself in the chair and crossed his thin legs. "Now let's take that chief mate—a good sailor but he could hide behind a corkscrew! Nobody's been able to pin it on him yet, but he's got a racket with the lumber in these deckloads. Every trip he has some dumb kid saw the serial numbers off the pieces used for shoring up the load. They go over the side and bumboats pick them up. Later he meets the thieves in a saloon and cuts up the take. He probably spreads it around with the other two mates to keep them quiet. You can skip Peterson. He's the brightest officer of the bunch, but how could he be normal with a face like his? Poor bastard! Who knows what misery he goes through! Then there's the third—a convicted conspirator with rumrunners, busted out of the service. A China Sea skipper—and one of the best all-around seamen in the merchant marine. But hardly the kind of guy you'd bring home to meet the family. Now let's take the steward. There's a fine, upstanding 'prick' if I ever saw one! The engineers have their rackets, too, with the oil and supplies. Why, even the deck boys have a racket on these ships."

Slim glanced at Sparks with interest. "What is it? I haven't heard about it yet."

"Carrying sacks of potatoes from the poop deck to the galley. You can make a deal to do that for the cooks and they pay off with a whole pie. I'm surprised you haven't worked that gag yet."

Slim grinned in anticipation. "Don't worry, I'll start in the morning!"

"Well, that's the picture, my boy, and it's not a bit exaggerated. All these tubs are alike—they stink! And so do most of the men who sail on them . . . from bridge to black gang."

Slim sat in silence for a few minutes, puffing slowly on the ever present cigarette. As the weeks had gone by he had wondered about the first mate and the lumber manifests. He remembered Edye's curious comment that Samson always sent the deck boy for the papers. He remembered the strange attitude of Slater in the lumber office and his concern that nobody saw the manifests but the first mate. At the time Slim sensed something strange in the relationship between the men. Now, after listening to the radio operator, he wondered if the two men were in cahoots. He wondered if Slater rigged the manifests so the missing timbers wouldn't show. Another thought suddenly crossed his mind: What could be in the sealed envelope that Samson had made him take to Slater? Could it have been Slater's end of the pay-off? He wondered if Edye thought something might be amiss, too, but had kept her suspicions to herself. He considered mentioning the possibility in a letter and, in the next instant, decided to keep his nose out of the affair. If the radio operator was wrong, he and Edye could both be put in an embarrassing and dangerous position.

Sparks had put on the headphones again and was copying down a message on a pad in front of him. He'd listen a moment, then quickly scribble a word . . . then another . . . and another, until the pad was filled with nearly illegible scrawl. Taking off the phones and replacing them on the hook, he studied the message for a moment. Slim looked at him curiously and waited for him to speak. After a moment he crumpled up the paper and tossed it in the round metal waste can.

"Looks like they're going to send marines to China. The insurgents are raising hell and threatening American property. That's what you oughta do, Slim. You want to see the world—join the Marines! We've got 'em in Nicaragua, too. Pretty quick we'll have leathernecks all over the world —protecting the new American empire!"

The radio operator twisted the corners of his mouth into a cynical smile. "That's the best racket of all. Get to be a tycoon, stake out a claim in somebody else's country, then when they squawk about your interfering with their economy, have the taxpayers send the marines to keep them from interfering with you!"

Slim was puzzled at Sparks' tone. There was a bitterness in it that he'd not detected before. "What's eating on you, Sparks? You sound like those guys on the soapboxes we heard in Pedro. You know, 'Fellow workers . . . unite . . . before the bosses strangle you!' "

Sparks relaxed and a self-conscious smile twisted his face. "I'm sorry, kid. Every once in a while I make speeches about the 'injustices in the world.' One of these days one of those guys on a soapbox is going to say something that makes sense and all of us who go to sea for a living will join his union. If it's done in the right way, it could make going to sea a respectable profession."

Neither of the men spoke for a moment. Each was preoccupied with his own thoughts. The headphones on the bulkhead scraped in a gentle arc as the *Tropic Trader* rose and fell with the long mid-Pacific swells.

Slim stretched his legs halfway across the small space and yawned. Suddenly, from back aft in the fo'c'sle, came a piercing scream that sent a chill through both of them. Slim jumped to his feet, hurdled the coaming, and leaned over the railing, listening.

Sparks was at his side. "What the hell was that?"

Slim motioned for silence. Back across the deckload they could hear heavy footsteps moving quickly on the steel deck. Several men had apparently run for the companionway and hurried below.

Slim looked at the radio operator. "There must have been a fight. I'm going back there and see. I'll let you know what happened!"

The deck boy ran to the starboard side of the boatdeck, and his heavy shoes clattered down the steel treads of the ladder. He jumped up on the deckload and raced through the darkness, leaping over the giant chain lashings that he sensed rather than saw. When he arrived in the fo'c'sle a strange sight greeted him: Jack, Otto, Spots, Ioway, Chips, Russian John, Rusty, and several men from the black gang were standing over the unconscious and completely naked body of the Shiek. Several of the men still held their poker hands. Jack stood over the dead-white form of the ordinary seaman and stared at it in disgust. He gave the Shiek's head a half kick.

Chips stepped up alongside of him. "All right, sailor, that's enough. Let's put the poor son-of-a-bitch back in his bunk!"

Jack pushed past the carpenter without a word and slowly walked out of the fo'c'sle. "I'd throw the bastard over the side!"

Slim moved close to Otto as two of the men picked up the Shiek and roughly shoved him into his lower bunk in the narrow passageway leading to the head. "What happened to him?"

Otto shook his head in disbelief. "If I hadn'ta seen it with my own eyes, I wouldn'ta believed it! I just threw in my hand and walked in here, when I see this miserable shit, ball-ass naked, hanging by his hands from the overhead beam. He's swingin' like an ape—got a hard on out to here—and he's yellin', 'I'm a lone wolf and it's my night to howl!' "

Slim looked down at the deck. The Shiek had been lying in a pool of urine, and its heavy smell filled the hot, dead air of the tiny quarters. Several of the men turned away indifferently and followed Hammer back to the poker game.

Otto made a grimace of digust. "Look at that mess! That's piss—*his* piss!" He jerked his thumb toward the Shiek's bunk. "Hammer came in and kicked his swingin' ass down onto the deck. The son-of-a-bitch got up and tried to piss all over us. That's when Jack hit him." Otto shook his head. "He'll be out awhile! Jesus, but that guy can hit!" He shook his head again and walked to his bunk. Taking a bucket, he sloshed the water on the deck to flush the urine into the scupper, but the persistent smell hung in the oppressive, heat-laden air and the deck boy gave up all thoughts of sleeping below.

He returned to the boatdeck and reported the incident to a disgusted Sparks, then walked aft and stretched out on the big rope table. The hawsers had been stored below, and the vacant grating made a high, clean resting place. The boy lay with his head toward the wake, so he could look up past the edge of the awning into the black dome of the night. He rolled his eyes up, and the inverted horizon slid into view. Away to the northeast he could make out a bright planet. He wondered if Edye could see it, too, and then remembered that they were nearing the International Date Line and the time difference was so great it was probably daylight in Wauna. After a time his neck became stiff and he pulled his head back up onto the rope table and settled down to sleep in the comfortable warmth of the South Pacific night.

He had no idea how long he'd dozed off, when he was suddenly awakened by the roar of water on the overhead canvas and the cold splash of a tropical squall. Rising wearily from his resting place, he clumped down the companion ladder into the stifling fo'c'sle. In the bunk his body oozed and the bedding beneath him became soggy. The moisture seemed to release the odor of ancient sweat from the scores of unbathed, perspiring seamen who had lain there before him. Sleep was impossible, but in the fuzzy focused world just beneath the edge of consciousness the boy felt the beginning of a growing hopelessness. He thought of home in Berkeley, and of Wauna and Edye and of the wonderful excitement of her little body pressed against his that chill, dark night by the dock gate. He could feel the velvet softness of her lips and taste again their faint lingering sweetness.

Longing and desire tensed his middle and his groin, and he stirred restlessly and tried to turn his thoughts away. But the image of the girl grew clear again in the fluid darkness of his lidded eyes. He could hear her gentle voice, and then came a strange excitement as he realized that it was not Edye but the girl in the brothel in San Francisco and she was whispering to him not to be afraid. She was moving her perfumed naked body close to his, pressing her firm little breasts against his bony chest. Straining against him urgently for the last fraction of feeling. Then he was suddenly engulfed by a pulsing, pervading pleasure-pain that made his body rigid. He fought to prolong it and he could feel the girl struggling to be closer. He could hear her gentle gasping . . . feel her fin-

154

gernails in his flesh and her teeth biting his shoulder. The wave passed and his long body relaxed in deep exhaustion. Face to the wall, his right leg resting bent over his left, he slept in the wet warmth of his dream.

— 15 —

As a boy Slim had been accustomed to the searing dry heat of California's upper Sacramento Valley, but he was not prepared for the furnace-like fury of the overhead tropical sun near the equator. The temperature seldom dropped below one hundred degrees in the wheelhouse, the coolest part of the ship. Ioway, the deck boy, had got a second-degree sunburn through his light cotton work shirt, and even the hardiest of the seamen didn't dare work without a shirt until the sun was well past its zenith.

Slim couldn't understand how the firemen tolerated the blistering 130-degree heat below during their watches. He would see them come up on deck, sweat rags tied around their foreheads and necks, dressed in heavy wool shirts. They'd take a breather and sit in the shade of the main deck near the fiddley, getting what breeze there was to be had. The thirty- to forty-degree temperature change on deck actually chilled them after a two-hour watch in the fireroom.

The *Tropic Trader* had passed through the International Date Line, where it bulged eastward from the 180th meridian to avoid confusing the calendars in a number of important South Pacific islands. From the third mate Slim had learned that the line had been set by treaty among the world's mariners to compensate for the gain or loss of twenty-four hours (one hour of time for every fifteen degrees of longitude) in circumnavigating the world. The mate explained that, traveling west, a ship loses one day; traveling eastward, it gains a day. Slim got completely confused when Holst had tried to explain to him the relationship between time and arc, which is the basis for all positional computations on the globe. It wasn't until he'd got away by himself and drew the earth on a paper that he began to understand that, if one divided the three hundred and sixty degrees of the equator by the twenty-four hours

156

it took the sun to complete its journey, one found each hour was then worth fifteen degrees of equator, or arc. Once understood, he felt a glow of pride and a new determination to unravel another bit of the celestial riddle.

Several more days passed and the *Tropic Trader* continued to slip through the Pacific at two hundred-odd miles every twenty-four hours. The weather turned a bit cooler as the ship moved deeper into the Tropic of Capricorn and the south equatorial current began veering to the east.

The food got progressively worse, as did the stories. Jack played poker incessantly and, between hands, spoke of the bacchanalian orgy he'd planned for himself in Auckland. "Any takers? I've got a hundred bucks here that says I'll screw five broads and drink a full fifth of Black & White the first night ashore!"

There were no takers. The big carpenter looked at the ex-fighter without humor. "I've seen he-men like you before. After the second hump you wind up with yer cock in a sling. What the hell are you talkin' about—five times!"

Hammer looked at Chips with those cold blue eyes Slim had come to know meant trouble.

Rusty hit the oilcloth table top with annoyance. "Come on, will ya? Screw the dames when you get in port, but let's play poker now! Unless I get some of this guy's money, I'm gonna wind up givin' it a few jerks in an alley!"

Hammer's gaze slowly returned to the cards, but the carpenter continued to watch him. Jack played out the hand and dealt a new one.

In addition to Chips, Rusty, Spots, and Otto, the fireman called Mike had been sitting in the game for a week or more. He was a beautifully built, extremely handsome fellow in his early thirties. He had the sort of good looks usually associated with a he-man movie star. Slim remembered the shock they had all got during the first really warm days when they'd found Mike skipping rope on the poop deck, stripped to the waist. The man's body was completely covered with the most intricate oriental tattooing. The front of his massive and powerfully muscled chest was a vast panorama of delicate Japanese scrollwork which formed a border for a huge stylized chrysanthemum, worked in concentric circles from his navel. The lacelike border design extended under each arm and across the rib cage to the broad back. Here the tattoo artist had created a living masterpiece: a giant oriental lion, rampant and enraged, its dripping claws placed at the extreme out-

157

side planes of the shoulders. The lion's loins disappeared below Mike's belt line, but shipmates who had seen him naked swore that the tattooing extended all the way to his ankles.

Chips' comment was a mixture of admiration and disgust. "He's a beautiful thing! When he dies they oughta have him stuffed and mounted!"

Jack viewed the fireman differently. "If that guy had in the bank all the dough he's spent on that needlework, he'd own the goddamn ship!"

Rusty and Otto seemed disinterested in Mike's decorated epidermis. Ioway was repulsed by it. Slim was secretly curious. If he'd been asked, he'd have confessed to a desire for a small piece on himself—despite the fact that several of the nonmarked shipmates concurred that an unclean tattoo needle had been known to transmit both syphilis and leprosy.

As the poker game wore on, Spots grew more disgusted. Jack's winning streak seemed to be holding out and several of the men had borrowed from him in order to stay in the game. After losing all but two packs of cigarettes from the carton he'd borrowed from Jack, the fat little A.B. threw in his hand and left the game, promising to pay Hammer when the crew drew money in Auckland.

Slim, who had been leaning against the bulkhead, watching, took Spots' place at the messroom table on the same side as Rusty and Jack. Opposite Jack in the other corner was Mike, next to him sat Chips, and closest to the passageway sat Otto, opposite Slim.

When the deck boy moved into Spots' vacant place on the long bench, Jack leaned forward and grinned. "Don't tell me you're gonna sit in, Slim?"

The boy hesitated a moment, thinking about the little money he had left, but Hammer supplied the answer and the money. Tossing eight quarters down the table, he cut the cards and started to deal. "You owe me two bucks when you get paid. Okay?"

Slim looked at the quarters, stacked them in front of him, and nodded. "Okay, deal me in. I don't know too much about poker, but it's worth two bucks to learn."

Chips frowned at the boy. "It'll probably cost ya thousands of bucks before ye're through—and you'll still have plenty to learn! Ask me—I know!" The carpenter looked up the table at Hammer, then back at Slim. "He's the only guy on this ship that wins. Ye're gettin' yer lessons from an expert at least!"

158

Jack shook his head deprecatingly. "I don't know any more than you guys. It's just the way the cards fall! Get your antes in!" He deftly dealt the six hands around the table. "Who opens?"

The men sat in silence, studying their cards. Rusty spoke first. "I'll open for a quarter." He tossed the money into the center of the table.

Hammer spoke to himself. "Jacks—or better, eh?" He looked past Rusty at the deck boy. "You gotta beat jacks, kid, so be careful with my money!"

Slim studied his cards and decided to hold a pair of deuces. Across the table Otto made his decision. Chips thought for a moment, then tossed in his quarter and discarded two cards face down in front of him. Mike tossed in a quarter and folded his hand. The men asked for cards and the betting started. Rusty backed up his openers with another quarter and Slim dropped out with nothing. Otto folded his hand and tossed it in. Chips followed suit and so did Mike. The hand was between Jack and Rusty.

The ex-fighter, turned so his back was braced in the corner, studied his cards a moment, then looked at Rusty. "Okay—and up a quarter." He tossed the coin into the center of the table.

Rusty reached for the pile of change in front of him, neatly stacked up against the thin storm board that kept plates from sliding off the table in bad weather. "Here's yours and another one." He put two quarters on the pile with a determined gesture.

Jack smiled. " 'At's the way I like 'em! I'm not rich but I'm curious. Whatcha got?"

Rusty spread the cards into a wide fan and laid them on the oilcloth, revealing a pair of aces and a king, jack, and four of clubs. "My openers."

Jack shook his head sadly. "This is getting monotonous." He laid his hand down for Rusty to see and at the same time reached over and began raking in the money.

Rusty silently inspected Hammer's hand: aces and threes with a stray king.

Chips laughed in disgust and shook his head in disbelief. "All right, let's try it again. This can't last forever!" He tossed in the five-cent ante and the others followed.

Again Jack, who was banking the game, dealt the cards around and again Rusty had the openers. This time it was Otto who took the hand with a full house: threes and eights. Another hand went around and Rusty took it with three aces. Slim couldn't seem to catch any cards, and the antes kept eating away at his dwindling pile of borrowed money. Chips and Mike were the consistent losers, and the battle continued between Hammer and Rusty, who seemed squared off as the principal contenders. After an hour Slim ran out of money and threw in his cards. Keeping his place, he watched the game continue with the five men. Mike won an occasional hand. He seemed to be playing very cautiously, and Slim saw him studying Hammer very closely while the A.B. was engrossed in the betting. The big fireman hardly spoke. He indicated the number of cards he needed by throwing the discards in front of Jack, who quickly dealt him a like number. The ex-fighter was still winning, not spectacularly, but steadily—more often than any of the others. And each time he handled the cards, Mike watched him impassively, a long-ashed cigarette held firmly in his strong mouth. Slim couldn't tell whether or not Hammer was aware of the fireman.

Several times Jack went out of his way to joke with him. "Mike, we gotta fix this game so you can win. Otherwise we won't be getting any more of that good blackgang money. Right, fellas?"

Mike looked at the A.B. and indicated one card.

Jack paused before giving it to him. "One card." He winked at Chips. "I gotta be careful now and fill that inside straight for him!"

He flipped the single card across to the fireman, who picked it up and placed it at the left end of his hand. His face revealed nothing to the other players. Jack dealt himself three cards, holding only his openers. Ottto had taken two cards and Chips had taken the same. Rusty had taken two and folded. Jack opened with a dime. The others saw him, but the fireman raised it a quarter.

Jack looked surprised. "Jesus! Don't tell me I *did* fill that straight for ya?" He looked at Mike through partly closed eyes for a long moment, then made his decision. "Okay, we might as well make it a big one. Here's your quarter—and a half more!"

The others dropped out quietly and waited to see the outcome of what was obviously the strongest betting of the evening. Mike studied his hand for a moment, dumped the ash from his cigarette into the open-topped condensed-milk can and shoved it back against the sugar bowl and catsup bottle that were permanent fixtures at the bulkhead end of the messroom table. Directly above them an occasional breath of cool breeze came through the open port. During the long silence before Mike answered Jack's challenge, Slim could hear the low rush of the wash along the ship's plates. Mike's hand reached slowly toward the modest pile of cash in front of him. He fingered two quarters thoughtfully, then slowly added two more to the stack and pushed them deliberately into the center of the table. Jack pressed the corners of his mouth down in mock surprise. He spoke to himself. "This boy must have 'em!" He studied the backs of Mike's cards absently, as though thinking out his strategy; then, making a sudden move that startled Slim, he raised the fireman's bet another half dollar.

No words were spoken as the others watched the two men intently. Jack's face wore a smile, but his cold blue eyes were fixed intently on his opponent. The fireman returned his gaze steadily for a moment, then lowered his eyes to his cards. He inspected them carefully, weighing his chances. Then, straightening up on the narrow bench, he counted out the money in front of him and pushed it slowly into the pile in the center of the table. A low whistle of surprise escaped from Otto's lips and all eyes turned to Hammer. The A.B. inspected the proffered bet. "The bundle, huh?" The fireman made no reply. Jack looked at him intently, then slowly counted out five one-dollar bills and to it added thirty cents in change. He pushed the money toward the heap in the betting pile. "Okay, friend, let's see what ye're so proud of——"

Mike hesitated, then carefully laid his hand out on the table, a card at a time. The men leaned forward as Jack spread his out in front of him. The two men looked at each other's cards in silence; then, with an unpleasant smile, the A.B. reached slowly toward the money to rake it in.

As he moved, the fireman leaned forward. "All right, sailor, hold it!"

Mike had spoken quietly, but the dead-flat tone of his voice made Slim's scalp crawl. Hammer's hand rested on the money and the smile slowly left his face. The two men stared at each other in silence.

Chips stirred and turned to the fireman. "What the hell's eatin' you? He's got a full house, eights and aces. You caught threes and kings."

Without looking at the carpenter, Mike answered, "I also caught a lousy fink who plays with a cold deck!"

The quiet accusation came like a sudden shock that stunned the men at the table. The breathless instant prolonged, and time and the men seemed frozen. Then, with a lightning-like movement, Hammer seized the catsup bottle

161

and clubbed the fireman on the left temple. The bottle exploded its crimson contents over the bulkhead and most of the men at the table. To his horror, Slim saw a slash of deeper red appear on the fireman's gore-covered face. The man sat upright, stunned but conscious. Hammer released the jagged end of the broken bottle and discovered that the glass had cut a deep gash in the middle of his hand. As he looked at the wound it disappeared, covered by the crimson pool in the cup of his palm. He quickly clenched his fist and blood spurted between his fingers.

Holding his fists tightly clenched, he spoke quietly to the fireman. "All right, shit-head! Come into the fo'c'sle where there's some room an' we'll settle this right now!"

Slim watched him closely. There was no anger in his voice. Except for the language, he might have been challenging someone on a definition in the dictionary. But his eyes held every man in the messroom. They were unblinking, cold and confident. The pale blue irises seemed to glitter in icy anticipation as he waited for the fireman to answer. Mike lifted his head slowly and stared at the A.B. He looked down, and the bloody smear trickled from the tip of his massive chin, and a crimson tracery appeared on the white T-shirt stretched taut across his massive chest. He roused himself slowly and shook his head. Then, as the players rose from the table, he stood erect and moved toward the passageway. He paused, looked back at Hammer, then turned to his left and entered the seamen's fo'c'sle.

Men materialized from both crews' quarters and silently followed the pair into the scant clear space in the center of the area. The tattooed fireman stepped across the inverted wooden trough that covered the steering-engine cables and turned to face his assailant. Hammer felt for the trough with his foot and stepped over to the same side. The men stood facing each other for an electric instant—a scant two feet apart. Suddenly the fireman raised his hands. No one could tell clearly what happened. In the blur of brutal action that killed the unreal moment, Slim, like the others, could see no single move. It was over as suddenly as it had begun.

Mike lay unconscious, head against the cable housing, and Hammer stood looking down at him. No one spoke. Each man stared in blank disbelief at the beautiful physical specimen, reduced to a sprawling, bleeding hulk. The wounded side of his face was pressed against the rough red cement of the deck. From beneath his neck a ribbon of blood moved slowly toward the scupper, spreading gleaming crimson tendrils as it gathered momentum with each roll of the vessel. The corners of Hammer's mouth curled in a cruel smile. Raising his loggered foot, he kicked viciously at the unconscious head, pounding it up against the cable housing.

A wave of revulsion swept through Slim and an involuntary cry escaped from his lips. "Cut it out, Jack! Cut it out! You'll kill him!"

Hammer replaced his partially raised boot on the deck and turned slowly toward the deck boy. There was no expression on his face, just that ice-cold blue gleam that sent fear coursing through Slim. Like a bull trying to make up its mind to charge, the big A.B. stood, his chest heaving slightly from the murderous exertion of the past moments.

Slim felt his arms and legs slowly turn to lead. He knew the feeling. It was the same one he'd often had in those frightening dreams that tormented him as a child: mortally threatened and unable to move . . . impossible to escape from the path of the oncoming disaster which in real life had now taken the form of a man without a conscience, without a single one of the moral restraints that would set him above a brute. Panic seized the deck boy —not because he was afraid of physical harm, but because he was confronted by an immutable force that could hear no reason save its own. Slim instinctively understood that his cold, methodical destructiveness could be triggered by countless challenges that would set in motion the machinery with which the man gave vent to the hatred pressures that had built up inside him since his earliest frustration. Without knowing why, the boy understood its impersonal nature and the understanding compounded his fear. Slim's eyes blurred as he struggled to keep them on Hammer. He could feel the pressure of the man packed behind him in the small space and then he grew aware that it was lessening; that they were moving away from danger while he, trapped by his own immobility, waited alone for the onslaught. And then quickly and quietly a blue-denimed hulk loomed between him and Hammer.

It was the ship's carpenter. "All right, brave guy! Get out of here!"

Slim was nearly pushed off his feet as the men hastened to move away from what seemed certain to be a titanic struggle. The boy found himself backed against Hammer's bunk. His own was directly above. Without turning, he stepped on the edge of the lower bunk pipe and slowly raised himself up off the deck. From this position he could look over the carpenter's shoulders to Hammer, standing in the growing pool, being fed by the sanguineous springs beneath his victim's beaten head. Without fear the carpenter waited for Hammer's move. As the two stood facing each other, a stillness enveloped the fo'c'sle—a stillness so filled with tension that the scrape of Hammer's heavy boot sent a nervous start through each man. Still holding his right fist tightly clenched, he pushed his way out of the fo'c'sle to the passageway, turned aft, and climbed the companion ladder to the poop deck.

Chips turned slowly and faced the direction of Hammer's retreat, as though expecting him to return. When it was apparent that he'd gone topside, the carpenter moved to the unconscious fireman and kneeled on one knee beside him. With surprising gentleness he turned the big fellow on his back and looked for a moment at the crimson pulp of the wound. Pulling a crumpled handkerchief from the back pocket of his faded dungarees, Chips blotted the wound. As the cloth touched the cheek, the clean edge of freshly severed flesh appeared. Slim, who had kneeled beside the carpenter, felt momentarily sick and dizzy as he realized that the shattered bottle had gashed completely through Mike's face, from cheekbone to the middle of the lower jaw. The lower edge of the long cut sagged down into the oral cavity, revealing strong white teeth, and the seeping blood trickled into the fireman's throat from both edges of the slashing incision.

Without knowing whom he was ordering, the carpenter spoke to the boy at his side. "Hurry up—go get the steward. This guy's badly hurt!"

Slim hardly knew how he'd crossed the dangerous deckload in the deep midnight darkness, but he found himself on the portside of the main deck. Breathing heavily from the excitement and exertion, he knocked on the steward's screen. The man had turned in some time earlier and was apparently in deep sleep. The boy knocked again, but there was no answer. He tried the handle, and the varnished frame swung inward. Slim stood a moment, his hand on the door, peering into the darkness of the stateroom. The yellow glare from the glass-bowled midship lights sent a pale, glowing shaft through the open porthole that shed a sickly light on the stifling, cluttered interior. In the deeper shadows of the built-in bunk Slim could make out the sprawling form of the steward, clad only in shorts,

164

lying in the tangled folds of a soggy sheet. The air was dead and filled with the humid musk of unclean sweat.

The boy called urgently. "Mr. Pugh! Wake up, sir! A man's been hurt—he needs help!"

The steward's half snoring stopped in mid-breath and he lay motionless in the bunk. Then with a start he sat up, struggled free of the sheet, and swung his pudgy white legs over the edge of the mattress.

There was anxiety in his sleep-thickened voice. "Whaddaya want—whaddaya want? What'sa matter?"

"It's Slim, the deck boy, sir. One of the men back aft has been hurt. He needs help or he'll bleed to death." The boy spoke quickly and waited for the steward's reply.

"All right, all right. What happened to him? How'd he get hurt?"

Slim wished the man would turn on the cabin light so he could see him more clearly. "They were playing poker and one of the men hit him with a bottle, sir. His face is cut clear through and he's bleeding badly."

The steward wormed his moist feet into a pair of worn raffia slippers and stood up. Though Slim could not see him too well in the oppressive gloom, he could sense the rising tide of indignation in the narrow-shouldered, pot-bellied, spindle-legged little man.

When he spoke, repressed rage shook his high-pitched voice. "D'ya mean you came here and woke me up just because two of those wild animals got into a fight over cards? Do you mean to tell me that—*do* you?"

The ridiculous look and sound of the moist little fellow would have made Slim laugh if the more serious picture of Mike lying bleeding on the fo'c'sle deck hadn't been so vividly etched in his mind. His answer to Pugh was a plea to reason.

"Chips asked me to call you. The man is badly hurt. He won't be able to stand his watches. Please bring some bandages and see if you can't fix him up—at least stop the bleeding!"

The rumpled, sweaty little steward reached for the switch on the bulkhead above the bunk, and the sudden flare of light made Slim squint painfully. Taking a towel, the man began blotting his face, neck, and chest.

"Now you listen to me, sailor." He shook the towel menacingly at the deck boy. "I don't care who sends you. The regulations are quite clear! I have no responsibility to render first aid to any man on this ship, unless his injury

165

was inflicted during the course of duty! Y'understand that?"

Slim nodded and started to speak, but the steward cut him off. "Now you go on back there and tell Chips to take care of the man any way he can, but he gets no help from me! Now go! Get out of here and let me get some rest!" He tossed the sweat-dampened towel into the small porcelain basin in the corner, next to the foot of his bunk, and snapped out the light.

Slim stepped over the coaming and out into the welcome freshness of the night. He paused for a moment outside the door. Nothing would be gained by running back to the fo'c'sle. Quickly he made up his mind. Running across the after end of the main deck, he shot up the ladder to the boatdeck and hurried to the door of the radioman's quarters.

Sparks was seated at the desk with the headphones on, lost in the squealing, staccato babel of his wireless world. The sudden slam of the screen startled him and he jerked off the headset. Taking the cold stub of a cigarette from his mouth, he said, "I'll have that door removed if it slows you up."

Slim ignored the gibe, and the story of the fight tumbled from his lips as the radio operator listened intently.

"That chicken-shit little bastard and his goddamned regulations! I used to think he was just a 'prick,' but if I called him that now I'd be doing that worthy organ a grave injustice!" He moved toward the door. "Come on —maybe the place is unlocked. I don't think anybody's been in there for years!"

They stepped out on deck, and the radio operator tried the ringed brass handle that lay flat against the door. It turned and he pulled it open. A wave of suffocating, stale, medicinal-smelling air enveloped them. Sparks groped for the light switch and turned it on. The bare little room was filled with a sickly yellow light from an ancient, dust-covered bulb of inadequate wattage. The place was absolutely bereft of furnishing except for the two pipe bunks with their stained, straw-filled ticking, a basin served from a small water tank on the roof deck, and the large chest of medical supplies to the right of the doorway.

Slim dropped to one knee and tried the top of the chest. It was securely fastened by a heavy built-in lock. The keyhole looked like an ordinary trunk lock that would accept a round key with a hollow shank. There was no way of picking the mechanism or of prying the lid open without doing much damage.

Sparks stood up slowly. "I'll tell you what you'd better do——" He interrupted the beginning of his own suggestion with a question: "Who's on the bridge now—which officer?"

Slim looked at his watch. It was twenty minutes past midnight. "The third mate—Holst."

"He's a good guy! You better go up on the bridge and see what he wants to do about it. Tell him I sent you, if you're worried!"

Ducking around the end of the boatdeck structure that housed the radio shack and sick bay, Slim hurried through the dark maze of davits, ventilators, and stack guys that cluttered the top deck. Reaching the forward end of the boatdeck, he grasped the cold rungs of the ladder that scaled the heavy steel starboard king post. With the smooth agility of his new profession he slipped down the ladder until his feet hit the deck with a gentle metallic thud. He paused for a moment to look up at the bridge, hoping to see the third mate out on the upper wing bridge. Avoiding number three hatch, he started for the base of the bridge ladder.

A voice came from the deep shadows of the main deck directly beneath the bridge. "Where ya goin', kid?" It was Peterson, the second mate, who had just completed his watch.

Slim hadn't seen him standing there. The boy stammered in confusion. "I was . . . well . . . I . . . gotta see the third, sir!" He finally got the words out.

Peterson walked over to Slim. His loose, wide stance easily braced against the slow roll of the ship, he looked at the boy in amusement. "You overslept, eh? You're late for wheel watch—is that it?"

Slim shook his head vigorously. "No, sir. I don't stand night watches yet. I was going to tell the third that one of the men got badly cut in a fight. He needs attention and the steward won't give it to him." He blurted out the words in one breath.

Peterson's face grew stern. "All right—tell me how it happened."

Once again the deck boy described quickly the details of the fight. As he finished, the second mate ordered him to follow. They made their way aft to the fo'c'sle. Chips had put a towel under the fireman's head and ripped off his gore-soaked skivvy shirt. The blue-green clashing dragons

167

were smeared with a dark crust of dried blood. The horrible gash lay open as Slim had last seen it. The fireman was regaining consciousness and his glassy eyes moved slowly to each of the silent men bending over him. If he felt pain, he gave no sign. The wound oozed blood from a hundred severed capillaries. Chips rinsed out the handkerchief in a bucket of crimson water and tried to keep the blood from clogging up the victim's throat.

The lanky second mate knelt beside Chips and inspected the wound in silence. Then he looked at Slim and barked an order. "Fredericks! Go tell that steward to open up the sick bay. That's an order from me! Then tell Sparks to see if there's a passenger ship around anywhere with a ship's surgeon. This guy needs sewing up!"

Slim waited an instant to see if there were more instructions, then raced forward. When he got back to the fo'c'sle Chips, the square little A.B. called John, and the second mate were helping the big fireman to his feet. He seemed fully conscious and capable of moving. Holding Chips' soaked handkerchief to his left cheek, his head tilted to that side, he moved slowly between the three men toward the companion ladder to the poop deck. It seemed to Slim that the trip forward along the deckload took an eternity.

When they reached the main-deck ladder leading up to the sick bay, the mate spoke to Slim again. "Go on up ahead and see what Sparks has to say!"

Slim shot up the ladder and into the radio shack. Sparks was sending a long message at the key and he ignored the boy until he had finished. Listening intently, he motioned Slim to a chair. After a moment he took off the headset.

"The closest ship is the *Sierra*. She's about 950 miles north of us, heading for San Francisco. Her captain advises us to do what we can and run for Auckland." Sparks hung the headset on the bulkhead hook and rose slowly. "He also sends his regrets!"

Outside they heard voices as the two A.B.s and the officer helped the fireman up the ladder. Slim stepped out on deck and held open the door to the sick bay. They put Mike in the dingy lower bunk. The steward, dressed in blue trousers, a rumpled undershirt, and slippers, was trying one key after another from the many that hung from a large wire ring. It was obvious that he did not know the purposes of half of them. Finally one slipped into place and the lock turned. He raised the lid and peered inside. Slim noticed that the man had not once looked at the injured fireman. He bent over his keys, as though to shut out any picture other than the one immediately before his eyes. Slim watched him fumbling with packs of gauze encased in protective paper, brittle and yellow with age. He saw several bottles of antiseptic and alcohol standing in special compartments, but the man made no move to take them out. A half tray covered one end of the big chest. In it were two pairs of blunt-nosed surgical scissors, their blades slightly angled from the handles. Also Slim recognized a pair of hemostats, the clamps used by surgeons to compress the ends of bleeding veins and arteries. He'd seen them in the sterile cabinet in his doctor's office. There was a glass jar containing a roll of threadlike material and another smaller one holding three needles. In another bottle was a small, sharp instrument. An adhesive-tape label was marked: "Lancet."

"Fer Chris' sake, steward, what are ya doing—counting the stuff?" Peterson spoke over his shoulder as he helped Chips change the bloody rag that had long since lost its identity as the carpenter's coarse but clean handkerchief. "Give us some gauze pads—or some cotton!"

Slim waited for the steward to comply, but the man seemed incapable of decision. And then, to his horror, Pugh turned ashen-gray, slumped down on the edge of the chest, rested there for an instant, then fainted in a soggy heap on the deck. Slim stood looking down at him for an instant, wondering what to do. Then he saw the mate's outstretched hand, waiting. Peterson hadn't seen the steward pass out. His eyes were still on the bleeding fireman, who was beginning to gag on the blood that trickled down his throat. Slim's arm shot into the medical chest. Reaching a package of gauze pads, he ripped the paper off and placed it in the mate's outstretched hand. Then, taking the dead weight of the steward by the arms, he dragged him over to the doorway and propped his head over the coaming in the outside air. Both the carpenter and the third mate looked around in surprise.

Chips snorted in disgust. "How do you like that?"

Sparks came out of the radio shack and started to enter the sick bay. He started as he saw the steward's wispy bald head wedged between the coaming and the screen door. "Oh, for Christ sake! Now what?" Sparks asked the question of no one. Stepping over the prostrate form, he entered the sick bay and addressed the second mate. "I can't raise anybody who can help, sir. The *Sierra*'s too far away to make it. I've been trying for a shore station in the

169

North Island, but there's no answer. I don't want to send out an emergency signal unless it's ordered, sir."

Peterson looked up over his shoulder. "For Christ sake, no! The ship isn't sinkin'. Keep sending CQs and we'll do the best we can in here!"

Sparks mumbled a curt "Yes, sir," stepped over the limp, lumpy form of Pugh, and returned to his station.

Slim followed him out on deck. Holding the sick-bay screen open with his foot, he hoisted the unconscious steward over the low coaming and laid him along the after railing of the boatdeck.

Sparks stuck his head out of the radio shack. "You better come in here and take my fresh water. The bucket's clean. I don't think there's any water in the topside tank. If there is, it's a hundred years old!"

The boy took the proffered bucket and returned to the sick bay. Peterson looked at it and nodded approval. Slim watched him as best he could in the dim light, made dimmer still by the shadow of the upper bunk. Without asking, the boy reached over the kneeling men and lifted the mattress off the top pipes. New light came down through the springs and Chips grunted, "Good boy." Both men kept blotting at the wound. The fireman lay on his right side, facing them, the left side of his face up. His eyes were open and he blinked occasionally, but no sound came from his blood-caked lips.

Suddenly a retching spasm seized him and a trickle of dark hemoptysis ran from the corner of his mouth. He'd swallowed a lot of blood and it was beginning to make him vomit. Peterson cursed quietly and wiped the mess from the man's chin and from the ticking. Slim popped out the door and returned in a moment with several towels borrowed from the radio operator. He pushed one of them under the fireman's chin.

"I don't think he's bleeding as much, sir. It's beginning to coagulate."

The second mate nodded. "I wish there was something we could do to close this thing up. We can't sit here and hold it for a week—that's for goddamn sure!"

Chips grunted in approval. Then he straightened up with an idea. "I'm goin' for'ard and get a cluster light so we can at least see what the hell we're not doin'!"

As he went out on deck, Peterson called after him: "You'd better bring an extension cable, too. You'll have to bring the juice up from the main-deck outlet!"

Chips didn't answer. They heard him growl at the steward, who had apparently come to and was trying to go below.

Slim squatted on his heels beside the second mate and took a gauze pad from the dwindling supply resting in the remnants of the torn package on the edge of the berth. Without asking, he carefully inserted the pad in the fireman's open mouth and pressed the sagging cheek upward, until the two edges of the slash were flush.

"This'll keep the blood from going into his throat, sir. If he gets any more, he'll get real sick."

There was something in the boy's manner and tone that made Peterson turn his head slowly. In that long moment he studied the boy's serious face at close range and found an earnestness and intelligence of which he'd been only vaguely aware. Slim felt the mate watching him as he gently took the soaked pad from the fireman's mouth and deftly replaced it with a fresh one. His fingers worked quickly and surely as he applied the pressure from inside the cheek once more and forced the edges of the wound together again. And then he heard himself speaking, as though there were two of him: one watching and one acting.

The Slim that watched heard the Slim that acted say to the mate, "Sir, if you'll let me, I think I can fix him up until we get to Auckland. I feel sure I can—if you and Chips could help me——"

The Slim that watched tried to call out—to stop the Slim that acted, but he could find no voice and he heard the other self speak again. "I've had some training in first aid, and I've worked with hurt animals. I think I could do it, sir, if I could have a few minutes to go through that chest."

To the Slim that watched the other voice seemed unreal, like the voice in a vivid dream. And then the mate spoke, and the dream was reality and Slim was one again and moving toward the first-aid supplies.

There was a strange eagerness in the boy as he inspected the contents of the big chest. Quickly he removed two bottles: one labeled "Alcohol, pure grain" and the other "Cresolagen." Reading the label, Slim discovered the bottle contained a concentrated carbolic acid solution that could be mixed with water in varying amounts to make a powerful antiseptic. He removed a bottle of iodine and a packet of swabs, the bottle containing the surgical needles and the one containing the threadlike sutures. Chips entered with a large cluster light, hauling the heavy rubber cable

171

after him. The sick bay was flooded with hot, white light from the six big bulbs. The carpenter secured the work-lamp to the overhead bunk pipes, and its heat quickly filled the little space.

Indicating the deck boy, he spoke curiously to Peterson. "What's the kid doing?"

The mate replied without looking, "He thinks he can patch up this guy. Something's gotta be done—he might as well try. He's got good hands. We'll help him. You better get some clean water."

The carpenter looked from the mate to the boy, frowned in disbelief, then took the bucket of red-stained water and disappeared outside. He moved quickly for a big man, and they heard his feet rattle down the ladder to the main deck and on down the tapered end of the deck-load to the scuttle butt in the shelter deck. He came back in a few minutes and set the bucket on the deck beside Slim. The boy quickly washed the porcelain basin. He used the antiseptic to clean it thoroughly. Next he laid out the surgical supplies, the closed top of the chest serving as a work area. Opening the sutures, he found the fluid had leaked from the bottle and the material was brittle-dry. He looked for more and, finding none, quickly went out, tell-ing the second mate that he'd be back in a moment. He ran to the fo'c'sle.

Jack was sitting on the edge of his bunk, his cut hand soaking in a bucket of soapy solution. He didn't speak, neither did the deck boy. Slim opened his locker, grabbed his sailor's sewing kit, and rushed back to the sick bay. Taking a spool of thin white silk thread from the packet, he quickly placed a length of it through the flat, thin eye of the smallest surgical needle and let the short end hang clear. Into the basin he poured half the contents of the Cresolagen bottle and added an equal amount of water from the bucket. He immersed the needle and thread in the solution and let them soak while he took a moist pad and cleaned the congealing blood from the outside of the fireman's face. The bleeding was definitely slowing down. He worked easily and efficiently, and as he moved about, organizing the things he'd need, the boy felt a new happi-ness, a sense of importance—of usefulness—of being needed; and with it came a determination to do *this* job better than he'd ever done any other. He was only vaguely aware that the sight of the ugly wound no longer repelled him; that he was, in fact, following the advice once given him when he rebelled at studying medicine: to regard the

172

human body as a machine that needs repairing. The trick was to use all the techniques to effect the repairs without tormenting the patient. A sudden thought occurred. What about a pain killer, or an anesthetic of some sort? Certainly the fireman was a stoic, but would either of them be if the needle had to penetrate aware flesh? The thought made him cringe inside. He went back to the first-aid chest, removed the things from the top, and opened it again. Taking each of the bottles, he held them up to the light and quickly scanned labels on pills and ointments, including blue ointment for the treatment of a common sailor's affliction, "crabs." He reached for one bottle that appeared to be labeled "Chloroform," but on closer inspection it read "Chloral Hydrate fluid—12 oz."

The second mate turned to the boy. "What are you looking for, kiddo?"

Slim answered with simple matter-of-factness: "Something to deaden the pain."

Chips offered a suggestion. "I've got some whisky back aft. We could give him a big slug and goof him up a little. It'd make it easier——" He added an afterthought: "—for *all* of us!"

Slim had been reading the label on the last bottle. "Never mind. This'll do it. That's what it's for." Aloud, he read from the instructions: " 'Sedative dosage, one teaspoon = 5-7½ gr. Hypnotic dosage, 2-3 teaspoons = 15-22 gr.' "

Peterson spoke up. "Better give him *four* teaspoonfuls —he's a big guy!"

Slim took one of the flat paper cups he'd set out with the other supplies and by eye measured out four generous teaspoonfuls of the fluid. Adding enough water to make a large mouthful, he carried it carefully to the bunk. Chips and the second mate turned Mike over on his back and propped him partially upright. Slim gave him the cup, guiding his hand toward his mouth. The fireman tipped his head back and to the right side and gulped the sedative quickly. He shuddered, and the boy thought he might retch it up, but it stayed in him and the men gently lowered him back on the bunk. Slim changed the gauze pad that he'd packed inside the fireman's cheek and waited for the medicine to take effect. A quarter of an hour passed and Mike was still conscious. After a few more minutes he closed his eyes and seemed to relax. In half an hour he was sleeping heavily and Slim was ready to go to work.

The word had been passed around and curious members

of the crew had climbed quietly up to the after end of the boatdeck. Slim could make out their dark silhouettes against the night, could see the pulsing glow of their cigarettes as they watched and waited, could hear the low murmur of their occasional conversation. The second mate paced back and forth, smoking and cursing quietly. Chips stood by the bunk, watching the fireman. The first engineer, a stocky ruddy-faced Scotsman named McNair, stood by grimly, looking at his injured man—a man he could ill afford to lose in the undermanned crew.

A chair, borrowed from the radio shack and covered with a clean towel, served as the table on which Slim laid the gauze and the threaded surgical needle. A low footstool brought him down to the level of the anesthetized fireman.

The boy had washed his hands carefully in the antiseptic solution in the basin and had shaken them dry, although he felt it was a bit too late for such precautions after the primitive first aid that had already been rendered.

As he moved to the stool the men backed away to give him room. Chips stayed by Mike's head and helped Slim pull it over to the edge of the bunk, where the wounded cheek was more readily available. It was difficult to move easily and still avoid hitting the pipe rail of the upper bunk. Slim and Chips were both forced to work in cramped positions. The other alternative would have been to take the fireman to the petty officers' mess and use its facilities for an operating table, but the man was too heavy to move up and down ladders.

Dipping a thick gauze pad in a cup of alcohol and water, the boy reached inside the fireman's open mouth and sponged it free of clotted blood and seepage. He dropped the stained pad and took a fresh, dry one. As he inserted it with the two fingers of his left hand, he forced the fleshy cheek away from the teeth. Applying gentle pressure, he then pushed the inside of the penetrating gash upward, until the severed edges protruded like two raw, misshapen lips. Reaching for the surgical needle, he touched its point to the flesh, about a quarter of an inch wide of the top of the wound, on the side nearest Mike's left ear. The needle made a small indentation in the skin but did not penetrate. Slim felt a tightening in the pit of his stomach, and Chips shot a quizzical look at him as he gripped the sleeping fireman's head in big hands. The boy hesitated a fleeting instant, then with a quick, sure movement he forced the razor-sharp cutting edge of the curved needle completely through the flesh until it penetrated the pale skin on the opposite side of the wound. Pulling the silk suture, to which he'd applied mineral jelly, Slim left an inch of end protruding from the original needle hole. A tiny dot of blood welled around the thread. Next he took a pair of surgical scissors and cut the suture an inch away from the opposite side of the wound. An involuntary sigh escaped him and he wiped a rivulet of sweat that trickled down the side of his nose. Chips reached over almost gently and blotted the boy's forehead with a towel.

Slim worked quickly now—with confidence and with the common sense that was one of his priceless heritages. If Slim had ever spoken of it, most people would have laughed, but there had never been a time since his early teens when he'd faced a crisis alone. His grandmother had been a devoutly religious woman. But hers had been a practical, almost metaphysical approach to God and she'd firmly believed in the continuity of the spirit and personality. She had taught Slim to call on the wisdom of God and of his resourceful forebears, and this lesson gave him strength as he bent over a task that would have been impossible for him six months before. There was no fear now, no uncertainty; no revulsion at the sight of the terrible wound. The boy felt a growing exultation as the needle pierced the flesh, leaving behind the thin blood-tinged tails of silk that would draw the incision together.

Chips knelt, holding the fireman's head firmly to prevent an involuntary motion. Peterson stood over them, peering down tensely, watching every move the boy made, for he knew well that the responsibility of the decision had been his. Sparks stood to one side, his thin jaw grimly set, and never once took his eyes off Slim. Outside in the dark the others watched and waited.

The line of untied sutures grew slowly behind the moving needle. When Slim reached the point in the gaping slash where the bottle's edge had penetrated the entire cheek, he pushed the edges of the wound harder to make them protrude and deftly forced the needle through both sides, so the top and bottom edges of the cut flesh could be pulled squarely together. On went the task under the blazing lamps of the cluster light, whose heat made an oven of the sick bay. Chips took over the task of blotting Slim's face when needed, until the needle penetrated the last of the severed flesh at the point of the jaw. Snipping off the final tail of silk, the boy returned the surgical scissors to the towel-covered chair and sat upright for a mo-

175

ment, stretching his spine. Then, moving quickly because there had been a change in the rhythm of Mike's breathing, he began to pull the incision together and tie the ends of the threads. As though instructed by some unseen master surgeon, the boy's fingers reached first for the ends of the suture that would close the gaping center of the wound. Gently he pulled the threads into the first half of a square knot. Motioning to Chips to take a pad, the boy placed it against the inside of the cheek and instructed the carpenter to hold it in place with his forefinger. But the carpenter's finger was so thick it bulged the wound and Slim had to hold the inside edges of the mucous membrane flush by building them level with the gauze placed between the inside of the cheek and the teeth. Carefully he pulled on the crossed ends of the thread.

The fireman's face was pale and the fine, crimsoned tails lay like living things against the dark, subcutaneous shadow of his close-shaven beard. Ten times the boy's strong, slender fingers deftly looped the thread, gently tugged the edges of flesh together, and completed the knots, until the long incision was closed. When the last thread had been tied, the boy paused to inspect the work. Beneath each stitch the edges of the flesh met squarely, but between the ten closeset sutures it rose in little puffs. Taking a narrow piece of gauze, Slim folded it into a cigarette-like roll and laid it along the length of the wound. Then, placing a dry gauze pad over the entire area, he secured the bandage in place with wide strips of old adhesive. Sparks had cut the tape for him and had tried to renew its holding power by patting the sticky side with alcohol.

Satisfied that there was nothing more to be done, the boy rose wearily from the stool and stood looking down at the fireman. Then he gathered the instruments from the chair and placed them in the basin of antiseptic. Chips collected the blood-stained gauze and wrapped it in the old newspaper that had served as a surgical waste receptacle. He handed it out the door and one of the men heaved it over the side. He offered Slim a cigarette and held the match for him. The boy dragged deeply and rolled his head from side to side to stretch his taut neck muscles.

Chips looked at him and smiled. "Are we through, Doc?" The big carpenter squeezed his thin neck affectionately in his huge hand. "What a hell of a sailmaker you'd have made!"

Second Mate Peterson studied the boy quietly for a long

176

moment. "What the hell are you doin' on a ship?" It was more comment than question. Then he moved toward the door. "You men break now. I'll stop in and see him later. Slim, go get some rest. I'll have you relieved of your watch tomorrow so you can take care of him." Peterson stepped over the coaming and disappeared forward toward the bridge.

The boy took a last look at the heavily slumbering fireman, then he too stepped out into the night. The bosun and several of the men moved back silently to let him pass. He walked slowly to the portside, past the radio shack, and made his way forward along the boatdeck until he came to the galley bunker. It was here that he'd completed his first task as a deck boy. He sat down heavily on the small canvas hatch cover and stared aft. Silhouetted against the glow of the covered cluster light he could make out the boxlike silhouette of the little deckhouse that contained the radio shack and the sick bay. There he'd completed his first task as a man. And then something inside let go. His shoulders sagged, an ache seized his throat, and a warm flood streamed from his eyes. Alone in the night, comforted by the darkness, the boy found release in the quiet blessing of manly tears.

– 16 –

Overhead, fleecy cumulus clouds raced their shadow selves across the dark water and beneath each billowy break a crowd of sparkling sunbeams cavorted merrily on the moving crests of the restless sea.

Slim went topside to the poop deck, took the reading from the taffrail log, made a note of it, and hurried to the bridge. He arrived at exactly eight bells, and both the second and third mates were sighting through their sextants, trying for a noon latitude sight. It was difficult and frustrating work, for the hot, tropical weather had given way to the cooler, uncertain weather of early autumn in the reversed seasons below the equator. In the language of the navigator, "the declination of the sun was north." The *Tropic Trader* was twenty-one days out of San Pedro and only 86 miles from Auckland, New Zealand. The crew had taken to wearing heavier clothes the past forty-eight hours.

Most of the work had been devoted to getting the ship ready for her arrival at Central Wharf. The booms were topped, the running gear rove; the thick hempen hawsers had been brought from the rope locker and coiled down on the fore and aft decks; emergency mooring cables were readied, and the last two days would be spent cleaning and freshening the paint on the superstructure. The first mate had issued orders in the captain's name that the *Tropic Trader* was to be clean and shipshape for her visit to the port of Auckland. Slim had been taken off the day watch and deck work, so he could tend to the injured fireman, but Holst had assigned him to the midnight watch so Warndahl could relieve Hammer on the four-to-eight. The ex-fighter's cut hand was useless. Slim had finally persuaded Jack to let him take care of it, but the A.B. refused to go to the sick bay where Mike was still confined. The boy brought antiseptic dressings aft and changed the bandages twice a day.

178

As for the fireman, he had refused to stay flat after the first day. Peterson and McNair confined him to the sick bay, where he sat brooding or playing solitaire between visits from Slim. The boy kept him under mild sedation with small doses of chloral hydrate and occasional aspirins. Feeding him was the biggest problem. It was impossible for the man to open and close his jaws. Chico made eggnogs of condensed milk, and Slim fed him through a length of glass-gauge tubing forced into the right corner of his mouth. The look of the wound disturbed Slim. Seeping blood had formed an ugly, soft, scablike covering over the stitches and it was almost impossible to tell how the healing had progressed. At Slim's suggestion Sparks had radioed the port captain in Auckland, who had checked with the health authorities. Their physician had judged the appearance of the wound to be normal, as described. There was considerable swelling and tenderness over the whole left side of the fireman's face, but there was no visible evidence of infection. And so the *Tropic Trader* plowed on, short-handed above deck and below. The poker games had stopped and men were washing clothes and getting ready for their first shore leave in twenty-four days.

Rusty had gone back into the messroom after the fight three nights earlier and picked up the deck of cards that Jack had used in the game. He had studied them carefully, inspecting their backs for telltale marks that might reveal their suit and value, but there were none visible. It was while Rusty was cutting the cards that he accidentally found out their secret. The deck was tapered—one used by professional gamblers. When properly handled, it was possible for an expert to pull out the threes and eights during the cut and locate them on the bottom of the pack, where they could be dealt as Jack saw fit. In thinking back over the game, Rusty remembered the constant recurrence of those cards in the winning hands. He passed the word to the men and Hammer was branded a "cheat." No one confronted him with the accusation. Chips had advised another course: refuse to sit in a game with him and refuse to honor their debts. The men quietly agreed.

The estimated time of arrival in quarantine for the freighter was noon on Sunday. The intervening days seemed endless. In his free time Slim tried to write home. He started one letter to his mother and father in Berkeley, but tore it up. He couldn't get Edye off his mind. Finally he gave in and began one to her. He had trouble with the salutation. He wanted to use an affectionate greeting, but each time he put it on paper it felt wrong. But then so did "Dear Edye." You just didn't address a girl that way—at least not a girl who had eagerly sought your arms and your lips. He finally settled on "Edye dear" and slowly began an account of the past three weeks. He filled several pages with the highlights, minimizing his part in patching up the fireman, showing obvious pride in progress at the helm and with some of the basic navigational formulas. At the end of the letter, he wanted desperately to speak of his loneliness. He wanted to make her understand how much he missed her and to reassure her that what he had felt and said that last night in Wauna had been the truth. He wanted to ask for her reassurance, but he couldn't bring himself to put any of these things on paper. He was positive a letter—perhaps several—would be waiting for him in Auckland. He'd wait until he'd read hers before he wrote something that might sound ridiculous. He finished off with a paragraph that left many things unsaid:

"I'll be hoping for a letter from you when we arrive in Auckland on Sunday. I don't suppose the consulate will be open, so I'll have to wait until Monday. No mail was delivered to us in San Pedro but the second mate, Mr. Peterson, has been kidding about stopping for letters in mid-Pacific at the 'mail buoy.' I guess deck boys go through the same jokes every trip. It gets kind of lonesome out here sometimes, so you can imagine how good it will be to have a letter, especially from you. Please give my best regards to your mother and dad. You were all wonderful to me and I'm not very good at saying things, but I guess you know how much it meant. I'll write you from New Zealand and send you some picture postcards like you asked. This is all for now—please write soon. We'll be going to Wellington, Dunedin, Bluff, and then over to Hobart in Tasmania and then to Adelaide in South Australia. I'll let you know where we go from there—probably Manila, Hong Kong, and then San Francisco again. Your affectionate and footloose friend, Lewis."

The boy reread the last paragraph, folded the paper for the envelope, and put it in his shirt pocket. He made his way wearily into the fo'c'sle, and in the gray light of early dawn slipped off his clothes, stepped carefully on the lower bunk to avoid waking Hammer, and hoisted himself up into his bedding. Pulling the worn spread that served as a screen, he snuggled into the blankets and thought of

Edye and the letter he knew would be waiting. Before long he sank into a deep slumber, taking with him into that boundless world the feel and sound of the girl and the sweet ache of anticipation.

— 17 —

When Slim came off watch at 4 A.M. Sunday morning, the night was clear and comfortably cool. Ninety miles to the south lay the port of Auckland, former capital city of New Zealand and now its principal center of commerce. Two points off the port bow, some thirty miles ahead, lay Great Barrier Island and Cape Colville. Every half hour the three mates had checked positions carefully, searching for errors, correcting for the confusion of currents born in the Coral and Tasman seas that boiled around the bleak volcanic reefs rimming the North Island of New Zealand.

To Slim the experience was absorbing. During his two hours at the wheel the course had been altered from minute to minute, as the officers plotted and replotted. The boy set his jaw and resolved to do a perfect job as quartermaster. As new courses were given him, he repeated them crisply and professionally. The third mate watched surreptitiously and, though his face betrayed none of it, he felt a growing pride in the serious-faced kid and promised himself that he would accelerate Slim's lessons.

Slowly the burdened sea-weary old tramp moved southward into Hauraki Gulf, passed Rangitoto Island, and steamed into beautiful Waitemata Harbor. Then the city of Auckland suddenly came into view. The surprise of the scene was breath-taking. Each man felt it and reacted. They lined the rail to stare longingly at the city. To each of them it had a different meaning. Some were returning to familiar territory and the mixed emotions of previous adventures. To Hammer it meant a chance to drink his bottle of scotch and make good his prodigious boast; to Warndahl it meant a vile orgy and the basis for endless exaggerations. To Spots it meant another losing bout with his conscience and the gin bottle; another snoring, seeping, oil-soaked hangover—and another pledge to be broken in the next port. To Rusty and Otto it meant a chance to pursue their earthy pleasures in private, to Russian John more days of tedium, for he seldom left the ship, to Chips a chance to drink good ale and stout with old friends and to visit with his favorite lady—a barmaid in the Waverly Hotel. To Mike it meant more pain and tedium in the hospital, to the officers, added duties and little time off—and to Slim it meant all the things a first foreign port can mean to an adventurous boy nearing nineteen. It meant a unique thrill which would never again be quite the same, for, as time went by and ports disappeared astern, he would become less the wide-eyed boy and more the aware young man. He would learn that no matter what color the skin, how strange the tongue, how odd the land, human nature never changes. Happiness and sorrow, gentleness and brutality, generosity and greed, prejudice and compassion are the common blessings and burdens of all men. But for the moment the edge of his excitement could not be dulled, even by the aching impatience of the past three weeks.

At the quarantine station the *Tropic Trader* ran up the yellow flag, dropped anchor, and the government doctor came aboard. The crew was mustered on the starboard side of the main deck and each man was given a brief inspection. The doctor looked at Hammer's hand and advised attention from a private physician ashore. Up in the sick bay he quickly inspected Mike's wound, shook his head in amazement, and went to the bridge to fill out the necessary clearance papers.

A tug came alongside and, continuing dead slow, the *Tropic Trader* was brought up to the end of Central Wharf adjacent to the Ferry Terminal, almost at the foot of Queen Street, Auckland's main thoroughfare.

Slim took his place with the second mate and the rest of the after gang for the docking. He had been so absorbed in the work that he'd hardly noticed the gathering crowd of curious townspeople who had drifted out onto the wharf through the great iron gates. From the midship main deck he and the others looked down on the well-dressed families, still in their late summer attire, who strolled slowly along the length of the vessel. From up on the higher fo'c'sle deck that towered over the street, Slim could hear the good-natured calls of some of the men, trying to attract the attention of the girls who stood back against the long dock shed in bashful groups of twos and threes. He could see them laughing among themselves, obviously enjoying the attention of American sailors. They

183

looked very attractive and a bit old-fashioned. One or two of them carried parasols, which reminded Slim of the girls in the illustrations of Booth Tarkington's *Seventeen*.

The high past-noon sun was hot and a number of the strollers sought the narrow shade near the buildings or beneath the tall gantry cranes that towered along the dock. Most of the men aboard were burned a deep bronze from the weeks of tropical sun. Slim had taken it easy and had not peeled. The golden brown of his taut young hide glowed with a sheen of perspiration and the flush of abounding good health. His deep tan was accented even more by the shock of sun-bleached hair—the color of clean straw—and the hazel-gray of his clear eyes. He worked at his task with eagerness, looking forward to setting foot ashore. Cocked down over his right eyebrow was a salty, squared, Navy "whitehead" that he'd worn all through the mid-Pacific. Stripped to the waist, clean, faded blue dungarees tightly belted around his lean muscled middle, Slim looked very much like the ideal young sailor depicted in recruiting posters. He heard the low-spoken comments of his shipmates about the women and girls on the dock, but paid little attention to them. When the gangway was secured and the cluster light set over it, the bosun knocked the men off for the rest of the afternoon. Slim started for the fo'c'sle to wash and change, but Chico intercepted him at the after end of the main deck. Looking around to make certain that no one was watching, the smiling little Filipino sneaked the deck boy two large oranges. "Take thees, Sleem. Eets good bait—por the ladies!"

The boy took the oranges, stuck them in his hat, and tucked it in the crook of his arm. He could no more have put the fruit in the pockets of his skin-tight dungarees than he could have put both feet in one shoe. Thanking Chico, he walked across the deckload to the poop.

Chips was moving some wooden pallets from the top of the chain-lashed timber. When he saw the deck boy he straightened up and smiled. "How ya doing, Doc?" Ever since that night in the sickbay, the big carpenter had taken to calling him that. Slim understood that it was Chips' own affectionate nickname and that it signified his new status with the senior member of the crew.

The boy smiled warmly. "Fine, thanks, Chips. I'm going to get cleaned up now and go ashore for a look around."

The carpenter nodded in approval. "Me too, soon's I clear these turnbuckles." He pulled some loose planks

184

aside and called after the boy, who had moved toward the companionway. "Have you got a lady staked out yet?"

Slim stopped and leaned against the poop-deck rail. "Nope. I haven't tried."

The carpenter looked at him appraisingly. "A good-lookin' young kid like you can have his pick. And let me tell you something, boy——" He jerked his thumb toward the wharf. "Those are nice girls down there. Don't get confused and think they're like the bums that hang around our waterfronts." He looked thoughtfully over the side for a moment. "Of course you'll find some pros down there, too, but not many. These are wonderful folks here in New Zealand!"

He spoke with simple conviction. There was nothing vulgar about the man. He was hewn from clear, strong stock. His natural dignity and obvious decency were the real source of his strength. These were the qualities that Hammer sensed, did not understand and therefore feared; inversely, they were the ones that attracted the boy. He suddenly remembered two letters that a friend had given him to people in Auckland.

"I've got an introduction to some folks down here. They work for a photo developing concern here in town."

The carpenter furrowed his brow and mentally listed the businesses he knew firsthand. "Must be Suckling's up on Queen Street. Go meet 'em! You'll probably have a good time."

Slim answered over his shoulder as he resumed his way below: "I'll probably go see them tomorrow. They won't be open today." Slim looked at his watch and checked it with the clock on the tower of the Ferry Terminal. He liked the looks and feel of the city already and he'd not yet set foot ashore. But the air was sparkling and clean and the ferry wharves and terminal seemed like miniatures of his own San Francisco. He felt at home here; even the surrounding country reminded him of California. He was glad they would be here for a week or more. He could guess the stay when he'd heard the second mate grumbling about the leisurely pace of the local stevedores. "They cut this whole goddamn load, sawed it to length, and loaded it aboard in less time than these buckos will take to unload half of it! I'll be unfrocked and frigged if I know how to hurry 'em up!" Slim hoped the conscientious second mate wouldn't find a way.

Ducking quickly down the companionway, he washed carefully, using the fresh water he'd drawn the night be-

185

fore. When the boy came back into the fo'c'sle from the head he found Jack sitting quietly on the edge of the lower bunk. The big A.B. was trying to undo the bandage Slim had put on his cut palm.

"What are you taking it off for, Jack?"

Hammer continued his clumsy effort to remove the gauze. "The goddamn thing itches. It's drivin' me crazy!"

Slim set the bucket on the deck, pulled the footstool close to the bunk, and indicated that he wanted to inspect the wound. Hammer held out his hand without looking at the boy and Slim untied the square knot at the thick wrist. Unwinding the bandage carefully, he exposed the deep cut. Several days before a puslike ooze had been coming from the wound, but now it appeared to be closing. It had a much healthier look, Slim thought.

"It's better, Jack. The itching may be a sign that it's healing. You oughta go see a doctor, though."

Hammer looked at the boy almost reluctantly. "According to the scuttle butt, you're the best doctor around. What did they do with that son-of-a-bitch in the sick bay?"

Slim was surprised by the question. It was the first time Hammer had even alluded to the fireman. "He's coming along okay. The doctor's coming aboard to take him off."

Hammer's mouth twisted into an ugly smile. "They better get him off. The lyin' bastard! Next time I'll kill 'im!"

"Forget it, will ya? It's all over with! Right or wrong, you beat him—now forget it!"

The A.B. let his right hand rest on the boy's knee, palm up. He looked at him, as though weighing his words. Fishing a cigarette out of his pocket with his left hand, he slowly shoved it into his mouth. Slim lit it for him and tossed the match on the deck.

Hammer took a deep drag and, as he spoke, his words were punctuated by thin, gray wisps of smoke. "What do you mean, 'right or wrong'?" He emphasized the last two words.

The boy fought his way back from the edge of fear and looked directly at the man. "I mean that it doesn't make any difference whether *he* was right or *you* were right. You settled it with him. Why keep after him?"

Hammer narrowed his eyes. "I asked ya what you meant by 'right or wrong'! Do *you* think I was cheating?"

The boy shrugged his shoulders. "Look, Jack, I don't know much about cards. All I know is what the guys are saying."

"Okay! What *are* they saying?"

"They say you used some kind of a phony deck so you could pull out cards you wanted."

A sardonic laugh heaved Hammer's heavy shoulders. "Who said that—which guy?"

Slim thought quickly. He knew the accusation had been made by Rusty, who had the proof in his locker, but he didn't want to precipitate another fo'c'sle brawl and have to patch up still another victim of the man's ruthless urge to destroy.

"Nobody in particular. The guys *all* think that."

Hammer looked down at his cut hand and tried to clench the big fist, but the pain stopped him. "Well—they're right! But fuck 'em! If I hadn't used my own deck, one of those bastards would have rung his own deck in. Every trip it's the same story. Only this trip it was my turn!"

Slim rose from the stool and went to his locker. Taking out a jar of improvised wet dressings and some new gauze, he seated himself again in front of Hammer.

"They don't want to play any more, Jack."

Grinding out the cigarette butt, Hammer rapped Slim's shoulder with the back of his left hand. "I'll make you a bet, kid. I'll bet ya my half in the ship's safe against yours that those shit-heads'll be playin' poker with me again as soon as we head for Frisco—maybe sooner. You wait and see!"

The boy made no comment. Before he had finished with the bandage, several of the men came in and started cleaning up. They all had the same complaint: "Nuthin' to do and nuthin' to drink on Sunday in this Christ-bitten place!" Tomorrow they'd all change their tunes and a few of them would find ways to scare up bottles, even on Sunday.

When Slim finished, Hammer asked where he was going. "I've got a letter to some people here. I'm going to look them up."

A smirk of disbelief crossed Hammer's face. "You got friends all over. Makes a handy excuse when you want to travel alone, don't it, kid?"

The boy tried to conceal his annoyance. It was the second time Hammer had put him in this position. After the experience in San Francisco he was not anxious to become a bosom shipmate of the cold-blooded ex-fighter. After watching him knock out the stevedore and mutilate the fireman without giving them a chance, he was certain he didn't want to develop the relationship, for he knew that

Hammer just as easily might turn on him for some fancied injustice.

"Look, Jack. I'm trying to be a good shipmate. But I don't like boozing it up in whorehouses. I don't think you'd like the kind of girls I like——" He realized his mistake as soon as he'd made it and Hammer immediately took advantage of it.

"If you mean the kind of dame I saw you layin' it on in Wauna, you're wrong, pal. Them I like just *fine!*" The innuendo in his voice was mirrored in his broad smirk.

Slim felt a flush of anger color his face. "I told you that girl was a family friend. I like her very much and I'm going to see her again. Not because I want to do anything to her—but just because I like her—very much!"

Hammer studied the boy's face and the smirk slowly faded from his own. "Okay, kid, you play it your way, but you'll find out soon enough about these dames." He laughed bitterly to himself, then continued, "Your *friend* up in Wauna may be different, but I've seen a lot of guys get conned by those snooty 'nice girls' and wind up with a full house!"

He didn't attempt any rebuttal. He knew that a "full house" meant coincidental cases of gonorrhea and syphilis. He'd heard Warndahl's endless and contemptible tales of his encounters with "society dames" who had chased after him because they were unsatisfied by their sissy mates and how he had refused their insistent begging because they were more promiscuous than common whores. He had listened reluctantly, only vaguely understanding that the perverted seaman was subconsciously justifying his own filth and licentiousness by trying to reduce to a status below his own the decent women who were repelled by him.

Slim could feel Hammer watching him as he went about changing to freshly scrubbed dungarees and clean blue shirt. The boy had no special plans, and it was apparent to the A.B. that he was not getting slicked up to go "on the prowl." Slim slipped the letter in his pocket, although he had no intention of presenting it, and left the fo'c'sle. As he turned into the foot of the companionway, he could hear shouts and raucous laughter. When he got topside, he found Rusty and Otto leaning over the rail, calling down at several girls on the dock. The men were holding apples enticingly, pretending to throw them. Slim understood now what Chico had meant when he smuggled the two precious oranges to him for "bait."

Three of the girls were giggling and whispering among themselves. Two others were standing back, watching. One of the girls had a quiet, serious manner and seemed unamused by the broad flirtations.

Slim walked over to the rail to watch the game and suddenly found himself involved. Otto grabbed him by the arm and hauled him close beside him.

"Hey, baby! Look what I got here. If ya don't like us—maybe ya like 'em younger. He's a devil with the ladies, too! Ya shoulda seen him when we loaded this lumber—had every cutie in town chasin' him—all the way back to the ship. How about it, Rusty?"

Rusty went along with the game. "That's the truth. They'da chased him right into the fo'c'sle if Otto and me hadn'ta beat 'em off and saved him!"

Slim tried to pull away in embarrassment, but the two shipmates held him securely. The girls looked up and were overcome by a new wave of giggles.

Otto turned his attention to the quiet girl who was standing back against the dock shed with her companion. "Hey, bashful—yes, you with the big eyes——"

Rusty leaned close to Otto and added parenthetically, "And the big tits——"

Otto laughed and added, "And the shapely ass——" Then, aloud, he addressed the girl again. "What do ya say, bashful? You wanta take this sailor? If ya want him, we'll throw him down to ya. You'll love it—just like the other girls did! How about it?"

They pretended to hoist the protesting Slim up on the rail. The girl watched without changing expression, then both of them turned deliberately and began to walk slowly toward the gate.

Otto called after her: "Don't go away mad, sweetheart. You don't know what you're missin'!"

Slim felt foolish, but he knew the ribbing was good-natured. He felt sorry for the girl, who was certainly not a pickup. He pulled away from the two seamen, who let him go with a parting shot.

"Go get her, kid! Those quiet ones are the best! Take it from a couple of old pros!"

The boy dismissed the joke with a sorry smile and crossed the deckload as Rusty and Otto continued their attempts to line up dates.

After twenty-four days Slim felt happy to set foot on land again. At first it felt a bit strange. As he walked toward the broad street that paralleled the waterfront, he looked at the curious strollers along the dock. Several of them called greetings to him and their soft New Zealand accents seemed very much like the English, sometimes with a trace of cockney. Some of them sounded vaguely Scottish. He liked their overt friendliness and responded in kind. Except for their pleasant accents, so unlike the usual American twang, they might have been the folks he'd known most of his life in Red Bluff and Proberta in the northern Sacramento Valley. They fit comfortably into the picture of similarity that had struck him upon his first view of the city.

Reaching the dock gate, he walked through it and turned right under the towering bow of the ship. As he passed the great stone pillar at the end of the fence, he nearly collided with the two girls who had recently beat a retreat before Rusty's loud exhibitionism. They both started perceptibly and the thin-lipped little blonde in the pink cloche hat giggled. The girl the A.B.s had called "the quiet one" looked at Slim directly for an instant, then turned. He thought she had been about to speak. Suddenly he realized the awkwardness of the situation. In confusion, he tried to find something sensible to say. "Hi——" The girls looked at each other but didn't answer. Slim waited and stifled a smile at the ludicrous mental picture of the two girls springing into each other's arms for protection against the wild American sailor.

"Listen . . . I . . . uh . . . I'm sorry about those two fellows. They were just clowning around. They're kind of fresh, but, believe me, I didn't know they were going to do it!" Again Slim waited for an answer.

The girl with the big brown eyes that tipped up at the corners blinked several times and opened her full, moist lips, as though trying to frame a reply. But it was the smiling little blonde who spoke first.

"Oh, that's all right, laddie—we're used to it. If it gets too bad we just walk away, that's all!" She flicked her handbag in a gesture of disdain, then laughed. "It does get a bit thick at times, you know."

Slim nodded sympathetically. "I'll bet it does! I know those guys!" As they stood facing each other he suddenly felt that he ought to make amends, somehow.

He tried to make the invitation sound casual and impersonal. "If you would like to see the ship closer, I'd be glad to walk along with you. I don't think the fellas will bother you if you're escorted."

The blond girl looked up at the tall boy eagerly. "Do you s'pose we could go aboard and look around a bit?"

Slim cocked his head uncertainly. "Gee . . . I can't take you aboard, miss. Only an officer could do that."

A little shrug bounced the girl's shoulders. "That's a pity. Officers don't bother much with young ladies in their teens." She reached into the braided white handbag, took out a powder puff, and pulled it down both sides of her nose with quick little gestures. "Oh, by the way, I'm Lyla —with a *y*—and this is Marge."

Slim hadn't intended to, but he found himself reaching to shake hands. "I'm Lewis Fredericks—they call me 'Slim.'"

Lyla giggled behind her hand as her eyes roved up and down the deck boy's lanky frame. "I wonder whatever for!" She gave his hand a quick little shake. The dark-eyed girl, who was much the prettier of the two, held out her hand and Slim took it in his. It felt soft and pleasant after the nervous squeeze from Lyla's thin, agile fingers.

"I could walk you down along the dock and explain the ship to you—if you'd like."

The girls glanced at each other quizzically for an instant, then Lyla voiced their unspoken decision. "We've seen lots of grubby old ships—from the outside." She laughed ruefully. "That's about all there is to do in Auckland on Sunday—that and go to church—or walk in Albert Park."

Slim smiled at the way she said it. "There's not much more to do where I come from. Sunday is Sunday—all over, I guess."

An idea struck Lyla and she brightened a bit. "Know something we could do?"

Marge's big eyes opened wider and from her alarmed glance it was apparent that her friend's plans were being improvised.

"We could show this nice young gentleman our world-famous 'royal bumps.'"

Slim looked puzzled and waited for an explanation.

Marge seemed about to veto the proposal, but Lyla continued, "The only thing is, it's a bit early in the day for it. It's really better to do it just before teatime."

Slim was completely baffled. He was about to try a tentative question when Ioway came swinging around the corner whistling his inevitable embellishment of the latest popular hit from back home. When he came upon his shipmate and the two girls, he broke off in the middle of a note, his lips still pursed. Without a trace of self-consciousness he walked up, as though joining a group of old friends.

"Hi . . . I was looking for you!"

The girls thought he had meant to include them and looked puzzled.

Slim began the introductions. "Lyla, this is Horatius Edwards." The girl was giving Ioway an impertinent going-over. When she heard the name she stopped abruptly and looked at Slim. "Horatius?"

Slim nodded.

She turned back to the boy. Her tone was awestruck. "Gracious!"

Marge shot a warning look at her.

Slim continued, "And this is Marge . . . Marge . . . Horatius . . . only I think you'd better call him 'Ioway' like we do!"

Lyla, still taken aback, murmured, "Well, I should jolly well think so——" The look of concern on her face changed to a sudden smile and she put out her hand. "In case you didn't hear, it's Lyla—with a *y*."

Ioway took her hand, then turned to the other girl. Reaching out his big hand, he grinned at her. "I know! You're Marge—with an *M*." He laughed at his own joke, then bounced up and down expectantly on the balls of his feet.

Slim watched him and fought back a smile. "Cocker spaniel" is right, he thought. "Where were you going, Ioway?"

The boy looked startled. "Hey! I'm lookin' for you. Didn't I tell ya? The second wants to see you—up in the sick bay. You better get goin'!"

The girls seemed disappointed, and a sudden thought worried Slim. He wondered if something had happened to Mike. He knew the doctor was scheduled to come aboard and look at the fireman and probably order his removal to the hospital. He was afraid that he might have to stand some sort of official inquiry that would rob him of his time ashore. As he stood uncertainly trying to make up his mind what to do about the girls, he could see that Ioway was fairly bouncing with excitement at being in his first foreign port. The questions came pouring out of his mouth so quickly that he couldn't remember which girl was which. Ioway was close to Slim's age, but his puppy-like friendliness made him seem considerably younger. Physically he was a bit heavier and several inches shorter. All in

192

all he added up to a very pleasant-looking young man. Slim watched Lyla's appraising eyes and felt sure that she'd agree. Marge, who seemed a year or so older than Lyla, watched Ioway with mild interest, but Slim felt her eyes on him and when he turned he caught her questioning gaze.

He spoke with sudden inspiration. "Look, I've got an idea. I'll go back aboard and see what the mate wants, then I'll come back and the four of us can find something to do. Okay?"

He waited for the girls to approve, but Ioway gave them no chance. "Good idea. Get goin' so we don't waste the whole afternoon!"

Slim left them and walked quickly back through the wharf gate. As he hurried along beneath the high, weather-dulled topsides, he found himself anxious to be done with whatever the second mate had set out for him and return to the girls. He had been increasingly aware during the brief conversation that Marge was very attractive. In the full bloom of young womanhood, she possessed the voluptuousness that made men look a second time. Her broad, deeply tanned face was serious, and in repose the tipped-up, vaguely oriental eyes and the full, red lips lent a misleading sultriness to it. Her soft black hair was pulled back simply across her ears and caught in a full knot at the smooth nape of her neck. She wore no hat and the sun glinted along the carefully combed strands at the crown of her head.

Climbing the gangway suspended diagonally against the rust-streaked hull, Slim gained the main deck and turned aft. The bosun, who'd had little to say since the second mate placed Slim on special sick-bay duty, smirked as he passed. "What's de matter, kid? De wild natives scare ya?" The rough laughter followed Slim, as he rounded the after end of the main deck and headed up the ladder to the boatdeck. The second mate was waiting. "Fredericks, the doctor wants to ask you some questions." A sinking feeling hit Slim's middle.

As he stepped over the low coaming and entered the gloomy little room, he saw the fireman stretched out in the bunk, his wound exposed, and a smallish man in a dark suit, gently probing the stitches.

The mate introduced him. "This is Fredericks, Doctor. He's the one who did this job."

The physician turned on his stool and looked at the boy. He seemed weary, but when he spoke his voice was surprisingly deep and vibrant. Innate kindliness modulated its tone. "Come over here, lad." He indicated a second stool.

Slim crossed and seated himself and the doctor looked at him closely through a pair of dusty, rather old-fashioned steel-rimmed spectacles. "Mr. Peterson tells me you performed this little operation."

"Yes, sir. I thought something should be done and——"

The man interrupted him. "You were quite right. Something should have been done!" The doctor's tone made Slim fear what was to follow. "What made you think you could do a job of skin surgery like this? Have you had any training?"

There was no hint of censure in the voice, but Slim could not rid himself of the nagging guilt. His mouth felt dry, and he licked his lips nervously and tried to swallow before he answered. "I've never had any medical training, sir. I thought maybe I could do it because on the ranch in northern California we used to sew up animals that got ripped on barbed-wire fences. And I used to stitch up the incisions of new pigs after they were castrated." The boy felt miserable and speech was difficult. He paused a moment, then continued, "I hope I didn't do anything that can't be fixed up?"

The physician blinked over his glasses and his face broke into a broad smile. "My dear young chap, the incredible part of it is that nothing need be fixed up! You did everything precisely right! If you hadn't done what you did, this man might have lost his life or at best been hopelessly disfigured. As it is, with a little bit of work at the hospital, he'll be back with you in a few days—and in a year I predict he'll have a remarkably small scar for so large a cut!"

Slim felt the tension leave his middle, and his shoulders sagged with relief. He wanted to smile, he wanted to thank the doctor, he wanted to say something to Peterson, but he could find no words. The jumble of thoughts at the unexpected turn of events left his mind a blank and he just stood looking into space, blinking.

The second mate jarred him to action. "Well, what's the matter—are you deaf? Say something!"

The boy's face broke into a sheepish grin. "I'm sorry, sir . . ." He glanced at both the officer and the physician. "I'm very thankful that everything turned out all right ——" He paused, looked at the second mate again, then added, "For *everybody!*"

The doctor rose wearily and wiped his hands on the end

194

of a shabby towel that had been lying across his knee. "There's only one thing more I'd like to know. What did you use for a pain-killer—and what did you use to sterilize the needle and sutures?"

Slim described in detail the steps he'd taken to prepare the wound and the method he'd used in closing and dressing it. He brought the equipment from the chest.

The doctor inspected it and listened with obvious interest. The fireman watched the boy with fixed fascination and heard for the first time the details of the experience he'd gone through while knocked out by a massive dose of chloral hydrate. He lay on his side in the bunk, his heavy tattooed left shoulder and arm lying limply on a thin blue Navy blanket.

When Slim finished, the doctor chuckled to himself, then looked once more at the patient. "I'll wager he went through more pain having those impressive murals pricked into his hide than he did having you work on him. It's a remarkable job, young man. The medical profession may have lost a fine talent when you chose the sea. No matter! There are times when I'd gladly change places with you!" He wadded up the towel and placed it on the bare springs of the upper bunk. "We'll put a fresh bandage on your friend here . . . and get him off to the hospital. In the meantime, if any of your shipmates need minor surgery at sea, they may trust you completely—especially, I should think, if a castration were indicated!"

— 18 —

Slim found Ioway and the girls where he'd left them. While he'd been with the doctor, Ioway had told the girls about his feat with the surgical needle. They had cringed at the details but were visibly impressed, and when Slim returned, the atmosphere was much friendlier.

As he had left the sick bay the second mate had stopped him and asked whether or not he'd drawn money. Slim had replied that he didn't think any would be available until the following day, whereupon Peterson had reached into his pocket and taken out a New Zealand pound note.

"That's worth four dollars and eighty-eight cents in our money, kiddo. When you draw yours, you can pay it back to me."

Slim had taken the unfamiliar paper bill, thanked the mate and promised to return it the following day. He could have waited until the steward, who also acted as purser, got the books ready, but he would have lost several precious hours. Most of the other men wouldn't get their money until it was too late to spend it, even if recreation places were open on Sunday.

And so with a pound in his pocket and a girl on the dock, Slim was ready for his first excursion in a foreign port. It was to be an experience he'd never entirely forget.

Ioway was full of curiosity. "Hey, Slim, tell us what happened with the second! Was there any trouble? What did the doctor say? Is Mike okay?"

Slim laughed. "Which question do you want me to answer first?"

Ioway made a gesture of impatience. "All of them, ya damn fool!" He put his hand up to his mouth suddenly and shot a worried look at the girls. "Excuse me——"

Their laughter tinkled pleasantly. Lyla pushed him gently. "You're such an eager one, Horatius!" Turning to Slim, she urged him to answer. "He told us what a job you did. Go on . . . tell us about it. Is the tattooed chap all right?"

Slim reluctantly gave them a brief account as they walked toward the Ferry Building and turned up Queen Street. When he finished he stopped walking and looked around. "Say, where are we heading for, anyway?"

Lyla winked at Ioway. "Do you think we ought to tell him, Horatius?"

Ioway furrowed his brow in mock consideration and announced his decision. "Sure, let's tell him. He's old enough to know!" Before Lyla could speak, a frightening thought seized the boy. "Oh my gosh, I forgot something! I've gotta talk to Slim. Excuse me—excuse us just a moment——" As he apologized he pulled Slim aside a few steps. Leaning close, he whispered with pained concern, "Geez, Slim, what am I gonna do? I told the girls we'd do the 'royal bumps' with them, and I don't even have a penny. Do you have any money, or shall we try to get out of it?"

Slim grinned and put an affectionate arm across the boy's shoulder. "I think the good Lord takes care of fools and deck boys! Mr. Peterson let me have a pound just before I left the ship."

Ioway looked relieved and smiled ruefully. "You gotta watch me. I go jumping into things without looking— sometimes."

Slim nodded in hearty agreement. "That's for doggone sure! And by the way, what in hell *is* this 'royal bumps' business?" Ordinarily Slim didn't swear, but a few small four-letter words had found their way into his vocabulary and they came out at those times when more than ordinary emphasis was needed.

Ioway looked blank. He spoke slowly to himself. "You know sumpthin'? I don't know——"

Slim glanced at the girls. Lyla was trying to listen while pretending to look in a shop window.

"Well, let's find out. We can always say 'no.' "

The deck boy shook his head sadly. "Not to that little blonde, ya can't!"

Lyla had made it clear that Ioway was her escort. When the boys rejoined them, she linked her arm possessively through his and steered him up the left side of Queen Street. The two of them exchanged a constant stream of laughter and chatter. Slim and Marge fell in behind and walked along slowly, enjoying the last warm patches of sun that slipped through the irregular tops of the old-fashioned buildings on the opposite side of the street.

When Slim looked down at her to see whether or not the quiet girl was enjoying or merely tolerating his company, she returned the look with a friendly smile. He felt there was something almost mysterious about her. She looked as though there might have been a strain of Polynesian blood in her background. He imagined signs of it in the dark hair and eyes, the full red mouth, the even white teeth, the broad face, the undeniably feminine body, and the easy grace with which she moved. Slim could imagine her full, round body wrapped in a sarong, her hair flowing and caught with blossoms. The picture excited him, but it also brought a sudden pang of guilt and he forced his thoughts back to the first walk with Edye—and the last one—the night they'd said "good-by" at the dock gate. Then he remembered the letter he should have mailed and the one that would be waiting, and wondered where the consulate was located. He thought about asking Marge and decided not to. He felt the girl looking up at him. When he turned his head he caught a fleeting trace of concern and saw it quickly change to a little smile. Something about this girl disturbed him, but the sensation was not unpleasant. He struggled against it, for she troubled his conscience and the need to struggle vaguely annoyed him.

At the end of the first block, Queen Street narrowed down and the Victorian buildings lining the way reminded Slim of the older parts of San Francisco. Until the boys grew accustomed to the left-hand traffic, they were constantly wandering over to the right, while the girls patiently tugged them back into the proper lane. As they threaded their way through the strollers and avoided the occasional cars, Slim thought it was time to end the mystery of their destination.

Catching the girl gently by the arm, he stopped her. "Listen, do you mind telling me just what this deal is that Lyla—with a *y*—is getting us into?"

The girl smiled at him and steered him to the opposite side of a narrow street before she answered. "I think little Lyla's got you boys a bit confused, hasn't she?" The helpless look on Slim's face was answer enough. She took his hand and held it in both of hers, like a mother reassuring a frightened child. "The 'royal bumps' are really not so terrifying. Most of the girls and boys here in Auckland enjoy them—especially since Luna Park has been closed." She looked up at him, all innocence. "I thought you Yanks were all such daring ones—ready for anything?"

Slim grew defensive. "We are! Only we have a funny habit of liking to know what we're getting into!"

The girl hesitated a moment, as though gauging his temper, then broke into laughter. It was the first time Slim had been aware of her voice. It was an exciting sound, he thought, rich and musical—filled with warmth and an intensity that made him uneasy. One more experienced would also have recognized in it the voice of a young woman capable of real tenderness and deep passion. Slim was pleasantly surprised at the sudden evidence of humor in the girl. He saw it now in her gleaming eyes and at the upturned corners of her lips. He heard it in her voice as she spoke again.

"What on earth do you think you're 'getting into,' as you put it?"

Slim grinned and shook a finger under her nose. "We'll be getting into nothing at all—unless you give me a straight answer!"

The girl's eyes moved from Slim's face to the tip of his extended finger. She reached up and closed her hand around it. "Better point that somewhere else, or you'll have me cross-eyed!" She pushed his finger gently to one side and released it. "All right! The mystery will be revealed!" She looked at the other couple who were still engrossed in animated conversation. Taking his arm, she turned him to face the opposite side of Queen Street. "If you'd really like to know what you're getting into, I'll tell you. See that autobus up there in the next block?"

Starting him across, she steered him through the lazy Sunday traffic. "That's what you're getting into! An autobus!"

His mystified look made the girl laugh again. In a moment the battered old vehicle, its destination labeled with a strange Maori name, ground to a noisy stop and the four of them got on. There were a number of young people already aboard. All seemed in a holiday mood and the bus was filled with the low murmur of masculine voices and the high, merry obbligato of feminine laughter. They found two empty doubles toward the rear. Ioway and Lyla crowded into one and Slim and Marge squeezed into the other, directly behind. Slim had trouble making room for his long legs and the girl crowded over in the corner nearest the window to make more space.

It did little good and she laughed at him. "Those are the most impossible legs I've seen. How on earth do you ever manage?"

Slim looked down at the awkward tangle of shins and thighs and smiled ruefully. "They're the only ones I have!" He tried shifting his legs inside the seat so he could angle toward her, but quickly gave up and turned away, letting them dangle in the comparative freedom of the aisle.

Marge looked at him sympathetically. "I don't know why they insist on growing you Americans so big. Is everything in your country like that?"

Slim considered her question for a moment and a pointed answer made his eyes twinkle. "Absolutely everything—and especially our curiosities! By the way, that reminds me, not that it's important, but where are we going?" He asked the question innocently, as though the subject had just arisen.

Marge looked contrite and patted the back of his head maternally. "We're being mean, aren't we? All right, then, we're going on a bus ride to the countryside." She made the words sound like a rhyme. "At the end of the line we'll stop and take tea. Then we'll come back again—that's all. Doesn't it sound frightfully exciting?"

Slim's suspicious sidelong glance made her laugh again and she raised her right hand in an oath-taking gesture. "I swear on His Majesty's personal Bible, it's the truth!" She held the oath sign, waiting for Slim's reaction.

He kept his eyes on her intently. "Okay, we're going on some sort of a picnic, but just where do these mysterious 'royal bumps' come in?"

Marge's big eyes grew sad, but a smile twitched at the corners of her mouth. "Oh dear me, those 'bumps' again. Well, I may as well tell you. There's nothing we can do to avoid them. We're trapped now—in this miserable bus—and we'll just have to keep our chins high and see it through."

Slim made a truculent gesture and settled down as comfortably as possible on the skimpy cane seat. It was slippery from the polishing of hundreds of bouncing backsides and he had to wedge his knees against the frame of the seat ahead. He twisted his right arm, raised it over Marge's head, and clung to the back of the seat. Ahead of them, Ioway and Lyla were laughing and adding trivial tributaries to the growing stream of small talk. They seemed to be enjoying each other and Slim watched them with a touch of envy. Apparently Ioway had no curiosity at all about their destination. It was enough for him that he was having another adventure to write home about. His life was all cut out and planned. There would be very few uncertain moves—at least in the foreseeable future. He'd finished all the education he wanted. He'd probably marry a home-town girl, raise several kids and bushels of corn, and be perfectly happy as a true son of the midwest. He had no burning ambitions—no real convictions about anything but farming. In short, he understood the life he'd chosen and hence was comfortable and secure. An unexpected afternoon with this attractive, energetic, little daughter of New Zealand suited him to perfection. It quite obviously suited Lyla too.

When Slim turned to Marge she was staring absently out of the window. If she could see his reflection watching her in the half mirror of the dirty glass, she gave no indication. She seemed occupied with her own thoughts and Slim decided not to interrupt them.

Her preoccupation gave the boy his first good chance to look at her. When he'd first seen her, standing in the back against the dock shed on Central Wharf, he had noticed that she was obviously attractive. But now, sitting within inches of her, he was aware of the real impact of her quiet beauty. He'd overheard Lyla tell Ioway that she'd never known Marge to "talk so much" and he was certain from the girl's gentle teasing that she was enjoying their time together. He was too—even though the poignant undercurrent of longing for Edye was still there, as it had been for so many weeks. It was the teasing that had reminded Slim of Edye. The boy felt the uneasiness of one who suddenly feels he is reliving a past experience. The emotions felt the same, but the setting and characters had changed. As he watched Marge he looked for any similarity to the girl in Wauna. He found none. They were two distinctly different types. Only the urge to tease seemed the same. He wondered fleetingly whether or not it was a technique for flirting that girls practiced on young males they found attractive.

It was just such an easy encounter, such friendly and disarming persuasion that had led him to his first bed with the clinically curious little brunette art student back home. It had not been a particularly rewarding experience, although he'd found himself with her often. It was more satisfactory than his experience with the prostitute in San Francisco, but both had exacted their secret penalties of worry and guilt. None of those naked nights could compare with the thrill of just being with Edye, of setting the table with her, of drying dishes, of comfortable talk in the kitchen, or of walking with her in the chill night, holding

201

her in standing embrace, lost in the sweetness and excitement of her eager kisses. The remembering brought the ache to his throat again and he tried to shake off the image and the feel. He also tried to understand why this girl, sitting so close to him, had evoked these memories and whether or not the feeling of excitement that came with them might not also be something every male feels in the presence of a girl who attracts him. As Slim watched her in the window he was assailed by the compounded guilt of having failed Edye, of finding this girl appealing, and of acknowledging a desire to feel more of her firm, brown shoulder resting inside the circle of his braced arm.

And then suddenly that arm was wrenched free of its hold and both of them, caught off balance, nearly tumbled into the aisle. A shout went up and the bus was filled with the tumult of swaying bodies, the deep-throated bellowing of the men, and the excited screams and laughter of the girls. In the seat ahead, Lyle clung to Ioway and, with shrieks of delighted laughter, the boy hung onto her with one arm and clung to the seat in front with the other. Slim found himself holding Marge closely. He could feel the cushioned softness of her bosom against his ribs as she leaned against him for support. Recovering his balance, he braced his feet against the seat on the opposite aisle and collected himself as best he could. Marge was smiling and closing her eyes tightly as the rickety little bus roared down the second in a series of steep roller-coaster hills affectionately called the "royal bumps." Slim wondered that the vehicle could hold together under the punishment given it by the rough roadbed and the heavy-footed driver. The steep plunges and sudden ascents lasted for another few moments, then it was over as quickly as it had begun. The steaming bus and the screaming girls simmered down to near normal as the road leveled. They bounced and jounced another country mile and jerked to a halt in front of a rustic cottage. The driver stepped out and stood by the door to collect the fares. When Ioway and Lyla stepped down, the deck boy indicated his companion would pay for both couples. Slim offered the man the pound note.

He refused it with an offended look. "Wot's this—wot's this—a pound note? The lad must think I'm a blinkin' banker!" He addressed the remark to no one in particular but was obviously pleased with the scattering of good-natured laughter.

Slim's face flushed. "I'm sorry, it's the smallest I have."

The wiry little driver, with the suggestion of a cockney accent, looked at the boy with pretended pity. "Oh, God bli'me—wot a shame! I'd like to have a few *small* pound notes like that! Wouldn't you, folks?" Then, with a trace of annoyance, he waved his hand toward the cottage. "Go in there and get it changed, bucko. You're 'oldin' up the parade 'ere!"

Marge opened her handbag and spoke softly to the boy. "I have some coins. You can return it later." She handed the driver two florins for two round trips, took the flimsy paper-ticket receipts, and handed them to Slim. "Come along, let's go in so we'll get a proper table!"

The place was small and homey, probably patterned after an English wayside inn. The two couples found a table by a window—one the girls apparently favored. As he helped Marge into her chair Slim found himself wondering how many times she'd brought her friends to this place. A little twinge of jealousy stabbed him. He dismissed the thought as unreasonable, but the feeling persisted until Marge leaned over, her face still flushed and smiling with the excitement of the ride, and patted him reassuringly on the hand. "There now, my timid Yankee friend, the 'royal bumps' weren't so fearsome, after all, were they?"

Slim put his free hand over hers and held it there a moment. "Most frightening thing I've ever been through! Don't tell me we have to do it again, going back?"

Marge bit her lip and cocked her head to one side uncertainly. "You *could* walk, I suppose——"

Ioway looked happily across the table. "He's a fool if he does!" Taking Lyla's hand and placing it in his, he added, "I think it's a real fine way to get acquainted!"

The little blonde looked at him archly. "Why do you think we invented it, silly?"

They both laughed, and Ioway edged his chair closer to the corner of the table and draped himself comfortably nearer his girl. A neat gray little lady stopped by to take the order. Marge and Lyla chose tea and biscuits and, upon the recommendation of the girls, Ioway and Slim ordered their first fish and chips.

Lyla apologized for the local blue laws that prohibited serving alcoholic beverages on Sunday. "It's a bit stuffy, but it's better than your ridiculous prohibition! Tomorrow you can get a handle of half-and-half or a bottle of Speight's ale. As a matter of fact, *I* could do with a bit right now!"

Ioway took out a package of cigarettes and offered one to the girl.

She looked at it eagerly for an instant, then shook her head. "Nice girls don't smoke in New Zealand, and I've got to be a 'nice girl'—at least here in a public place. Someone might snitch to my father!" She leaned forward to impart a confidence. "He'd have my head stacked up in Albert Park if he caught me smoking! That he would!" She bobbed her pink cloche hat with a gesture of finality. "But a little later—when it gets dark out—I might just be persuaded to try one of your impossible American cigarettes." She turned her head close to Ioway's and gave him a fleeting wink. "How about it?"

The deck boy expansively offered to give her a whole carton. The thought of the gift made her gasp. "Oh my! I'd be the richest girl in Auckland. I could sell them for a fortune! But that wouldn't be very proper, would it?"

Marge grew impatient. "Lyla, what in heaven's name has got into you? You're talking like a tart!" Her voice was soft and low, but there was no mistaking the note of reprimand.

Lyla looked abashed but recovered quickly. Her voice seemed to be imparting a confidence. "Marge's my conscience. If it weren't for her I'd come to no good end. I'd probably set up shop selling illegal Yankee cigarettes and use the money getting quite properly screwed every night!"

Ioway looked stricken. His hand froze in the act of raising the cigarette. With jaw sagging open he looked at the girl in unblinking disbelief. Slim twisted nervously in his chair and pretended he hadn't heard, but he knew the girl could see the shock on his face. He stared at the trim little blonde in silence and tried to reconcile what he saw with what he'd heard. He had the feeling that his ears were playing tricks on him and that nothing had really been said at all.

Lyla looked slowly from one to the other and her expression grew puzzled, then concerned. "Oh, God have mercy on my soul! What have I said now?"

Ioway scratched his head and blinked vacantly. Slim frowned and fumbled for words that wouldn't come. Marge looked at both the boys with a perplexed smile. Lyla watched them, too, but as the awkward silence prolonged, a trace of defiance set on her face. "Well, all right, laddies! Maybe I am a trifle open-mouthed about things, but what's so horrible about owning up to a taste for a bit of booze?"

Ioway shot another surprised look at Slim, and expressions of relief slowly spread over their faces.

Slim found his voice first. "Look, Lyla. We just didn't understand. You see . . . uh . . ."

Marge, eager to end the awkward moment, broke in. "The simple truth is, Lyla—I've told you before—nice girls don't drink—or at least if they do they don't go around talking about it."

Slim continued, "It's not the drinking——but you use some different words down here in New Zealand—well, not really different. They're the same words we use, but they have different meanings. Like at home it's perfectly all right for us to say 'bloody'—but in England it's a——"

As he spoke the word, Slim saw both girls recoil. A little shudder ran through Lyla and she dropped her eyes in embarrassment. The sentence faded out, unfinished. Marge looked around quickly to see if anyone had overheard, then motioned Slim to silence. "That's a horrid word to use, even if it doesn't offend in the States!"

It was Slim's turn to feel embarrassment, but it changed to anger which shone in his eye and hardened the edge of his voice. "All right, now, that's enough of this damn nonsense!"

The girls flinched. Slim continued, "So the word I just used is rough down here! Up where we come from the word Lyla used is just as rough. I'm sorry we showed it, but you kind of shocked us. Now let's forget the whole thing." He fumbled in his pocket for a cigarette and was fishing for matches, when Marge lit one and held it for him.

When she spoke, her voice was soft and contrite. "I'm sorry I buffed you. I guess perhaps we should both learn to speak each other's English. There seems to be a bit of confusion. I gather that when Lyla said she'd use the money to get 'quite properly screwed' you didn't understand. Down here it means two things—getting paid, or getting 'tipsy'—a little bit drunk."

Each time Slim heard the word it jolted him.

Lyla was nodding at Marge in righteous agreement. "Gracious me, that certainly is a small thing to get so upset about. I can't imagine what it could mean in the States—unless it's some form of horrible torture?" She waited expectantly.

Slim shot a warning look at Ioway, who was on the verge of open laughter. The boy struggled to control himself but exploded in a series of short squeaks as his heaving lungs forced the air out between his tightly compressed lips. Giving in completely, he let out a huge guffaw that turned everyone in the room. He smothered his mouth in his napkin, his shoulders shaking and his attempt at control turning his face lobster red. The girls watched him uncertainly, then Lyla's eyes widened and her expression underwent a change from complete bewilderment to horrified understanding. She clapped both hands over her mouth for a second and looked helplessly at Marge. The words were gasped—addressed to no one. "Oh my God! Now I know! Oh my God!" She rose from the table, snatched her handbag, and ran quickly from the room. Marge excused herself and hurried after her.

The girls were gone for nearly ten minutes. The woman who served took the food back to keep it warm. When they returned to the table, Ioway had composed himself and Slim was sitting dejectedly, feeling that the whole afternoon had been spoiled. The boys self-consciously helped them into their places, and as Slim sat enjoying his first fish and chips, he thought several times that he detected an amused smile in Lyla's eyes as they met Marge's.

The trip back to Auckland was fun, but the first excitement was gone. When the little bus raced up and down the steep inclines, the girl passengers shrieked with practiced fright and took the opportunity to cling closely to their escorts. Slim put a protecting arm around Marge, who settled comfortably against him, her head almost touching his cheek. As they plunged over each new crest she closed her eyes until the bus reached the bottom. Lyla hung onto Ioway with both arms and made no pretense of being frightened.

Back in town once again, the embarrassment about words gone, they glowed from an afternoon of good fun. But as they stood on the corner an awkward silence fell over them. Slim didn't know whether to extend the day into the evening or to go back aboard ship. Ioway's mind was made up for him.

Lyla broke the impasse by linking her arm through his. "Look here—two's company and four's a crowd. Let's give them a little time to get acquainted. Come on, sailor, we're going for a boat ride." She started to haul Ioway off in the direction of the Ferry Building, but he stopped and turned to his shipmate with a pleading look. Slim didn't understand at first and then remembered that Ioway had no money. Reaching into his pocket, he took out a handful of coins and began examining them.

Marge smiled at his confusion and picked out five shillings. "That's enough for them to ride to North Auckland a dozen times!"

Ioway took the change and once again happily started off on another adventure with the persistent and ubiquitous Lyla.

Slim looked at Marge expectantly.

She slipped her arm through his. "Would you like to stretch those long legs of yours for a while?"

He looked down at her and got that same strange feeling he'd experienced with Edye—of having always known the girl. It disturbed him that it could happen with two different girls. And they were very different, he told himself. Edye—bright, lovely, vital, full of fun—a dancing little flame that flickered but never failed. And Marge—lovely, too, but dark and smoldering, with a veiled humor that seemed to contradict the quiet shyness. Marge was warm underneath, he suspected, like a bed of glowing, black-topped coals. She fell in beside him. After a few blocks she turned him into a steep little street that led up to Albert Park. Slim liked the feel of the hill and its neat houses braced against the sloping walks. At the top they crossed into the park. It was almost dark, but Slim could see down over the sprawling city to the waterfront. As he stood watching, lights began blinking on. He could see the small shapes of the ferries slipping out of their berths and heading out into the bay, and the sight touched off a tinge of homesickness for San Francisco. Here it was, stretched out below him, in miniature. He felt strangely at home, even in the midst of this mild relapse into loneliness. The quiet girl at his side seemed to understand and said nothing. He was barely aware of the gentle pressure on his arm.

After a time he turned away and they walked along in the darkness. An empty bench invited them to rest, and Slim smoked for a while in silence. Grinding out the butt, he pulled his left leg up on the seat and faced Marge. He looked at the girl, but she turned her head away and looked down into the darkness. After a time she spoke—very softly. "I know what you're thinking, Slim——"

He leaned forward to see her better. "How come? Do you have a crystal ball or something?"

"No, but I have what all women have—a little thing called 'intuition.'"

"All right, when am I thinking?"

"You're thinking that Lyla and I planned it this way—I

mean, being alone—aren't you?" She couldn't see the slow smile grow on Slim's face, but she felt his strong fingers close lightly around the soft column of her neck. He shook her gently. "That's not intuition, girl. That's a guilty conscience!"

She reached up and took his hand away. "I think I had that one coming to me!" Slim noted a new lilt in her voice as she continued, "As a matter of fact, it *was* planned. Lyla planned it because she wanted to go skipping off with Ioway. She's crazy about Yanks." Her voice suddenly sounded small and worried. "You're not angry about it, are you?"

Reaching over, Slim took her hands in his. "I'll let you in on a big secret. I think it's just fine. How about you?"

The girl sat in silence for a moment. "I haven't met many of you American boys, but if you're a fair sample, I like it fine too!"

Slim knew that the next turn of the conversation could determine the future course of the evening. Even though he felt vaguely guilty, he was glad for the girl's company, for it helped pass the hours more quickly until Monday. He knew he wanted to see her again while the ship was in Auckland. They'd have a week to get acquainted—if she cared to see more of him. But he didn't want to force her.

When he spoke, there was gratitude in his voice. "Thank you, Marge—thank you very much for those few kind words." He got up from the bench and turned to face her. She took his outstretched hand and he pulled her to her feet. "Let's go find some food. Those fish and chips have worn out. How about you? Aren't you hungry?"

"Not very—really." They walked along Princess Street, skirting the park, and then turned down toward the center of town.

"There's something you ought to know, Slim——" Her tone was ominous. "This is not a great country for eating places, especially on Sunday. We'll be lucky to find the fish-and-chips stall open on the ferry wharves."

Slim shrugged. "Anything tastes good after the food on the ship."

The streets were almost deserted. They walked along the waterfront, past the *Tropic Trader*'s shadowy black hull rearing over the high iron dock gates. Slim could make out the head of the gangway in the bright glow of the cluster light. He could see one of the men on watch, slumped on top of the main bunker hatch. They passed under a permanent awning, and Slim read the legend:

208

"Waterside Loan Company." Painted on both ends of the sign were the traditional three balls of the pawnbroker. The boy chuckled to himself.

Indicating the sign with a flip of his finger, he grinned at Marge. "On the pay we get, I'll probably end up in there before the week is out!"

"Take it easy and you'll make out, laddie—and just remember, Ioway owes you five bob."

The reminder made him start. "Hey! I owe you two of those silly-looking things too." He stopped and reached into his pocket. A crumpled bill came out with a fistful of large coins. He held out the money to Marge. "Here, take the ones I owe you."

She made no move. "You really don't owe me a thing, you know."

"Oh yes, I do!" His tone was emphatic. Turning toward the dim street light, he examined the change and picked out two large silver coins. "Here, take these—and no arguments!"

The girl refused the money and Slim could see the amused twinkle in her dark eyes. "Oh dear me, you do need someone to take care of you. I gave the chap two florins, and you're trying to make me take two shillings. That will never do!" She laughed softly at Slim's confusion. "Now put it away. When we get to the Ferry Building, I'll give you a lesson in the value of New Zealand money. Come along now." She linked her arm through his and directed him diagonally across the street to the big ornate terminal.

It was nearly nine o'clock when they finished. By nine-thirty they had walked back from Queen Street to Karangahapi Road, a broad avenue that led off at an angle toward Grafton Bridge, which spanned a deep depression called "the gully." They turned into a narrow street, and Marge stopped before a small red-roofed house surrounded by a low, well-tended boxwood hedge.

"This is home, Slim."

They stood quietly in the night, aware of their closeness, but neither moved to make the moment anything more than convention demanded of two young people concluding their first date.

Slim found Marge's hand in the dark and held it firmly. "I was a real lucky guy to meet a girl like you the first day in port. Thank you for everything, Marge, and I hope we can get together again."

"I hope so too—but you don't even know my name."

For the first time Slim realized that he'd never thought to ask. "Hey, that's right! Do you mind telling me at this late date?"

The girl pulled her hand gently from his and stepped away. "My name's MacLaine. . . . Please call me again!" She deliberately emphasized the rhyme.

Slim watched her go quickly up the dark walk and climb the short steps.

She spoke quietly from the deep night shadows. "Good night, Slim—and thanks for everything. You're wonderful!"

He heard the door open and close and then the lights flared up behind drawn shades. He stood a moment, then turned down the little street and headed back toward the waterfront. Moving quickly along walks that somehow seemed familiar, he felt happy. It had been a good day. Tomorrow would be a better day, for he would read and reread every precious line of the letter he knew would be waiting from Edye.

19 —

The bosun turned the crew out on deck at seven in the morning to free the forward load of its heavy chain lashings and shorings so the stevedores could begin the unloading operations at eight.

Slim worked with Rusty, clearing the loosened chains and dragging them forward to the fo'c'sle deck. When the turnbuckles had all been opened and the ends separated, the bosun singled out Slim to carry the chains down the narrow steel ladder and stow them below. The locker for the chains was in the forepeak, which could have been reached by opening the booby hatch on the fo'c'sle deck. But the bosun had no intention of letting him do it the easy way—for that matter, the proper way—for if he had, Slim would have got ashore much earlier in the day.

He set his jaw and went about the bone-bending job of bucking two-hundred-pound lengths of heavy chain across the rough top of the load and lowering them down through the tapered slot in the timbers to the small open clearing of well deck. Then, climbing down, he dragged each chain through the watertight door and forward to the locker in the very bow of the ship. There he raised them overhead and draped them across large metal hooks bolted to the steel partitions. The boy's arms and shoulders were tormented with a burning ache, and even in the cool morning air he was drenched with sweat.

Several times the bosun struck his head in and looked around critically. Slim worked with a pair of heavy horse-hide gloves he'd bought in San Pedro. The man looked at them and smirked. "Whatsa matter, kid, you afraid of hurtin' dem soft hands on dese chains?" The boy didn't answer but kept doggedly at the job. Up on deck he heard the winches start and knew that the stevedores had come aboard and that the first slingloads of timbers would soon be dangling in mid-air, making their erratic way down to the dock.

At eight bells the crew was knocked off for breakfast. Slim was the last one to be called. Half an hour later the men were working on deck again.

Chips had told Slim that when a ship carries a deckload on a long voyage it was customary for the bosun to let the men have some time ashore before starting the routine cleaning which must necessarily await completion of the unloading. He allowed the men would have ample time, for New Zealand dockworkers had the reputation with American shipmasters of being the slowest in the world. Chips figured that most of the unlashing would be finished by noon and the chances of being given the rest of the day off seemed good. Slim worked as quickly as he could. Several times he saw the carpenter watching him struggle with the great chains. He knew what the man was thinking. It was obvious that another hand helping Slim would have accomplished the work in half the time without imposing any dangerous strain on either. There were men who might easily have been spared, but the bosun invented things for them to do.

At noon the lashings and shorings had all been freed. Those that had first been cleared were stowed, and the dockworkers had long since begun the unloading at the after end of the forward load. Slim knocked off for lunch with the others. No word was passed about time off. The men finished their meal in silence and waited for the bosun to turn them out again. At twelve-thirty he stuck his head in the messroom and gave the crew liberty until eight the following morning, except for those men who were given gangway watch. They, too, were free to go ashore, so long as they reported back in time for their tedious four hours of keeping off unauthorized visitors and tending the lines as the tide raised and lowered the ship.

The bosun started to leave, paused, then turned back and spoke to Slim. It was an obviously planned afterthought. "Hey—you—Fredericks! You ain't goin' nowhere till ya get dem chains stowed! Ya unnerstan'?" He smirked at the boy and waited for his answer.

Slim looked up from his coffee cup as the man spoke. He heard the words, felt the sting of their injustice and the rising heat of his own anger. He clenched his teeth slowly, and the muscles in his jaw made taut cords beneath the smooth, tanned skin, but he said nothing. He looked at the bosun dispassionately and, taking his gloves from his back pocket, pulled them on and rose wearily from the table. The bosun waited a moment longer, then disappeared.

Chips watched the boy and said nothing. Otto made a dry spitting noise with his lips. Rusty cracked his knuckles and glowered at the vacant doorway. Hammer stared at the place the bosun had vacated, and there was that same ice-cold glaze in his eyes that the men had seen when he struck Mike with the bottle. He had the look of an impersonal murder machine. Spots shook his head sadly at the injustice and the Shiek sat slumped over his cigarette, his darting eyes watching each man from beneath his lowered brow. Ioway blinked and cleared his throat needlessly.

Slim made his way forward and began fighting the heavy chains again. He'd been working about an hour when Ioway came forward, dressed in his shore clothes. "Hey, Slim——" he called through the fo'c'slehead door, and his voice had a hollow, metallic echo. "You in there?"

Slim strained to lift a heavy link over the stowing hook and exhaled the breath he'd been holding. "Yeah! Come on in——"

Ioway picked his way around the cables and spare hawsers coiled in the gloomy shelter and stuck his head into the locker. "I think the bosun stinks. You shoulda heard the guys when you left. They'd like to kill him!"

Slim smiled bitterly. "Maybe that'll give you a rough idea of how I feel!"

Ioway nodded sympathetically. "Listen, I haven't forgotten the loan. I'll give it to you later when I get some change."

Slim dismissed the obligation with a wave of his glove.

Ioway continued, "I'm going to locate the American Consul and see if there's mail from home. If you like, I'll check and see if you have any. Okay?"

Slim removed his right glove and reached into the back pocket of his rust- and paint-stained dungarees for a handkerchief. Mopping his wet brow, he smiled warmly at his friend. "Thanks, Ioway. I'd appreciate it. I think I'll get through about four o'clock—if I keep after it."

The younger boy looked at the heavy chain lashings hung by their middles in double strands. "The guy has no right to make you do this alone. I asked him if I could stay and help and he said he didn't want me hanging around the ship—whatever that means."

Slim snorted in disgust. "I wouldn't hang around here, either, if I didn't have to! You better get going now. I'm expecting a letter from a friend in Oregon. I don't think there'll be any from the folks. They don't know where I am yet." Slim remembered the unposted letter to Edye

213

that lay in his locker. He knew Ioway would pass the big post office on Queen Street but there was no envelope for it, so he decided not to ask him to address and mail it. Besides, he didn't want the boy to read what he'd said to Edye; not that it was anything to be ashamed of, but because the girl was a part of his life that he was unwilling to share with anyone on the ship. Ioway looked at his own clean clothes uncertainly, then offered to help in spite of the bosun's order. "I could stay down here out of sight and heave them up on the hooks——"

Slim felt the same warm affection for the boy that he'd feel for a younger brother. With a grateful smile he declined the assistance and sent his friend on his way.

As he left the forepeak, Ioway called back to him: "Listen . . . I gotta date with Lyla this afternoon. If we go out tonight, I'll come back to the ship first—if there's any mail for you. Okay?"

Slim poked his head around the locker door. "Okay, pal." As Ioway stood silhouetted for a moment in the water-tight doorway Slim called after him: "Hey, I meant to ask you. How'd you make out with your little blond friend last night?"

Ioway stopped. His tone was uncertain. "All right—I guess—but boy, she sure is forward!"

Slim smiled. "What do you mean, forward?"

Ioway put a finger up to his mouth. "Well, when I kissed her good night, she got so excited she bit my lip!" He pressed the side of his lower lip gently. "It's still sore."

Slim spoke with exaggerated sympathy. "Aw gee, Ioway. I'm sorry to hear it. There's one thing, though—a blond's bite is seldom fatal—especially if you bite 'em right back!"

Ioway made a quick gesture of disgust. "Aw, to heck with ya. I knew I shouldn'ta said anything!" He could hear Slim's fading laughter as he climbed up the stepped ends of the deckload and disappeared toward the gangway.

At four o'clock the bosun came forward and stuck his head in the forepeak locker. He chuckled when he'd obviously taken the boy by surprise. The repressed anger nearly escaped Slim's lips, but he held himself in check and drove his burning muscles still harder. The man made no comment, but as he went out on deck his broad, Slavic face was wreathed in a satisfied smile.

By quarter of five the job was finished. Twenty two-hundred-pound chains hung in double strands from the steel stowing hooks; two tons of thick galvanized linkage had been pulled across the deck, lowered to the forepeak, and hoisted six feet to their hangers. When the last chain slid over its hook, a low moan of fatigue escaped from deep down inside Slim's tormented body. He half sat, half fell on a coil of steel cable, rested his forearms on his legs, and lowered his head loosely between his shoulders. He stayed like that for fully five minutes, then got up wearily, closed the locker door, and climbed to the fo'c'sle deck.

As he walked aft on the portside he passed Hammer, who had relieved Warndahl on gangway watch.

"Hi, Jack, did you see Ioway come back aboard?"

The A.B.'s answer was a shake of his head.

Slim looked at the soiled bandage on his hand. "Did you get ashore to see the doctor yet?"

Hammer lifted his hand and inspected it front and back. "Naw. It's okay. I'll see him tomorrow. You change it tonight."

It was the first time that the seaman had directly asked the boy for help. Slim noticed that his face was flushed and the smell of beer was heavy on his breath. But he seemed perfectly sober. Slim knew he'd be relieved by Otto or Spots for supper.

"When you come aft I'll take care of it. I won't get ashore until after mess."

Hammer grunted in agreement and Slim continued toward the crew's quarters. The boy had no heart for going ashore. He'd been fighting a growing fear that Ioway had found no mail for him at the consulate and had decided to stay in town with Lyla. He washed and shaved mechanically, without really caring whether or not he left the ship. He ate supper with the few men who were aboard by choice or duty and returned to the fo'c'sle to finish dressing.

He was putting the last of his shaving gear in the locker when Ioway burst into the room. He was flushed and out of breath. In his hand he clutched a thick packet of letters; there must have been a dozen of them, Slim thought. Which one would be Edye's? The thick one on the top of the bundle, he hoped. In an instant the whole gloomy, agonizing day had disappeared, and the young night became bright with hope and the promise of weeks of sweet dreams fulfilled between the lines of her closely filled pages.

He tried not to appear eager; he tried to sound casual, but as he spoke he could hear the edge of excitement in his own voice. "Hey, Ioway, I gave you up! What'd you come back for?"

The deck boy fumbled with the latch on his locker. He'd tucked the letters under his arm to free both hands for the task. He answered Slim over his shoulder as he kneeled on the deck. "Lyla's waiting on the dock. I had to come back for a coat. It's getting chilly out there!" Taking the letters from under his arm, he placed them on the shelf. "Boy, I hit the jackpot, but they'll have to wait. I'll read 'em later!" Straightening up, he glanced at Slim. "Hey, how about coming along with us? Lyla says Marge is home. We could go and pick her up—and have some fun. We'll be okay for money. There's a letter from Pop. He said he'd send me some—there'll be a bill in there all right!" He snapped the lock and stood up. "How about it, mate?"

Slim barely heard the question. The hope that had welled so quickly in him at the sight of the letters began to fade and he fought stubbornly against the insistent, unwanted intrusion of the truth. He knew the answer before he asked: "Did you ask for my mail too?"

The deck boy jammed a long arm into the sleeve of his jacket. "Yeah, I did, but there wasn't any." As he pulled the jacket over the other arm he added, "And there's been two mail boats from the States, too—the *Tahiti* and the *Aorangi*. Boy! I wish I could have seen her. She's the Union Line's new motorship—four screws—eighteen knots. She's the fastest ship on the Pacific run!"

Slim heard the boy's words echo in his mind: "two mail boats from the States, too—the *Tahiti* and the *Aorangi*." Two chances for a letter from Edye to reach him, if she'd written; two chances for his secret hopes to become exquisite reality; two chances to find the answer to the questions he wanted answered with all his heart; two chances to have his tormenting doubts and fears allayed. Two chances gone now, no chances left; nothing to wait for, nothing to hope for—nothing but the sudden, stabbing pain of disappointment, more excruciating than the burning that still seared his back and shoulders muscles that had rebelled under impossible burdens. And now his heart rebelled under an impossible burden and he turned away without speaking. Walking into the passageway, he climbed the companion ladder to the poop deck and stood alone in the hooded glow of the dock lights, struggling against the choking ache that rose in his throat, clamping

216

his strong jaws tightly, forcing his blurred eyes to see through the moist margin of tears he refused to let flow.

As Slim clenched the soot-streaked rail, staring down into the oily black undulation of the harbor, distorted light reflections danced their lunatic antics to the senseless syndrome of thoughts that raced through his mind. Anger, self-pity, recrimination, remorse—each educing its own violent emotion, until the turmoil became unbearable. Doubling a fist, he struck the pipe rail with its fleshy hammer, and the dull, repetitive pounding made the metal rattle in the dark margins of the night.

Ioway, unseen in the shadow of the companionway, was alarmed. Not understanding the nature of the struggle, he understood his friend's need to struggle alone. Quietly he tiptoed across the steel deck and stepped up on the deadening surface of the rough timbers. Making his way hastily forward to the gangplank, he rejoined the waiting girl.

Time passed and the boy stared, unseeing, into the night. From the distance came the hollow hoot of ferry whistles and the muffled panting of steam tugs pushing their tumbling bow waves across the harbor. Away toward Mechanic's Bay he heard the toylike shrilling of a narrow-gauge locomotive butting miniature boxcars onto the dock sidings.

For a while the sounds were indistinct notes in the half-heard cacophony of the waterfront, but as the boy's unleashed emotions spent their force he began to emerge from the chrysalid prison of his pain.

He pushed himself back from the rail. His face felt drawn and his lips were dry and apart, his jaws relaxed and weak from the effort of his aimless invective. He looked around at the unfamiliar silhouettes of what had been, only an hour ago, a city of hope—a place to be impatiently gained by sailing at snail's pace along the trackless miles of sea that linked these two different worlds. Slim had bound those endless miles together with the tender memory of a girl. And now the bonds had lost their tenderness and, as he struggled to free himself, they gained the power to hurt. He turned aimlessly from the rail. He had called himself a fool for building his world a day at a time, a dream at a time, and he wanted desperately to be told that he was not a fool. But there was no one to talk with and there were no dependable, well-practiced escapes; no places of forgetfulness; no comforting confessionals where a man could dilute his pain with the pain of others and in so doing relieve some of the torment. He walked

217

slowly across the dim-lit deckload toward the gangway. He didn't see the slender outline of the radio operator draped on the after rail of the boatdeck directly above him.

"Hey, Slim! What are you doin'? I thought you were ashore——"

The boy looked up and saw the end of Sparks' cigarette glow brightly from a long drag and he heard the breath behind the smoke escape with a hissing sigh.

"Hi, Sparks——" His voice was flat and hoarse and his throat felt full and dry.

The radio operator heard it too. "Come on up a minute. I'll go ashore with you. I haven't been on the main stem yet."

Without enthusiasm Slim crossed to the ladder and made his way up to the boatdeck. Sparks had gone inside. He was digging his old sweater from a drawer beneath the bunk. He looked up at the boy, started to look back in the drawer, then slowly turned again.

"Jesus, sonny, you look as happy as a pallbearer with two broken arms! What the hell's the matter with you?"

Slim shrugged. "I'm beat, I guess—been a rough day."

Sparks chuckled to himself as he pulled the sweater on and buttoned the long row down the front. "I think Divine Providence sent you to me, Junior, 'cause I need a little cheering up too. Let's go to one of those genteel saloons I've been hearing about and have a beer. What d'ya say?"

Slim remembered Marge had told him about the bar in the Waverly Hotel. It had been closed the day before, but it would be open now, and he led Sparks up Queen Street and turned into the narrow alley that led to the side entrance of the place. It looked very much like the old saloons at home that had managed to keep their doors swinging on prohibition beer and soda pop. There were empty metal trays nearest the door where the free lunch probably had stood earlier in the day. Behind the long, dark mahogany bar, with its customary ornamental edge and long brass rail, was a massive mirror framed in crude neo-classic carvings. Several large brass-bound wooden handles protruded straight up from the back edge of the bar, and the back bar itself was lined with a field of large glistening glasses standing on clean strips of linen toweling. The far end of the room was divided into a family bar where people were eating and drinking. An amply built, openly friendly blonde barmaid presided. She was wearing a rose-red velvet dress and crisp white apron. The square low-cut neckline framed her bulbous, soft white breasts, which seemed capable of comforting the heads of at least two careworn patrons simultaneously.

She smiled broadly as the pair entered, and Sparks whispered out of the side of his mouth, "Get a load of those teeth. They look too good to be home-grown!"

Slim felt the beginning of a smile fighting the set muscles of his face. They found a place at the almost deserted bar. Sparks took out his pack of cigarettes and laid them before him. Settling one foot comfortably on the rail, he ordered two handles of half-and-half. Twisting around on one elbow, he surveyed the place critically. "Not bad . . . not bad." He punctuated his comment with a positive nod of his sandy head and twisted his mouth down in begrudging approval. Picking up the foam-topped stein in front of him, he drank a long draught and smacked his lips in appreciation.

Slim had watched the barmaid take the two tall glasses and fill each of them half full of rich brown stout. Then, pulling another of the well-polished handles, she filled the tops with sparkling, golden ale, expertly timing the stream to produce a creamy head. It was the first time the boy had ever been served real brew. He'd had the green, ether-needled beer served in the blind-pig joints in Emeryville and South Oakland, but it had always upset him and left him with a throbbing headache. But this was different. He could tell by the rich, sweet aroma and by the crystal clearness that this was the careful brew of experts with a tradition to maintain—the tradition of good English ale. The boy lifted the glass, buried his upper lip in the cool foam, and drank. Wiping his mouth with the back of his hand, he let the aftertaste linger in his mouth.

Sparks watched him with interest. "How do you like your first 'awf-'n-'awf'?" He pronounced it with the exaggerated broad *a* of the English musical-hall comedian.

Slim managed a small smile. "Okay." He took another swallow. "Tastes real good——" A small air bubble slipped out of his throat and surprised him.

Sparks laughed and winked at the barmaid. "You drink too fast, and those swallows'll fly south!" He shook two cigarettes out on the bar and offered one to the boy.

The woman held the light for them. "You two lads must be off the American ship?"

Sparks gave her an incredulous look. "I knew it! The cigarettes gave us away. You couldn't possibly tell from our accents!"

The barmaid looked puzzled; then, getting the point,

laughed with the radio operator. Sparks picked up the change from a ten-shilling note, left sixpence on the bar, and motioned Slim to follow. They carried their glasses to a vacant table and sat down.

The radio operator stretched out his skinny legs and slumped comfortably in the chair. "I've been sittin' on my ass for so long, I've forgotten how to stand."

The chair felt good to the boy too. His muscles still ached from heaving four thousand pounds of chain. Some of the bitterness had gone. In its place had come a leaden disappointment and he could feel the physical pain again. They sat in silence, each occupied with his own thoughts.

As Slim drank, the radio operator watched him closely. After a time he put in words the question that had been growing in his mind. "Slim . . . what's eating you? You sick or something?"

The boy looked up from the glass quickly. "I'm okay. Why?"

Sparks shook his head sadly. "For a guy that's okay, you look like something off the wreck of the *Hesperus*. What happened to you yesterday after you left Peterson?"

The boy wondered why he would ask that particular question but decided to answer honestly. "I was out with Ioway and a couple of girls."

Sparks raised his eyebrows. "Where'd you meet 'em?"

"On the dock—but don't get me wrong. They were okay."

"Sure they were, and so are you, with your chin draggin' on the deck. Tell me something, Slim. Did you get into some sort of trouble?" The radio operator liked the tall, rangy kid who came from the suburb adjoining his town. He was genuinely interested, and Slim felt his sincerity and the warm glow of appreciation it engendered. The boy looked down at the scarred oak table and pushed the beer glass through a series of quarter turns by its heavy handle. "I'm kinda low, I guess—but not from any trouble with a girl—at least not a girl in *this* town!"

Sparks followed up the boy's lead. "You didn't get a letter from that kid in Wauna telling you you're going to be a proud papa, did you?" There was real concern in the radio operator's voice.

Slim jerked his head up in surprise.

Sparks raised his hands in a placating gesture. "Now wait a minute. I'm not casting aspersions on your lady's virtue! But it happens, you know, even to nice kids! And brother, you ain't worried until you've worried about

220

that!" He wiped imaginary perspiration from his brow. "Did you hear from her?"

Slim shook his head without looking up. Sparks watched him for a moment, trying to read the boy's thoughts. "Did you expect to hear from her?"

The boy stared at his unfinished beer, then he nodded. "Yeah . . . I guess so."

A knowing smile spread across the radio operator's face, and his intelligent eyes twinkled with quick understanding behind his horn-rimmed glasses. Pulling himself up straight in the chair, he leaned across the table and put a hand on Slim's arm. "Okay, Junior, now we're getting somewhere. Spit it out in papa's hand! You really fell for that kid, didn't you?" He waited for the boy to answer. There was none. To Sparks, silence was the best possible answer. "You know something? When you told me about her, I thought you'd forget all about it by the time we hit the next port—but you didn't, did you?"

Slim reached across his body with his right hand and slowly squeezed the aching shoulder muscle that ran to the left side of his neck. He seemed to be struggling for an answer. After a time he looked up. "No, I didn't forget her, but I wish I *had!*" The boy took another long drink and drained the glass.

Sparks got up, carried the big empties to the bar, and had them refilled. He offered the boy a cigarette and waited for him to continue. Slim touched his index finger absently to the fresh, foamy cap and watched it draw up into a creamy little point, like the frosting on his grandmother's cakes. He seemed to have made a decision as he raised his head and looked across the glass at Sparks. He started slowly from the beginning and recounted the details of his meeting with Edye, the lunch, the two evenings at her home, and the farewells on the dock that had been seen and overheard by the eavesdropping Hammer and Otto. He told of her promise to write and of her apparent interest in seeing him again. He confessed completely his own feeling for the girl and the eagerness with which he had awaited the letter that had not arrived. He told of his own unmailed letter and of his anxiety to make it sound just right. He spoke without emotion and the radio operator listened quietly.

At last, when Slim finished, there was a long silence. His face was slightly flushed from the beer, which eased his tension and made the recitation less of a chore. He felt stronger, relieved; and when he looked at the radio opera-

221

tor's thoughtful frown, his gratitude deepened into something akin to affection. He felt that no matter what he told the man he would not be censured or derided; that the seeds of understanding would ripen in the warmth of their growing friendship and in time bear the welcome fruit of wise counsel. He needed and sought that counsel now.

Sparks drummed his fingers on the handle of the empty beer mug. Slim knew that he was packaging his thoughts. He knew Sparks as a man trained to deal in fact. From long conversations and from hours of listening to the debates with Stokes, which the English fireman delighted in calling "cerebral cricket matches," Slim also knew that his legal mind was equally concerned with motives.

A faint hope still lingered beneath the cold overlayer of doubt that Sparks, having heard the facts, would support with incontestable logic the correctness of his own first appraisal of Edye and find in her silence some worthy and reassuring reason for not keeping what Slim had felt to be a promise.

Sparks lit a fresh cigarette and looked at the boy through narrowed eyes. His was the manner of one making certain that the target was squarely in the sights before firing. "Slim, let me ask you some questions——"

The boy waited for the first one, like a key witness waiting for cross-examination.

"You knew this kid three days. Right?"

"That's right—two and a half, to be exact."

"Two and a half, then. When you first kissed her, did you take the initiative, or did she?"

"She did. I didn't even think there'd be a chance."

"Okay. How long has she lived in Wauna?"

"All her life."

"That would be about seventeen years. Right?"

"Something like that——"

"How long has she been working at the lumber dock?"

"Off and on for a couple of years. Why?"

"You'll see why in a minute! Now then, let me ask you to take a calculated guess with me. How many ships load lumber at that dock in a year, would you say?"

Slim was puzzled by the question, but he judged that an average of two a week pulled in, counting the steam schooners. He wrinkled his forehead and rubbed his hand over his unruly blond hair. "About one hundred a year—more or less."

Sparks confirmed the estimate with a positive nod. "That's pretty close. Now then, let me ask you this. How many young deck boys and cadets come into that dock on those ships? Just take a wild guess."

A sickening ache cramped the pit of Slim's stomach. Sparks, with cold, elementary logic, was making him face the simple truth he'd been struggling to avoid ever since the night in the bunk when loneliness and doubt had first visited him. He had turned his back then and had clung to the pillow, relistening to each word she had spoken, finding in them the truth he would need to reaffirm, time and time again, until he could face her with the eagerness and uncertainty of a long-separated lover, fearful that the dream had become the friend—its inspiration a stranger.

Sparks prodded him to answer. "Go on, just take a guess. How many cadets and deck boys do you think hit that dock?"

Slim struggled with the mental arithmetic and with the impossible sum it produced. "Maybe—uh—uh—maybe a hundred." His voice was barely audible.

"Easy a hundred!" Sparks shifted his position in the chair and prepared for the second round of questions.

"All right. How big a place would you say Wauna is?"

Slim shook his head. "It's pretty small."

"You're damn right it is. No movie theater, no dance hall. Maybe a lodge hall. Cold and wet as hell for half the year."

Slim could no longer refuse to see what the radio operator was driving at and he wanted to cry out in protest: "Facts are cold. . . . Logic is cold. . . . Two and two makes four—but you're not adding figures, you're adding people, and people don't add up like figures. They don't all behave the same way—*all* the time. They're all born, they all live, they all die, but *while* they live they don't all live the *same* way. They don't feel and think like *machines*." He thought of the arguments he'd used on his own doubts. What about his own mother and father? Love at first sight at Glacier Point in Yosemite Valley while his father had been an engineering student at the University of California, working his way with a summer survey gang. They'd celebrated their twentieth anniversary just a few months ago, but after their engagement they hadn't seen each other for almost a year—and still their love had grown. His mother had been Edye's age then; she'd known what she wanted; she'd meant it when she returned his father's love—and their love became such that envious friends called them the "happiest married couple in California"— and they were! There'd been no logic in their love; they

223

just loved, in spite of family opposition, economic obstacles—in spite of everything! His mother had been the prettiest girl at the hotel. She'd worked there to supplement the family income. Hundreds of eligible young men had come into her life, too, but their numbers and compliments and attention meant nothing to her. She'd found her man and she'd wait for him—and she did.

Slim clenched his jaws. He looked at the empty beer glasses, and they seemed to have two outlines. It annoyed him and suddenly he wanted to sweep them out of his way. His arms twitched, their muscles straining to strike out but held in check by the remnant of reason left in his aching brain. Sparks' voice droned on, doling out monotonously logical sentences that were plainly labeled truth by their very logic. And the boy struggled to hear without feeling.

"Like I said, it stands to reason—kids are pretty much the same all over. The boys gang up on the new girl in town and the girls gang up on the new boy in town. Only in this case the other girls didn't have a chance because she saw you first. She's in a good spot to see fellas first! And make no mistake about it, Junior, you're pretty good to look at—and since you've filled out, it's getting better!"

Slim felt guilty that in the midst of his misery he could feel a flash of pleasure at Sparks' compliment.

"And so it's reasonable to suppose the girl *would* be friendly. Who the hell's more exciting—you young stags who have the look and smell of adventure about you or poor goofy Elmer who plays on the local football team and works in the hardware store on Saturdays? You know the answer! She'll probably wind up marrying Elmer! She's known him all his life—and he's around. He's always around, and you guys who send her letters with foreign stamps make her a glamour girl at the post office and with her friends, but you won't be there on that warm summer night down by the river when Elmer finally wears her down and gets his hand in her pants! But Elmer will be there—*real good*—and you guys'll be the memories that let her tolerate the big oaf the rest of her uninspired days!"

Slim listened, and the unspoken protest closed on his chest like a vise. Suddenly things were transposed: reality had gone again and this was the dream. Sparks was his conscience lashing back at him with a thousand stinging truths—binding his arms, gagging his lips, blinding his eyes. The room went out of focus; the sounds distorted and the murmuring river of reason narrowed into a raging torrent that roared past his ringing ears, its pounding pressure pinning him against the chair, holding him there—an unwilling prisoner of the truth. With a squealing scrape, the chair shot out behind him and the empty glasses shattered against the dark wooden wall, flung there by the violent sweep of his arm.

His body shaking, he towered over the scrawny radio operator. "Shut up, God damn it! Shut up!"

The few people in the bar froze where the words had caught them. Nobody breathed or made a sound. Sparks sat clenching the arms of the chair with knuckles trembling from the effort, a strange smile—half surprise and half fear—caught in transition by muscles shocked to sudden immobility. He looked up at the boy and saw a stranger glaring down at him, and the boy looked down and saw nothing but the blurred and stricken remains of his last hope. Slowly the long, muscular arms lowered to his side. Without seeing or feeling, he walked a wavering course across the still hushed room, stumbled off the sill, and disappeared into the night.

— 20 —

The young sailor listened to the uneven cadence of his heavy shoes on the sidewalk. He listened with an odd detachment and he smiled as a long interval between steps was followed by several quick ones. He could feel his feet hurry to get under him before his body leaned past its center of gravity. He tried a few steps with his eyes closed and laughed to himself. "Boy, this sea is sure rough—hope we don't roll over——" He didn't recognize the buildings that moved indistinctly past him. Reaching a corner, he stopped and fumbled for a cigarette.

The match gave him trouble and a friendly voice spoke out of the night: "It's a bit thick out, sailor. Would you like a lift back to the ship?"

Slim tried to focus his eyes. He blinked and shook his head, for he felt certain he could not have seen such a man. Clad in a long blue coat, he was wearing a tall white pith helmet. Slim wanted to smile and say, "Dr. Livingstone, I presume——" but he shook his head again, accepted the proffered match, and mumbled. The words felt thick. "No, thanks, I'm awright—jus' gettin' a li'l air——" The policeman stood by him for a moment, then moved away as quietly as he'd come.

He didn't know how long he'd been walking when he came to the top of a long hill. His legs were suddenly very weary and he sat down heavily on a low cement wall that bordered a small garden. He squeezed his eyes together and opened them. Things were clearing a little and were staying "put," unless he turned his head too quickly. Then they glided into place silently, like errant kids late to the school line. He closed his eyes, shook his head, and took half a dozen deep breaths of the chill night air. For a time he sat trying to think, but his brain refused any but the random, disconnected fragments that moved through it in slow motion—a morbid medley of hurtful half-remem-

226

bered words—and then he heard Ioway saying, "Hey, how about coming along with us? Lyla says Marge is home. We could go pick her up . . . pick her up . . . her . . . up . . ." The voice seemed like a receding echo.

Slim shook his head again and pressed his fingers against his ears, closing them to shut out the ghostly sound. He thought of Ioway and he smiled foolishly. Good ole' Ioway . . . He never hurt anything . . . he just wags his tail at everybody . . . Ioway's a pal . . . and Lyla's a pal . . . with a y . . . no, Lyla's a pal with a p— —— He squeezed his eyes closed to erase the thought. No! That's not right . . . that's not even nice . . . but Lyla's a pal, all right . . . and so's Ioway . . . and so's Marge. Marge is a pretty pal . . . she doesn't hurt anybody . . . she's quiet . . . and she has pretty eyes . . . and very pretty hair . . . and very pretty mouths! He shook his head in frustration. No, not mouths . . . lips . . . and she has very pretty . . . very pretty . . . everything! I gotta find Marge . . . and if I find Marge I'll find Ioway and Lyla and they're all pals . . . with a capital P——

Slim got up unsteadily and looked around. Off to his left was Grafton Bridge and the gully. He was quite near them, which meant he was quite near the little street where Marge had taken him the night before. He walked a block more toward the bridge and recognized a tall, steep-roofed house on the corner. He turned into the street which sloped gently across the contour of the hill and found himself before the little iron-roofed house with its neat boxwood hedge. The shades were drawn, but the lights were on and he could see an occasional shadow move across their dark green translucence. He wondered if the elongated silhouette could be Marge. Perhaps it was her father. He stood on the packed-earth walk, trying to make a decision. The little path to the front door was short and straight. He could make it in three steps, but his steps were still a little uncertain. He turned away from the house and walked to the corner again. A weak street light cast its pallid glow in a diffused circle around the intersection. Lifting his arm, he looked at his wrist watch. It read eight o'clock. Eight o'clock was early at home, but somehow it seemed later here—maybe too late to go to her house. And maybe he would embarrass her with her parents, especially with his breath heavy with the sweet reek of ale and stout. He licked his lips and ran his tongue around the inside of his mouth. It felt cottony and he was thirsty; his hands smelled of tobacco and he felt unkempt,

227

even though his clothes were fresh and he'd taken a warm sponge bath in his bucket. He felt his face and it was freshly shaved; then he remembered the Waverly Bar and Sparks, and his jaw snapped shut. A glistening perspiration broke out on his forehead and he felt its clammy dampness beneath his collar. He blotted his face with his handkerchief and, wrapping it around a finger, ran it around the inside of his neckband. It smelled of the cheap shaving lotion he'd used earlier, spreading it generously on his face and neck and under his arms. Hammer had watched him using it once and told him he "smelled like a French whore." He remembered thinking that if it were true, he'd rather smell like that than like Hammer! He stuffed the handkerchief back in his pocket and looked down the little street.

Then, making his decision, he walked quickly and directly back toward the house. He paused for an instant at the opening of the hedge, covered the path in three long strides, and reached the door. He heard a man's voice and it startled him. Then he smiled to himself as he recognized the tinny, deliberate King's English of a radio announcer. He rapped loudly several times and waited. The radio suddenly cut off and there was a long silence. He rapped again on the wooden frame and it sounded like the booming reverberation of a kettledrum. He wished he hadn't struck so heavily. Then he heard quick footsteps. A small porch light switched on overhead and the solid front door opened slightly. He saw Marge's face, questioning and fearful.

"Marge, it's me—Slim. I'm looking for Ioway and Lyla. Are they here?"

The door opened a little more and the girl looked down at him in disbelief. "Slim! What on earth are you doing out here?"

"I'm looking for Ioway. I got tired of being alone. I thought he said he and Lyla might come up here——"

The girl seemed embarrassed and ill at ease, as though she wanted to hide behind the partly opened door. "Lyla and Ioway are not here. I saw Lyla in town this afternoon, but she didn't say anything about visiting——"

Slim felt foolish. He wished now that he'd turned away the first time and returned to the ship. He should never have let Marge see him in this condition, and from her manner he surmised that she, too, wished she hadn't seen him.

His brain still felt dull and the things he started to say

seemed wrong. He decided to retreat as gracefully as possible. "Well—I probably misunderstood. I didn't mean to just come barging in. I guess I took you by surprise, so I'll——"

She broke in before he could finish. "I should say you *did* take me by surprise! I look a perfect sight. I was just getting ready to wash my hair——" She opened the door a few inches more and looked at him intently. "You look a bit of a sight yourself. Don't you feel well?"

Slim hesitated a moment, debating the possible answers, then decided to tell something close to the truth.

"I had a rough day. A lot of things happened, and I think I had a little more beer than I—than I'm used to——"

The woebegone look on his face and his desolate tone made her smile. "Oh, gracious, Slim—they should tell you Americans about our strong New Zealand ale!" She pulled the flannel robe tightly about her and opened the door wide. "See here, if you don't mind looking at a horrid mess, you can come in for a minute—and I'll make you some tea."

The magic word "tea" suddenly transformed the girl into a ministering angel and the boy docilely obeyed her quick little order. "Come along, come along—I'll get a chill—and don't fall up the steps!"

It was an unpretentious home, with a friendly feel about it, very simply done in what Slim thought must have been family furniture several generations old. It had the look of modest, solid respectability that he'd come to associate with the homes of older relatives in his own family. In the wide, vertical cream stripe of the beige wallpaper, Slim made out garlands of depressing little roses that reminded him of a room on the ranch in which he had convalesced from a serious childhood pneumonia. He could never look at that particular kind of flowered wallpaper without feeling depression and despair. It was not to be looked at in his present mood and he turned his eyes away to Marge, who was leading him to a chair.

"You're going to have to sit here for a moment, my unexpected friend, until I get myself put together. I won't be long."

Slim sank gratefully into the restful embrace of the club chair and his heavy heels slid out straight along the worn nap of the faded Axminster carpet. He let his head loll over and smiled wanly at the girl. "I won't move—word of honor——"

She looked at him appraisingly for a moment. "Word of honor—I don't think you *can!*" With a sympathetic smile she moved toward a door at the opposite end of the room. "You contemplate your sins now, while I put up some water and do something about my hair."

She disappeared through a swinging door which Slim guessed must lead to the kitchen. He tried closing his eyes, but opened them after a moment to stop the swinging sensation. Rising wearily, he swallowed hard to rid himself of the squeamish feeling at the pit of his stomach. A cigarette tasted flat and he put it out after a few puffs. He hoped that Marge would be prompt with the tea; the thought of the clean, amber liquid appealed to him. He made a wry face and wondered why the British always had to louse it up with milk, which made it look like underperked coffee.

Wandering aimlessly around the room, he inspected without much interest a number of small pieces of bric-a-brac and some faded color lithographs of Gainsborough and Corot. At one end of the room a photograph hung on an inverted V of twisted wire suspended from a flat brass S-hook, its top half buried in the unseen trough of the picture molding that bordered the room a few inches below the ceiling. Its plain dark oak frame was surmounted by two crossed draped flags, the colors of Great Britain and some unfamiliar regiment. A small brass plate was engraved with the legend: "Sergeant-Major Francis William MacLaine, 42nd Regiment, Royal Highlanders, Glasgow, 1891." Slim smiled at the ferocious-looking warrior. He remembered the awesome name the Germans had given Scottish soldiers during the war in France—"The Ladies from Hell"—and he remembered the account of their charge in Arthur Guy Empy's book, *Over the Top*. He'd read the book from cover to cover several times, and when he and his childhood friends used to dig trenches in the fields and simulate charges with rubber-tipped bayonets fixed to their Daisy air rifles, he had always worn the kilts his grandmother had made from an old plaid scarf. An old knitted "tam" that had once belonged to his mother completed the uniform, and he played his part with such enthusiasm that a friend's broken wrist resulted in a sternly imposed and permanent armistice.

Slim sank onto the long sofa and fought an overpowering desire to put his head down. His body felt worn, inside and out, and he wondered what he was doing here. He wished he could crawl into his bunk, pull the threadbare curtain across it and slip into merciful oblivion. He knew he was fighting a losing battle. Taking a newspaper from the low table, he quietly spread it at one end, put his feet up carefully, and lowered his body painfully to a prone position. He bent his right elbow and used the fleshy inner side of his arm for a pillow. He closed his eyes and opened them and the room held still. He closed them again. A quiet sigh escaped through his partly opened lips, taking with it some of the aching tension. He slipped quickly across the indefinable border separating consciousness and troubled sleep and the diminishing sounds of the one world segued to the soothing music of another, long since passed into the vastness of memory. He heard his mother's soft, trained soprano sadly intoning the words of a song about an ailing doll that she used to sing to him when he succumbed to one of his small-boy maladies: "I've got a pain in my sawdust . . . that's what's the matter with me——" He could feel a gentle hand stroking his fevered brow and settling the covers and he felt secure and comforted. Out of her selfless devotion and his selfish acceptance had been created a profound peace.

The girl sat on the floor beside him, resting her arm on the edge nearest his head. She saw the strain fade, leaving a face in repose—one she'd not seen before—and the seeing begot the feeling and the feeling begot the deed. Her hand brushed the stray hair from his forehead, then deftly undid his laces. She put the heavy shoes beside the unintended bed and pulled a crocheted afghan over his unshod feet.

The quiet night grew older and the quiet girl, made bold by the deepness of his slumber, leaned close and touched her lips lightly to his cheek and they trembled there like the petals of a crimson blossom, quivering before the insistent pressure of a freshening breeze. As her head bent over the boy, a cascade of soft, sweet-scented hair tumbled over his face, and beneath its dark, gleaming canopy her heart quickened with the first stirring of a newborn passion.

A sympathetic little smile pouted the corners of her lips, and she lifted the confusion of silken strands away and, raising her head, carried them back and let them fall over her shoulders. She tried to look at Slim's watch, but its face was pressed between his wrist and the sofa. Rising noiselessly, she looked at the clock on the silver cabinet at the opposite end of the room. It was going on toward midnight and she had a fleeting fear that she should have wakened the boy long since—that he might be overdue aboard ship. Making no effort to be quiet, she leaned over and called his name softly. She tried several times; but, except for a short interruption in the even breathing, he remained oblivious to everything around him. She pursed her lower lip and frowned; then, taking the tip of her finger, she gently tickled the end of his nose. She laughed softly when he wrinkled his face and brushed it with the back of his left hand. The finger traced its ticklish pattern around the edge of his ear and down his cheek, then lightly across the strong curve of his upper lip. Again his arm raised in an annoyed gesture and he brushed his face. She called his name again and his breathing suddenly stopped. His eyes opened wide and stared, unblinking. As Marge leaned over him, the first thing he saw was the loose overlap of her robe. His eyes rolled sideways as he followed the seam to the belt; then, as he turned his head stiffly to the left, his gaze traveled upward, over her full, round bosom, to her smiling face.

"Well, sailor-boy—you've had quite a little nap!"

At the sound of her voice Slim batted his eyes and sat up with a startled expression. "Hey! What happened?" His voice was thick and heavy with sleep. He looked down at his feet, caught in the tangle of the afghan, and regarded his empty shoes with a puzzled look.

Marge removed the hobbling cover and tossed it into a nearby chair. "Nothing happened——" She spoke reassuringly, in a tone one would use with a child awakened in fright. "Nothing happened at all—except that you slept off your first little binge on our excellent brew!"

Slim rubbed both eyes with his fists and gave in to an immense yawn, then ran his fingers through his rumpled hair. "Fine thing!"

Marge was not quite certain what he meant, but she defended him against his own judgment. "It *was* a fine thing! Best thing in the world that could've happened to both of us. You got rid of your headache, and I had time to do my hair."

Slim hadn't noticed until she spoke, but now he looked at her face, framed in its dark, misty-edged cloud, and he thought he'd never seen anything so beautiful in all his life. Marge watched his expression change from mild curiosity to open admiration, and her large tipped-up eyes tipped still more from pleasure. Taking a short length of lavender ribbon from the pocket of her robe, she slipped it back of her neck, gave it an expert tug, and with that special magic known only to women produced a flowing pony

232

tail of glistening jet. Slim straightened up and stretched the slump from his long frame. His left arm tingled from its cramped position under his head and he massaged it, pressing his thumb deeply into the resisting muscles.

He stood unsteadily and looked at the girl reproachfully. "Marge, you shouldn't have let me stay. You should have kicked me out of here!"

The girl raised her eyebrows defiantly. "Indeed I should not have. You don't think for a moment that we want tipsy American sailors wandering about our neighborhood in the middle of the night. And besides—I would have been dreadfully lonely!"

An alarming thought struck Slim and he looked quickly around the room. "Oh my gosh! What about your family? I've gotta get out of here or they'll——" He interrupted himself, when he realized with a sudden shock that Marge was still in her dressing robe. "Hey, look at you! You're not even dressed!"

She pointed to his feet. "Neither are you!"

Slim looked down in panic.

She tucked the overlapped edge of the robe tightly under the soft cord belt and tried unsuccessfully to control a giggle. "Oh, my poor darling, don't worry! You'll not be compromised. We need good men down here, but we don't go about getting them that way!" She reached up and put her hands on his shoulders, gently forcing him back to the sofa. "You're safer here than on your ship. My family is down in Wellington and they won't be back until Sunday." She disappeared into the kitchen and returned in a few minutes with a tray. "It's a bit late for tea, but I'm too thrifty to throw it out."

Slim sat in one of the deep leather chairs, his stocking feet resting on the corner of the sofa table. He balanced a nearly empty teacup on one broad arm and, bracing himself in the corner, finished the last of a sweet roll and smiled contentedly. Marge sat on the big sofa, her hands cupped in her lap, cradling her saucer. She had been watching the boy respond to the strong, steeped brew, watching the young physical machine recover from its recent abuse. She had no way of knowing what was troubling his spirit, but she had sensed from the effect the presence of some hurting cause and she wanted to put her arms around him, pull his head down and comfort him. Instead, she looked at him with a mischievous smile and a teasing twinkle in her eyes. "You know, Slim, it's not good form to put your feet on the furniture, but we'll make an exception in your case. I've never seen anyone look so comfortable!"

He regarded her uncertainly for a moment, not entirely sure whether she was joking or using roundabout diplomacy. Holding the balanced saucer by its edge, he lifted his feet down carefully and sat up in the chair.

The girl made a regretful little cry. "Oh, Slim, I didn't mean——" Pressing her lips with determination, she got up, gathered his long legs in her arms and, with a little groan of effort replaced them on the table. "There now! Don't take me so literally!" She took the cup and saucer from his hand and for a moment stood looking down at him thoughtfully.

"Of course, in all the good books and cinemas, this is the place where the domesticated 'little woman' always brings the pipe and slippers—but we're just out of them. Will a cigarette do?"

It would, Slim thought, and he reached in his pocket for one. When he took out the box of safety matches, she put the cup and saucer quickly on the table.

"Oh no—let me! It's the least I can do!" She took the box from him and slipped a match out. Seating herself on the arm of the chair, she struck it and held it to the end of the cigarette. He dragged the smoke through and she lifted the match to her lips. With an exaggerated "poof" she blew it out. Smoothing his hair, Marge made no attempt to conceal the feeling that had filled her since she first sat on the floor beside him and watched the pallor leave his lean, young face.

Slim looked up and was struck again by her beauty. He'd thought before that she looked like the travel-poster idealization of every dusky native girl he'd ever seen; still there was nothing alien about her. Perhaps it was the eyes so slightly slanted at the corners, or the jet-black hair that created the illusion—or her generous mouth and the strong even teeth revealed by her smile. A part of her attractiveness came from the feeling of quiet repose—of assurance and of easy friendliness; and to these qualities he responded against his desire, for they felt the same as those that had bound his thoughts and dreams so constantly to Edye.

As he looked up at her now, there was none of the new restraints left—only those older ones that lay deep in the fabric of the boy's upbringing. And as their eyes met and held, those strong threads strained and were suddenly parted by the very stresses they'd been woven to restrain.

He slipped his arm around her and pulled her unresisting body gently down onto his lap. She half turned and leaned back, and the robe slipped open, revealing her smooth, tanned legs, gracefully slung over the arm of the chair. Slim's long arm moved slowly around her and she allowed her body to be pulled close to his. Their faces were so close that he could feel the warmth of hers, and as he looked into her deep brown eyes he saw nothing but willingness . . . and waiting. He pulled her still closer, and his lips found hers and rested lightly on them for a breathless instant; then a rising tide engulfed them and for a long time they were together in a world bereft of everything but feeling. When his arms eased their hold, she rested her head against his shoulder, and her soft hair caressed his cheek and tenderness interfused with ardor. His hand pressed very gently against her cheek and slipped under her chin. He raised her face and turned it to his, and his lips brushed her brow and lingered on the petal-like softness of her closed eyes, then trailed down the bridge of her nose and eagerly sought her just-as-eager lips once more, and the still mounting passion welded their lips together again. The pressures of their long-pent desire smashed and held each against the other, and in their opened, eager mouths they whetted their unbearable desire with the torment of love's lingual allegory.

As she felt the boy move beneath her, her own body responded until the writhing could no longer be contained. . . . She wrenched herself from the viselike embrace, stared at him with frightened, pain-filled eyes, then let her body slump against his. She lay there very still and her voice was a low sob. "Oh, Slim . . . Slim! Whatever are we doing?"

After a time her hands sought his face again and caressed it, gently at first; then, with the eagerness of hungry things seeking to slake an insatiable appetite, they moved across his head and neck and grasped through his clothing at his shoulders and arms and down his lean ribs to his waist. His hands sought the fullness of her breast, but the light flannel offended and he groped for the encircling loop of cord around her middle. Freeing it, his hand traveled under the folds and found another, smoother garment that extended up to her underarm. His fingers explored the soft skin of her shoulder and found the thin strap. They pushed, trying to force it over the willing flesh, but it held tightly by its strong-stitched tethers. The girl's shoulders heaved impatiently. The narrow band pressed deep into her flesh and suddenly parted. Eager fingers slipped beneath the silken edge and forced it down, finding at last the soft smooth dome of her breast and caressing it with restrained passion. Her lips found his again and her body twisted eagerly to lay more of its feeling self against him and, through the union of trembling hand and breast, another promise was born. Her hand lay still at his waist until it, too, sought its satisfaction against bare flesh. He felt its urgent movement between them as the fingers fought stubborn shirt buttons and found themselves frustrated by the length of cotton undershirt. They pulled at the fabric that seemed to have no end. Giving up, they discovered the belt buckle, and her body raised to make easier the loosening of its leather bonds. A snap and a row of buttons gave way before their hurried probing, and at last they found the hard muscles of his belly and their nails dug at the smooth skin eagerly, as though to keep it from slipping away. Her lips still held in loose submission against his, her hand found its way down his groin and grasped with wondering fingers the throbbing moisting maleness of him. They lay very still in the chair, hardly breathing; then, with an anguished cry, the girl slipped from his lap, grasped at his clothes, and pulled him from the chair. Quickly she led him through the door.

– 21 – Twenty-four hours out of Auckland, the *Tropic Trader* pushed south and east past the Bay of Plenty on a course laid to clear the jutting headlands of East Cape and the Mahia Peninsula, before turning southwest again for the run to the lower tip of North Island and the capital city of Wellington.

The sailing had been sudden and unexpected. A large warehouse several blocks from Central Wharf had caught fire in the middle of the night and two thousand cases of precious gasoline had gone up in the roaring inferno of deep red flame and oily black smoke. Ships in the nearby docks had been backed out to the safety of Waitemata Harbor.

Aboard the *Tropic Trader,* only recently cleared of their covering of deck timbers, lay the close-packed cases of the largest shipment of gasoline ever to be sent "down under." The captain, remembering well the added danger of the drums of liquid dynamite, made his decision to leave Auckland and discharge the case oil in Wellington for trans-shipment back up the coast. Since the dangerous cargo had been intended for the blazing warehouse, the consignees had no choice but to agree. And so two days before their scheduled sailing date she left her temporary anchorage and headed out to sea.

Slim and a number of others who were ashore had to be taken out to the ship in launches. As he stood his lookout, huddled behind the black apron plate in the extreme bow of the ship, the boy remembered those last frantic hours now. He had been with Marge, as he had been each night after that first one. They had been in each other's embrace when the harbor whistles and sirens had begun their frantic warning. They had dressed quickly and hurried down toward Waterfront Road, guided by the ominous glow rising behind the taller buildings of the business district. Slim remembered, as they walked and sometimes ran toward the fire, that it must have looked very much as San Francisco had looked that early morning in 1906 when the earthquake had set off the holocaust that had destroyed most of the city.

When they got to the foot of Queen Street, the whole city was awake and watching. He pushed his way through the milling people toward Central Wharf in time to see the *Tropic Trader* backing out into the harbor, a puffing, tall-stacked tug nosed against her bow. They both had understood. He held Marge and kissed her eagerly, as though to make the memory last until he could rejoin her. Both would wait impatiently for the night they knew must follow this frustrating dawn of disaster. She brushed her lips against his ear and, with an urgency in her low voice, repeated their private little couplet: "The name's MacLaine —*please* come again——" The words sent a shivering shock through his body, so newly filled with the ringing vibrance of an instrument performing in perfect pitch. He crushed his lips against hers again and disappeared into the awe-struck crowd standing like silent mourners before a giant funeral pyre. That was the last he'd seen of her.

Chips, Otto, Rusty, and Hammer were all ashore, standing at the head of Central Wharf, looking at the retreating ship. Hammer, looking pale and drawn, had sworn softly. "Sonuvabitch! I missed out all around. I coulda stayed in that dame for a new world's record." Chips arranged for a small launch, and an hour later they climbed the tricky pilot ladder to the forward well deck. Nobody said anything to them, for they had been on their own time. They went to their places and turned to the task of getting the ship settled in the anchorage. The decision to sail had been made a few hours later. There had been no way to get word to Marge.

Slim wondered now, as he stood huddled in the chill night, whether or not she had waited and, waiting in vain, had walked back into town to discover the truth. He realized with a sickening start that he didn't even know the name of the street on which she lived or the name of the place where she worked. He knew it was in an office, but he'd never heard the name of the firm. Except for her name and a hint at her age—six months older than he— there had been no time to find out anything about her except the unbelievable beauty of her body—its eager, passionate desire to enclose his with encircling arms, the hurried, whispered words, and then the short, frantic gasps that signaled the onrushing pain of their erupting pleasure.

And in the quiet union that followed he remembered how secret muscles had contracted around him, as though to hold him in place forever. Slim tried to force his mind to the task at hand. He answered the bells obediently, and his muffled call reassured the mate huddled behind the protecting dodger on the wing bridge. After two hours Warndahl relieved him on lookout with his usual obscenity.

Most of the off-watch men were in the messroom, hunched over coffee mugs, grumbling post-mortem complaints over pleasures now dead and philosophical oaths over promised ones now stillborn. Slim crawled into his bunk, tired from the continuous work of completing hastily done—often half-done—tasks that resulted from the forced sailing. The booms were all topped and ready for unloading in Wellington. All that remained was to clear the forward hatches to expedite removal of the unwelcome gasoline. The *Tropic Trader* was estimated to arrive at noon on the following day, and the third mate had guessed that the stay in Wellington would be prolonged to about eight days, even if the dockworkers could be induced to unload on overtime.

Peterson had cursed New Zealand's United Federation of Labor and the idea that it was spreading to other ports in the Pacific. He was particularly vehement about an Australian seaman named Bridges who had hit the San Francisco waterfront a few years before and had become the spokesman and leader of what the mate called "the radical bastards that want to take over the shipping lines and docks and make flunkeys out of the owners and masters!" Holst had listened to Peterson's dire predictions patiently for a long time, and Slim had never heard him express an opinion one way or the other. He just listened, a small smile-wrinkle in the corner of his squinting, sea-gray eyes, and puffed on the butt that was perpetually wedged in the corner of his strong mouth. Slim had listened and remembered an earlier conversation with Sparks when the radio operator had railed against the abuses being perpetrated by shipowners on the public and on professional seamen alike. He also could hear again a fragment of Holst's warning to the bosun the day he'd stopped the Russian-Finn from thrashing him for leaving his work to see the Columbia River pilotboat: "Whenever a young kid wants to make a career in this lousy, stinking merchant marine, encourage him! Maybe someday these bright young punks, as you call them, will make things a lot better for the likes of you and me!"

The boy wondered who was right, where the truth lay, which side he was really on, and how the choice of that side might affect his future efforts to study for a mate's ticket. That day seemed a long way off. Much closer was the memory of Marge, and it brought with it again an aching loneliness—keener than the one that he'd felt for Edye, keener and made more burdensome by the hungering lust in its longing. He tried to drive his thoughts back to the ship and the work and the third mate's oversimple explanation of the principle of the bow-and-beam bearing he had taken with the pelorus and stop watch. Slim tried to remember the number of degrees in each of the two angles in the calculation; instead he rememberd the gentle curve of Marge's hip as she lay on her side, facing him, watching him smoke in the calm quiet that always followed the raging storm of their passion. He could feel his hand move over its smooth, tanned skin and he remembered wondering how the girl had managed an all-over tan, and felt vaguely ashamed of the white skin that lay below the line of his belt. Marge had laughed and explained that during the height of the summer season, in December and January, she had always spent several weeks at her family's "bache" on Rangitoto Island. A "bache," she had explained, was a sort of beach house, and there were very few of them on their particular beach; so, in the privacy of isolation, her family had taken to bathing and sunning in the "altogether."

As he had lain with the breath of chill on his back, he remembered wishing that he and Marge could spend their hours in that same sun-drenched isolation—a South Sea paradise with nothing to do but satisfy in each other the ageless need to love and be loved. He turned on his side and he could still feel the tingling memory of her lips and the wonderful low sound of her voice as she found deft little ways to make him feel his growing masterfulness. He felt begrudgingly grateful to Hammer for a piece of half-sober advice the A.B. had given him in the San Francisco coffee shop that night after his first adventure in a whore-house: "One thing you gotta remember, kid, with a dame—if you're gonna get your money's worth out of her —you gotta let her know who's the head man! They wanta be bossed and bulled, and they won't give a shit for ya unless ya do! You just remember that—show 'em who's on top!"

Slim wondered why he had remembered the crude advice that first night with Marge. It was as though Hammer

240

had been standing in the shadows, coaching him through those first self-conscious minutes. He remembered again the surge of confidence he'd felt when he first realized that he was taking the lead, setting the pace, controlling the eager body beneath him . . . and the new assurance that had grown in him when he discovered that he could hold off his own agonizing urgency by concentrating on the feel of her breasts against him, the feel of his lips buried in her hair and of her open mouth and teeth working against his neck and shoulders, until she had signaled the moment of meeting and the tidal wave of their ecstasy engulfed them. He tossed impatiently in the bunk and struggled to erase the memory and the feelings that made them unbearably vivid, and another fragment of advice, heard in the more distant past, floated to memory's surface and lingered:

"If you can dream—and not make dreams your master; If you can think—and not make thoughts your aim; If you can meet with Triumph and Disaster And treat those two impostors just the same . . ."

He could still hear his grandmother intoning from the ruby-red, leather-bound booklet by Rudyard Kipling that she maintained held distilled, between its twin covers, the essence of all human truth. He finally slept the deep sleep of exhaustion and was roused from it a scant hour later by the call to "hit the deck." He ate a small mountain of dismal pancakes, covered with the sulphur-sweet syrup and rancid butter. He'd got used to the taste now and ate well, but without relish. Three cups of strong coffee warmed him and, when he turned to on deck, his body felt almost alive again.

The lingering memory of, and concern for, Marge stayed with him all during the day and the night and he found no relief from the painful awareness until it was dulled by the flurry of activity that attended picking up the Wellington pilot at the entrance to the beautiful harbor. The arrival time had been well estimated, and at noon the *Tropic Trader* was being warped alongside a lone pier across the harbor from the main docks and business district. The remote unloading site had been selected as a precaution because of the inflammable cargo. It was Saturday, but because of the emergency caused by the Auckland fire and the promise of welcome overtime at bonus wages, the stevedores were standing by to begin unloading. Slim was grateful when the second mate chose him to tally the cases as they came out of the hold.

Peterson stood beside him part of the time and looked

with wonderment at some of the damaged cargo. He swore softly to himself. "Holy Mother of Christ, it's a wonder this tub didn't blow to the moon a dozen times, with all those fumes down below! And those bastards scratchin' matches on the 'No Smoking' signs!"

At five o'clock the men stopped the unloading and the bosun had them rig the hatch covers across the gaping hold to protect the cargo from threatening rain.

There had been little time for Slim to look around. Ioway had gone ashore with Mr. Pugh to help with errands in connection with purchasing fresh provisions. Usually someone from the steward's own staff would have done this menial work for him, but the two colored cooks and the Filipino mess men tried to avoid shore leave in New Zealand and Australian ports because of the curiosity and antagonism their presence caused in these countries known for their "all-white policy." With the exception of the Maoris, whose status was much like that of the American Indian, Slim had not seen a single dark-skinned person in Auckland. From fo'c'sle talk he had learned that even the British ships that hired Lascar crews did not permit those men ashore in these ports. New Zealand and Australian pioneer stock was not to be outnumbered by the prolific natives and Orientals that surrounded them; nor would their daughters and sons dilute the strain by having access to even an occasional liaison. The hard-won foothold on the islands and on the outermost fringes of the Australian continent had been too precarious and costly to risk losing by the gradual infiltration of alien blacks, browns or yellows.

The attitude was not a new one to Slim, who well remembered the furor caused in northern California when the Hindus had been brought in to show the local whites the complicated techniques of raising much-needed rice during the World War. Any local girl found consorting with a Hindu was ostracized. A few had been horsewhipped with their Hindu lovers. After the war many of these brown men labored in the railroad section gangs and Slim used to enjoy watching them, their fine, dark faces topped by pastel turbans. To him they had seemed a patient and uncomplaining people who could work long hours in the parching, hundred-degree temperatures that seared the Sacramento Valley. He couldn't understand why people hated them. He'd listened to the townspeople at the general store, half frightened by the "gospel-truth" tales they told of the Hindus' secret, barbaric rites, and later he had listened to his grandmother's understanding explanation of these unfortunate people and of the great gifts of thought they had given the world and he'd felt sorry for them and tried to be friendly. For this some of the boys had called him "a nigger lover" and he had run for home in tears. In time the Hindus drifted south to the Imperial Valley and the railroad imported Mexican peons and the local prejudice found new targets in the Yaquis and "greasers," as they called the stocky, bronzed men who labored under their sweat-stained straw sombreros. Only the Chinese, who had drifted north in the gold-rush days, seemed to be immune from prejudice and hatred. When the boy had wondered why, his grandmother had smiled sadly and said, "Because we're used to them, I guess. . . ."

Slim dragged his thoughts back to the clip board and the long tally lines of cases already hoisted from the holds. It would take all day Monday and Tuesday to unload them at the present rate, and after that would come the unloading of the cargo originally scheduled for Wellington. A million feet of timber would come off the after well deck, and through its uncovered hatches would come the cases of canned goods and other general cargo that had been put aboard in San Pedro. Slim guessed that the *Tropic Trader* would be there the full eight days. He wondered how land travelers got to Auckland and how much time and money it would take by boat. His loneliness for Marge was growing, just as it had for Edye when the ship had left Wauna. He was aware of the sameness of the feeling, but he put the obvious comparison from his mind, using the reluctantly accepted arguments on himself that Sparks had so recently used to enrage him. His frustration was complete when he remembered that he had no means of contacting her, either by mail or by telephone, for want of addresses or, for that matter, her father's given name. Perhaps Ioway had taken Lyla's address; he was an enthusiastic, if not inveterate, letter writer, and through the little blonde he could get word to her. The hope cheered him and he waited impatiently for the younger deck boy to return to the ship.

It was after seven when Ioway finally came aboard. Slim had just finished supper with the crew and was cleaning up his locker. The boy burst into the fo'c'sle and clouted him on the back. "Hey, do you believe in miracles?" He waited eagerly for an answer.

Slim shook his head glumly. "Not on Saturdays. Why?"

243

"Well, you will when you hear this!"

"Okay, I'm willing to be converted. Go ahead and try——"

He felt a little impatient and not much like playing games with Ioway. He wanted to find out Lyla's address and be left alone to write a letter to Marge.

Ioway wagged his head incredulously. "I still don't believe it myself, but the steward bought me dinner tonight——"

Slim's tone was skeptical. "Bought you dinner? Where —in the officers' mess?"

"Nope. He bought me dinner ashore—at a place called the Ritz—a real snazzy joint!"

Slim laughed at the boy. "I can tell you one thing, Ioway. You belong to a very exclusive club!" He tried to make the next words sound casual. "By the way, you wouldn't happen to have Lyla's address, would you? I want to write the kids a note and I forgot to get either of them."

Ioway searched his mind, then a pained expression crossed his face. "Geez, Slim, I forgot to ask!" He spoke slowly, as though trying to remember. "She kept me flyin' around the countryside so fast, I don't think I ever wrote it down, but I know the name of the street. She lives on Airdale Street. I'll never forget *that*, 'cause Otto asked me if I was going out with a dog!" He paused a moment, then shook his head. "I don't remember the number. I don't even think I saw one. I was only there a couple of times, and I never went in." The boy reached for a notebook in his inside pocket. "I've got to remember to take more names and addresses. I've met some *real* nice people already!"

He replaced the little book and suddenly grasped at his side pocket. "Hey, fer Pete's sake! I nearly forgot something!" He reached in and took out several envelopes. Handing them to Slim, he explained, "These are for you! They were at the Consul-General's office when I went up there with Pugh. They stayed open for us on account of the gasoline cargo, I guess—'cause the chief mate was there too!"

Slim didn't hear a word Ioway had said after "These are for you——" He took the envelopes from the boy with hands that fought to keep from trembling, and his body suddenly felt numb. He had never seen the handwriting, but he knew it was Edye's. He looked at the postmarks and saw they bore cancellation dates that were less than a week apart—the first letter having been mailed the same day he sailed from Wauna. He stood holding the letters, and Ioway watched him with a puzzled frown.

"Hey, what's the matter? You're holding those like they're gonna blow up!"

Slim looked up quickly with an embarrassed smile. "Oh? Yeah—I just didn't expect to get any mail——"

Ioway dismissed it philosophically. "That's how it goes. You didn't get any in Auckland, and I didn't get any here." He kneeled down on the deck and opened his locker. "I'm going to a movie with Spots. D'ya want to come with us?"

Slim put the letters on his bunk. "No, thanks. I'm going to stay here and read my mail."

Ioway shrugged and snapped the lock. "Prob'ly just as well. It's that stage actor, John Barrymore, in something called, *His Lady*. Doesn't sound very exciting, but there's nuthin' else to do." He rose to his feet, waved a farewell over his shoulder, and disappeared into the passageway.

Slim was alone in the fo'c'sle. He thought of climbing into the bunk and drawing the spread across the wire. But the light was poor and curious shipmates coming in might try to find out what he was doing aboard alone on Saturday night. He thought of going to the sick bay. He put on his coat and went topside. Looking forward, he could see the light in the radio shack and stopped. He didn't want to talk with Sparks; at least not until he'd had a chance to read the letters. He'd seen him only once since the night in the Waverly Bar. They both had ·been contrite, and Sparks, in accepting Slim's apology, had also offered one for what he termed his own "courtroom manner." The old friendship had not only been reinstated, but in truth had grown considerably.

Sparks had concluded the reconciliation with an earnest appeal. "I got started on a real prosecutor's summation, son, and I couldn't stop. Question my methods if you will, my friend, but not my motives! All I really intended to do was snap you out of it."

Slim *had* understood, just as it had been clear to the radio operator, that his friend's outburst had been brought on by long uncertainty, bitter disappointment, a dead-tired body—and too much ale. But there was one thing Sparks had not understood about himself and his motives: and that was why he'd taken such unholy pleasure in trying to destroy his friend's romantic image when, knowing something of the quality of the boy, he had acknowledged all

245

along that—logic to the contrary—his own appraisal of the girl could quite possibly have been wrong; also, why had he gone about the task with such ruthlessness? The radio operator could not know the whole answer, because he could not acknowledge the whole truth that, once revealed, would have taken the ugly form of jealousy. Love for a girl was something that Sparks had never admitted to in his life. Without knowing it, he was jealous of anyone who could feel it; of anyone with the honesty to declare it. When the man admitted that he hoped he'd been wrong about Edye for Slim's sake, he didn't know that he hoped it for his own sake too. He was still to discover that the fallibility of his elementary logic carried in it the promise of his own deliverance—a chance to be free to give and accept the thing he most feared and most needed: the acknowledged love of a woman. Women had loved him and dominated and bossed him, and he had fled from them and the pattern of life into which they had forced him. In defiance he had closed his ears to their pleading and had "gotten even," had asserted his own bitter independence, by making them watch the tragic waste of the years he'd spent in *their* chosen profession. He had not reached the place for seeing that the waste of life was his own, not theirs; that love cannot be wasted, but fulfills its ultimate purpose in the loving.

Slim stod in the darkness of the poop deck, his sheepskin coat collar pulled high around his neck, and watched the silhouette of the radio operator moving across the open door. Turning, he went back down the companion ladder and headed toward the empty messroom. The door of Chips' stateroom stood open and the dim overhead light in the alleyway cast a pallid beam into its vacant interior. Chips would be ashore and likely would not return until late. Slim stepped across the low coaming and switched on the light. Closing the door, he seated himself on the lower bunk, lit a cigarette, and settled down to read the letters.

He opened the one bearing the postmark of the day that the *Tropic Trader* had drifted away on the current and disappeared into the low-hanging veil of river fog. He remembered how the mist had given the docks of Wauna a dreamlike quality, and it was this impression that had become the tenuous background of the fantasy he'd fashioned from the events of those unreal days. Even as the boy had struggled to give his dream outline and form he had sought to avoid a painful prescience which, after asserting itself in a hundred tormenting ways, had finally triumphed in that moment of bitter disappointment in Auckland. Now, as he sat with the letters in his hand, scarcely believing their obvious fact, the ghost of the old fear came to live with him again during the moments in which he hesitated to open them, lest their contents deliver the *coup de grâce* to a hope reluctantly reawakened. He turned the letters over in his hand. There were three of them—three letters—three chances—three chances too late. He gritted his teeth. Weeks of waiting for them, then disappointment. A week with Marge, and now these letters. They suddenly seemed like intruders, each filled with its own stinging rebuke. As he pried a finger under the loose upper corner of the flap, he thought bitterly that, a little over a week before, the act would have carried with it an exquisite uncertainty. Now the finger, moved by fear, pried under the lid of a new Pandora's box in which the only thing *not* left was hope.

The easy rolling loops of her handwritten return address lifted under the pressure and the flap opened upward behind his knuckles. He pulled out the folded pages of pale blue and looked at the neat lines of closely written words. He scarcely breathed as he read the opening salutation: "Dear Lewis." "Edye dear," he'd written in the unmailed letter, and she'd written "Dear Lewis". . . . "Dear Lewis" —the polite salutation of the head of the Math Department advising him that he'd have to make up credits in geometry. "Dear Lewis"—the matter-of-fact opening of a letter from a distant cousin in Denmark whom he'd never met. "Dear Lewis"—the matter-of-fact opening of a first letter from a girl he barely knew—and then, as he read on, his eyes moved more quickly along the lines and growing bewilderment shone in them and a little frown furrowed the flesh at the top of his nose.

"Dear Lewis," he read, "I'll bet I've tried a dozen different ways to start this fool letter to you! I used up so much paper, I was beginning to think I couldn't afford to write! 'Dear Lewis' looks so cold and 'Lewis dear' sounds like something your maiden aunt who keeps Persian cats would write when she encloses a dollar on your birthday. 'Lewis darling' is out of the question because, if I did use it, you'd think I'm a shameless hussy—which, of course, I am!"

Slim chewed on the side of his lower lip and looked up from the page. He stared absently at the bulkhead, then closed his eyes and wondered at the familiar sound of the words—not the words themselves, but the odd little undercurrent of their humor, the unsettling sound of them as they came alive in his mind. It seemed again that this girl, who had been so little in his arms and so long in his heart, had never been away. But even as his hands felt the paper, his eyes saw and his ears heard the words; the girl who had been so long in his heart retreated before the image of the girl who had been so long in his arms, and again the sound and feel of the girl who was *not* a dream came flooding into the tossing sea of his memory like the backwash of the tidal wave that had first engulfed them. Anxiety and desire and guilt compounded a reaction that glistened his body with a sheen of small sweat. He opened his eyes and forced them back to the letter.

"It was funny last night after you left, Lewis." She'd crossed out the name "Lewis." "I'll be dad-burned if I can call you 'Lewis' on paper. I can call you 'Lewis' on the hoof, all right—but it's just too formal and distinguished on paper and 'Lew' is impossible, because it reminds me of the girl in the *Shooting of Dan McGrew!* It doesn't make any sense, I know, but then a lot of things don't—like why I'm sitting here scribbling away on my best blue paper and not saying any of the right things! I just can't figger it out!" She followed the exclamation point with a series of silly question marks that made Slim smile. He began the new paragraph.

"As I started to say, it was funny last night after you left—Slim (There! I went and called you Slim!) But I got all bollixed up——" Bitterness twisted the smile as he remembered the word she had used that night at the dock gate: "I ought to hate you, you know! You came along and bollixed up all my fine plans for little old me!" The score was even now, he thought. Edye had done a little "bollixing up" herself. "I wanted to write as soon as I got home—and I tried to—but what I said sounded too 'schoolgirly.' I tore it up, like ten times! And what is more, you consarned long drink of water, you kept staring at me all night with that silly grin of yours! And Mom didn't help matters any either. She kept sticking her head through the door with a real 'mother hen' look, asking me if everything was all right. It's only because I'm so brave that I kept smiling and saying, 'Yes, Mother dear,' and it's only because I'm such a coward that I cried half the night. You see, Slim, I didn't want to have to watch that ugly old boat of yours go sailing away—and that's why I ran back inside the office this morning when I heard the whistle blow. Please don't ever do that to girls. They hate fare-wells and, besides, they look so ugly with red noses."

Slim's head nodded slowly and his hands relaxed and lowered the letter. He squeezed his eyes shut and sat sub-merged in a black sea of anguish. He couldn't separate the hurts and fight them off one at a time with reason, for there was no reason left to battle the calamity of coinci-dence that was unfolding. It *had* been Edye on the lumber dock that morning and she had fled from the things they both were feeling, and now he understood that it had been easier for him, because the ship had physically taken him away, while she had been caught in the midst of those constant and relentless reminders. He turned the next page, and even as he read, his eyes were searching the lines ahead.

"And so I know that by the time I get these words out of this stupid pen it will probably be too late to get them to you in Auckland. I called Portland this morning to ask them about mail boats to New Zealand, and they told me that it might be too late to catch the *Orangee* (?) (I know that isn't the way to spell it!), so I'm going to try to get it on the *Niagara* in Seattle. They told me it would be safer to address it to Wellington, because if I missed the *Tropic Trader* in Auckland the letters might follow you all over the South Pacific. And because you men are all alike, the first thing you'd think is that I'm a girl who can't be de-pended on and dismiss the poor little hick with a shrug of your broad shoulders (that need a little more meat on them) and go dashing off with some hula dancer! And by the way, I think I ought to warn you that our home-grown girls may not be as glamorous—but they stay young a lot longer!"

She had ended the sentence with the letters (advt.) in brackets. Slim reread the lines about men being "all alike" and the caution about "hula dancers," and again more re-cently remembered words formed their soundless syllables in the maelstrom of bitter-sweet memory: "I have what all women have—a little thing called intuition." He wondered why men didn't have this gift or whether, back in the be-ginning, they'd been given a choice and had chosen logic. If that were true, he thought they'd been robbed! He read the lines again, looking for more meaning. Perhaps it was intuition or simple logic born from some past experience of her own and of the sort Sparks had suggested in the saloon that night. It seemed unlikely that a girl would waste three letters on a passing amorous adventure, but then again she might have written it for the same self-protective reasons that had let him admit the possibility of an "Elmer" in her life. It's less painful to lose if you know the odds against winning are impossibly high. But he admitted the possibility that the reference was coincidental —just another expression of her irrepressible humor; another manifestation of the gentle teasing which had awakened in him the urge for affectionate roughhouse.

It was this unself-conscious aspect of the relationship from their first moment together that had made it so easy and natural to take her in his arms that night. But then it had been easy to take Marge in his arms, too, but for different reasons. The feeling for Marge had been restrained at first, then charged with passion, and the feeling for Edye had been filled from the first with a wonderful easy warmth—a sort of protective belovedness which held in it the promise of passion, but a passion tempered by infinite tenderness. This was the feeling that had pervaded his longing during the weeks at sea. He had wondered during those lonely times, when his impounded prurience had sought release, why he could never let it relate to Edye. Even in his dreams she would become another: a Boots or the art student or a composite stranger, but in any case a willing stranger whose unashamed labor in his service left no harrowed bed in which to propagate the anxious seeds of guilt. He could not drive his mind to any liaison with Edye that exceeded the extremes of his actual experience with her; whereas, in the time since he had been torn from Marge, scarcely a waking or sleeping hour had been free of physical longing for her. He could feel tenderness for her, too, but the passion came first. He wondered what would have happened had there been the same opportunity with Edye, and he knew the answer through the intuition he had conceded to this girl but had denied himself. The answer reassured that bigoted part of his boyishness rooted in pioneer mores.

The young man who had so lately been a boy and the boy who had so lately become a young man struggled with the fact of these two young women without recognizing them as the heads and tails of a bright new coin which, properly spent, could add much to his richness. He weighed the coin now, mostly aware of its intrinsic value and the pleasures to be gained in the immediate spending.

His eyes traveled quickly over two more pages of "local items," as she called the general chatter. Her generous use of punctuation marks and cartoon-like symbols of emphasis lent an animation to the letter that matched the well-remembered lilt of her voice and imparted an almost audible quality to the words. The last full page he read more slowly:

"What with the twenty pages in the wastebasket and the cramp in my poor fingers, I think it's time I tried to end this. As I read back over these lines I can see I've written a veritable 'gold mine of drivel' and I'm sure each precious word has held you spellbound! Please forgive me, Slim. I'm trying to say a lot of things that just aren't coming out—or, if they have, perhaps they're 'between the lines,' where I hear most of the interesting things in the world are, anyway! So, if this has bored you, try there—you may find something!"

As he read the words he felt an old urge to take her face gently between his hands and erase the seriousness he remembered in her eyes with the warm humor in his own. From the page there appeared again the dim outline of the dream so carefully built through all those hopeful days. But the old hope was tinctured with self-shame now—shame for the doubt he had allowed to flourish in the cold light of Sparks' reason and in the dim light of his own. Here in his hands were some of the words he'd waited to hear. If he *had* heard them sooner, he wondered what might have happened—or might not have happened—and the wondering unleashed an unwelcome flood of longing for Marge.

Slim folded the letter and returned it to the envelope. He had read the closing paragraph several times and thought again of the lines as he opened the second of the three letters.

"If you insist on being a sailor," she had written, "then I suppose I better practice up on being a sailor's sweetheart. I understand you must have one in every port and I don't want to be a discredit to you or to our fair city. 'By now—and try to remember to write! Edye."

She had begun the second letter "Dear Slim" and had told him that it had been directed to San Francisco to catch another trans-Pacific mail boat listed in the Portland paper. "I don't know why I'm so determined to keep you in reading matter, my fine sailor boy. I turned down an 'invite' to go over to Longview and see Marion Davies in *Quality Street*—so I could sit in my lonely room and entertain you with a sparkling array of wit and humor, like it says on the cover of Nye and Riley's famous old book. But somehow I don't feel funny. I'll bet I *look* funny, though—sitting here chewing the end off my pen. Mom just told me to be careful and not get splinters in my tongue. She says it's sharp enough already! Maybe she ought to write the letter!

"There's a new ship in today—another grimy old tub like the *Tropic Trader*—only it's called the *West Katan*. Where on earth do they find those names? Why can't they name ships after people—like the S.S. *Lewis Fredericks* or the S.S. *Edith Morrison*? Of course that could make problems, too—like if they named a ship after one of the girls I went to school with. How would you like to be captain of a ship called the S.S. *Ophelia Clodd*? Oh well! I guess everyone has a problem or two—but the biggest problem I've ever had is you!"

Slim could see her sitting at the desk, frowning and making a serious mouth. The picture made him smile to himself as he read on:

"If you like playing 'Twenty Questions,' I've got about that many for you—and if you know the answers, then I will too! Questions like: Why does a serious, sober, hardworking office girl prefer to sit home and write letters to a wandering sailor, when she could be sitting in the movies with a wayward country boy? Do you suppose it could be because lately, when she sits with wayward country boys, her mind begins to wander?"

Suddenly Slim saw a distressing picture of Edye and Elmer sitting in the last row of the darkened house. Elmer was trying to put a big paw on her knee, and a feeling of anger swept over him when he imagined Elmer looked like Hammer. He forcibly shook the picture from his mind and read on:

"The next question is: Why does this same sober, industrious girl feel lonely each night when she comes out of the office and looks back at the dock gate, in spite of herself—or wants to sit for a moment on those grubby stairs? And another question might be: Why does she keep looking for a letter from said wandering sailor boy when she knows darn good and well that there couldn't possibly be one—at least not for weeks—and maybe not at all. That's a horrible thought! I'll put it right out of my mind! And there are at least seventeen other questions too, Slim, and they all seem to be about the same thing—namely, about a sad girl named Edith Isabel Morrison, who was minding her own business, putting things in the office vault, when a tall, blond stranger walked in. If I'd known what kind of guy he was I'd have locked the safe—with me in it! But I guess that wouldn't have done any good—because knowing you now, you'd probably have cracked it or stolen the combination! This is all pretty silly—and I probably won't send it—but I'll go ahead and write it anyway because it makes me feel better. I just don't know why this has to happen to me. Why did you have to be a sailor? Why couldn't you have been the Watkins man? Then I'd know that every so often you'd drive up in your horse and wagon and I could buy some vanilla and sneak looks at you—and wonder what I saw in you. But this way, I'll never know when that rusty old tramp is coming up the river—and when it does I'll probably be in Bellingham, visiting Grandmother! But you wouldn't be on it, anyway, because they'll probably make you the blond god of some South Sea island and you'll be sitting in your BVDs under a palm tree, clapping your hands for more coconuts—or girls or something. Ugh! What a disgusting sight! Not you! I mean all those fat native girls wiggling around. Oh, Slim, promise you won't?"

As quickly as the anger had come at the picture of Edye in the movies with Elmer, whom he could cheerfully garrote Sparks for having invented, a wave of laughter came. Slim found a big smile on his face—one that felt like staying—and it was the first one in a long, long while that had been there as truly as it was now. There was something about this slender, pretty pixie of a redhead with the tiny waist and the big green eyes that always had made him feel like smiling—from the moment she had walked with him to the little café on the main street of Wauna. Whatever it was, he knew he'd not felt it with any other girl, anywhere. For the first time in a week he thought of Marge without the full bitterness of longing. Marge had a sense of humor, too, but not like Edye's—a happy, laughing, teasing, taunting humor that poked fun at everything and everybody, but at none so much as at herself. Marge was the quiet one, who made love with her mouth open and her eyes closed and only occasionally let low, throaty laughter slip from her lips.

Slim chuckled at the ridiculous picture of himself—half clad, under a palm, crown on head, clapping for more dancing girls—and he laughed out loud at her admonition. He could see her and hear her saying it to him. It was the first clear picture of Edye he'd had since they stood in the kitchen under the glare of the big overhead light and had done the dishes. He could see her now, scratching the lines on the paper and acting out every question mark and exclamation point—and the first traces of wonderful warm tenderness reappeared.

Slim hadn't heard the footsteps in the passageway, and when the door opened he jumped and cracked his head on the bunk above.

Chips was startled too. "Hey, Doc! What the hell are you doin' in here?" There was no anger in his voice, just surprise.

Slim clutched the letters and stood up with an embarrassed smile. "Gee, I'm sorry, Chips. I thought you'd be gone awhile and I came in here to read some letters where I wouldn't be bothered." He started for the door. "I'll shove off now——"

The big carpenter looked at the letters and grinned. "Stay put, kid. If you got letters from yer girl, that's good. If you got 'em from yer family, that's better." He nodded emphatically. "There's lotsa girls around this man's world but only one family . . . and they go too quick." He slipped off his store-bought jacket and loosened the black tie knotted beneath the collar of his clean blue denim shirt. Slim stood in the doorway and listened. "My family's dead . . . nobody left now. But ya get used to it after a while."

He threw a loose clove hitch in the tie and put the loops over the paint-loaded hook that some long-departed ship's carpenter had screwed into the white tongue-and-groove bulkhead. "You get letters from your family?" He poked a big thumb in the direction of the loose sheets Slim still clutched in his hand.

The boy looked down quickly at Edye's neatly written pages. "No . . . I didn't. This is from a girl friend in Oregon."

A knowing smile spread across the carpenter's huge roughhewn face. "Must be a *special* girl—if you don't want to be disturbed! Well, go ahead and read. If they were in Norwegian, I'd ask ya to let me read 'em too!" His booming laugh filled the room. "I used to get letters from a girl in Oslo. I was a fool to let her go. I stayed out too long. Always figured I needed more money. And when I went back, another fellow got her—with half the money I saved!" He chuckled at the turn of fortune. "That was twenty-five years ago. I bet if I saw her today I'd pay the other fellow to take her—no?" He thought a moment, then a new roar of laughter came rolling up from his barrel chest.

Slim grinned at the big fellow, but sensed something pa-

254

thetic about his eagerness to know about the letters. He had tried not to show it, but Slim understood.

Chips tested the length of his whiskers with the palm of his hand. "I got a nice friend here in Wellington. Took me the whole damn afternoon to find her. I'm gonna shave and fix up nice and we have a good time." As he unbuttoned his shirt he gave the boy a penetrating look. "Did you have a good time in Auckland? Did you find a good woman?" He waited expectantly.

For a moment Slim was uncertain, then he decided to answer directly. "Yes, I did."

The carpenter batted him on the shoulder with the rolled top side of his fist. "That's good. Did she give you a good time?"

Slim understood the sailors' meaning of "good time" and he nodded. "Yeah . . . I had a real good time."

"That's fine! A man needs a good time . . . with a good woman who knows what she's doing! But remember something—don't marry these women! Lay with 'em, but don't marry 'em. They're just like sailors—always on the move! You remember that! They don't expect nuthin' from you— just a good time!"

Chips picked the shaving gear off the shelf and filled the little white porcelain bowl with water from the bucket under his bunk. Slim waited for more of his direct, good-natured advice, then took advantage of his preoccupation to leave.

"I'm going to go now, Chips. Thanks for letting me use your place here—and for the advice about women, too!"

The carpenter answered without turning, and his big voice was muffled in a handful of water. "That's all right, kid. You just remember, that's all!"

Slim stepped over the coaming, out into the alleyway, and closed the door behind him. "Lay with 'em—but don't marry 'em." More words to remember, more things to think about, more doubts to settle or have settled. He wondered why he could have spoken about his nights with Marge, even indirectly. He walked back into the fo'c'sle. It was empty, so he sat on the edge of Hammer's bunk and opened the last letter, which had been postmarked a little over two weeks before.

"Slim darling (see how brazen I'm getting?): I had a horrible thought. I mailed that second letter and I really hadn't meant to. I was so tired when I finished it, I just naturally put it in an envelope and sealed it—and the stamps and everything were already on—so I just swallowed hard and let it go, anyway. I know you must think I'm an idiot—and I just happened to think of something else. Suppose you get *this* letter first? Then you'll really think I'm an idiot! In which case I might just as well be one and tell you that I love you—very, very much, Lord help me! Golly, hurry up and write—please, huh? Edye."

— 22 — Slim walked along the quiet waterfront until he came to Lambton Quay, the main street of Wellington. Again he was struck by the similarity to San Francisco. The look, feel, and smell were almost identical as the threatened rain had turned to a fine mist that hung in shimmering yellow halos around the street lamps and slicked the paving blocks into a mosaic of uneven black mirrors. Finding the post office closed and no place to buy stamps, he carried the unmailed letter back to the ship and spent the rest of an aimless evening adding pages to it.

On Sunday he and Ioway spent the entire day exploring the city and the surrounding sights. Long afternoon hours were spent in the Botanical Gardens and, after an indifferent dinner back aboard ship, they pulled on their heavy coats and climbed to the barren top of a large hill overlooking the harbor and the city. Seated on damp stones, they looked out over the breath-taking panorama of twinkling lights that stretched away into the distance to blend with the paler lights of mist-veiled stars still down on the horizon. The Southern Cross blazed like an inspiring beacon, and Slim sat in silence and wondered how many pairs of eyes were looking at it at that instant and whether or not there was any place in the equatorial seas where a sailor could observe the Southern Cross and the North Star simultaneously.

Ioway watched him curiously as he stared up into the black dome of the night. "It sure is pretty, isn't it?"

Slim pushed the end of his cigarette into the moist soil. "Yeah. It looks like the stars look up in the mountains at home. Feels like you can reach up and stir them with your finger."

They sat in silence again. After a time Ioway heaved a little sigh. "You know something? I'm having a good time all right, but I'll be glad when we head back for the States. How about you?"

257

The remark surprised Slim. "I'm in no hurry. What's the trouble—homesick?"

"Oh no! Nothing like that—but this would sure be an uncomfortable way to live your whole life."

Slim nodded. "I'd hate to have to spend it in a fo'c'sle like some of these guys, but I don't think it would be so bad if you were an officer."

Ioway pulled his coat collar up a little higher around his neck and scrunched down into the warmth of the lining. "Are you seriously going to try for a mate's license?"

"Sure, if I've got brains enough to learn the navigation. Why?"

"Oh, you've got brains enough all right. If you ask me, I'd say you've got too many brains to waste them out here! I'll tell you one thing—I don't envy any of these guys! Me, I like my comfort!"

Slim thought before he replied. "Well, I'll tell you something, Ioway. It was good enough for my grandfather—and he had more than his share of brains—and after he got to be an officer he had his comfort, too, even on sailing ships."

"Sure he did, but you told me he quit and got married the first chance he got!"

"Yeah, but not until he was almost forty—and with what he'd learned at the Royal Naval Academy in Copenhagen and out at sea, he came to America and got a fine job as a construction engineer. I could do the same thing —after I get a master's license. I could probably get a good shore-side job with a steamship company, too—if I got tired of the ships."

Ioway shook his head in resignation and sadness. "I don't see why you don't finish up and go on to medical school. You should hear what the guys said about the way you patched up Mike. They call you 'the doctor'—they say you're a 'natural.' They're right, too, Slim. I didn't see you do it—and I'm glad I didn't—cause I'd probably throw up. I got a weak stomach for things like that, but it must have been wonderful!"

"I've got a weak stomach too, mate!"

"Yeah, but you *did* it! And you didn't throw up, either!"

"I wouldn't bet on it!"

There was disbelief in Ioway's voice. "I don't believe it! You didn't get sick, did you?"

Slim smiled in the darkness. "Well, not really, but I sure as hell could have!"

"Yeah, but that's just my point! You went ahead and did it, and if you really knew how, it would get easier each time!"

Slim turned and placed a hand on the arm Ioway had wrapped around his hunched-up knees. "Listen, Mister Fix-it, I don't know about doctors, but for me it would never be easy to see people all busted up. Maybe they *are* like machines that need fixing, but machines don't groan when you grind their valves. People do—even brave ones! No, thanks!"

Ioway considered Slim's argument and felt it necessary to press his point. "But you don't have to be a surgeon. You could be just a plain medical doctor—or one of those child specialists, like that famous guy in San Francisco you were telling me about—what's his name?"

"Dr. Porter. He saved my life when I was a kid."

Ioway's voice was challenging. "Well, can you tell me any *better* work?" He waited for Slim's answer.

"Look, Ioway, if somebody brought a kid to me that was dying and I couldn't save it, I'd want to lie down and die too. I don't think I've got that kind of guts. I agree with you—and I agree with my family too—it's a wonderful career if you're tough enough to take it. I don't think I am!"

There was a note of finality in his voice that made Ioway hesitate. After a time he tried another tack. "Have you heard about how Mike's coming along?"

"He's doin' fine. He's going to rejoin the ship here in Wellington this week."

"How's he going to get here?"

"McNair's fixed up passage on one of the coastwise passenger ships, I guess. I heard him talking to Peterson about it on the bridge the other day."

"Geez, I hope he and Hammer don't get into any more trouble. That guy's murder!"

Slim got up and stretched his arms. "Come on, let's get back——"

Ioway rose, and a shiver shook his well-padded frame. "Boy, I'm cold! How come? I've got a lot more beef on my bones than you."

"I don't know. Maybe you've got thin blood."

Ioway grinned at him in the dark. "Thanks, Doc! How much do I owe you?" He laughed as Slim's sudden punch on the shoulder nearly upset him.

Slim set the pace with long, loping strides. At the bottom of the hill Ioway was puffing and perspiring from the exertion. "Hey! For Pete's sake, slow down, will ya? Those long legs of yours get rolling and nuthin' stops 'em!" He caught up with Slim and stood panting. "Man, you must be made out of rawhide. I watched you with those deck chains in Auckland. Don't tell me you're not tough! You're the toughest guy I know! You just won't admit it!"

Slim grinned and eased his pace. In a few moments they were down on Lambton Quay again. They turned right and followed the main street along to a point that Slim thought would be opposite the *Tropic Trader*'s dock, then turned left down the gentle hill to the waterfront.

The Shiek was on the gangway watch. He made no sign that he'd even seen the two deck boys come aboard. As they walked aft to the fo'c'sle Ioway made a wry face. "That guy gives me the creeps. I wish to God he'd get lost!"

It took the full eight days to unload the remainder of the forward deckload and the case oil originally destined for Auckland. The poker games had started again on the first rainy week night. Hammer had been right. After the second night he was sitting in again, but this time the cards were bought from the ship's slopchest. No one mentioned the fight or the tapered deck that had caused it.

Mike rejoined the ship and Slim changed the dressing each day, using supplies and instructions sent along by the Auckland doctor. The boy was surprised when he saw the wound. It had healed almost completely and the stitches were gone. In their place were two neat rows of dotlike scabs paralleling the cut, marking the points the needle and sutures had penetrated. Mike had told him that there had not been much pain and that when the stitches were pulled out the doctor had used an anesthetic. There was no denying that the man would carry a long scar down his face for the rest of his days, but it would not be as bad as Slim had pictured it. Mike, never an articulate person, thanked him with difficulty and genuine feeling and presented him with an English leather garrison belt secured by a large metal buckle bearing the enameled coat of arms of New Zealand. The boy was touched and a little embarrassed by the fireman's gift and in turn had found no easy words of thanks.

Under orders from the first engineer, the black gang was forbidden to play cards with members of the deck department. Slim was relieved by the decision worked out in joint conference with the bridge. Occasionally he would wander over to the portside quarters and watch the black-gang poker games. He knew he was welcome, but most of his free time was put to good use studying the navigation problems Holst had sketched out for him. Even Peterson had handed him some work to do and had let him know that his questions would be answered "if they're not too goddamn ridiculous!" Many hours were spent with Sparks and Stokes. Slim preferred to listen to the two of them go at each other than go ashore to see the finest movie made. And there were hours spent writing to Edye and getting the letters posted in time for the mail boats. There were other, less pleasant, times when Slim tried to use reason to fight his longing for Marge, only to give up in quiet despair at the sudden awareness that the arguments sounded disturbingly like the ones Sparks had used and applied as logically to either girl. Several times he'd thought of asking Sparks to wireless Auckland to see if Lyla could be located at her home on Airdale Street, but each time he put it off, hoping that Ioway might get a letter or that one might come from Marge herself.

Sparks had got a radiogram off to Edye, telling her that letters were on the way. Slim did not understand the empathic nature of his concern for her, but he could guess, he thought, at the emptiness of her hours alone. With each letter it had been easier to unburden his heart, and many of the pages flowed from his pen with an ease and unself-consciousness that surprised him. Most of the time he found that he could speak of his love and that something of the tenderness he felt was miraculously transmitted to the pages which, weeks later, would send exquisite little shivers of longing through the girl as she read them in the quiet of her room and treasured each well-remembered word. But there were other times when the pen hung over the paper and the waiting words were dammed up behind a barrier of memory that separated today from the reservoir of memories stored up during those yesterdays with Marge.

The memory of them whetted the edge of an ancient appetite and he grew angry with himself for not being able to deny his hunger. He argued that there had never been any desire or inclination on his part to use the word "love" in connection with their affair. Then the muffled ears of memory heard her agonized murmuring as he fanned to white heat the flame of their pleasure. The word had been "love," but love was not the word for those moments; the word, he thought, had been a simpler one. He struggled against the memory, even though there was nothing shameful or unclean about it; but it was heavy and unhappy—a restless emotion in which there was no real peace. He had known it all along and he didn't try to deny it. He thought about both girls, and the difference was clear. His feeling for Edye was light with gaiety, bright with humor, lit by the unexpected flash of poignant love that was now openly acknowledged.

Slim had written one letter in which he'd confessed his affair with Marge and the apparent reason for it, and had asked her to forgive him or forget him, as she saw fit. When he reread it, he tore it up and the reasons for doing so that came tumbling into his brain were troublesome, for his honesty might cost him Edye, or at least become her license for an action about which he couldn't bear to think. Slim had no way of recognizing his own first serious encounter with society's reluctantly admitted double standard, whose single purpose is the rationalization of man's rampant maleness. Without his knowing, it had motivated the decision to destroy the pages. And so he lived with his uneasy conscience like a gladiator in the ring with two opponents, either one of whom he knew he could best, but battling against a lurking fear that, together, they could be his undoing.

There had been no more letters in Wellington, and the *Tropic Trader* had nosed out of the beautiful harbor, crossed Cook Strait separating the North and South Islands of New Zealand, and had headed slowly into thickening weather for the 365-mile run south to Dunedin.

Slim was back on his regular work now, standing the four-hour wheel watch and filling the rest of the time at day work on deck. Holst had kept him on the midnight-to-four watch also, which meant the deck boy was now working the full day of an able-bodied seaman.

The wind was south-southeast at twenty knots and the sea, piling up before it, slammed into the blunt plumb bow a point or two off the port and exploded in white fans of feathery foam that curled over at the top and swept back across the decks in trailing rainbows of mist.

Slim braced himself at the wheel as the helmsman's grating began sliding under his feet. Holst leaned on his thick forearms, his officer's cap pushed well back on his head, so that the shiny black leather sunshade cleared the wheelhouse glass. He looked out ahead at the low bank of dirty gray clouds that moved in along the high, rocky coast of South Island and after a time he walked to the helm and peered into the binnacle.

"Hold her up into it a little so she won't blow off."

"Yes, sir." Slim turned the wheel a couple of spokes to port as the bow rose from beneath another white-capped wave and plunged into the gray-green trough. He could make out the glistening black oilskins of the bosun and three men who were sledging the wedges tighter against the batten strips of number one hold. He was glad to be in the snug shelter of the wheelhouse when the sea boiled over the well deck and buried the men to their knees in its pummeling wash.

Holst wedged a fresh cigarette into the corner of his mouth and produced his magic flame again. Slim wanted to ask him how he did it. It happened faster than the eye could follow and, though he'd seen the man do it a couple of hundred times, it always startled him.

Putting the match in the condensed-milk can, the third mate peered into the compass again. "It's a little harder holding her in this kind of weather, huh?"

"Yes, sir, but it's fun trying!"

"Do you find most of the ship's work fun?"

"Some of it, sir."

"Like stowing deckload chains up forward?"

"No, sir, that wasn't much fun." His voice was even, with no hint of self-pity. He knew the mate never spoke without a reason and he tried to figure out what Holst was driving at now.

"How long did it take you, Fredericks?"

"All day, sir—until quarter of five."

"Did you get ashore at all?"

"Yes, sir, about eight o'clock I think it was—with Sparks."

"Did you get drunk?"

"Not exactly 'drunk,' sir, but a little dizzy, I guess."

"What were you drinking?"

"Half-and-half, sir."

"How many did you have?"

Slim began to feel worried. He wondered why this particular line of questioning? Had someone told the third mate about his unintended binge—perhaps seen him wandering up Queen Street in Auckland?

"I had three handles, sir."

"Sounds like you learned to drink the beer and speak the lingo at the same time."

Slim grinned and peered down into the binnacle top.

"That's what Sparks called them, so I figured that was the right name."

"You forgot to say 'sir.'"

The boy looked up, startled. "I'm sorry, sir——"

Holst forced a straight face. "I've been counting. You called me 'sir' fifteen times in the last fifteen minutes. That's a record on this bridge!" He walked over to the boy and laid a hand lightly between his shoulder blades. "Fredericks, you're going to turn out all right. Unless you foul yourself up along the line, I think you might make a good merchant marine officer. That's what you want, isn't it?"

Again Slim felt the warm glow of appreciation and the curious feeling akin to affection for the stocky little third mate whose reputation for cold-bloodedness was said to be second to none in recent times. He could never reconcile what he'd heard with the officer's behavior toward him. The legend didn't seem to fit the man—not as Slim knew him.

"I'd like to be an officer, sir—if I'm smart enough to learn all the things I have to know. Sometimes I get a little worried about it. I'm not very good at mathematics."

Holst chuckled. "Neither am I! The whiz on this ship is Peterson. But you can get the hang of it after a while. It's a formula. Once you learn all the moves, you can figure out any sight on the globe. It's not as tough as it looks. The biggest danger is errors in your arithmetic." He reached inside the open front of his khaki jacket and tugged at his belt. "You've got to check everything completely through at least twice, and even then there's a chance that you'll make the same damn-fool mistake over and over again and put her up on the rocks. There's no such thing as being absolutely positive in navigation—remember that!"

Holst walked back to the window and leaned one elbow on the frame. "After all's said and done, you might forget to allow enough for the set of tides or currents or winddrift." He pointed forward. "This southeast weather that's hitting us on the port bow is driving us inshore all the time—so is the surface water. That course you're steering now has the correction in it. But maybe it's not enough. As long as we're running in daylight, there's not too much danger, except for unmarked offshore rocks, but these charts are pretty good. At night—that's another story! I'd take her way off east, just to make sure. It's easier to make up time than to salvage a ship!"

Holst turned his back to the glass and leaned both elbows on the sill. Slim had never heard him talk so much and for the first time he was aware of a slight German accent in his speech. The voice had a low, easy tone that was pleasant to listen to.

"Fredericks, let me ask you something."

"Yes, sir?"

"You have a pretty good temper, haven't you?"

The question was totally unexpected. A sudden confusion of thoughts alarmed him as he remembered the outbreak in the Waverly Bar. He wondered again whether or not someone had seen him smash the glasses. He knew Sparks would never have mentioned it. Perhaps the owner had come to the captain for damages or filed a complaint with the police. Sparks had said nothing about any problem—and surely he would have known, for Slim had left him sitting there when he staggered out. The third mate watched the boy and waited quietly for the answer that took a long time in coming.

"Yes, sir. Sometimes I do get . . . uh . . . sort of hot under the collar."

"Have you ever gotten mad at anybody on board except the bosun?"

"Only Sparks, but that was a misunderstanding. It was my fault. If there's any trouble, sir, I'll be glad to square it up. I still have some money coming——"

Holst's sea-gray eyes squinted into narrow lines. "I don't know what you're talking about. Did you bust up some saloon?" A little smile of anticipation widened the corners of his mouth and he took the stub of the cigarette from his lips and held it. "Well, go on—what happened?"

It took a while for Slim to lift his head from the binnacle and look at the officer. "I broke a couple of glasses. I guess I was mad—mostly at myself. It was my fault—not Sparks'! It wasn't about anything very important, sir."

The mate lowered his arm from the sill and walked closer to the binnacle. Leaning a hand on its shined brass top, he looked directly at the boy. "That's the second time you've told me something was your fault. The first time was outside the Columbia River bar when we were picking up the pilot and Boats got on your tail. Now you say you were wrong again. Were you, or do you just like taking the blame? Do you always think everything is your fault?"

Slim tightened his lips into a straight line and swallowed hard. "No, sir. I don't think I'm always wrong. But I was taught that when I *am* wrong I should own up to it. So I try to—if I really am wrong!" His tone was matter-of-fact as he continued, "The other night in the Waverly Bar I had too much beer. I didn't know it was happening. Then Sparks told me some things I'd asked to hear, and I got sore when I heard them. I shouldn't have lost my temper, but I did. Sparks and I are okay. I talked with him the next day."

"What kind of things did he tell you?"

"Some things about girls, sir."

"Oh?" Holst raised his eyebrows. "What kind of things?"

Slim hesitated, as though trying to find the right words. "Discouraging things, sir." He emphasized the first word.

The third mate looked at the boy for a surprised instant, then his shoulders began to heave with soundless laughter. He turned and walked out on the starboard wing bridge. Slim flushed hot and felt miserable. He damned himself for a complete idiot! The words hadn't come out the way he'd intended. He hadn't wanted to say anything about the incident at all, but his own guilty conscience had led him into a trap. He quietly cursed and determined not to get caught off base again. Holst was gone for several minutes and when he stepped over the coaming into the wheelhouse his face still bore the traces of the booming laughter that had trailed off downwind, unheard in the gusty roar of the wing bridge.

"How old are you, Slim?" It was the first time he'd called the boy by his nickname.

"Almost nineteen, sir."

"Know anything about women?"

"No, sir!"

The mate smiled again. "I'm fifty-one—and I don't, either! What did the radio operator tell you that discouraged you about women?"

Slim frowned. He was uncomfortable and hoped that after Holst had finished laughing at him he'd change the subject. "Well, he said that most of the time you can't depend on them, if they're the kind that go out with sailors."

The mate covered his lower face and rubbed the gray stubbled cheek with his fingers. "I wonder what would happen if I told that to Mrs. Holst?"

Slim looked up from the compass, where he'd been hiding his head like an ostrich. "I don't know, sir."

"Well, I can tell you! She'd call me an idiot for not finding it out thirty years ago!" He turned back to the boy. "I don't know what I can say to you, son, but you'll probably find out that there are as many different kinds of women as there are sailors. I gather Sparks must have blasted one that you liked pretty much, right?"

The boy's eyes lowered to the binnacle. "Yes, sir."

"Did you think Sparks might be right about her? Is that why you blew your stack?"

"I wasn't sure, sir. Some of the things he said made a lot of sense, but I guess I didn't think they fit this particular girl."

Holst seemed to consider something for a time. Then, with a quick gesture of resignation, he began: "When men talk about women, you have to listen, not only to *what* they're saying, but to what makes them say it. A man who likes women and gets along with them will tell you that most women are great. From where he stands, that's the truth. Guys who are afraid of women will tell you that they're liars . . . bosses . . . cheats . . . anything to justify their attitude toward them. The guys who talk nothing but filth about women and figure they'll all whores—and that's a hell of a lot of guys on these ships—are filthy, themselves. They try to make every woman as dirty as they are. I'll tell you one thing, Slim. A woman doesn't love like a man—she loves a lot more. A man who's got a woman really loving him can make her into almost anything he wants, depending on the kind of person he is. If he tries to take her too far, she may call a halt, but she'll give him plenty of warning first."

Slim thought the mate had finished, but he began again. "Goin' to sea is a hard life for a married man. And it's a hard life for a single man, too, if he has anything to him. Any man needs to get laid once in a while. Men are built like that. I guess women who marry seafaring men know it and sort of close their eyes and pretend it don't happen. And unless the guy is a goddamned fool and gets dirtied up, she'll never really know—or she'll think she don't. A lot of other wives close their eyes, too, when their nice respectable white-collar husbands come home early Sunday morning. Those are the ones that blow up—not because they find out their husbands are cheating—but because they can't stand the rest of the town knowing it!"

He walked over and peered into the compass again, then continued: "A sailor is kind of like a traveling salesman. There are lots of things about both that are no good. And a lot of guys make bad mistakes finding that out. If you play it right, you can have a good home and a good career at sea—but it takes a little doin'! This should be an honorable profession, but in the States most people think sailors a lot of bums! They're partly right and it's partly their fault. But there's still a great chance in the merchant marine for young men who have guts enough to make a real career out of it. This is the only major country in the world that considers going to sea a lousy profession. In Great Britain and Germany and the Scandinavian countries a merchant officer ranks with doctors and lawyers. Those countries depend on the sea. Without the merchantmen, they'd starve. Over here we let the other guys' merchant service do the work. If they never came sailing into our ports, we'd still have more than we need of everything. That's the goddamn trouble! But one day they're going to wake up—maybe before it's too late. Maybe kids like you can wake them up—who knows? But just remember, Slim, you *can* live a good life and still go to sea!"

Holst spoke the last few words directly at the boy, then turned and busied himself at the workshelf at the after end of the wheelhouse.

Slim looked at the chronometer and noticed he had been listening to the mate for nearly half an hour. He concentrated on the compass, checking the ship's movement almost automatically. He'd got the feel of the helm much more quickly than he'd expected in those first confusing days out of San Pedro, when Holst had made good his promise to let him steer.

At three-thirty Slim rang seven bells and for the first time since Holst had started his surprising monologue he noticed that the low, heavy clouds were almost upon them. The sea was considerably rougher and the men had left the forward well deck. Nearly every wave was washing across it.

Off to his right the boy could see the coast line. The sun was low behind the snow-tipped, serriform mountains that ran like a prehistoric spine along the length of South Island. Ioway, who had become the ship's unofficial tourist guide because of his unquenchable thirst for details to fill his letters home, had told Slim that the range was called the Southern Alps. The highest peak was Mount Cook and he'd even gotten the correct altitude: 12,349 feet. Slim had been impressed, for they compared with the highest in the States.

The third mate took the binoculars from their box on the wall and stepped out into the full force of the strengthening gale. Spray was coming up to the wheelhouse now and the windows were streaked with erratic rivulets of water, leaving behind a jackstraw tracery of salt that made seeing difficult. Standing in the lee of the structure, the third mate trained his glasses on the shore line and after a time stepped back inside to make an entry in the day book. Slim thought he could see a town off the starboard beam. His supposition was confirmed when Holst mumbled, "That's Kaikoura over there. We're not making much headway against this slop!"

At three forty-five the first mate came up on the bridge. He nodded to Slim and checked the course on the compass and on the blackboard. The two officers spoke quietly for several minutes and then went out on the bridge to fix the pelorus on its stand. Together they took a series of bearings and Mr. Samson disappeared into the chartroom to put the information on the coastwise chart. At eight bells Hammer, back on regular watch again, relieved him at the wheel.

As he took over, he spoke to the boy. "Watch yerself goin' aft. It's sloppy back there."

Slim had wondered about the after deckload and whether or not the lifelines had been tightened. For most of the trip they'd become loose rope snares that could put a man overboard in the darkness. He thanked the A.B. and stepped outside. The force of the wind nearly knocked him off his feet. Staggering to the ladder he clung to the rails with both hands as he eased his way down to the main deck. Once behind the shelter of the deckhouse, it was not so bad. He looked into the galley and saw Mr. Jones and Mr. Bones balancing themselves skillfully as they prepared the evening meal. Chico looked up from his scullery work and waved. "Hi, Sleem!" Ever since the impromptu operation in the sick bay, Slim had become the little Filipino's special friend. Slim smiled and saluted, then grabbed the rail again quickly. Making his way to the after end of the deckhouse, he paused at the base of the ladder to the boatdeck and decided to postpone the trip aft across the slick timbers. He'd visit the radio operator instead. Climbing the ladder, he crossed the after end of the boatdeck and rapped on the heavy door.

Sparks opened it partway and stared owlishly into the light. "Hi, pal, come on in." Pushing the door completely open, he secured it against the bulkhead and closed the inner screen door. "It's time I let some air in this place, anyway!"

He was right, Slim thought. The room was filled with a pungent, blue-gray haze.

Sparks waved at a briar pipe resting on his desk. "It's

that goddamn thing. I bought it in Wellington. I used to try to smoke one when I was in college, but I always had to spit, and there was never any place to do it, so I quit."

Slim picked up the pipe and smelled its bowl. The acrid odor came from a mixture of burned varnish and a blend of aromatic Turkish and Latakia tobaccos. The combination was revolting.

Sparks hiccuped unexpectedly. "And that's another thing it makes me do!" He belched and wiped his mouth with the back of his hand. "Filthy habit. I'll give the stinking thing to Stokes. It'll serve him right!"

Slim laughed at the radio operator and offered him a Chesterfield. "Here, smoke one of these and get back in shape again!"

Sparks reached for the pack. "Thanks, I will. What're you doing up here?"

Slim shrugged. "Nothing much—just got off the wheel."

The ship pitched suddenly. The radio operator closed his eyes and shuddered. "If I ever quit these ships, I'll murder the first guy who even says the word 'water.'"

The boy remembered that, like Ioway, Sparks never really got used to the pitch and roll. Each time the sea roughed up a little, both of them wore anxious looks. So far, with the exception of the big ground swell coming down along the Pacific Coast, they had been sailing on near-smooth water with only an occasional surface chop. But this was different. The weather outside had all the sound and feel of a respectable storm.

Slim knew that Sparks got whatever reports were available. He was curious to know what lay ahead. "Did you get the weather today?"

The radio operator reached over and took a carbon copy from the basket. "Got this last night from Dunedin."

Slim read the message that Sparks had typed on the battered machine bolted to the end of his desk: "WIND S.S.E. 30 KN. TEMP. 6:00 P.M. 55DGS-F. CLOUDY-RAIN."

Slim read the wind force aloud: "South-southeast thirty knots? That's a pretty good blow."

Sparks flopped into his swivel chair. "If you stoop over upwind, it'll come whistlin' out your ears!"

Slim laughed and held out the paper. "You got this report twenty-two hours ago. This is *their* weather we're getting now——"

"Well, what the hell? I'm generous. Give it back to 'em!" Sparks made a deprecating gesture. "I'll take that nice flat stuff myself!" He swung around and took the headphones off the hook. Clamping them on, he flipped a switch on the tall panel to his right and listened. After a moment he slipped them forward on his temples. "Nothing but hash. I heard the oyster dredgers talking off Stewart Island a couple of hours ago. It's rough down there, too."

Slim knew that the island lay off the southernmost tip of New Zealand. It was the last jumping-off place for whalers heading down into the Antarctic waters.

Sparks leaned back and yawned. "They're staying out, so I guess it isn't getting any worse."

Pushing himself up from the bunk, the deck boy braced himself against the roll. "If we're going to get anything bad, it'll probably come when we cross the Tasman Sea. The guys tell me that's the worst in the world."

Sparks nodded unhappily. "They're right! I've been across a couple of times, from Wellington to Adelaide. It's pretty nervous water!"

Slim walked to the door and steadied himself on the frame. "Guess I'll shove off and snooze a little. I gotta break today. It was too rough to work on deck."

The radio operator snorted. "I'm surprised the bosun doesn't have you up for'ard hosin' down the anchors!"

The ludicrous picture made Slim smile. "Maybe he hasn't thought of it yet." He stepped outside and pulled the screen shut behind him. "See you later!" Half sliding across the after end of the boatdeck as the ship wallowed up the side of a deep trough, he made his way down the ladder. Looking aft, he could see the spindrift swirling across the glistening deckload. The lifelines were hanging limp, their jury-rigged wooden stanchions leaning at odd angles, their soggy loops dragging on the timbers.

Waiting until the ship took another long roll to starboard, Slim ran quickly aft, hurdling the chain lashings as he went, and grabbed the poop-deck railing just as another sea came swirling over. He closed his eyes as its chilling spray pelted him, and hung on till the roll to starboard began again. Then he scurried to the shelter of the companionway. Down below, he stripped off the wet jacket and the close, warm air felt good.

— 23 — The bad weather held through the night, and when Slim came off the wheel at 4 A.M. the seas were still roaring across the foredecks. The ship had been making a scant five knots and the estimated time for the run had been extended to nearly fifty hours.

After breakfast the crew worked below, cleaning the fo'c'sle and the messroom. The time dragged by until eleven-thirty. Then Slim washed up, picked at a lunch for which he had no stomach, and, pulling on his oilskins, reported to the bridge for his watch. Holst gave him the first two hours on lookout, and the buffeting wind and stinging spray cleansed him and brought welcome relief from the heavy paint odor in the confined quarters.

Off to the starboard were the high headlands of Banks Peninsula protecting Port Lyttelton and the city of Christchurch, which New Zealanders called "the most English town out of England." Later, he could make out the entrance to Akaroa Harbor as the *Tropic Trader*, now on a more westerly course, plowed along the outer edge of Canterbury Bight with Dunedin still two hundred miles ahead.

Here and there the scudding clouds, tearing apart in ragged fragments, let pale rays of sunlight through to the sea. But the force of the wind continued, holding in it the threat of a painfully slow passage.

At five o'clock the following evening the ship dropped anchor in Port Chalmers, at the extreme lower end of the Dunedin River; in reality, the so-called river was an eight-mile-long estuary that penetrated southwest into the hilly amphitheater of Dunedin itself.

Slim was quietly grateful for the calm water in the shelter of the anchorage. As they stood on the poop deck Peterson pointed out the largest dry dock in the Southern Hemisphere. It appeared to be a huge cement basin sunk in the water. A ship was being repaired in it—a strange

272

looking vessel called the *C. A. Larsen*. From the second mate Slim learned that it was a factory ship that accompanied the whalers into the Antarctic. The vessel was being converted to an icebreaker and supply ship for the polar expedition about to be undertaken by Commander Richard E. Byrd of the United States Navy. Slim knew that some of the general cargo due to be discharged in Dunedin was destined for the *C. A. Larsen* and would eventually end up with the explorer in Little America.

Since no vessels were permitted to proceed up the narrows after dark, the *Tropic Trader* swung at anchor during the night and got under way again at seven the next morning. By ten o'clock they were alongside and the stevedores began unloading.

For most of the time the weather was blustery and uncertain and the time passed slowly for the men. Slim made the usual shore trips with Ioway and several with Sparks. He liked these cities in New Zealand and was struck by their marked similarity. Dunedin and Wellington were situated almost identically; blue-green hills, burned brown in patches by summer sun, rimmed beautiful harbors, red sheet-metal roofs topped the neat rows of houses standing back from small, well-tended front yards. The modest homes stood shoulder to shoulder on streets that followed the contours of the hills encircling the bay. Slim thought the houses looked like red-capped rooters seated in rows in the curved bleachers of a stadium. The main part of the city revolved around a hublike park. From this, six streets radiated like the spokes of a giant wheel and around the outer rim stood office buildings, civic buildings and a magnificent cathedral. The city was one of the best laid out Slim had seen, and one of the cleanest in a land of clean cities. But there was little diversion for the men beyond the picture house, the museums, several bars and the never-ending quest for pleasant company.

Both Slim and Ioway drew several days of cargo checking. When the front part of the remaining deckload had been taken down to the level of the hatch coamings, the crew uncovered number four hold. From it came cases of general cargo, mostly canned fruits from California. Slim discovered that many of the cases had been pilfered. The petty thieving that apparently happened in San Francisco during the loading that took place before he'd joined the ship. He remembered now the night Otto had called Hammer out of the fo'c'sle to show him something, and suddenly he understood the source of the mysterious cans that both of the men kept secreted in their lockers.

While the ship was still in Auckland, the heavy timber shorings from the foreward deckload had been hauled into the gloomy shelter deck beneath the main deckhouse. Now the first mate ordered the bosun to similarly dispose of the ones no longer needed on the after deckload. When the timbers had been stacked into an impressive pile of clear pine, Slim and Ioway were given a six-foot crosscut saw and ordered to saw an inch off the branded ends of each. The resulting small blocks were carefully saved; then each timber was given a new identification mark with red paint.

When the job was finished, the mate came below with the bosun and checked the branded serial numbers on the sawed-off ends against numbers on a long sheet. Slim recognized the paper as one of the manifests he'd seen in the lumber office in Wauna. After the tallying had been completed, the butt blocks were thrown into a dark corner of the closed-in deck and the shortened timbers were braced and lashed to keep them from shifting into a rolling sea. Slim thought about confiding his suspicions to Ioway, but dismissed them as a figment of his imagination. Samson had gone about the task as though it were routine and there was nothing in the bosun's manner to indicate otherwise.

At the end of the third day the timbers stowed over the tops of number five hold had been cleared off, leaving only the two eight-foot loads on either side of the open hatch. Again pallet slings and cargo nets dipped into the gaping maw and came up filled with cases and sacks. Little by little the confusion of cargo lowered, until the first level of the 'tween decks had been cleared and the crew was called to remove the wooden hatches that covered the dark abyss of the lower hold. In another two days that space was cleared of most of its cargo, revealing the rounded top of the steel housing that ran down the length of the hold, forming an enclosed alley in which the great propeller shaft rotated.

It was a week before the *Tropic Trader* was ready to sail again. They cast off at noon on the seventh day and headed down the river for Port Chalmers. The big whaling ship was still in dry dock, and several British freighters, which had arrived during the past few days, were loading produce destined for England. Slim recognized one of them as the motorship *Challenger,* which had been tied up next to the *Tropic Trader* in Wellington. He had visited aboard her then, and had traded magazines and cigarettes with several of her crew. She'd carried a few passengers and Slim remembered the flurry of excitement that had run through the fo'c'sle when someone had spread the rumor that among the passengers was a troupe of English chorus girls bound for Australia. He smiled as he remembered, too, that the "troupe of girls" had turned out to be the somewhat overripe peroxide blond wife and partner of a small-time juggler who played the fringes of the Empire's vaudeville circuits. This had not deterred the eager Warndahl from a series of inventions, one of which concerned an alleged affair with a lady juggler—while she was juggling—and the other with a girl acrobat who could bend double and place the soles of her feet on the top of her head, which, according to the lascivious Swede, presented a number of unusual advantages.

Chips had listened reluctantly with the others and had finally risen in disgust and blasted the man with some biting sarcasm. "Warndahl, either you're the greatest cocksman in the world—which I doubt—or you're the sickest —which I think! The next thing we know you'll be tellin' us how ya tied yer cock around the mast to keep from being washed overboard in a storm, causin' you to miss a chance to screw a passin' mermaid!"

The men had guffawed at the carpenter's barb and the Swede had assumed an injured air. "The sonuvabitch! He's done worse'n I have! He's just too fuckin' phony to admit it!" But Chips had made his point and the man was temporarily silenced.

Headed southwest again, the old tramp ran a few miles offshore on a course laid to the tiny fishing village of Bluff.

Clinging to a narrow hem of flat land that skirted barren hills, it was one of the most dismal ports that Slim had seen. They unloaded a few cases of general cargo from the small number three hold, just aft of the bridge. Slim checked the cargo out and noticed that it was mostly engine and machinery parts for the fleet of oyster draggers who worked in Foveaux Strait between the southern tip of New Zealand and Stewart Island. These rough, dismal waters that lay only slightly north of the same latitude as Cape Horn were the southern entrance to the Tasman Sea and some of the richest fishing and oystering grounds in the world. Several of the men who had been in Bluff and nearby Invercargill told fantastic fish stories of blue cod taken on bent nails and pork rind, so eager were they to swallow any bait.

Again Warndahl rose to the occasion with a devastating adventure which began when his ship had once laid alongside the oyster fleet at Bluff's lone dock. He told of eating three dozen of the giant raw oysters sprinkled with catsup and of their aphrodisiac effect and the calamity that had been caused when the crew ranged ashore in search of relief. According to the Swede, the population of less than a thousand had fled to their homes and barricaded their women inside. The fruitless foraging ended in a roaring binge in the little two-story Bay View Hotel, which was still advertised as the "most southerly hotel in the world." Warndahl sadly admitted that the outcome had been disappointing to most of them, with the exception of himself and another shipmate, who had gone to the hills and had taken turns holding a reluctant ewe. For this fabrication Rusty had threatened to swear off mutton forever and have the man committed to a "nut house." The rest of the crew had agreed. They loathed the vile-mouthed A.B., but they were bored and he fascinated them with the appalling scope of his depravity. In a society that could be tolerated for long only by the most insensate, and with his own roots deep in its filth, Warndahl was one of its most flourishing examples.

Slim came off day work at five and changed into fresh clothes. He decided to find food ashore, if possible, and headed toward the lone main street that paralleled the waterfront. Turning to his right as he left the pier, he walked along the drab shops, made dingier and more melancholy by the cold, low-hanging clouds, and came to the Bay View Hotel. He paused before the little building, confused by its double entrance, and finally chose the door that opened into the flattened corner of the cement structure. The first floor had been ornamented to simulate large stone blocks. Stepping inside, he found himself in a small bar. Several men were drinking and his heart sank when he saw that one of them was Warndahl.

Thinking he hadn't been seen, he turned to leave, but the A.B. called to him. "Hey, lover-boy! Where ya goin'?"

Slim hated the nickname. He also hated being trapped into spending any time ashore with the Swede. Most of the others avoided the man and made no effort to conceal their contempt by refusing to accept his drinks or offers to look for women.

Slim stopped in the door. "I'm looking for a place to eat. I don't feel like drinking."

Warndahl left the bar and came over to him. "This is it, sweetheart—best food in town!" Turning, he called loudly to the woman behind the bar. "Fix up some food for my boy here, will ya? Give him the best ya got. He's a special friend of mine!" Taking Slim by the arm, he steered him across the little room. The boy wanted to pull away but hesitated to show his dislike for the man in front of the others. None of them were from the ship. They appeared to be local workers and dredgemen—quiet fellows, drinking and speaking easily among themselves. When Warndahl had called to the boy they looked around, then returned to their conversations. It was obvious to Slim that the Swede had been drinking for a while and that his efforts to inject himself in their conversations had been rebuffed. Warndahl's nearly empty glass stood well apart from the others, who had moved to the end of the bar.

With his grubby hand still holding Slim's upper arm in a grip intended to convey determined friendliness, Warndahl fished a ten-shilling note out of his left pants pocket. Shoving it toward the woman who was in conversation with the men, he held up two fingers. "Let's have two more beers!"

Slim pulled his arm away. "Look, Vic, I don't feel like drinking. I just want to get something to eat."

Warndahl smiled and shook his head vigorously. "Nobody eats with Vic Warndahl unless he drinks with him first! I'm buyin', kid. Come on, drink up!" He looked at the woman. "Hurry up with those beers, cutie, the kid's dyin' of thirst!"

The plain little woman looked at the Swede without humor and began to fill the glasses. In the mirror Slim could see the men at the end of the bar interrupt their conversation and turn slightly. There were five of them— medium-built, wiry men whose clothes bore the dark smudges of coal. They wore soiled caps and beneath their rough jackets were heavy black knitted sweaters with collars high around their throats. Their faces were curious and not unfriendly. Placing the two glasses in front of Warndahl, the woman took the ten-shilling note and turned to a drawer to make change.

The Swede picked up the near-empty glass and drained it, then raised the fresh one. "Come on, sweetheart, let's drink it up good!" He smiled and reached down, giving the boy's backside an affectionate little squeeze.

Slim twisted his body away and there was no mistaking the annoyance in his voice. "Look, Vic, I told you—I'm not drinking. I don't feel like it. Thanks just the same."

He started to leave, but the A.B. caught him by the arm again and turned him roughly back to the bar. The smile he had worn had changed to a smirk. The forced good-fellowship in his voice was gone and the words that started coming from his ugly lips were edged with menace. "You're not drinkin', huh? You mean you're not drinkin' with Warndahl, don't you?"

Slim looked at the man's bleary, washed-out eyes. They were mean, like the inflamed eyes of a dangerous boar. He saw for the first time that they were very much like the bosun's; the same cruelness gleamed in them. Suddenly he felt for the Swede what he'd felt for the bosun that day off the Columbia River. He wanted to erase the face—to make it disappear. He knew Warndahl could see the growing feeling of loathing on his face. He looked him directly in the eye for a long moment, then turned again and began walking toward the door.

"Hey, kid." The Swede's voice was low. "You know what I think? I'm beginning to think you don't like your old shipmate." As he continued, his voice grew louder. "You know how I can tell, lover-boy? By the expression you get on your face when I'm talkin'. You look like you smelled a fart!" He spat out the last words as Slim reached the door. "You know something else I think, shit-heel? I think you're a queero! I think you and your ass-hole buddy, Ioway, are corn-holin' together. That's what I think. And so do a lot of the guys! What do you think of *that*, sweetheart?" A laugh started to explode from him— the same staccato bursts Slim had heard during that first seasick encounter with the man months before. It had infuriated him then, as sick as he was, and each time since, its maniacal quality had filled him with more revulsion. It struck him in the back now, like a blow. The vile accusation that preceded the laughter had little or no meaning, just the galling, taunting sound was all that mattered, and suddenly Slim decided to do something about it. As he turned, his body was filled with a strange coldness—the coldness of a man about to commit a premeditated crime, the coldness he'd felt as he aimed his rifle at a rattler. Looking at Warndahl, he smiled an open, obvious smile, but what the Swede saw in the boy's eyes erased the smile from his own face.

"You want to drink, Vic? Okay, let's drink!" He covered the distance to the bar in three long steps and picked up the full glass. Holding it out, as for a toast, he looked at the Swede. "Come, Vic, pick up your glass. I thought you wanted to drink?"

He smiled as the A.B.'s expression turned wary and he slowly reached for the other glass. Raising it uncertainly, he clinked it and carried it to his lips. His eyes didn't leave the boy's as he swallowed the first mouthful. Slim let the rich beer flow into his mouth until it was full, then, without warning, he compressed his cheeks and spat the whole lot into Warndahl's face.

Before the A.B. realized what had happened, the boy put the mug on the bar and drove a left and right hand into the ugly face. He felt the fists hit the cheek bones and he felt the taut snap in his own shoulders as frustration and weeks of loathing suddenly unleashed a lashing force through his arms. As Warndahl reeled back, dropping his beer, Slim followed, sending home hooking lefts and snapping, driving rights that traveled with a deadly rhythmic purpose. Warndahl sprawled backward into a chair. It collapsed under him and he crashed in a stunned heap on the floor, his head beneath a square table. He lay still for a moment, then raised himself up on one elbow, his mouth hanging open and blood trickling from a bad cut on the left side of his lower lip. Slim backed off and waited for him to get to his feet. The men at the bar scrambled to the safety of a doorway, and the woman ran out of the room.

"All right, Vic, get up! We're not finished drinking yet!" Slim barely recognized his own voice. It was cold with quiet rage and he felt good—better than he'd ever felt. His arms were strong and free, his brain was crystal-clear, and every muscle in his body was eager to finish what had been started. He wanted to kill this sprawling, slobbering mess of vileness that lay on his ass, blinking at him. *"Get up!"* He kicked the sole of Warndahl's shoe. "Get up, Vic, and let's do a little more drinking! Come on, sweetheart!" The words came from his lips like a curse.

The Swede shook his head and touched his hand to his bleeding lip. Then the daze began to leave his piglike little eyes and hatred inflamed them. An odd grin twisted his mouth and he spoke softly. "Kid, you just made a bad mistake. I'm gonna kill you fer that!"

Slim stood over him and waited for the man to get to his feet. Pulling himself up, he stood uncertainly for a moment, shaking the fuzziness from his brain. His hands were open and poised to grapple, for Warndahl, like most

279

rough-and-tumble fighters, knew little of the science of using fists. He moved slowly toward the boy, and the effects of the alcohol seemed to have disappeared.

When he was just out of range of Slim's arms, he suddenly kicked at the boy. Slim sensed rather than saw the foot coming and, in the fraction of a second it took to travel, he pulled his pelvis back slightly and the toe grazed the front of his trousers. He heard a roar of protest go up from the men who had moved back to the end of the bar. At the same time he saw Warndahl's big open hand descending, like a blunt blade, toward the base of his neck. Instinctively his arm went up and the blow landed on the thinly covered bone of his left forearm. It was like a blow from an ax, and all feeling left it. Slim backed away a step and, as he did, the Swede, with a roar of rage, charged at him.

The boy waited, arms at his sides, until the man was almost on him; then he dropped suddenly and let Warndahl's stomach hit his left shoulder. Reaching out for the legs and heaving upright at the same time, he threw the big sailor over his head. He fell to the floor like a log and lay still for a moment. Suddenly he scrambled to his feet again. There was no method in him now—just the undisciplined, destructive urge of an enraged animal seeking to destroy its tormentor. Slim backed off a step or two and waited for the new charge. It came immediately. He let the stocky Swede get almost to him, then stepped to the side and drew himself up like a *torero* avoiding a charging bull. As the man's outflung arm reached in vain for him, he turned to his right slightly and his long leg shot out, entangling Warndahl's feet.

The off-balance momentum carried the roaring Swede into the tables at the far end of the room. He turned and stood there, heaving, and the anger came from his throat in growling sobs. He looked around for a weapon—something to lay his hands on—anything to strike with or to throw. Slim saw the man's burning eyes come to rest on one of the heavy glass steins at the end of the bar. For the first time he felt a flash of fear. He knew that as long as the heavier but far more awkward A.B. kept charging he was in no great trouble. But if the man should hurt him with a thrown glass and close with him, he'd be lucky to get out with his life.

His own partially filled stein was on the bar, a couple of feet to his right. His arm shot out and grabbed it, deliberately spilling its contents. "All right, Warndahl, go ahead, get it!" He nodded to the other glass.

The Swede stood uncertainly. He flashed a quick glance at the potential weapon out of the corner of his eye, without turning his head from the deck boy. Slim knew that if he threw first and missed, Warndahl would have the only weapon left—not just one, but five of them. Warndahl knew it, too. He knew the five-to-one odds worked in his favor and he knew that if he could force the boy to throw first he'd probably be able to kill him. That's what he wanted to do. After all, there were plenty of witnesses that the kid had spit beer in his face—provocation enough for a fight, provocation enough to kill a man in self-defense.

He smirked at the boy. "Okay, ya fuckin' fairy! Let's see how good your aim is! Go on—throw it! Throw it— and when ya do, I'm gonna rip yer throat right out of yer long skinny neck!" His voice raised to a roaring crescendo, egging the boy on, trying to force him into a move.

Slim stood poised and ready. He could hear the sound of Warndahl's antagonizing filth and he could hear other words running through his head like some unseen person whispering and coaching him from the side: "Keep your eye on the ball! Keep your eye on the glass. If you watch it, you can duck it. You have to use your head now. Don't make any mistakes."

Warndahl stood watching him, smiling and running his tongue across the split lip. He spat the crimson saliva on the floor. "See that blood? For every drop I spilt, you're gonna spill a gallon!" He pressed his mouth gently with the back of his left hand and looked at the red blot it left.

The room was absolutely quiet, there was no sound save Warndahl's heavy breathing. The five coal-smudged dredgemen watched from behind the rounded end of the bar. Slim was barely aware of them. The whispering voice continued to speak: "He's mad—you're cool. Outwait him, kid, outwait him. He'll make his move in a minute. He hasn't got brains enough to stay still. Keep calm—keep still. Outwait him—outwait him——"

Slim's eyes didn't leave the Swede, who stood with his feet apart, his arms down and out a bit from his sides, like a wrestler. "So you're not going to throw it, huh? You're gonna wait until I make a move, huh? Well, all right, ya fuckin' stuck-up punk, I'll make a move!" His arms reached out suddenly and he stepped toward the glasses on the end of the bar.

Slim waited until his hand nearly reached them, then his

281

own long right arm went back. With eyes boring along the target line, he sighted and threw with all his strength. The heavy mug traveled like a rifle slug and exploded in the midst of the standing glasses. In the same instant Slim leaped along the bar and aimed a whipping right at Warndahl's bloody jaw. He felt the crash of his knuckles on the chin and he felt the bone in the Swede's face resist the blow, almost as though it had come to meet it. The boy's left hand swung in a looping hook and crashed into the Swede's temple, and the right crossed again and smashed into the jaw. For an instant the man stood still, arms hanging limply at his side; then he slowly collapsed to the floor.

Slim stood looking down at him and had trouble breathing. He felt as if a giant band had been squeezed around his chest; as if someone were trying to force the ribs to collapse beneath his broad, lean shoulders. And then he heard the carpenter's voice.

"Okay, kid, that's enough! He's had it." The voice was gentle and sounded very near, and then Slim realized Chips had seen the last of the battle and had let him go on until it was finished. Now he had his big arms around the boy's chest, pulling him away.

Slim felt weak and fought to keep his body from sagging. Every ounce of strength and concentration had gone into those last few minutes. They seemed timeless now and unreal. Warndahl, unconscious on the floor, bleeding badly from the mouth and from a cut on the cheekbone, looked unreal, like a defeated villain in one of the movies he'd seen at home. Even his own part seemed like something in a dream, no more real than the imaginary things he and Edye had done in the vivid fantasies he'd shared with her during the long nights at sea. Only Chips seemed real. But there was something new in his voice.

"Order a couple of whiskies. I want to look at this mess down here——" He walked to Warndahl and bent over him. Reaching down with one big hand, he grabbed the A.B.'s coat front and hauled him to a chair. He put the unconscious Swede in it as one would lift a sack of grain. Propping him against the dark wall, he slapped the man's face between his huge hands. After a moment Warndahl opened his eyes and blinked stupidly. A groan escaped his lips as he tried to turn his head.

The carpenter straightened up and watched him for a moment, then returned to the bar. "He's all right. He'll live, worse luck!"

The woman had returned to the room and stood at the far end of the bar with the men, looking at Warndahl in disbelief.

Chips called to her. "Ma'am, if the boy hasn't upset things too much around here, can we please have a couple of shots of Canadian rye?"

The woman looked at him uncertainly but made no effort to move.

Chips smiled reassuringly. "It's all right, ma'am. It's over now. There won't be any more trouble. I'll pay for the mess here, too." He indicated the broken chair and the fragments of glass glistening on the bar and the floor.

The woman looked uncertainly at the carpenter and then to the customers. One of the fellows nodded. "Go on, Effie, give 'im a whisky. I daresay 'e needs it after that go!" The others mumbled in agreement and the woman took a bottle from the back bar and poured two shots.

"Better pour another one for *him*." The carpenter jerked his head in the direction of Warndahl. Taking the whisky, he handed one to Slim and held the other up. "Down the hatch, mate! You earned it!"

Slim looked at the small glass for a moment and could feel it start to tremble in his hand. He raised it quickly and gulped its burning contents before Chips could see.

The carpenter grinned. "Don't worry about the shakes, kiddo. That happens to all of us!" He tossed down the contents and motioned for two more.

Before the woman could comply, the front door burst open and a uniformed policeman entered.

"Now then, wot's goin' on 'ere?" He closed the door and stood looking around in the gloom. Everything appeared quiet and he was puzzled.

Chips turned to him and smiled. "It's too late, officer, but ya missed a hell of a good fight!" He put his arm over Slim's shoulder. "Meet the new world's champion!"

The policeman suddenly saw the Swede slumped and bleeding in the chair. "Look 'ere now, wot's all this?" He walked over to the seaman and inspected him closely; then his eyes traveled to the collapsed chair and the floor strewn with jagged pieces of glass.

The woman answered his question. "It's like I told you, 'Arry. That one"—she indicated Warndahl—"come in 'ere and started drinkin' and after a time the young one 'ere" —she caught her breath and inclined her head toward Slim—" 'e come in, too, and the one in the chair tried to get 'im to drink. The boy didn't want to, then the bloody

283

one—I beg yer pardon—begin using such a filthy mouth as I 'aven't 'eard in all me days! And the young chap 'ere took a drink and spit it straight in 'is bloomin' face. And if you ask me, it served 'im quite properly right, too!"

The policeman listened to the woman, who gasped for breath as she spoke, then walked over to the boy. "Is that the way it went, laddie?"

Slim blinked and the whisky still burned in his throat. "Yes, sir——"

Chips lit two cigarettes and handed him one. As he reached for it, he saw his right knuckles for the first time. The skin had been pushed back along their length and tiny little flecks of blood tried to force their way through the raw hide. They felt cold. He was also aware of his left hand for the first time. The whole forearm felt numb and some of the skin was gone from the knuckles, too.

The officer waited for him to take a long drag. "Well, I guess we could cart you two off for disturbin' the peace, but we don't 'ave a very comfortable gaol 'ere in Bluff. Suppose we do this. Suppose we just say we'll settle with the nice lady 'ere for the nuisance to her furniture and glasses and forget the 'ole thing—mindin' you, of course, that it don't 'appen again?"

Chips smiled and reached in his pocket. "Thanks, friend! This kid's a deck boy on the *Tropic Trader*. He's a good one, too." Pulling out a pound note, he laid it on the bar and turned to the woman. "Will this take care of the damages, ma'am?"

The woman blinked at the big carpenter, then looked down at the money. "A pound? Oh, it won't come to that! The glasses are only sixpence apiece and the chair was a bit rickety, anyway. I'd say 'alf of it would be more than enough!"

"Okay, ma'am, half of it is yours, and five drinks come out of the rest." Turning to the policeman, he added, "And if he'll have one, make it six!"

The man looked at the bottle uncertainly, then took off his helmet and tucked it under his arm. "Well, I thank you, sailor. I'm not against a bit of whisky now an' then" —he indicated his uniform—"but these are not exactly my drinkin' clothes—if you know wot I mean!"

Chips smiled and raised a second glass. "These are *my* drinkin' clothes, so here's to His Britannic Majesty!" He tossed the drink off in one swallow and smacked his lips with appreciation.

At the other end of the room Warndahl stirred and sat up painfully.

The carpenter called to him: "There's a shot on the table, Warndahl—better take it!"

The Swede turned uncomprehending eyes to the glass and looked at it for a moment. Then, reaching over, he lifted it to his mouth and drank it.

Chips watched until he put down the glass, then walked over and stood looking down at him. His voice was low and deadly earnest. "Vic, can you hear me all right?"

The bloodied A.B. looked up at him, then nodded his head.

"Good! Because I want you to listen to every word." He paused to make sure Warndahl was registering. "You got beat in a fair fight that *you* started. You got what every one of us on that ship has been hoping you'd get ever since you first started shootin' off your rotten mouth. If you ever so much as look wrong at that kid again, I personally am going to beat you until the coronor won't be able to tell what it was that got killed! Y'understand?"

The Swede sat slumped in the chair, staring at the floor. He made no sign that he'd heard. Suddenly the carpenter reached down and grabbed a fistful of his coat. Jerking him to his feet, he asked the question again. "I asked you: 'Do you understand?'"

Warndahl nodded his head once and stared at the big hands holding him erect.

"Okay—now get out of here and stay out—and stay away from the kid!" He pushed the A.B. from him and waited.

The Swede teetered unsteadily, then walked slowly across the silent room. He paused at the door held open by the uniformed policeman and stepped out into the night. He had not turned his head when he passed, and Slim had watched him with a growing feeling that he didn't quite understand. It was a feeling close to pity.

– 24 –

The *Tropic Trader* sailed at dawn the following morning and by late afternoon was eighty miles out into the Tasman Sea, bound for Hobart, capital city of the island of Tasmania.

The weather was changeable, with gusts whipping the tops off the seas and whistling through the ratlines. Banded alto-cumulus clouds corrugated the high vault of the sky, and near the horizon the backlight of the setting sun touched their edges with gleaming silver.

Slim had shared his watch with Warndahl as usual, and the third mate had noticed the abrasions on the Swede's face, his badly cut lower lip, and Slim's iodine-stained knuckles. He had given Ioway the keys to the sick bay and told him to get some medication for the A.B. When Slim had relieved the wheel after the first two hours, Holst had asked a question. Like most of them, it had come unexpectedly.

"Who's fault was it *this* time, Fredericks?"

Slim had answered without hesitation. "His, sir."

"Where'd it happen?"

"In the hotel bar, sir."

"Who won?"

"I did, sir."

"He's heavier than you. How'd you manage it?"

"I got lucky, I guess, sir."

"Could you—'get lucky' again?"

"With him? Yes, sir."

"How do you know?"

"He gets too mad. He doesn't use his head."

"Not good to lose your temper then, is that it?"

"That's right, sir."

"Is it all settled?"

"As far as I'm concerned, it's settled—if he lays off."

"Do you think he will?"

"I think so, sir."

286

"Why?"

Slim hadn't wanted to say anything about the carpenter being present, but from Holst's questioning he wondered if perhaps the word had got to the bridge and the third mate had simply used the obvious injuries as an excuse to open the questioning. He had taken a moment before he answered.

"Well, sir, Chips came in at the end of it—and told Warndahl that he'd better not make any more trouble."

"Was that the way he put it?"

"Those weren't his exact words, sir, but I think—— Well, anyway, Vic got the idea——"

"Knowing Chips, I imagine he did! Did he help you any?"

"No, sir, not during the fight. Warndahl was out cold when I saw him. He pulled me away after it was over."

Holst had been staring straight ahead out the wheelhouse window while he'd been questioning the boy. He had turned and walked over to the compass before he spoke again, and when he did they were the last words spoken during the watch. "Where'd you learn to fight?"

"I never did, sir." His answer had caused Holst to turn and look at him sharply. Slim had added, "I mean . . . I never had real lessons, sir. When I was a kid we used to box and wrestle on the ranch, and I learned a few tricks from the wranglers. They're sort of dirty tricks, in case a guy doesn't fight fair."

The mate had smiled and mulled the boy's words in his mind before his next question. "Did Warndahl fight fair?"

"No, sir."

"Did you?"

"I wanted to, sir——"

"But you had to fight his way, is that it?"

"Yes, sir."

"And you beat him?" The last words had been spoken to himself. Holst had checked the compass once more and gone out on the port wing bridge. He had stayed there until Mr. Samson had come up to relieve him.

It was dark when Slim finished supper. Nobody in the messroom made any reference to the fight, but there was a new note in their voices as they spoke with him of the ports that lay ahead. The Swede had not appeared and the talk was noticeably cleaner. Chips had told them about the encounter and, knowing something of his enthusiasm for yarning, Slim suspected the details the carpenter had personally missed seeing had been filled in with some colorful fiction. The cards were broken out and the boy sat in. Before, he'd always felt like an amateur and the men had watched him carefully, expecting mistakes. But now it was different. When he lost a hand nobody said, "Tough luck, kid, you shoulda dropped out when ya seen his jack showin'." Now he played each hand as best he could and took his winnings when he could. He was sure it was beginner's luck, but at the end of the night, even with Hammer in the game, Slim was money ahead—good, solid British sterling—four pounds, six shillings of it, worth twenty dollars, ninety-seven and two tenths cents in American currency. The carpenter grinned broadly when Slim raked in the money and left for his 4 A.M. trick at the wheel.

On his way to the bridge Slim stopped back in the messroom. Folding a ten-shilling note, he tossed it up the table to the carpenter. "Chips, here's the money I owe you from last night. Thanks a lot!" Before the big Norwegian could protest, the boy disappeared up the companionway.

He took the first two-hour lookout alone in the eyes of the ship, and the time passed quickly as his thoughts ranged over the events of the past twenty-four hours, then turned to Edye and the possibility of more letters from her. He'd read those first ones till he knew them by heart; especially the third one, the shortest of them all: "Suppose you get *this* letter first? Then you'll really think I'm an idiot! In which case I might just as well be one and tell you that I love you—very, very much, Lord help me!"

The remembering did wonderful things and he could almost see her pixie-like loveliness and hear her lilting voice —laughing a lot, mocking him, threatening, sorrowing— and knowing the effect of the sorrow on him and loving him, too; for, from the very first, the unexplainable affection had made itself felt and had shone through everything she'd said. He'd felt the same thing, but was less gifted at conveying it to her, and now he hoped he'd been able to do so in his letters, though he still felt a bit like a schoolboy when he saw "love" written out on the paper.

And in the midst of his thoughts of Edye, Marge arrived to torment him and the memory excited him, too, and for a time—as it often did—the happiness that was Edye gave way to the longing that was Marge.

The wind hit hard against his face in the black night and back over his right shoulder he could see the dim lunar glow through the threadbare eastern edge of the cloudy canopy. Out ahead, nothing but the night—the unpredictable, buffeting gusts—and the ghostly manes of whitecaps riding full tilt into the black sides of the ship.

When Slim answered the faintly heard bell, with the deeper tolling from the bow, the call of his muffled voice trailed off downwind, unheard on the bridge. The lights were bright at the mastheads and occasionally Holst's flaring match reddened the dead black of the wheelhouse windows.

Warndahl relieved him on lookout and Slim noted that the third mate called him to the bridge before the Swede was sent forward. He left no chance for an incident in the dark that might reopen the trouble. Slim was not worried about the possibility. He knew that if anything happened to him on watch that could possibly be connected to the A.B., Chips wouldn't hesitate to charge the man openly with murder. He felt certain Warndahl was not fool enough to try. Knowing that Holst was also in possession of the facts further eased his mind, and he gave the Swede little thought.

When he turned in at half-past four in the morning there was no sign of the approaching sun. He looked for it, back along the tenuous ribbons of boiling foam that lined the edges of the wake. Up ahead the high clouds lost themselves in deepness of the night that gave no hint of the nature of the new day. But the barometer did, and the first mate watched it fall and noted its reading in the log.

At seven o'clock Mr. Peterson made an unusual round of the decks, probing with the slender yellow eye of a flashlight at battens and wedges and coils of line and at turnbuckles on the after deckload. At eight o'clock he worked out the dead-reckoning position with the first mate and took the command of the *Tropic Trader*. He went about his duties with the usual meticulous attention to detail. He probably would have, even had he known it was to be the last sea watch he would ever stand.

– 25 –

The crew was turned out on deck early, and the bosun set all hands securing hatch covers, rewedging battens, tightening turnbuckles, and making certain everything was shipshape for the storm that was looming ahead.

Sunrise had confirmed the warning given by the rapidly falling barometer. The glass tumbled from 30.02 inches to 29.82 inches of mercury in less than six hours, and the wind that had been blowing steadily from the south for the past twenty-four hours had hauled around a bit toward the east. It was numbing cold on deck, even with wool watch sweaters under heavy work shirts. The clinging oilskins transmitted the chill of the Antarctic blast through to the skin. As the men huddled in the cramped canyons, between the after deckload and the coamings of number five hold, sheets of white spray exploded against the rusty side plates and shot upward thirty feet to have their tops ripped off by the wind and hurled down across the timbers onto the deck. Torrents gushed out of the long cracks between the timbers and slender, salty streams dripped off the vibrating chains that ran overhead across the top of the load.

As the wind hauled around more to the east the seas began striking the ship on the port quarter, and the hull reacted with a curious waddling motion as the stern squatted and sidled into the lead-gray valleys between the rolling mountains of foam-streaked water.

Samson and Holst, dressed in storm gear, hugged the lee of the main deck and descended to the open well deck around number four hold. Motioning to the bosun, Samson ordered the stowed timbers brought out from the shelter deck. Slim turned to with the others and, two men to a piece, they lifted the ten-foot lengths of 12 by 12's and laid them out along the deck plates. A barrier was to be built across the forward ends of the remaining load to keep it from sliding forward and loosening the chains. The task was nearly impossible for there was nothing to brace to but the main deck bulkhead a good thirty feet forward. The timbers had to be butted end to end along the deck, extending aft to the face of the load, until they met the wall of uprights. Then, lighter 6 by 12 diagonals were braced from the deck timbers up to the top of the barricade. There was no chance to secure the entire face of the load. It was a poor job, but the best possible under the circumstances.

When Slim left the deck at eleven-thirty to get some food before standing his wheel watch, Holst told him to eat in the petty officers' mess amidships. The steward was unable to get hot food aft. The boy stuck his head in the galley and passed the word to Chico, then stepped into the athwartship passageway and went into the messroom. He'd only caught glimpses of it before, but now he found that it was not unlike the crew's eating quarters, except smaller and considerably cleaner. Bolo, the second mess boy, brought him his food.

The rolling had steadily worsened and he had to brace his feet and hold the plate from sliding along the length of the oilcloth table. The coffee in his half-filled cup slopped over. He wondered about Ioway, who had been looking green around the gills all morning. In the enclosed little messroom with no chance to see out, he knew the country lad, lately turned sailor, would have a bad time. He wondered how Sparks was making out, and in the midst of his wondering the radio operator poked his head around the corner.

"Jesus! Do you mean to say you can eat that crap in weather like this?"

Slim looked up and nodded vigorously, his cheeks filled with an immense half-chewed chunk of gristled boiled beef. Sparks sat down heavily and balanced a filled coffee mug off the table to keep it from spilling. He sipped at the black stuff and looked at the boy's emptying plate with a baleful eye. His thin, stooped body, encased in the old school sweater, instinctively stayed plumb as the table and bench tilted dangerously with each roll. The look changed to woeful wonderment as Slim bolted a square of half-stale plain cake and washed it down with the last gulp of coffee.

"If you get sick and have to puke up those chunks, boy, they're gonna break your neck the hard way—from the inside! Oh, to be young again and have cast-iron guts!"

Slim laughed at him and looked at his watch. He still had ten minutes to get to the bridge. "What do you mean, 'be young again'? You've gotta few good years left—before they have to shoot you!"

Sparks blinked at him thoughtfully. "I'll pay *you* to shoot me right now. How much do you want?"

Slim grinned at a sudden thought. "Why don't you ask Stokes? He'd do it for nothing!"

The radio operator looked dejected. "Oh well, maybe I'll live through it—I always have!" He sipped the muddy black fluid and stared absently at the table cover. After a moment he lifted his eyes and spoke. "This isn't going to get any better, Slim. I've been workin' a couple of ships around here. The *West Islip* is north of us about two hundred miles and she's beginning to get it too. There's a limey collier hove-to west of us. Afraid his coal will shift and founder him. Doesn't look too good, m'boy."

Slim got up and pulled on his oilskins. His hip boots were turned and folded down below his knees. He hated to stand the two-hour watch in them. They were heavy and chafted him, but he'd need them on the wing bridge for lookout.

"One thing I can't understand, Sparks. Why the devil do they unload everything in the forward holds and leave almost all the other cargo aft? Geez, our bow is sticking up in the air like a canoe with a fat Indian in the back!"

Sparks came close to smiling at the picture of the stern-heavy tramp. "I'll tell ya how that happens, my observant friend. It happens because these old tubs never know where their next cargo is comin' from. Consequently the mates never know where to stow the stuff. If they put a cargo for Auckland in the bottom of the hold and stow on top of it for Adelaide, how the hell are they gonna get it out, if Auckland turns out to be the first port of call? It's the goddamnedest puzzle you can imagine, and I'm glad that radio operators don't have to solve it!"

Slim immediately understood the problem this posed for Peterson, whose responsibility it was to allocate the cargo to the different holds and make certain it was properly stowed. Apparently the deckload had gone on first, because it was the first cargo the owners had been able to get for the *Tropic Trader*. Inversely, the cases of gasoline had been put on last for the same reason. And now the old tramp was laboring in a heavy quartering sea, her bow drawing a scant six feet of water and her stern still deep with deck cargo. Slim understood that the rolling was exaggerated, because the center of gravity had been raised by the high afterload and the generally shallower draft. She behaved like top-heavy wagonloads of hay on an unlevel country road. He'd seen many of them turn over in a twisting rut. There were some pretty deep ruts out there, too, he thought, and Sparks had been thinking the same thing.

"I'll tell you one thing, buddy-boy. I'll be damn glad when we get the timber off this tub and she levels up again. You should feel her swing up in the shack! It's like Coney Island!" He got up from the bench and turned toward the door. "Come on up when ya get off watch. You can hold my head!"

At four o'clock Hammer relieved him and he left the bridge. He stuck his head in the galley and joked with the two smiling cooks about the high quality of the food in the petty officers' mess, then turned the after end of the deckhouse and climbed topside to visit Sparks.

There was no answer when Slim knocked at the heavy varnished weather door. He waited a moment, then went around to the window on the portside of the shack and looked in. Sparks was sitting with the headphones clamped to his head, his eyes squinted against a smarting plume of smoke that rose from a short butt and washed against his cheekbone and forehead. His head was cocked slightly and bent in deep concentration as he scribbled. He started when he saw the boy's face pressed against the window and motioned to him to come in. Even though he was sheltered from the brunt of the gale by the port lifeboats, Slim had to lean hard to make headway. It took all his strength to hold the door open long enough to let him squeeze through. Inside, he slipped out of his weather gear and pulled off his boots. The cement deck felt good against his heavy wool socks. He lit a smoke and waited for the radio operator to finish. The little shack was swinging through space in a giant arc, like a stuffy nest in the topmost branches of a wind-lashed tree.

Sparks listened and wrote for a full ten minutes before he took off the receivers and hung them on the hook. He studied the messages for a time, then rewrote several words to clarify them.

Offering the paper to Slim, he said, "Here, read it and weep!" But before the boy could take the pad, he changed his mind. "I better unscramble it for you. The net of it is that a hell of a lot of ships are in trouble or tryin' to avoid it. Listen to this: The *Cape Deneb* is hove-to at Half

293

Moon Bay, with six feet of water in number one hold and smashed hatches on number two. The *Anthracite King* is sending SOS's with a shifted cargo and a twenty-three-degree list. There's nobody near enough to reach her within twenty-four hours' steaming, but the *Tahiti*'s goin' to try. There are half a dozen trawlers runnin' for Tasman Bay in Cook Strait and there's a lot of hash I can't read—too far away—but, brother, there's plenty of trouble around us!"

At no time since he'd first sailed had Slim been afraid of the possibility of a storm, but hearing Sparks read off the names of ships—very much like the *Topic Trader*—who were in trouble in these same waters, he felt his first real uneasiness. Only twice since he'd been aboard had there been even a token lifeboat drill, although one was required each week. The men hadn't bothered to swing the four big boats out on the davits so they could be lowered. But even if the crew knew what to do and the davits functioned properly, he doubted that a boat could be launched in the seas that were running.

The two sat in silence, exhaling long plumes of blue-gray smoke, each immersed in his own thoughts. Suddenly Sparks clamped the receiver on his head again. Slim had heard nothing.

"Somebody's calling right next door!" Reaching over, he flicked a switch and turned on his transmitter. In a moment he was engaged in mysterious conversation. The exchange of dots and dashes went on for several minutes, then stopped as abruptly as it had started. The radio operator turned off the equipment and replaced the headphones on the hook.

"That's the *Clarendon*. She's two miles south of us, heading for Invercargill. She says it's worse out ahead!"

"Two miles south? We ought to be able to see her!" Slim moved to the door and opened it partially against the wind. Sparks grabbed a handful of papers from the wire file basket on the desk. "Hey, you're blowin' the place apart. Either stay in or go out, will ya?"

Murmuring a small apology, Slim went out on deck and wedged himself in between the two port lifeboats. Off to the south, and just about opposite, he could see the top masts and part of the funnel of the other vessel. She appeared to be a little Australian or New Zealand coaster, about two hundred feet long and loaded to the gunwales. As Slim watched her, she raised into full view on the crest of a huge wave, then disappeared into the trough again with nothing revealed but her uppermost works. As the little vessel rose to meet the next wave broadside, she rolled so far that the boy could see the top decks of her bridge and midship deckhouse. He watched her wallowing along for several minutes, until the chill drove him back inside.

As he re-entered, Sparks raised his hands in a gesture of disgust. "I thought your corn-picking friend, Ioway, was the tourist on this trip!"

Slim looked at the radio operator and a twinkle came into his eyes. "Geez, but you're getting to be a grumpy old poop. Haven't you got any adventure left in your soul?"

Sparks mustered up something that he thought passed for a scowl. "Not a goddamn ounce on days like this! And not very much on the other days, either!"

It was five o'clock when the boy left the radio shack and went aft to the fo'c'sle. Most of the men were in the messroom, trying to drink coffee, and Hammer was working on a gambling board of some sort—a game Slim hadn't heard of, called "Chuck-a-luck." Otto and Spots had wheel watch and lookout with the chief mate. It was dark on deck. It had grown darker much earlier than usual as the sun went down behind the wall of thick black clouds that stood high on the horizon. The running lights and range lights had been lit before he'd left the bridge at four.

The only off-watch seamen who were not in the messroom were Russian John, Warndahl, and the Shiek. The others smoked and grumbled and cursed the weather and the food and the muddy, undrinkable coffee. About the coffee Chips was the most vociferous, for without a cup instantly available he suffered the only really unbearable inconvenience and deprivation possible in his well-adjusted fo'c'sle life. Slim had never seen the man in such poor spirits.

"I'll tell ya something. If that steward don't send one of them goo-goo's back here with a bag of that powdered cow shit they use for coffee, I'm gonna go up and get it myself!"

Rusty shrugged indifferently. "What good would it do ya? Ya hafta know how to take that goddamn doo-hickey apart and clean it first. Otherwise ye're just gonna get the same old tobacco juice out of it!"

Ioway, who would have sold all the coffee in ship's stores for one tall glass of fresh milk, offered another suggestion. "I'll tell ya what. If one of you guys will come along and watch for me, I'll take half a bucketful from the officers' pantry. They got good coffee there, I'll bet!"

Before anyone could take him up on his offer, the men were nearly thrown from their seats by a sudden, sickening roll that tipped over the salt and sugar containers and sent the catsup bottle rolling the length of the table.

Nothing was said for a moment, then Chips spoke and his voice was grave. "I wish to God they'd head 'er up into the weather a little more. With this stern so heavy, we're gonna get pooped by one of those big ones. We're so light forward, she ain't recoverin' fast enough."

Rusty looked at Chips and asked a useless question. "Whose bright idea was it to load out everything up forward and leave us stuck with half a deckload, for Chris' sake?"

For the first time Ioway began to suspect why the ship was behaving so badly, but he wanted to hear his suspicions confirmed. "That's kinda dangerous, huh?"

Chips smiled at the boy without humor. "No, kid, it ain't a bit dangerous. Ask John here what happened when they did that with a load of pit props bound for Cardiff." He indicated the square little A.B. by his side.

Ioway looked puzzled. "What are pit props?"

"Pit props are the timbers they use to shore up the sides of coal mines in Wales. They're heavy, like this stuff, and just as tricky to load securely."

The men waited for John to begin his narrative, but the quiet, rectangular man sat and stared into his empty coffee mug. Chips waited, too, and after a time undertook the story himself.

"He's not much for talkin' unless it's Norwegian, but I'll tell ya what happened. It was on a Limey coaster half our size, in weather like this. All of a sudden she squatted deep, took a big one over the stern, and rolled to starboard. The lashings let go and the load shifted. That was the end of her! John here hung onto one of them props for the whole night before they come out and got us."

Rusty shot a suspicious glance at the carpenter. "Got 'us'?"

Chips hadn't intended to let slip his own part in the adventure. He looked embarrassed. "Well, we shipped together on that trap. I don't want no more of that!" Indicating the deckload with a thumb aimed over his shoulder, he shook his big head unhappily. "I don't like the looks of that load face where the shorings are. A good sea over the deck could lift all them braces. They're the ones that got all the strain, too."

The men talked quietly and from time to time fell suddenly silent as they braced themselves against a deep roll. Through the heavy glass of the closed port, Slim could see black water cover it momentarily when the ship lay over to the starboard.

For the past several minutes the boy thought he'd heard the rumble of distant thunder. He heard it again as the ship heeled over to port and wallowed down into another of the deep, restless valleys. He turned his head and looked toward the passageway, knowing that outside sound would come down the companionway and echo in the short steel area leading to the messroom. After a moment he rose from the bench and squeezed past Rusty and Ioway.

Chips looked up at him curiously.

"Where you goin', Slim?"

The boy answered without looking. "Topside. I want to see what's going on. I keep thinking I hear thunder."

Chips waved his hand in a belittling gesture. "There's no thunder around here this time of year."

The words were hardly out of his mouth when Slim heard the distant rumbling again. This time they all heard it. It seemed to fill the hull.

Chips listened intently for a moment, then rose quickly from the bench and joined Slim. "Come on, I'll go up there with you."

Together they climbed the narrow companion ladder and opened the steel weather door against the full blast of the quartering gale. Since Slim had come below, the sea had made up noticeably, and even in the dark he could see the boiling white tops of the waves as they came rushing diagonally toward the high counter. He felt the edge of fear again as he watched a big mountain of foaming water rush out of the darkness, stand poised for an instant, as though making up its mind to crash down on the poop deck, then disappear a few inches below the scupper rails as the stern rose slowly to meet it.

Again the deck plunged down and tilted hard over to the port, and again came the rolling sound of distant thunder. The intermittent rain that had been driving almost parallel to the surface of the sea had stopped momentarily, so the two men moved forward and looked over the deckload. They hung on and their feet slid beneath them as the *Tropic Trader* squatted and rolled again, and this time the distant noise made both of them stop breathing. It was not the thunder of a seasonal squall, but the muffled rumble of

297

cargo shifting and moving below decks in number five hold.

The same horrified thought struck both men at the same time and Chips bellowed it into the wind. "Jesus Christ Almighty! It's them drums of dynamite. They've carried away!" He turned toward the companionway for an uncertain instant, then bellowed at Slim, "Go to the bridge and get the second mate and the bosun. Go like hell!"

Before the carpenter finished the sentence, the boy was on his way. Crossing to the starboard side, he jumped off the top of the load down onto number five hatch and ran forward.

When he hopped down off the top of the hatch the roll of the ship smashed him into the side of the deckload, but he kept going, past the winches and the mainmast, until he came to the cleared deck around number four. He barely remembered climbing to the ladder and running to the bosun's stateroom, just aft of the fiddley. He pounded on the door and it seemed like an eternity until the man, dressed in his long underwear, opened it.

"That dynamite's come loose in number five! Chips says to get back there in a hurry!" He paused long enough to see the unbelieving look on the man's face and then turned toward the bridge. He heard the heavy slam of the stateroom door behind him. Running around to the portside of the bridge deck, he pounded on the second mate's door. It opened almost immediately, and Peterson, dressed and ready for his watch, stood wedged between it and the inward-opened screen.

Slim was out of breath and the words came in gasps. "Sir . . . the dynamite's let go in number five. Chips asked me to get you and Boats right away!"

Peterson's reaction was instantaneous. The door slammed shut from the wind and reopened instantly. Clutching a flashlight, the second mate bolted over the weather coaming, and again the wind slammed the door behind him. Following Slim, he half ran and half slid along the lee side of the main deck, until they came to the starboard after well-deck ladder. They retraced Slim's steps of a moment before and arrived at number five in time to find the bosun, still in his underwear, directing the removal of wedges behind the forward end of the hatch coaming. Chips had taken the red-handled emergency fire ax from the fo'c'sle wall and was using it with giant smashing blows. He swung at the tough hardwood wedges that held the folded edges of the heavy canvas covers securely behind the long iron batten bar. As he worked and the others waited with unbearable impatience to fold back the canvases and lift off the thick, wooden covers, the hollow thunder of heavy steel rolling on the 'tween deck filled the men with unashamed fear. They knew—and it was unnecessary to put it into words—what could happen if the high explosives, packed in those double-walled steel containers, should hit hard enough to detonate. It would happen so fast, there would be no time for terror. A blinding blast would shatter the night, and its yellow-orange flash would light the bottoms of the low, scudding clouds for one terrible instant; then wailing winds and the foam-flecked water would be the only witnesses to another tragedy at sea. Perhaps some of the men on the bridge would survive for a time, as John and Chips had once, by clinging to a timber. But for the others—no chance. There would be no time for Sparks to get off a radio message. There would be no search made until the *Tropic Trader* was reported overdue at Hobart, sixteen hundred miles west. By then even the surviving timbers and broken bits of wreckage would have drifted many miles to the north and east on the wind-driven surface water, speeded by the swing of the Australian current. Slim wanted desperately to run to the radio shack and alert Sparks, but in the anxiety of waiting for the last wedge to loosen he dared not speak.

At last Chips' ax was still, and eager hands clutched at the long metal batten bar, lifted it from behind the cleats, and heaved it aft, where it fell with a ringing rattle across the top of the hold. Other hands ripped at the mitered corners of the heavy tarpaulins and pulled them loose. Like men turning down the top covers of a giant bed, they folded the forward ends back along the top, exposing a row of thick gray boards with flat metal handles countersunk at both ends. Chips and the bosun literally tore the center ones loose at the forward end of the hatch coaming, exposing a gaping hole directly over the narrow steel ladder. Peterson jumped up on the covers and lowered himself into the opening, his feet feeling for the rungs. From the opening, the thundering roll of the steel drums on the thin steel 'tween deck was deafening. The bosun and Chips followed, then Hammer and Warndahl.

Slim found himself beside Ioway and made a sudden decision. He half shouted into the boy's ear, "Get up to the radio shack and tell Sparks to stand by! God only knows what's going to happen!"

Ioway hurdled the winch head and disappeared into the night. Slim was the last man down. His feet found the ladder easily, for this was the first hold he'd been down that day Ioway had come aboard and the bosun had set them to cleaning up the rotten copra. The stench still lingered faintly in the close air.

As the boy half slid down the ladder, the rungs rattled under his heavy soles and he hit with a dull thud the wooden hatch covers that closed off the deep pit of the lower hold. The noise was terrifying and the sound of shouting voices blended into an echoing, metallic roar that robbed the words of their meaning and set cold fingers of fear clutching at his guts. He could see nothing at first but the swinging beam of the flashlight and the flashing glimpses of the men who ran through it. Holding fast to the ladder, he didn't know where to begin or what to do. Suddenly the ship gave a sickening lurch to port and the roar of rolling drums mingled with the shouted warnings of blind men playing for their lives in a deadly game of bowls. Something made Slim move—something he felt rather than saw. With a mighty pull he hoisted his legs clear of the hatches an instant before a drum crashed into the base of the ladder. He felt the steel give and he clung to the rungs as they leaned in under him at a crazy angle. Lowering himself, his feet came to rest on the top of a rounded container, and his legs slid astride it as one sitting on a horse. It had landed athwartships, its longitude along the vessel's roll. As the ship leaned far over to starboard again, he could feel it straining to turn, and he used every ounce of muscle to keep it from rejoining the deadly avalanche. His eyes strained to accommodate to the darkness and he almost prayed aloud for light. He could see the second mate's flashlight playing across the deck and, above the tumbling rumbling din, he could hear the agonized groans and the growling cries of men clinging to the explosive steel monsters that dragged them blindly back and forth through the hellish din. He knew there were twelve containers, but he had no way of knowing how many had carried away.

As he sat astride the drum, his hand felt something hanging over the ladder rung. It was a length of worn rope. A sudden hope soared in him as he pulled it free with his left hand. It felt at least eight to ten feet long—enough, perhaps, to loop around the drum and secure it to the ladder. Working frantically, he led the lifeless hemp around the end of the big steel drum and beneath the edge that was raised above the deck by the container's own rolling rims. Tying a quick slipknot, he pulled it up tight and secured it to the side of the ladder. He repeated the process at the other end of the drum, waiting to make his moves until the ship had recovered from heeling. The second loop he tied back to the ladder and pulled it up with all his might. Throwing a clove hitch around the rung, he waited to see whether or not the line would hold. The drum was wedged flat against the narrow coaming that formed a four-inch lip around the lower hold, but the hatch covers filled in all but an inch of the space; not much to rest the big circumference against, but something at least. Remembering the wedges, he scrambled up on deck and stuck a number of them in his belt and pockets and raced back down into the dark. He took three of them and drove them under the drum with his heel, wedging it tighter against the bent base of the ladder.

From overhead he heard Ioway call his name. He shouted up to him, "Go forward and get a cluster light and some flashlights. Ask the officers for their lights!"

Ioway's answer was lost in the chorus of warning shouts that went up as the ship took another sudden, plunging roll and the deafening clatter began again. From somewhere in the darkness he heard a man yell in terrified surprise, and in that deathly still instant before the juggernauts reversed their courses he heard a low moan. Someone had been hurt badly. He shouted into the black nothingness, "I've got some wedges!" and threw them toward Hammer, whose voice came from the starboard side of the hold. He heard them hit and skid along the deck. Then he heard Peterson shout, "Never mind the wedges! Get some lumber down here—quick!"

Without answering, he scrambled up the ladder again and ran forward to the shelter deck. He knew it would be useless to get the heavy timbers. They would be too big to wedge under the drums and would themselves become lethal enemies, skidding around in the dark. Grabbing several pieces of dunnage, he ran aft and lowered them into the hold by their ends, letting them drop the foot or two to the deck.

As he released the last piece, he shouted below, "There's dunnage at the foot of the ladder!" Hurrying forward past the winches and mast, he gathered another armload of six-to eight-foot lengths of 1 by 6 soft pine and carried them back to the hold. As he started forward again, he heard men running along the starboard main deck and saw

Ioway and Holst carrying a cluster light. He remembered the weatherproof electrical outlet just outside the fo'c'sle door. It was nearly buried under the end of the deckload. He rushed aft and stuck an arm in behind the timbers. His fingers found it and fought to unscrew the paint-stuck cap. It was difficult to get a good hold on it. Turning his body around, he reached in with his left hand and got a better purchase. Twisting with every ounce of energy in his long arm, he forced the cap until it gave way slowly and finally broke free.

Jumping up on the hatch, he called to the third mate, "Sir, it's Fredericks. I've got the outlet cleared. Give me the cable and I'll hook it up!" There was no answer, but Holst bolted across the top of the hatch and slapped the socket into his hand. Turning back, the mate bagan paying out the long rubber cord while the boy set the end in place and screwed up the collar. Suddenly the light blazed to life and was lowered into the opening.

When Slim reached the ladder, Ioway was lowering the cable to Holst, who was down on the 'tween deck. Slim leaped to the rope table at the base of the mast and grabbed a large coil of heavy manila. He groped for a free end and realized that it was the bull rope still rove through its blocks. He ran back to the hatch and found the ax which Chips had let fall to the deck. Just as he used to lop the head off the Thanksgiving turkey, he drove it cleanly through the strands and it struck sparks as the blade met the steel deck. Looping the heavy coil over his arm, he ran aft again and climbed back down the ladder into the roaring din.

As he moved into the blazing circle of light, the deafening echoes became the booming accompaniment to a macabre dance of crouching men whose distorted shadows moved frantically on the deck and across the curving rib and slats of the hold. His eyes fell on the line he'd lashed around the drum that had nearly crushed his legs, and his heart sank as he saw how worn it was—a piece discarded by the stevedores in San Pedro as unfit to secure cargo. The scene became a series of impressions—brilliant, contrasting flashes—like someone showing magic lantern slides too briefly to be clearly seen. He made out a number of the drums standing on their ends and he could see two men securing the lashings. One of them was Chips.

As the ship rolled deep into another trough, three of the steel drums wrenched loose from the men. One tipped and careened toward the wooden hatches. Striking the coaming obliquely, it seemed to leap into the air and its sharp edge crushed the old wooden covers like kindling broken under a heavy heel. Instantly Peterson and Rusty ran for it and somehow managed to get it back on the deck. Slim joined them with the rope and, handing it to the second mate, kicked fragments of dunnage under either side. The mate threw a loop around the end nearest the broken hatch and brought it along the top of the container. Next he threw a hitch over the opposite end and led the rope across to the slats along the side of the hold. As the ship's roll started the drum back to the starboard, he hauled the line tight until the thing was snug against the ribs. There he tied it off, as Slim and Rusty kicked more wedges under its rounded sides.

The operation had been done in less than thirty seconds, but already other drums were on their erratic, destructive journeys. The boy saw Holst and Hammer heave one of them up on end and hold it in place by brute force, until the ship recovered and rolled to starboard again. Warndahl, white as a ghost, stood with his right arm hanging helpless at his side. A stabbing shock went through Slim as he saw the lower forearm hanging away at a grotesque angle. He remembered his brother's arm when he'd broken it badly in a fall from a horse. He'd had the same sensation then. But there was no time to do or say anything. There still remained two loose drums. With Rusty and the second mate he held grimly onto one of them, and its tremendous weight dragged the three of them sprawling across the deck. He let go as the container smashed into the coaming and rolled up on the wooden hatches. It came to rest in the break made by its predecessor, and Slim could hear the fractured wood give under the great weight. When the ship rolled to starboard again, the three of them heaved it off the hatches and tried to break its force, but it went crashing into its upright mates. There was no thinking about the possible explosion. There was no thinking about anything but the immediate job at hand. The consequences had long since been forgotten after the first horrified awareness of what was happening. The men worked now with scarcely a word. The glare of the cluster light had revealed with dreadful clarity the impossible problem before them; and they struggled against the monstrous weight and prayed the rough, curse-filled prayers of men who plead to God for help with lips that know only blasphemy.

As the drum smashed into the row standing on end,

303

Slim kicked a short piece of dunnage under it and felt in his pockets for another wedge, but there were none. Waiting to make certain the roll to port hadn't started again, he loosened the board and turned it endwise, shoving it under again to make a fragile lever. He heard Peterson mutter "Good" as the three of them grabbed at the outer end and pried up against the thing to prevent it from rolling back onto the hatch. Out of the corner of his eye he saw that Holst and Hammer had stopped the last drum with the help of a third man he hadn't seen before—Square John.

Slim felt the deck lift beneath his feet as the *Tropic Trader* wallowed over the top of a great wave and slid with a sickening swing down its weather side. The deck slanted alarmingly and suddenly the drum began to move. As they strained upward on the flimsy lever, it snapped with a rifle-crack. Slim dived over the oncoming monster like a football player going over a charging opponent. He turned as he fell and saw the explosives hit the coaming, bounce into the air, and smash down on the broken hatch. As they watched for a hushed instant, one end of the heavy hatch cover broke entirely away and fell free down into the gaping abyss below. They heard its hollow clang as it bounced off the top of the steel shaft alley and lodged in the lower hold. Somehow the remaining piece hung in place, wedged by its neighbors. The horror of the next possibility was inescapable. Leaving Hammer and Square John to hold the last upright drum, Holst half slid down the sloping deck, and the four of them heaved the deadly thing off the covers just as the starboard roll began. It wrenched free, rumbled across the deck, and crashed full into the secured drums with a force that caved in both of their outer shells.

The ship lurched back to port, and before his unbelieving eyes Slim saw two broken hatch covers sag for an instant, then crash thirty feet down into the lower hold. A gaping hole was left in the 'tween deck hatch, easily large enough for the drum to drop through. No one needed to be told in that instant what could happen next. No one had to be told, as the deck lifted again and inclined steeply to port, that for the past, frantic, unbelievable few minutes they had been the principal players in a living miracle. No one had to be told that the stuff was nitroglycerine, with a stabilizer added, and that it could be detonated by a sharp enough blow; the drums had already absorbed dozens of blows and only God himself could tell them why they hadn't all been blown to kingdom come.

Slim would never have a clear recollection of what happened in those next few seconds. He felt the deck rise to an unbelievable steepness. He braced himself against the roll and saw the drum coming at him. He was aware of Rusty and Holst beside him, and he remembered feeling the weight of the container against his thigh for a jarring instant as it passed. He remembered the warning shouts and he heard Peterson's voice, but no actual words. He saw Holst trying vainly to change the drum's direction as it headed toward the broken hatches. He saw Rusty slip and fall beside him. He saw the open hatches and the black pit beneath them, blacker still in the white glare of the cluster light. And then he saw the hatches no more and the great steel container stopped dead against the coaming. There had been no grinding thud. He saw Peterson's legs sprawled strangely on the other side of the drum. He felt the ship roll to starboard again with that same sickening, swinging motion, and he saw the drum begin its smashing return. He remembered catching the metal lip and straining against it with Holst and Rusty and tripping on the dunnage and finally tipping it on end, and he remembered someone passing a rope around it. And then it grew quiet. There was no sound in number five hold, not even the whistling screech of the wind reached down below; just the distant rhythmic rumble of the great shaft rotating in its rounded steel prison in the bottom of the lower hold.

Second Mate Peterson lay still, his body pressed against the edge of the steel coaming, his pale, pock-scarred left cheek forced grotesquely against the metal. His faded blue eyes were open wide and stared, unseeing, into the void. His khaki sweat-stained officer's cap lay crumpled near his head, and as they watched his long neck seemed to stretch and his body pulled away from it in a slow convulsion. A low moan came from his open mouth, but there was no change of expression on the dead-white face. He lay against his own limp left arm; his right arm was flung back over his thin hips. There were no marks on his body or on his clothes, except the adhesive oil smudges to which bits of deck rubble still clung.

The third mate spoke and his voice was quiet, but the words echoed, vaultlike, in the nearly empty hold. "Get some line and make sure those things are secure. Boats, you and Chips tend to that. The rest of you better help

305

over here." He knelt down beside his fellow officer and watched him. Motioning to Slim, he indicated the second mate's right wrist. "See if he's got a pulse."

The boy took the limp wrist between his fingers and probed for the telltale throbbing below the base of the thumb. "His heart is beating, sir, but it's going awful fast!"

Holst took the wrist clumsily, and forced his stubby index finger into the white flesh. Feeling nothing, he slipped his hand under the second mate's chest and felt with the flat of the palm. After a moment he looked up. "He's breathing. I think he's busted inside. Help me turn him over."

Slim dropped down beside the mate, and gently they turned Peterson over on his back. He was completely limp. Again a slow convulsion stretched the long neck away from the body and the loose mouth seemed to open a bit more. A tight groan came from his throat. It was the hollow retching of a straining stomach about to give up its contents. The sound made Slim feel sick and lightheaded, for he sensed the presence of death. The other men gathred around the injured mate in a silent, helpless circle and braced themselves as the ship continued its unceasing roll.

It was Chips who broke the silence. "That makes two men we gotta get out of here."

Holst turned a questioning look at the carpenter, who pointed toward the bottom of the thin steel ladder. Slim turned with the others and saw Warndahl, his left arm linked through a rung, leaning head down against its bent frame. The broken right forearm dangled helplessly and the man seemed about to drop.

Holst clenched his jaw and cursed through his teeth. "Those goddamn slipshod bastards in Pedro are to blame for this!" Addressing the silent men around him, he ordered the Swede assisted to the sick bay. Then, turning to the bosun, he issued more orders. "Rig up a stretcher and get Mr. Peterson out of here. Move him very gently. I don't know what's wrong with him, but a sudden move could kill him. Chips, you work with Boats. Fredericks, go to the sick bay and get those bunks ready. I don't think any of us can do a goddamn thing now—but we can try. Before you fix up the bunks, tell the radio operator to contact a doctor anywhere he can. We need help. All right—get moving!"

Slim made for the ladder. Warndahl's good arm was still hooked through it and he hesitated a moment. The Swede raised his head. It was the first time their eyes had met since the fight, and the boy could see the pain in them. "They're going to get you out of here in a minute, Vic."

The A.B.'s lip was still swollen and the battle marks were visible on his jaw and cheekbones. He spoke thickly. "I'll get out of here myself, punk! Keep yer fuckin' hands offa me—y'unnerstan'?"

Slim continued to look at him for a moment and cut off the reply that was forming on his lips. Without a word he climbed up over the man's arm and out on deck.

In the radio shack he relayed Holst's order, and Sparks turned to the transmitter to begin his hopeless quest. Slim unlocked the sick bay, opened the medical supplies, and fixed the double-decked bunks. On his way to the bridge Holst had stopped by to give final instructions and went forward to report to the first mate, who was now standing Peterson's watch.

Hammer and Square John brought Warndahl to the boatdeck and forced the protesting Swede into the upper bunk. His broken arm lay twisted across the pipe rail. For Slim it was harder to take than the fireman's gashed face.

It was nearly an hour before they got Peterson out of the hold and up to the sick bay. Chips had rigged a small cargo net used for bringing commissary supplies aboard. To keep from bending his broken body, they had laid Peterson on one of the hatch covers, then placed the improvised stretcher on the net.

Slim cursed the rolling as his feet slid sideways along the slanting deck. It had taken almost fifteen minutes to get the second mate's clothing off. He lay in the bunk stripped to his shorts. His body was moist with perspiration, and the usually dead-white skin had a curious, bloodless look about it. When Slim felt for the pulse again, it was so faint he couldn't be certain whether or not he was feeling his own. Then, as he shifted his finger and dug deeper between the wristbone and the tendons, he felt the same fluttering, racing pulsations he'd felt in the hold. He counted the rate against the tiny second hand on his wrist watch and estimated it was close to two hundred beats per minute. He knew that normal was around eighty.

Chips helped him wrap the unconscious man in blankets and they rigged light cotton safety lines from the lower pipe to the upper one to keep him from rolling out.

Leaving the carpenter and Square John to watch the men, Slim went next door to the radio shack. Sparks was seated at the desk, sending a constant stream of code with mechanical precision. When the boy entered, he turned his head without interrupting the message and shook it negatively. After a minute he stopped and listened intently, then slid the headset forward on his temples.

"I can't raise anybody, kiddo. The air's full of hash! Holy Jesus-in-the-manger, every ship on the air's got problems. And for your information, the *Anthracite King* hasn't made a transmission for over an hour. I think she must have rolled over!" He shook his head in disbelief. "What a horrible son-of-a-bitchin' mess this is! What the hell are the likes of us doin' out here, anyway?"

He glowered at the boy and Slim could see the look of agonized helplessness in his eyes. He knew this radio operator, who pretended to be a cynic and impervious to the sufferings of his fellow man, and he knew how shallow the pretense really was—how much the responsibility of being the only link with help weighed on him. Sparks cursed in frustration and said with rough eloquence all the things the boy felt himself.

Slim had looked over the second mate's moist bluish body and had found no wounds, no evidence of broken bones, no single clue as to what had happened, except for a diagonal bruise across the lower left back side of his bony rib cage. No blood was coming from him that could be seen, and the men felt helpless and angry that nothing could be done for this ugly, ofttimes pathetic officer whom they all respected. Slim hadn't been able even to tell whether or not Peterson was suffering. The convulsions had stopped and the unfocused eyes stared wide open at the springs of the bunk above. His breathing was shallow and fast and seemed to catch at times and then resume with a faint gasp, as though laboring under some invisible burden. With Warndahl, the problem was simple—a badly broken arm.

Shoving the headphones back over his ears, Sparks listened intently again and his hand reached for the "bug," and its shiny black blade rattled between his thumb and forefinger. He was listening again and making notes on the ruled yellow pad before him when the third mate entered.

He spoke quietly to Slim. "Has he been able to raise a doctor yet?"

"No, sir. There's too much interference. He says a lot of ships are in trouble."

Holst looked at the boy sharply, then stepped behind the radio operator's chair and peered at the pad.

Sparks pushed the chair back impatiently. It bumped

the mate and he turned in surprise. "Sorry, I didn't see you——"

Holst dismissed the apology. "No luck?"

"I can't raise a goddamn thing! Everybody's hollerin' for help tonight!" He hooked one foot under the drawer section of the desk to keep his chair from sliding as the ship took a long, deep roll. "I'll keep trying, sir, but it doesn't look too good." He pulled himself in close to the desk again and picked up the pad. "The *Tahiti*'s our best chance. I can hear her calling the *Anthracite King*. She's been trying to raise her, but the collier's not transmitting —nothing for over an hour. The Union liners carry doctors, I think, but I can't get 'em to answer."

The third mate looked at the deck thoughtfully and ground out a short butt under his foot. Sparks regarded the circular patch of tobacco shreds without emotion and waited for Holst to speak. The officer doubled a hairy fist and cracked the knuckle joints. "All right, Sparks—keep tryin'." He paused at the door. "We'll be standin' two watches on the bridge until Mr. Peterson gets on his feet. I'm going to relieve Mr. Samson at twenty-two hundred. Let me know what goes on!"

Sparks glanced at the clock on the bulkhead. It read eighteen minutes to eight. It meant that the first mate would stay on the bridge until ten o'clock and that Holst would take over and stand six hours until 4 A.M. the following morning. Slim assumed the wheel watches for the men would stay unchanged. Holst altered the routine in the next moment, at least for him.

"Fredericks, you're on sick-bay duty again. I'll get one of the other men to relieve you. Stay with Mr. Peterson and your 'friend' there, and do what you can."

Slim nodded understandingly. "Yes, sir."

"Come on. I'll stay with you for a while." Turning to the radio operator, he added, "If you raise anybody, come in and tell me!"

Sparks grunted and turned back to his listening. Slim followed Holst out onto the after end of the boatdeck and ducked through the adjoining door.

Chips was bending over the second mate. When they entered, he motioned to them. He spoke in a whisper. "Somethin' just happened to him. His body kind of jerked. I think it's Fiddler's Green for him, sir."

The carpenter had referred to the mythical heaven that sea lore held was the final resting place for sailors killed in line of duty.

Slim bent over the blanketed form and reached under the edge for the second mate's left arm. Laying it across his chest, he pressed his fingers against the pulse. Again it was impossible to find. Holst and Chips watched closely as the boy probed and finally nodded his head slightly. He started to count the beats, but a sudden change in the quick rhythm made him look at the man again. His fingers probed deeper and felt a faint lifting under the tips, and then it disappeared again. Once again he changed the position of his fingers and dug the tips into the space between the bones, searching for the telltale surge that meant life. His fingers worked along the wrist almost frantically. Then he looked up. "Sir . . . I——" The words wouldn't come. Quickly Holst bent over his fellow officer and looked at the face, glistening with fine sweat. The bluish-gray pallor was more pronounced and the eyes seemed different. As the boy continued groping for the pulse he saw the eyes widen almost imperceptibly and then another change came over them. The blurred light faded, as though a dying flame had suddenly flared brightly, then flickered out. The long body sagged slowly, and Slim clutched hard at the wrist, as though to stay the hand of Death, which in that instant claimed the broken body and tortured soul of Second Officer Lars Peterson.

—26— "Let me outa this goddamn bunk!" Warndahl writhed under the heavy hand that held him flat. "No son-of-a-bitch in the world is gonna keep me lyin' in here with a stiff! Fer Chris' sake, the guy's been dead fer an hour and you want me to lay with him all night!"

He struggled again and struck at Chips with his left arm. The grotesquely twisted right arm lifted and a moan escaped the Swede's lips. He settled back on the straw-filled ticking, gasping for breath, and pain-sweat broke out on his forehead. His bloodshot little eyes rolled down toward Peterson's blanket-shrouded form in the bunk below, and the look in them was close to terror. The carpenter leaned on the A.B.'s chest with his hand and forearm and waited for the next outburst. Slim could see that the man's patience was nearing its end. Ever since the last weak spark of life had flickered and died in the second mate, Warndahl had been like a trapped animal, plunging in panic to escape the specter of death. His ranting curses filled the room with its vile sound, changing the boy's deep sadness into deeper anger.

Warndahl's eyes searched the little sick bay and his tormented mind sifted every possible way out and he knew there was none. The unreasoning rage broke forth again in another fusillade of such depraved filth that the boy jumped to his feet.

Reaching into the bunk, his long fingers grasped the Swede's throat, as the man had once threatened to grasp his. He struggled to control the grip and his voice trembled. "You filthy pig! You rotten, ungrateful slob! I should have put that glass through your slimy mouth!" His fingers tightened on the man's throat and dug in until he could feel the Adam's apple work up and down convulsively between them. "You oughtta be killed! Why do you have to live, when a man like him has to die? Why? Go on—tell

311

me, why? You're a rotten, mad dog, Warndahl—and a disgrace to the whole goddamned human race!"

He released the other man's throat with a shoving motion, as though to rid himself of it, and the carpenter pushed the boy gently away. The blazing anger in him blurred his vision and the blood pounded in his temples. He turned from the bunk and dragged deeply on a cigarette. In a few minutes he left the sick bay and stepped into the radio shack.

Sparks was still transmitting. He turned his head quickly when he heard the boy. "I raised somebody. Hold it a minute!" The key literally flew between his fingers as he completed his message and listened intently for the answer.

Slim stood at the end of the desk nearest the door, his long legs absorbing the motion of the ship.

The radio operator lifted one phone away from his ear and looked up. "I got the *H.M.S. Dunedin*. She's about ninety miles northeast of us, looking for the *Anthracite King*. They've got a Royal Navy surgeon aboard who will give us some instructions, but she can't come alongside. She's trying to get to the collier's last reported position."

The mate had told Sparks to continue trying to contact medical help, even after Peterson's death, in the hope that they'd be given some advice about caring for Warndahl's arm.

The advice appeared to be forthcoming, and Slim was ready. He had written a description of the fracture as best he could, using the first-aid manual to identify the bones involved. That paper was before Sparks now and the operator pulled it closer and began writing on his own pad. The boy moved to the opposite end of the desk and watched the message unfold in the operator's jerking scribble. The surgeon was asking for details of the accident.

Slim leaned down close. "Tell him we don't know exactly how it happened, but this is the end result." He pointed to the paper.

Sparks nodded and relayed the message in a stream of flying dots and dashes, then listened for the answer. As he began to write, Slim followed the words:

"APPLY OPPOSING TRACTION ABOVE BENT ELBOW AND FROM WRIST. SEPARATE BROKEN ENDS OF RADIUS AND ULNA AND TRY TO LINE THEM UP BY FEELING BREAK THROUGH SKIN. ONCE IN PLACE SPLINT TIGHTLY. HAVE A GO AT IT AND WE'LL STAND BY WITH YOU. COME BACK."

The radio operator's hand returned to the key and he acknowledged the message; then, turning to the boy, he handed him the paper. "Here you are, doctor! By the time we finish this trip we'll both have medical degrees!"

Slim took the paper and stepped quickly out on deck. He clung to the rail and let the cold wind plaster the damp clothes against his body and he sucked in great gulps of the moist air.

Heavy drops of rain beat against his face and trickled down across his lips. He licked at them with his tongue and let them drive into his open mouth. Looking down, he could see the square patch of light outlining the open hatches in number five hold. The bosun and some of the crew were still working down below, securing the drums. After a time a chill shook him and he turned and re-entered the sick bay. Chips was still braced against the upper bunk, holding the Swede, and against his legs the covered body of the second mate rolled loosely with the motion of the ship.

Going to the medical chest, Slim got out the bottle of chloral hydrate. He measured a double dose of the colorless liquid into a coffee cup and added an equal amount of water. Moving to the bunk, he spoke to the carpenter. His voice was low and the words came with effort. "Okay, we got what we want." He indicated the water-marked paper folded in his shirt pocket. "We gotta get him to take this."

Warndahl had turned his head and was listening. He tried to raise his head. "I ain't takin' nuthin'! I don't give a fuck-all what ya say. I ain't takin' nuthin'!" He tried to shove the carpenter's huge arm aside, but was immediately pinned down again.

Chips looked at the medicine, then back at the injured A.B. There was a note of finality in his voice. "Vic, you're going to take this now—one way or the other. How do you want it—shoved down yer throat while yer out cold or sittin' up like a man?"

Warndahl pressed against the arm and blinked at the overhead.

Chips waited for him to answer. "Okay, stupid! I don't like to do this 'cause yer jaw is already kinda sore—but out ya go!" He doubled his huge hand into a knuckled club and brought it back slowly.

The Swede's eyes rolled down and stared at the massive fist. Then, suddenly, he shook his head from side to side frantically and forced the words from his throat: "Don't hit . . . don't hit! Give it to me!" He turned his head to-

313

ward Slim, and his left arm reached across his body for the cup.

Chips, suspecting a trick, pinned the arm back down on the mattress.

Warndahl looked up at him imploringly. "I'll drink it, Chips . . . give it to me . . . I'll drink it!"

The carpenter looked at him warily, then slowly relaxed the pressure, and Warndahl tried to lift his head. Chips shoved his left arm under the man and raised him a few inches. Reaching for the cup, Warndahl downed its contents and shuddered at the aftertaste. Chips eased him flat again and moved back a step.

He looked at the boy. "Is that the same stuff you gave the fireman?"

Slim nodded. "I put in a little more." Taking the paper from his pocket, he unfolded it and handed it to the carpenter.

Chips studied it, then held it out, indicating the medical terms for the two broken bones. "Do you know what he's talkin' about?"

"Yeah. Those are the two bones in his forearm that are broken. I found them in the manual. When he goes to sleep, you've got to make splints to hold them in place." A sudden thought occurred to the boy. "Hey, wait a minute!" Turning to the medical chest, he lifted the top tray from the trunklike box and set it on the deck. Reaching into the bottom, he brought out a smooth, flat piece of clear white wood that had been rounded at both ends. "Got 'em!" In a moment he pulled out several more and two rolls of wide webbing. "This'll do it——"

Chips looked dubious at the narrow strips of splinting. "We oughtta split one of them in half, so's we have something to put on the sides. Otherwise them bones are gonna move between the planks."

Slim shrugged. He was in no position to disagree. The only broken bones he'd seen had been held in plaster casts.

Warndahl stirred and rolled his head toward them. "Fellas . . . do something for me, will ya?" His voice was plaintive and beginning to thicken. "Get me outta here . . . will ya? I don't care whatcha do . . . but get me away from the dead. Please, fellas?" His head lolled on his right cheek and his breathing was labored.

The carpenter looked at him thoughtfully, then turned to Slim. "We're gonna need some help, anyway. Ask Sparks if we can take him in there."

The boy stood uncertainly for a moment, then went to

the radio shack. Sparks returned with him and carefully they helped the Swede down to the deck. Inside the Swede half fell into the radio operator's bunk.

In less than an hour the arm was straight again, bound between the splints with a layer of wrapped webbing and anchored with a criss-cross of black electrician's tape. Warndahl slept heavily, completely oblivious to the uncertain, sometimes clumsy attempts to repair his broken bones.

Slim had volunteered to stay with the Swede. Chips had left to recheck the shorings on the deckload. His parting admonition had been short and to the point. "If he makes trouble . . . cold-cock him!"

Slim looked at the A.B., who so recently had turned from adversary to patient, and thought that there would be no more trouble from Warndahl for some time to come. It was past midnight and he felt he should give the third mate a report. Making his way forward along the boatdeck, he climbed down the samson post ladder to the top of number three hold and scooted across the slanting deck to the lee side of the bridge. He found Rusty at the wheel and no lookout on the wing bridge. Holst, dressed in oilskins, was apparently doubling this duty, too.

Slim reported in detail the setting of the arm under the remote guidance of the Royal Navy Surgeon, who had supervised the proceedings from the radio room of the *H.M.S. Dunedin.*

Holst listened carefully, then gave the boy additional instructions. "Mr. Samson is in Mr. Peterson's quarters, going through his effects to see who must be notified. You better stop by there and tell him what you've told me, then get back to the radio shack, unless he wants you to do something else."

Slim dropped down the ladder again and knocked on the door immediately below the captain's quarters. The first mate opened it and directed an inquiring look at the boy.

"Sir . . . Mr. Holst asked me to report to you on the condition of the injured seaman and see if I could be of any help here."

The mate motioned him through the door. "Step in!" The stateroom was almost identical to the one he'd seen when Samson had ordered him to attend to the manifest papers in Wauna. There were the same built-in bunk and lockers; the desk and chair and the wash basin and cabinet in the corner. The portholes looked out to starboard and forward across the well deck to the bow. On the desk stood several photographs. One was the picture of a proud-looking, tall, thin young man in the uniform of a lieutenant in the United States Navy. Slim saw the stripe and a half on the sleeve indicating he was at that time a "j.g." There were three ribbons on the left side of the jacket which Slim couldn't identify. This was Lars Peterson during the days of his highest hopes. Slim guessed the picture had been taken about 1918. The other photo pictured an elderly woman—probably his mother—and under the edges of its metal frame were stuck the corners of several curling snapshots, all of the same woman.

The first mate had been sorting through papers which lay in uneven stacks on the desk. "We'll try to hold a burial service sometime tomorrow. How's that A.B. making out?"

The boy repeated his report. The first mate listened without comment, then dismissed him to return to sick bay.

Sparks was leaning back in his chair, his eyes closed, when Slim entered. His glasses were lying on the desk and a cigarette smoldered in his hand, its long ash threatening to fall momentarily. It did as the boy spoke and the radio operator sat up with a start. He yawned and looked at Warndahl sleeping heavily in the bunk.

Slim felt guilty about putting the Swede in Sparks' quarters. They should have taken him back to the fo'c'sle and done the job back there. "We kind of loused you out of a place to sleep, didn't we?"

Sparks picked up his glasses and slipped them on. Shaking his head, he spoke through a gaping yawn. "Uh . . . uh. I'm like Thomas Edison—I cat nap. I couldn't stay on that goddamn shelf on a night like this, if my life depended on it. I'll sleep when we get into port!"

The boy sat down on the stool, braced his elbows on his knees and rested his chin in his cupped hands. "That may not be for a week or more in this weather. What's new—anything?"

The radio operator looked thoughtful for a moment, then swung back in his chair. "I think that coal ship is done for. Poor bastards! There's no letup in the weather. It's one of those early winter blows they get down here. It's apt to last for several days yet."

Slim sat up and leaned against the bulkhead, his feet wide apart with one foot braced against the leg of the anchored desk. "The mate says they're going to have services for Mr. Peterson tomorrow——"

Sparks exhaled a long breath and scratched the back of his hand with quick, sensitive fingers. "On this ship they probably won't even get that done right!"

He seemed lost in his own thoughts again, then after a time he spoke. "If you want to cork off for a little while, I'll keep an eye on Laughing Boy here! And if he wakes up and starts raising hell with that filthy mouth of his . . . I'll be only too happy to let him have it with my little ball-peen hammer!"

Slim hesitated and the radio operator urged him. "Go on, kid, there's no sense in both of us sitting around here owl-eyed. Can you sleep in there . . . with him?"

Slim stirred his rumpled hair with the flat of his hand and stretched. "I can rest a little, I guess——" He stood up and stretched his long frame. "Call me in an hour and I'll come and sit with you."

He pushed the heavy weather door against the rushing wind and went out on deck. The pale light shone through the square sick bay window and cast a pallid glow on the white railing. The rain had stopped now and there was no light shining up from the 'tween deck of number five hold. Slim pulled the door open against the weather and slipped inside. The room smelled musty and a trace of carbolic odor of the medical chest lingered in the air. Peterson's still form, concealed by the blanket, rolled stiffly from side to side, as the *Tropic Trader* rose and fell with the twisting pitch of the quartering seas. The boy stepped carefully on the edge of the lower pipe and pulled himself into the upper bunk. He stretched out on the straw ticking and stared at the yellowing overhead less than three feet above him. Reaching into his pocket, he took out a cigarette and struck the match on the aging paint. It left a brownish streak.

It was strange, he thought, that he had no feeling about being in the room with the second mate's corpse—no feeling, but one of pity for the man and the fruitlessness of the life he'd led. Peterson had either slipped or deliberately thrown himself under the explosive-filled container. In any case his action probably had saved the lives of some forty-odd men. Slim thought about those men now and what those lives might be worth. Were Hammer and Warndahl and the Shiek or Spots, too, for that matter, worth the life of one Peterson? If a life had to be sacrificed to save the others, why couldn't it have been that of the murderous ex-prize fighter, whose only honesty was to his own selfishness; or that of Warndahl, whose piglike little eyes could see nothing but the filth into which he transposed some of life's rarest beauties; or that of the Shiek—a strange, silent, brooding character from a lurid underworld novel—a man who walked alone? Why couldn't he have died alone—and by that sacrifice given meaning to his own life? Why was it Peterson—the poor pock-scarred cynic, whose sole triumph was an adding-machine brain that drove him to discharge meticulously his responsibilities to this rust-ridden tub of a tramp steamer that had been born of democracy's greatest emergency and launched too late to serve its cause? Why had Peterson given his life to save this ship and its men? Knowing Peterson, Slim thought he knew the answer. To the second mate the men were part of the ship and the ship was more than a part of his life: it was his retreat—his iron-bound world—and his devotion to it was the ultimate rationalization that made his life bearable. Without his ship he would have been without his life. Had he survived this last gamble, it still would have meant the end of life. The final responsibility for the security of the cargo was his.

Slim pinched off the glowing tip and dropped the butt on the deck. He closed his eyes and listened to the ship fight the storm. Something hanging on the thin wooden wall between the sick bay and the radio shack scraped along a pendulous arc, measuring in sound the complex geometry of the ship's motion. Lying at right angles to the keel, the boy imagined himself faced up on a giant seesaw that one moment tilted his feet high above his head, then dropped them below in a movement so fast that he felt weightless. The motion made him squeamish and he opened his eyes again.

He tried to think of Edye and the words of her last letter ran through his mind; and then Marge was there and a twinge of guilt evicted the vagrant longing and he felt ashamed that in the cold, harsh presence of death he could feel the soft warmth of her nakedness. He sat up suddenly and his rumpled hair touched the overhead. He looked at the brown-edged paper dial of his cheap wrist watch. He'd been in the bunk only a quarter of an hour. Turning on his side, he stretched out again facing the wooden bulkhead and his eyes wandered up along the joints in the narrow grooved boards. He reached out and pulled at the end of a paint-imbedded bristle. It came loose and left it's hairline imprint behind and the irrelevant words of a partly

318

remembered poem formed soundlessly on his moving lips: "We can make our lives sublime . . . and departing, leave behind us, footprints on the sands of time——" He tried to remember who had written it. It sounded like Longfellow, but he wasn't sure. Then more of the words came back: "Lives of great men oft remind us . . ." Was it "*oft* remind us," or "*all* remind us"? Again he wasn't sure, but he remembered the sense of the lines:

"Lives of great men," *something*, "remind us, We can make our lives sublime, And departing, leave behind us, Footprints on the sands of time." What happens to the men who aren't great? Men like Peterson and Holst and Sparks and himself? When the spirit leaves the body, where does it go, as his grandmother had told him and as most people believed? Is this life really just a chapter in the Book of Life . . . or is it the beginning, middle and end of the book? Is there such a thing as a soul? Or when the machine slows down and finally stops, does everything end with it? Do spirits live on only in the memories of those left behind? And what reasons to remember do we give those we leave behind? Is the spirit that survives in loving memory the spirit that lives in the Kingdom of Heaven . . . and is the spirit that survives in hateful recollection the spirit doomed to Hell?

Slim twisted uncomfortably and rolled over on his back. He put his hand palm up to shade his eyes from the open light.

He remembered Father O'Malley's vivid description of Hell: "a place of eternal torment for the souls of the wicked who repenteth not their sins!" The Reverend Theodore of the Anglican Church had put it differently: "Embrace the teachings of the Lord Jesus, seek his forgiveness and each of you shall find the true Heaven within you. Turn from Him and the torment of Hell shall abide in thee for the rest of thy days!"

He remembered Loy, the Chinese cook on the ranch, making his annual pilgrimage to the Chinese cemetery in Tehama to join with his countrymen in an ancient ceremony whose purpose was the perpetual veneration and "remembering" of those gone before, that their souls might be assured eternal life. He remembered the brick-bordered family plot in Oak Hill Cemetery, west of Red Bluff, where the remains of his own ancestors rotted in their wooden coffins, six feet below the carefully tended oleander trees, and the funeral cadence of a childish chant filled his ears: "The worms crawl out, the worms crawl in,

319

they crawl all over yer mouth and chin . . ." He shook his head to rid himself of the picture, but another picture came of his living family, puttering around with pruning shears and rakes each Decoration Day, and he wondered whether in the midst of their ritual labors they were quietly remembering, and in so doing were imparting life to those loved ones long departed. He could smell again the moist moldiness of the black earth and see the smooth tufts of pale green moss growing in the widening cracks of the older headstones.

Why does the newly turned earth of a graveyard smell of death and the newly turned earth of the garden smell of life? Why doesn't God reveal to all men the mystery of death, so they aren't afraid? Some men aren't afraid. Jesus wasn't . . . Peterson wasn't . . . but maybe Peterson was more afraid of living than of dying. The certainty of his life here could have been more frightening than the uncertainty of life hereafter. . . .

He'd heard his grandmother say those words when a widower neighbor had blown his brains out on a gravel bar down in Oat Creek one evening. Nobody had paid any attention to Old Joe. They thought he was shooting quail out of season. They didn't miss him until his mail piled up in the general store. They went looking, but the turkey buzzards had found him first. If Old Joe had a soul—and he remembered them saying, "he didn't have a soul in the world after Clara died,"—then he was probably getting the same rotten break in the hereafter, because nobody took the time to remember, except maybe that he used to drink too much, sometimes even Jamaica ginger.

Slim took his hand away from his eyes and the light made him squint. He wondered at the parade of thoughts and his face twisted in an expression of disgust. He wondered if he was going off his rocker. Swinging his feet over the edge, he lowered himself to the deck and walked to the door. The stale odor of sweat and antiseptic was heavy in the air. Forcing the door open, he stepped outside and let the weather beat against him for a moment; then, turning, he knocked on Sparks' door and went in.

The radio operator looked up in surprise. "You've only been gone half an hour. What's the matter?"

Slim dropped wearily on the stool. "I couldn't get to sleep. I couldn't turn my damn head off!"

Sparks shook his own sadly. "Boy, you got me beat! What the hell did you expect to do—drop off like a baby at a wake? I couldn't even sit in there for five minutes alone!" He wagged his head slowly and reached for a smoke. "Did it ever occur to you that you've been working too hard? Better stay here and help me stare at this stiff." He indicated Warndahl sleeping noisily in the bunk. "At least he's alive!"

The night seemed endless. The storm made relaxing impossible and each creeping hour on the clock was filled with sixty minutes of battling to keep upright and awake. Sparks listened on the headphones at intervals and once said he heard a distant distress call but couldn't identify the ship. He could hear the destroyer, *H.M.S. Dunedin,* still sending futile calls to the *Anthracite King.*

About a quarter past four in the morning the third mate came aft to the radio shack. Slim was dozing, head down on the desk, and didn't hear him until he was inside the room. He looked closely at the splinted arm, grunted his approval, and went to his cabin for the scant five hours' sleep which would be all he'd get until they replaced the second mate. At six o'clock the sky began to lighten and the intermittent rain stopped again. Slim looked in the sick bay and saw Peterson's body rolling stiffly to the motion of the ship. Pulling on his coat against the gray morning chill, he went to the galley. Mr. Jones and Mr. Bones were just beginning to poke up the glowing coals. He asked for and got a saucepan of hot coffee. Up in the radio shack again they sat letting the steaming hot liquid trickle down their throats. Warndahl was still sleeping soundly, flat on his back, his open mouth emitting intermittent hollow snores.

Sparks swung around in his chair and looked over at him. "What did you give the guy, anyway?"

Slim grinned. "Chloral hydrate. I gave him a real slug. I've had my bellyfull of that bastard!"

Sparks looked shocked and spoke with exaggerated seriousness. "Great heavens, man, watch your language! I do declare, I think this life is beginning to coarsen you!"

Slim chuckled at the admonition, but felt an odd little worry that Sparks' kidding might be on the level. He'd noticed that there were more rough words in his speech lately and he smiled as he remembered the first time his grandmother had heard him say "damn," when he'd been bucked over the corral fence. "Son, swearing doesn't make you a man. It just advertises to the world that you have a limited vocabulary!" He thought of the patrician little lady and mentally hugged her. He wished he could see her again.

321

Slim dropped the cigarette in the milk can and was surprised to discover that he'd smoked two packs during the night. Crumpling the empty foil-lined package, he tossed it into the wastebasket and rose from the stool. "Finish that coffee and I'll take the stuff back to the galley."

Sparks nodded and poured the last of it into his cup. He drained it and gave the empty mug to the boy.

As he came around the after end of the main deckhouse and headed for the galley, he saw the bosun and Chips. The Russian-Finn motioned to him and he walked forward carefully, leaning his shoulder against the bulkhead until the ship recovered from a deep roll.

The bosun's manner seemed subdued. "You gonna help Chips here. He wants ya to give him a hand sewin' da body in canvas——"

The carpenter looked at the boy inquiringly. "That don't bother ya, does it, boy?"

The bosun smirked. "Naw . . . dat don't bodder him. He likes to sew up people."

Slim braced his foot against the bottom of the bulkhead as the ship swung to port, and ignored the remark.

The bosun watched him and smiled. "If he's a real good boy, you can let him take de last stitch tru da nose——"

The carpenter was not amused. "All right, boy . . . let's go."

They moved aft and Slim left the pan and cups in the galley. Chico was there, but the ever present smile was gone and the little crucifix hung on the outside of his khaki work shirt.

He saw Slim looking at the cross and he pointed up toward the sick bay on the deck above. "All de boys, we pray for heem. He was a berry good hombre . . . berry good mon!" The little Filipino seemed to feel genuine sadness. "You going to hab funeral for heem?"

Slim nodded. "Yeah, Chico . . . as soon as we can."

"Bueno! . . . I come!"

Chips went aft to get his palm and needle—the glovelike device that enabled him to shove the heavy sail needle and waxed thread through the tightly woven tarpaulin that would serve as Lars Peterson's shroud.

They laid the canvas out in the gloomy shelter deck just forward of number four hold. Using a heavy pair of sailmaker's shears, Chips squared up the edges of a piece about nine feet long and roughly a yard wide. At the bottom end he folded the canvas back and mitered the corners, then began stitching the loose envelope that would hold the weights. These would lie beneath the second mate's feet and would carry his body, head up, to the bottom of the sea. Before Chips had finished the first stitching, the bosun came from the fo'c'slehead with several useless pulleys whose flanges had been broken. Chips figured the four of them weighed about forty pounds, sufficient to do their grim job.

It took about an hour to get the shroud ready. The first mate had ordered the body brought down from the sick bay. They went now to carry it with gentle awkwardness to the adumbral steel catacomb, where it would lie in restless state awaiting the cold embrace of the sea.

Slim knelt on the deck beside Chips and overlapped the oil canvas ahead of the needle. They had left the second mate in his khaki bridge dress and had sent the weather-beaten officer's cap to his quarters to be packed with his other belongings. Slim looked at the face, as they folded the heavy canvas down over it and overlapped the sides. His expression was gone; he seemed unreal and waxlike. Chips took the last stitches and tied them off with a series of looping knots.

As he cut the thread Slim asked him about the bosun's remark. "What did the guy mean when he said I should take the last stitch through the nose?"

Chips, straightening up with difficulty, slipped the tag end of thread from the eye of the needle. "He was talkin' about something they used to do in the old country when they buried a man at sea. The sailmaker took the last stitch in the shroud right through the corpse's nose to hold the body from slipping down into the bag, when it's tipped off the planks. They used to give the sailmaker a guinea for every body he wrapped. The paymaster would come and lift on that stitch to make sure there was a corpse inside. In the old days in the British Navy the sailmaker and his mates could make a lot of money after a battle! Sometimes they used to cheat a little!"

Slim gathered the trimmings into a heap and threw them over the side. Chips went forward through the shelter deck and returned with his long tool box. The bosun returned with him. Taking pieces of dunnage, he and the boy constructed a rough pallet seven feet long and three feet wide. The three of them lifted the body on it and looped it with light line to keep the shroud from leaving its final base until the moment of burial.

As they laid the tragic burden on deck against the athwartships bulkhead of the cold storage locker, the bosun growled, "It's a gottdamn good t'ing dis didn't happen up where it's hot. We'd have to stick him in wid de udder rotten meat to keep him!"

Chips looked at the man with open disgust and carried his tools forward. A sickening shudder shook the boy, and he quietly left for the sick bay.

— 27 —

Two days passed before the weather eased enough to permit the burial. It was as though the elements had entered into a conspiracy to keep Lars Peterson aboard his ship.

At eleven-thirty Mr. Samson came below and ordered the body removed to the forward well deck. It lay atop number two hold, the lines still looped over it and under the pallet. The first mate had brought a large flag down from the chartroom and, with the bosun's help, draped it over the shroud securing the ends beneath the wooden base.

All hands not on watch were ordered to report on the forward well deck at eleven forty-five. Some of the crew began drifting forward earlier and Slim saw among them, Warndahl with his splinted arm hanging in a sling and Mike, his face unbandaged now, his left cheek divided unevenly from cheekbone to chin by the long, rawish scar. Chico and Bolo were there and Jesus, the black gang's messman. They stood impassively, apart from the others, holding small rosary beads from which dangled little silver crosses. The engineering officers were grouped against the forward base of the bridge and nearby were Squirt and Brill, the two off-watch oilers. The ship's cooks stood at the top of the ladder with jackets over their long white aprons. Their tall chefs' caps flattened in the wind. Stokes and Sparks stood at the end of the hold, speaking quietly.

At exactly quarter 'til noon the small bell on the front of the wheelhouse rang once and Captain Hans Jensen, uniformed in his dress blues and protected by his great coat, moved slowly down from the bridge to the starboard side of the well deck. At a signal from the bosun, Chips, Hammer, Otto, Square John, and Spots joined him and raised the pallet from the covered hatch. Three men to a side, they lifted the body and rested the end of the pallet on the slack chain rail. The men gathered around as the

325

captain took his place at the head of the flag-draped bier. Removing his cap, he handed it to the first mate and from the pocket of his heavy coat he took a small Bible. Wind riffled the thin, gilt-edged pages, as he opened it to the purple ribbon marker.

He read softly and Slim could hear nothing but the murmur of his deep voice, intoning the words he had chosen as his farewell to the ship's most trusted officer. The first mate handed the captain's cap to a nearby man and walked slowly forward to the big bell on the fo'c'sle deck. Detaching the clapper cord, he stood facing aft, waiting.

As the *Tropic Trader* rolled more easily now, torn shreds of gray clouds passed low above the topmasts and the wind slatted the loose halyards against the ratlines. The sun slanted down from the northeast and struck through to the leaden waves, plating them with quicksilver that dulled and lost its moving sheen in the restless shadows between the crests. There was no sound, save the wordless chant of the captain's monotonous eulogy.

The men stood silently, braced against the force of the wind and the rolling deck. The Filipino messmen fingered their beads and murmured their voiceless prayers. High above on the wing bridge Slim could see the huddled head and shoulders of the third mate waiting for the moment his fellow officer would take his last leave of his last ship.

A sudden lull in the wind left the deck strangely quiet and the captain's voice, distinctly heard now, intoned from memory the last words to be spoken before burial at sea: ". . . and therefore our Heavenly Father, we commit this body to the deep, to be turned into corruption, looking for the resurrection of the body, when the sea shall give up her dead, and the life of the world to come."

Closing the book, he returned it to his pocket and grasped the two corners of the flag. At a nod to the bosun the men slowly raised the end of the pallet. High and higher it inched, as they held their breaths and waited for it to move. But the body refused to leave the ship. In desperation the bosun jiggled the boards slightly; then with sudden understanding he unsheathed his big knife, reached under the flag and slashed through the securing loops. As the last bond was cut the body began to move. It hung for an instant on the brink, then slid free and dropped soundlessly into the swirling sea. From high above came the hoarse, shattering blast of the ship's whistle and from the fo'c'sle deck, the dolorous tolling of the ship's bell.

Second Officer Lars Peterson had been consigned to the

deep, embraced forever by the trackless waste. To the very last instant he had struggled against the imperfect bonds which became symbolical of those other bungled lashings that were his final undoing.

As he walked aft alone Slim felt deep sadness mixed with anger at the injustice of the man's life . . . and death. He did not know the whole story of Lars Peterson's frustration, but from the beginning he'd been aware of its effects. The man was gone and in all eternity Slim knew that no ship would ever pass this exact spot again. In all eternity no man would ever know the precise resting place of his mortal remains.

The first time Slim had encountered death in his own family he'd asked about its nature and he remembered now his grandmother's graphic explanation. She had likened the life cycle to that of a tree which puts forth its leaves for a season, sheds them to fertilize its roots, then from the decomposed blanket at its feet, draws forth the renewed substance from which the leaves are reborn. And so a broken leaf had fallen from the tree of life, and Slim wondered how and when and whether it would be reborn.

Ninety hours had passed without a single full hour of sleep. The accumulated fatigue overpowered him now, and he fell into his bunk and slipped mercifully away from the aching and doubting and wondering of those past few days.

— 28 —

A change of orders caused the *Tropic Trader* to by-pass a waiting cargo at Hobart on the island of Tasmania and head on a more northerly course to Port Adelaide, South Australia. Mr. Peterson's death had been wirelessed to the owners in San Francisco and they were trying to make arrangements to find another qualified officer who could pick up the vessel at one of the ports to be called at during the next month or six weeks. In the meantime Captain Jensen had been on the bridge day and night, taking noon sights and assisting with the navigation.

Slim had got to see quite a bit of him, since he generally stayed in the wheelhouse for half an hour or so after Samson and Holst figured and compared their fixes. Slim couldn't rid himself of the feeling that the man was seriously and sometimes painfully ill, but when the captain spoke to the boy his voice was deep and warm. Something about him induced a feeling of pity in Slim. It was strange, he thought, but he'd felt the same emotion for Peterson and for Stokes, even for Warndahl at times; also for Russian John and, if he were honest, for Sparks, too. He seemed to sense a deep futility about them that made him wonder about himself.

During the days that followed Peterson's death Slim and Sparks had spent more time together than usual. Working as they had during those troubled nights, a bond had been wrought between them, and Slim found himself saying many things that had remained half-thoughts until spoken aloud. Sparks had unburdened himself too and, without shame, had confessed at least a partial understanding of the rebellion that had turned him toward the sea. Those were quiet hours filled with more understanding than conversation.

Stokes had spent several long evenings with them in the radio shack, but the edge of the arguments seemed blunted

328

and the man had no taste for introspection. Conversations had lagged and finally ended in aimless guessing about the next port of call or the nature of the next cargo.

In the fo'c'sle the reaction to Peterson's passing was less noticeable and, with the exception of the carpenter's occasional reference to the needlessness of it, the talk was limited to comments about Samson and Holst and about the captain, whom they dubbed a "strange one."

The games had resumed and Hammer had introduced his homemade chuck-a-luck layout. It was reluctantly adopted after the dice had been thoroughly tested and their revolving cage minutely examined. But poker was still the favorite diversion, and Slim sat in on most of the games and did his share of winning and losing. Warndahl's arm was useless but the bosun set him to painting bulkheads and straightening out gear in the lazarettes. The Swede ignored Slim, but showed a tendency to return to his tales of Olympian sex antics.

Nine days out of Bluff the *Tropic Trader* poked her blunt nose carefully into the narrows between Kangaroo Island and the Australian Mainland and headed into the sheltered waters leading to Port Adelaide. After a brief medical inspection the ship skirted a long stone breakwater and proceeded up the river to the dock. The weather had cleared and the sun's long winter rays warmed the decks and set heavy jackets to swinging on improvised hooks as the men secured the ship to the pier and rigged the gangway. The bosun kept them working on deck until four in the afternoon, then gave liberty to all except Square John who drew gangway watch.

Slim and Ioway headed for the railway station and made the five-mile run into the city of Adelaide. It was seven o'clock when they arrived in the center of town. Neither of them ever had seen such a place. Beautifully laid out, the city's commercial section seemed about a mile square, entirely surrounded by a belt of green park.

Though it was nearing winter, the bushes were well tended and still filled with a profusion of blossoms. The boys walked along until they found an eating place and quickly dispatched a sturdy mutton stew and several cups of strong tea. Ioway got a little self-conscious about ordering milk, when he was continually asked if he wanted it to drink. The question was asked in much the same manner that one would question the wisdom of eating a fuzzy worm.

"What the heck do they think I want it for—to fill my fountain pen?" Ioway's tone was mildly outraged.

They walked through the residential suburb of North Adelaide, crossing the lovely little Torrens River that meandered through the city between broad grassy banks, and, after a little window shopping, wandered back to the railway station and caught the last train to Port Adelaide.

Otto was on the gangway when they came aboard. He looked glum. Slim stopped and regarded him quizzically.

"You look like you lost a big one. What's the trouble?"

Otto shifted from side to side on the bunker hatch in mute annoyance. Finally he growled, "No trouble at all, mate! I was all set to stay ashore tonight when that fat rummy gets ginned up again and can't stand his watch!" He spat neatly between the rails. "Listen . . . you got the keys to the medical chest. Can't you slip some poison into his bottle and put the sonuvabitch outta his misery?"

Slim considered the proposal, then shook his head. "Wouldn't do any good, Otto. The way he spikes his liver, he can drink anything! The best thing to do is steal his mineral oil!"

He turned and started aft and the disgusted A.B. called after him. "I got a better idea—plug up his ass and let him drown in the stuff!"

When he entered the fo'c'sle he found the sodden lump of a man just as he always was after a binge: naked and oozing, a blissful expression on his pastry-puff face. He shrugged hopelessly and went to the messroom. Ioway had come in and was in the midst of a ribbing about his sex life. Apparently Rusty and Hammer had become bored with the cards and had sought other diversion. Slim felt sorry for his friend, but in the fo'c'sle you took your hazing the best way you could, and Ioway's inborn naiveté made him a perfect target. Conversations about his own sex habits embarrassed him to the point of helplessness. He'd been the butt of these jibes infrequently so far, because Warndahl had usually managed to turn the conversation to himself. But Rusty had a clear shot now and he fired another barb.

"Let me ask ya something, Ioway. We know Slim here does real good with the girls . . . but what the hell do you do? Every time we see ya yer climbin' a mountain or takin' pictures of statues in the park. Don't you ever get laid, or have you got some real nice way of takin' care of things all by yerself?"

Slim half expected Ioway to get angry at the dirty innuendo, but he just shuffled and grinned. Rusty paused a moment to see what would happen, then started again.

"Look, kid . . . you don't have to be ashamed. But ye're just about old enough to go with girls now, ain't he, Jack?"

Hammer looked at the boy appraisingly. "Could be———"

Rusty turned back to Ioway. "I'll tell ya what, kid. When's yer birthday?"

Ioway shuffled nervously.

Rusty urged him again. "Come on, pal, tell us when's yer birthday?" The boy looked pained and stared at the deck. He tried to back away again and bumped into Slim. "Look, fellas . . . I don't see what my birthday's got to do with anything."

Rusty's voice dripped with exaggerated understanding. "Of course ya don't, pal. How could you know that Jack here and me are playin' poker fer cigarettes, just so's we can save our money to buy ya a nice birthday present? Ya see, Ioway, there's somethin' ya don't understan' about us older fellas. When we see young fellas like you, we sort of get to feelin' . . . well . . . like we're yer big brothers. We want to take care of ya and see that ya learn everything the right way. Ain't that the truth, Jack?"

The ex-prize fighter had been listening with growing suspicion. But for the moment, at least, Rusty knew it was his show and he didn't wait for Hammer's confirmation. "Now, we been plannin' a little surprise party for ya . . . but it's gonna cost us a bundle. We want to make sure that yer gonna be here and not out snappin' them statues when the shindig comes off. How about it, Ioway, are ya gonna tell us?"

The boy shuffled and rubbed his head. Then, he reluctantly answered in the hope of shortening his ordeal. "I don't know how you guys found out . . . but it's next week all right!"

Rusty turned to Hammer triumphantly. "I told ya, Jack! I knew the captain wouldn't give us a bum steer! He's a wonderful man, the skipper!"

Slim waited to see what the A.B.'s practical joking was leading to.

Rusty reflected for a moment. "What day next week?" Ioway counted to himself, then announced, "It's on the tenth. That's Wednesday, I think."

Rusty looked stricken. "Aw . . . that's too bad! We'll be out at sea again by then, and ya just can't have a good party with all fellas—now can ya?" He smiled broadly at Hammer, who continued to watch both of them. Nothing in his face committed him to any part of Rusty's unclear improvisation.

"I'll tell ya what we'll do. We'll have the party tomorrow night!"

Ioway looked puzzled. "With girls——?"

Rusty made an expansive gesture. "With girls . . . with music. Why, we may even buy ya a new harmonica! How'd ya like that?"

Ioway thought a moment. "That'd be fine, fellas. I'd sure like to have one again. I miss that old one that went overboard." He referred to the original instrument that had slipped from his shirt pocket one night and gone over the side.

The A.B. nodded in agreement. "Dam' right ya do . . . and we miss it, too. Don't we, Jack?"

Hammer glanced quickly at Rusty, then back to the boy. There was a suggestion of a smile around his mouth.

Ioway was still puzzled about Rusty's proposal. "I don't see how you can have a party with girls. They're not allowed on board."

Rusty dismissed the problem with a gesture. "No trouble at all, pal. The captain's given us permission—just on account of your birthday. He figgers it will be good for the crew's morale . . . after all we bin through."

The uncertain look on Ioway's face lingered there in spite of further assurances from Rusty. It was still there when he finally beat a retreat to the fo'c'sle.

Slim waited until he was out of earshot, then seated himself on the end of the bench. "What the hell are you guys up to?"

Rusty turned on the innocent smile again. "Why, doctor, I'm surprised at you. I don't think you trust us!"

Slim's wary expression made them both laugh. Rusty looked at him for a moment, then turned serious. "Okay, Slim, I'll level with ya. I don't *know* what I'm gonna do. I was just havin' fun. But I'll tell ya somethin'. I think a good lay would be just the thing for that yokel. Nobody's told him ya can't wear it out pissin' through it! If I thought I could get a dame aboard—by Christ I *would* give him a birthday present!" He emphasized the idea with a slap of his hand on the oilcloth table cover. "He's a good kid—and I'll tell ya somethin' else. I really do miss that fuckin' harmonica. That was nice when he used to sit up there and play at night. He's good!"

332

Hammer nodded. "Too bad the kid can't get another one. He had one of those special jobs that plays anything. They cost as much as *he* makes in a month!"

Rusty thought for a moment. "We could take up a collection and get him one."

Slim watched the A.B. closely to see if the man was serious. "If you're on the level, I'll donate a buck . . . or five shillings or whatever it is."

Hammer straightened up and stretched his powerful arms. "You're dreamin'. None of these guys are gonna ante up dough for a harmonica for that kid. What ya gotta do is put the whole thing on a business basis. Like a raffle or something . . ."

"Sure, sure, but what the hell are ya gonna sell chances on—a shot at the bosun?"

Hammer raised his eyebrows. "That's not a bad idea——"

The two men seemed lost in thought, so Slim went to the pantry for a cup of coffee. When he returned, Rusty was listening with rapt attention to a proposal being outlined by Hammer.

"I made the trip on the *Louis Luckenbach,* and we loaded at Havana. That's where I saw it—only it was more like a peep show. They had a little runt of a guy with a tool out to here——" He held his palms roughly a foot apart. "They called him 'Hercules' or something. Anyway, for a couple of pesos ya could watch through the windows while he took on these dames. What a racket! Nothin' much happened 'cause he never stayed with one of them long enough to pop! But ya shoulda seen the tourists gettin' up the money to take a look! A lot of nice dames, too! I'll bet they went home and spit on their old men!"

Rusty looked puzzled. "How do ya figger we can set up *that* kind of a deal?"

Hammer spread his palms and smiled. "Easy, mate, easy! Instead of gettin' some guy, we get some broad and smuggle her aboard. We make a deal with her—give her ten shillings to show the kid what it's for. We tell her she's doin' him a big favor and gettin' paid for it. Then we set her up somewhere and sell tickets to the guys to have a look!"

Slim listened and stared into his coffee. In spite of himself he had to concede a certain begrudging admiration for the limitless variety of their larceny. It was obvious that if the plan could be brought off Hammer and Rusty stood to

333

make a nice profit. He thought about the boy and felt a little sorry for him, but he also wondered whether or not there mightn't be a certain virtue in the rough logic of these men. He knew they were not being malicious and that actually they liked Ioway for what he was—an over-grown, underfoot puppy who looked deceptively like a man. He also knew that if the ex-prize fighter made up his mind to organize Ioway's sexual instruction into a public spectacle, nothing would stop him short of Ioway's refusal to participate. But Jack had thought about that too.

"The only thing about this is—the kid's gotta be kept in the dark. Ya can't let him know that his present's gonna be a dame, and ya sure as hell can't let him know that anybody's gonna be watchin'." He shook his head sadly. "She'd never be able to get his cob up!"

"Suppose the kid don't want to touch her?" The dreadful possibility brought a look of concern to Rusty's face.

Hammer discounted the chance. "Don't worry! When we shove him in there with that dame standing bare-assed, he ain't gonna come out for hours! If I know them country boys, that dame'll be the happiest whore in Australia!"

Rusty was not convinced. Hammer looked at him closely. "What the hell are ya worried about? It's easy!" He leaned back and waited for the objections.

Rusty thought a moment, then presented the first one. "Okay . . . it's easy. Where ya gonna get the girl?"

Hammer gestured in disgust. "Where ya gonna get the girl! Fer Chris' sake, did you ever get into a port where ya couldn't find some hooker who'd go for money . . . or even for beer?"

Rusty conceded the point.

Hammer smiled. "Okay!" He squinted at the porthole. "The only problem's gonna be the place to have it. We can't bring the dame into the fo'c'sle. There's no place for the guys to look in with the ship layin' portside to. What we need is some place with a porthole on deck—like the bosun's cabin."

The men sat silently for a few moments, mentally canvassing the ship for a likely place.

Hammer suddenly sat upright. "Hey . . . I got it! I got it! Come with me!" He pushed past Slim and waited in the passageway for Rusty to slide along the bench.

Leading the way around the corner, Hammer stopped at the door of the carpenter's stateroom. It was closed and a light shone between the bottom of the heavy door and the weather coaming. Motioning Rusty and Slim to follow, he walked quickly up the companion ladder to the poop deck and crossed to the top of the deckload. He moved noiselessly across the end of the timbers, until he came to the narrow opening that had been left clear directly over the single porthole. They looked down into the space and saw Chips stretched out in his bunk, reading a magazine. No curtain was drawn across the porthole, for the carpenter assumed that the timbers insured complete privacy. The spot was made to order and Hammer had trouble concealing his delight. Back in the messroom he and Rusty completed their plans.

"The thing we gotta do now is get Chips to go along with the gag."

Rusty wagged his head vigorously. "Are you nuts? That guy won't even listen to ya!"

Hammer wet the end of his thumb and scrubbed at a coffee stain. He knew Rusty was right. The carpenter barely tolerated the erotic stories that Warndahl and the others fabricated during the long, dull days at sea. More than that, he kept his quarters spotlessly clean and the idea of some waterfront tramp entering his room would disgust him. If he ever found out she'd been in his bed, he'd probably flatten every man in the fo'c'sle who had anything to do with it. The plan was definitely out. The only way it could be accomplished would be to make certain Chips was going to be ashore. Hammer looked at Slim and the boy knew without being told what was on his mind.

"Look, Jack. If you're figuring that I'm going to get him off the ship, figure again! He and Square John go prowling together, if he goes with anybody!"

Hammer knew the boy was stating a fact and he left the proposal unmade. After a long silence the A.B. shrugged. "The only thing we can do is wait and see. We'll line up a dame and if he goes ashore tomorrow night we'll move in."

Rusty pulled a dirty handkerchief out of his back pocket and blew his nose loudly. Giving it one last smearing wipe, he returned the crumpled rag and leaned his chin on his knuckles. "This is a hell of a spot. If we make the deal with the dame, we may not have any place to put her. What happens then?"

Hammer grinned. "Don't worry, mate! We'll find something to do with her!"

Rusty twisted his mouth down in disgust. "I don't need it that bad!"

Slim watched the two men struggle with the problem that seemed almost certain to scuttle their plans. Hammer was scowling at the table top, his eyes darting from side to side while he created and discarded impractical plans for getting the carpenter out of the way. Rusty lounged back against the bulkhead and released a series of neat smoke rings which he impaled suggestively on the second finger of his right hand.

He destroyed the remnants of one with a jetted exhalation and addressed Hammer. "How much dough do ya figger we could take in?"

The A.B. took a minute for mental arithmetic. "Well . . . there's forty guys, give or take a few, and I know one thing fer damn sure—we ain't gonna get 'em all. Let's say we get twenty guys to go fer a buck apiece. That's twenty bucks, less ten shillings, which is about two bucks fifty. That means we clear seventeen bucks fifty. Cut that down the middle and ya got eight and a quarter apiece. That's almost a week's wages on this lousy scow."

Rusty seemed disappointed. "Jesus, I thought we could do better than that. How about askin' two bucks apiece?"

Hammer looked at him scornfully. "Two bucks! They ain't gonna pay that to *watch*. For two bits more, they can *do* it!"

Rusty blinked and fell silent.

Slim stifled a smile and got up. "Looks like poor old Io-way's going to be climbing mountains again, don't it?"

Hammer looked up at him belligerently. "Mountains, my ass! He's gonna be climbin' a dame . . . if I hafta give that big chisel-slinger a mickey myself!" He got up from the table and stretched.

The three wandered into the fo'c'sle and got ready to turn in. It was past one o'clock.

The next morning on deck, Hammer and Rusty watched the stevedores apprehensively as they began removing the remains of the deckload. They had begun early in the morning after the men had removed the jury-rigged shor-ings put up during the storm.

Slim and the others worked together, cleaning the rust and old paint from deck plates with long handled scrapers.

Hammer grumbled as he filed a new edge on his. "Look at those bastards! All of a sudden they gotta rush. If they keep this up, they'll have the whole goddamn load off and we won't have a place to watch from!"

Slim tried to reassure Hammer. "They won't get it all off today. They'll work the close stuff first."

Hammer looked uncertainly at a slingload of timbers dangling thirty feet in the air. "I sure hope yer right!"

Slim wondered how the plans were progressing. Hammer told him that Rusty was "passing the word" and that so far most of the guys in the deck gang and a few from the black gang had agreed. But they all wanted to make sure the girl was aboard before they put up their money. Under the circumstances, Slim thought, it was a reasonable precaution. Also they wanted the party to be held late, so they could get some time in the saloons before closing. Jack and Rusty had agreed that the affair would not be held before ten o'clock.

At supper everybody was in rare good spirits. Warndahl was more loquacious than he'd been for some days.

Chips watched the men suspiciously. "What the hell's eatin' you guys? You'd think you were all goin' to a weddin' or something!"

Hammer tried to hide his surprise and gave Rusty a kick under the table. Looking at the man with an innocent smile, the A.B. began his first attempt to learn the carpenter's plans.

"Jesus, Chips . . . I thought you knew! There's a hell of a picture playin' in town."

Chips finished a mouthful of rubbery beef and looked at Hammer balefully. "Now don't tell me you boys are all goin' to the movies?"

The A.B. looked up and down the table carefully, then spoke in a low, confidential tone. "If Ioway comes in I'll have to knock off, but I'll tell ya what's up——"

Rusty shot a startled look at his fellow conspirator and squirmed uneasily. Slim wondered what Hammer was up to.

"The truth is, Chips, it's the kid's birthday and we're gonna give him a little surprise."

The carpenter looked directly at Hammer without a change of expression and said simply, "That's a load of shit!"

The A.B. shrugged helplessly. "Okay. Why don't you ask the other guys? We're going to chip in and get the kid one of them fancy harmonicas like the one he lost overboard."

Chips clamped his jaws shut and looked around.

Rusty confirmed the story. "That's the truth. Of course we're doin' it as much for us as for him. It's goin' to be a long trip back and that music was nice. Wasn't it, fellas?"

A murmur of agreement ran along the table. The carpenter was unconvinced.

Hammer followed up. "Lemme ask ya something. Are you goin' into Adelaide tonight?"

Chips took his time about answering. "What's it to you?"

"Nothin'. I just thought if ya was, you could take the money and buy it for him."

Chips looked annoyed. "How the hell can I go around buyin' tin whistles in the middle of the night? Tell me that! And while ye're at it, tell me what the hell you guys are up to, anyway. The whole thing stinks from fish!"

Hammer made a little gesture of resignation. Slim had to admire the way the man played his part. He was capable of anything. There was genuine hurt in his voice.

"What the hell's the matter with ya, Chips? He's a sweet kid, and he gives us a lot of laughs. What stinks about wantin' to do something fer him? Like Rusty says, we're doin' somethin' fer ourselves, too. I seem to remember you sitting up there on yer big butt, hummin' yer favorite tune . . . or was that some other ship's carpenter?"

Just then Ioway came past the door, dressed in his shore clothes. Hammer jumped to his feet and startled everybody. Chips made no effort to hide his suspicion. Hammer sounded too concerned, as he questioned the boy.

"Hey, Ioway—where ya goin'?"

The boy stopped and turned back to the messroom. "I'm goin' in town for a while. I may take the train into Adelaide. The stores are open late tonight. They got something they call a late shoppin' night."

Jack held up his hand. "Hold it, kid!" He turned to the carpenter. "Did ya hear that? Late shoppin' night. Aren't you the guy that said the stores wouldn't be open?"

Chips stuck his jaw out belligerently. "All right . . . they're open. So what?"

Hammer turned his warmest smile on the man. "You know, 'so what,' Chips. You could do us all a big favor. Come on—how about it?"

The big carpenter sat perfectly still, regarding the cigarettes on the table in front of him. After a moment he lifted his eyes and looked at Hammer. "All right . . give me the money. If I go, I'll try to get that thing for you!" He started to rise and Hammer turned to Slim.

"Okay, kid. You heard the man. Give him the money . . . and while yer at it, tell him what to get!"

Slim blinked at Hammer in shocked disbelief. His eyes

338

traveled to the carpenter, then he looked up at Ioway, grinning in the doorway. He thought about the poker winnings in his locker. A good part of the money had been won from Hammer and Rusty and he held an IOU for more. Hammer bored into him with his cold blue eyes, but the smile on his face was friendly . . . and expectant. Rising slowly from the table, Slim went to the fo'c'sle and took twenty dollars in assorted bills and coins and brought it to the carpenter.

Chips held it and looked slowly around the table. Turning to the boy he indicated the cash. "Where'd you get this money?"

Before Slim could answer, Hammer cut in: "Where do you think he got it? It's a collection!"

Chips spilled the coins into his left hand and counted the bills. "Who'd you collect it from?"

The boy glanced at the others and searched for an answer.

Again Hammer supplied it. "He collected it from us . . . all of us. How about you addin' a little something to the pot, too?"

The man's audacity left Slim speechless.

The carpenter took a final count of the money and slowly put it in his pocket. "Okay, kid, come and tell me what you want."

Hammer echoed the words, "Yeah, Slim, go tell him what we want!"

Chips glared at the grinning A.B. "Listen, Hammer, maybe the boy's lost his voice and you have to talk for *him*, but don't try talkin' for *me*!"

The smile remained and the voice was agreeable. "Sure, Chips. Anything ya say!"

As Slim moved through the door, he heard Rusty call Ioway. "Hey, country boy! We got plans for you!"

The carpenter opened the door to his cabin and Slim followed him in. When the door closed behind them, the man turned to face him. "What the hell's all this crap about buying that kid an harmonica? Since when have you guys all got to actin' like yer runnin' a church social? Something stinks about this. Anything that crooked sonuvabitch touches stinks from dead fish! What's he up to?"

Slim did his best to tell the carpenter that Ioway had said something about having a birthday. He tried to convince him that the idea of getting the harmonica had just sort of "happened."

"Do you mean to say that those guys anted up *twenty*

339

bucks to buy that punk kid a present? Did they actually give you the money?"

Slim hesitated before he answered. He didn't want to tell the carpenter a lie, but he couldn't actually tell him the truth, either. "Well, . . . it all happened kind of fast so I—— Well, they asked me if I'd put up the money until Jack and Rusty collected it from the guys."

Sudden understanding spread over the carpenter's rugged face. Reaching into his pocket, he took out the bills and coins and handed them back to the boy. "So that's the pitch, is it? Well, now . . . I'll tell you what we'll do. Since it's yer money and not theirs, if *you* want to buy that corn-husker a toy you just get right on the train and go to town and get it yerself! I got other things to do!"

Slim looked at the money. He felt both relieved and foolish.

The carpenter waited for him to say something. "Well?"

"Look, Chips, I just went along with the guys. I'd like to see Ioway have a harmonica, but I sure don't intend to pay for it myself!"

"Well, that's just what Hammer had in mind, sonny. You know, I figgered you for a real bright kid, but I'm beginnin' to wonder. You sure as hell aren't very smart if you let that bullshirt artist talk you into givin' his party!"

Slim shoved the money into his pocket and turned to leave.

The carpenter stopped him as he reached for the door handle. His voice was gentler with a trace of a smile in it. "Slim, ya never get too old to learn—remember that! When ya get to be as old as me, maybe you'll learn that them guys are all crooks." As he started to unbutton his shirt, he added, "But I'll tell ya one thing. They gotta get up pretty goddamn early to fool this old carpenter! You hang onto that money! Let the kid buy his own tin whistle. He makes as much as you do! I'll see ya later . . . I'm goin' to town."

Slim opened the door and the carpenter closed the subject emphatically. "And I ain't goin' shoppin' fer toys, either!" He winked broadly and turned to his locker.

In the messroom Ioway was seated at the head of the table. His coat was neatly folded on the bench beside Hammer, and Rusty was lighting a cigarette for him. The boy was pleased and confused and Slim laughed at the expression on his face, as he sucked in the first big mouthful of smoke.

Hammer smiled benignly. "Go on, Ioway! Cigarettes don't stunt yer growth! Who the hell told ya that? Jesus, kid, ye're eighteen now—ye're a man!"

The boy made an unhappy face and closed his eyes as the smoke exploded from his mouth in a great cloud.

Warndahl, sitting with his splinted arm resting on the table, urged the boy on to another try. "Take it down into yer lungs, kid. Inhale it . . . go on!"

Ioway held the cigarette awkwardly between two stiff fingers. "Geez, fellas . . . I don't like the taste! None of my folks smoke. The only thing I ever tried was corn silk. That don't taste good, either!"

Spots, recovered but still wan from his last gin jag, sipped on a mug of black coffee. He watched the boy try again and gag while the others laughed.

"Ioway——" The fat A.B. spoke softly. "You don't hafta smoke to be a man. Leave him alone, fellas . . . he's gonna get sick!"

Hammer looked concerned. He reached over and took the butt from the boy's mouth. "We don't want *that* to happen! I'll tell ya what ya do. You guys take Ioway ashore for a little while, so we can fix up the place a little. Okay? Get goin'!"

Slim stayed aboard with the two A.B.s. When they heard Chips' door open and close, Hammer nudged the boy.

"Go on . . . walk up town with him. Make sure he gets on that train. I'm goin' ashore and line up a dame and Rusty's gonna rig the Jacob's ladder on the well deck. I'll bring her aboard from the work punt."

Hammer referred to a flat-bottomed scow used by the men to paint the sides along the water line. It had been in use all day and was still moored below the well deck on the starboard side.

Slim called after the carpenter as he went up the companionway. "Hold it, Chips. I'll walk up town with you!"

The Shiek was sitting sullenly on the bunker, doing his gangway watch. He made no sign of recognition as they went ashore.

Chips looked up over his shoulder at the man as they moved along the dark sides of the ship. "There's another little beauty! I've sailed with a lot of crews, but this one wins the whole shootin' match!"

They walked in silence to the railway terminal. "Are you really gonna spend yer money for that silly doohickey?"

Slim hesitated and felt the money in his pocket. "No, I guess not. You go on . . . I'll just take a walk."

The carpenter pointed a warning finger. "If I were you I'd put the money in the ship's safe! Those thieves'll rap you on the head for half of that!"

— 29 —

Slim wandered around the little town for a while. He saw Ioway and several of the men at a bar. They were toasting the boy with mugs of beer. Passing by, before they discovered him, he returned to the *Topic Trader*.

Rusty was standing in the shadows on the poop deck, peering down into the darkness. "Did the big bastard get on the train?"

Slim moved over beside him. "Yeah, he's gone."

"The sonuvabitch nearly fouled up the whole detail."

"Not for my money, he didn't!"

Rusty turned on him angrily. "What the hell are you kickin' about? This hasn't cost ya anything, has it?"

"Not yet, it hasn't."

"Well, it's goin' to right now. Get up yer buck!"

Slim reached into his pocket and pulled out a dollar in change. "Here it is, and don't forget it's paid."

Rusty jammed the coins into his pocket. "Don't worry, Buster, you'll get your peek along with the rest of us!" He peered down into the darkness again and listened. "Jesus, I wish that guy would hurry up. He's been gone an hour. Maybe he had trouble."

The night was clear and cold and Slim pulled his collar higher. They leaned on the railing together and listened to the harbor noises.

Rusty was growing nervous. "Look . . . you stay here and watch. I'm gonna take a run up to the pierhead and see if I can find him."

The A.B. slipped away from the rail, moved forward across the deckload, and dropped down behind its uneven end. Slim saw him climb the ladder and walk along the portside of the main deckhouse.

A quarter of an hour went by and then a soft whistle drifted up along the topsides. Walking to the rail, Slim peered down into the darkness. He heard the muffled

343

sound of an oar pushing through the water and the gentle bump of the boat against the plates.

Hammer called in a loud whisper, "Hey, up there! We got company. Drop a line and pull us around to the ladder."

Slim leaned far out over the rail. He could barely make out the dark rectangular shadow of the punt.

"Okay—hold it a minute! I'll get a heaving line." He ran to the locker by the capstan and brought the small coil. Loosening it, he lowered the heavy monkey fist until he felt Hammer take a strain on it.

"Let me have a little more—"

He payed out a few more feet and waited while the A.B. tied it through the towing ring. He could hear the metal rattle against the damp wood.

"Okay, haul us around—easy."

Talking in the line until he felt it grow taut in his hand, Slim leaned over the rail and slowly led the invisible passengers around to the Jacob's ladder.

Hammer's voice called up to him in a hoarse whisper. " 'Kay . . . tie it off!"

Slim made the line fast to one of the upright shorings and waited at the side. He could hear the rattle of the wooden rungs. Then he heard a girl's indignant voice. "No you don't, laddie. You go first!"

Hammer grumbled and the ropes creaked noisily under his weight. After a moment his head appeared above the timbers and he gave Slim a broad wink. Scrambling up on the load, he leaned over and extended a hand down into the dark. Slim crouched alongside.

The rungs rattled loudly and he heard the girl's complaining voice again. "Wot the bloody 'ell 'ave ya got me into?"

Hammer lay flat on the timbers and grasped at her hand. "Come on up, yer highness! I got ya into the easiest ten shillin's ya ever stole!"

The girl's head labored up over the edge of the timbers and the two of them all but pulled her up on deck. Slim couldn't see her clearly, but he heard the petulance in her voice as she pulled at her dress and coat.

"If you ask me, it's worth a quid to climb up the blasted ladder! Me—climbin' like a monkey! Why can't I come aboard like a proper lady?"

Hammer put an arm around her and hurried her into the shadow of the poop deck. "I told ya, we're giving one

344

of the boys a surprise party—and you're the present. He's never been with a girl. You're gonna teach him."

The girl made a try at straightening her hair and moaned. "Oh, my God in 'eaven, now I'm teachin' clawses!" She spoke with a broad accent. "Well, come on lads, let's get it over with." She stopped suddenly. "Now wait a minute! 'Ow about seein' the ten bob before we go another step?"

Jack tapped Slim on the arm. "Give her the money, pal. I'll give it to you later!" He couldn't see Slim's wry smile as he dug out a ten-shilling note.

She tried to examine it, but it was useless in the dark. " 'Ow do I know it's right?"

The deck boy leaned close to her and whispered, "Don't worry, lady, it's good money." He caught a suffocating whiff of cheap perfume. It smelled like the stuff that cowhands used generously on Saturday night in lieu of a bath. It made him shudder.

The girl turned to Hammer. "I like 'im—'e talks like a gentleman!"

"Yer date's a gentleman too, baby. Come on, let's go!"

Hammer led the girl carefully across the deck to the companionway. They paused in the deep shadow by its side. Taking Slim by the arm, the A.B. pulled him close. "Duck down there and make sure everything's clear. Hurry up—and where the hell's Rusty?"

"He went looking for you——"

Hammer cursed softly. "The stupid bastard!"

The girl pulled her arm free. "All right now, laddie, let's not start usin' language!"

Hammer snorted in disgust. "Go on, kid. We'll wait for ya!"

Slim dropped down the companion ladder and looked around. The black gang messroom was empty. So was the pantry. He poked his head in the fo'c'sle. The light was on, but no one was in the place except Russian John who was reading behind his curtain. Tiptoeing to the ladder, he whistled softly and waited. Nothing happened. He whistled again, louder. Still there was no sound. Puzzled, he started up, then stopped in his tracks. He heard the dull ring of heavy footsteps on the portside of the deck. Hurrying to the top, he nearly collided with the Shiek.

"Oh, hi! You startled me . . . I didn't see you!"

The sallow ordinary seaman looked at him strangely. "What's the matter with you, kid? Does my face scare ya?" He grinned in his sinister, movie-villain manner.

345

Slim forced a smile and tried to sound casual. "Naw! I just didn't hear you, that's all! You want a hand with the lines?"

The man sneered at him. "When I need deck boys to help with lines, I'll come runnin' to you first, kid, I promise!"

He walked over to the portside bollards and loosened the big hawsers. Slacking them off a bit, he redid the turns slowly. Slim watched and it seemed to him that the man deliberately took twice the time needed to do the job. When he secured the last hawser, he sat down on top of one of the bollards and lit a cigarette. Slim knew that Hammer and Ioway's "surprise" were crouching behind the big slatted potato box. He was afraid the girl would get troublesome if she had to stay hidden too long. Just as the boy was going to try to get the ordinary talking in hope of diverting him, the gangway rattled loudly and the Shiek got up. Flipping the cigarette carelessly down onto the dock, he walked slowly forward. Rusty met him halfway along the low deckload and they passed without speaking.

Slim was waiting for him at the companionway. "Where have you been? Jack's down below with the girl!"

Rusty didn't answer. He plunged down the companion ladder with Slim behind him. Hammer was just closing the door of the carpenter's cabin. He glowered at the A.B.

"A big fuckin' help you are! Where the hell did ya go?"

Rusty opened his arms helplessly. "I went lookin' fer you. Where did *you* go? Fer Chris' sake, ya kept me waitin' an hour! I thought somethin' happened to ya!"

Hammer scowled in disgust. "Do ya think these dames grow on trees? I had to buy the broad a couple of drinks before she'd listen to me! She knows what happens if she gets caught on a ship!"

Rusty looked worried. "We only got twenty minutes before they bring the kid back. Let's get those papers ready!"

"You get 'em ready! I'm goin' in there and talk with her. She's a cranky one!"

Rusty gave Hammer a warning look. "You keep outta her . . . no samples!"

The A.B. glowered and stepped back inside the cabin.

Rusty looked at the closed door uncertainly, then turned to Slim. "You got some paper and a pencil?"

"How much do you need?"

"Enough to make some tickets with numbers—twenty of 'em."

Slim went to his locker and got several sheets from the writing pad. They sat in the mess hall and tore them into squares. After they were numbered, he folded them into quarters and put them into his knitted watchcap. They had hardly finished the job when they heard voices on deck. The laughter and clatter of feet on the steel companion ladder told them that their "guest of honor" was returning.

The men were already in the alleyway when Jack stepped out of the carpenter's cabin. When they saw his wink, they fell quiet and stood smiling in anticipation.

Ioway looked at them curiously. "What's the matter, fellas?"

Hammer draped a heavy arm across his shoulders. "Nothin's the matter, birthday boy! We got a little surprise fer ya!"

Ioway watched him with an uncertain smile.

The A.B. turned to the men. "All right, Rusty, you take the guys up on deck until we're ready. Kid, you're gonna stay here with me!" He gave Ioway a comradely slap on the back that jerked the boy's head. "Okay . . . get goin', you guys!"

The men followed Rusty back up to the companion ladder. Ioway watched them leave and wondered at their hurry. "Why are they goin'? I thought we were gonna stay here in the messroom?"

Hammer smiled at the boy reassuringly. "Naw, I don't want them hangin' around 'til it's time for ya to open yer present." He clouted Ioway's back again and chuckled to himself.

Up on deck Rusty cautioned the men to be quiet. No cigarettes were lit, lest the watchman or the bosun—or worse yet, the officers—should come back to investigate the unusual activity on the after decks.

The watchcap was passed around and the men drew lots to see who would crawl down in between the timbers for the first look. Rusty went ahead of them and waited for Hammer to take Ioway into the cabin to meet his unexpected "birthday present." Above him were most of the crew from the deck gang and a surprising turnout from the black gang. In the dark Slim recognized Warndahl, Spots, Otto, Squirt, Brill, Rags, and Pete. Several others appeared quietly and took their tickets, after paying admission to Rusty. Slim drew slip number two.

With the ticket actually in his pocket he suddenly felt sheepish about the Peeping Tom business, even though the

347

whole thing was a gag on Ioway. More than half the fun had been in the planning.

Rags, the wiper on the second watch, had drawn the first number. He complained bitterly. "It's no good, drawin' low number at a thing like this!" He spoke with querulous authority. "Another thing! It's against the law to start until their clothes are off! Ya can't see nuthin' 'til then, anyway!"

Slim made no reply. He felt that the sooner he went down into the slot and got it over with, the happier he'd be. Actually he much preferred to stay on deck and stand lookout. Now that Ioway's birthday party was a fact, he was growing uneasy about the Shiek. He knew the bosun was aboard, too, and that he had a habit of wandering around on deck at night. The only thing in favor of privacy was the weather. It had turned very cold and the men were slapping themselves to keep warm.

Suddenly Rusty scrambled topside. "Okay, you guys . . . the first two!"

Rags nearly fell in his haste to climb down between the timbers. Slim dropped down and squeezed in beside him. They had to be careful not to get too close to the porthole. Slim could imagine what kind of a howl would go up from the girl if she were to discover the public nature of her performance.

Having to stay well back in the shadows, sharing the tiny space, limited the vision, and Slim could see very little. Ioway was apparently standing with his back to the porthole, facing the girl. He was not visible. But the girl was, and Slim got his first clear look at her since she'd come aboard.

Rags saw her for the first time also. There was disappointment in his voice as he whispered to the deck boy, "Aw, Jesus! A buck for this? She ain't so good!"

Slim was inclined to agree. The girl apparently had begun to wear a bit under the burden of her profession, though she appeared to be only in her late twenties. She might be even younger, Slim thought.

Rags fidgeted nervously. "Man, I've seen mosquito bites bigger'n them!" His tone was impatient. "Well, come on, girl . . . git goin' with the guy!"

Rusty called down from the top of the load. "Hey, what are you guys doin' down there? Hurry up, will ya?"

Slim was getting tired of the cramped quarters, and though he felt a small erotic excitement as the girl finished disrobing, it was no more than he'd felt when he saw his first so-called "French post-cards" in high school. He nudged Rags. "I'm going topside!"

Rags spoke vehemently. "Fer a buck I ain't gettin' outta here until something happens!"

Climbing up the ends of timbers, Slim stretched his cramped legs and buttoned his sheepskin coat tightly around him. Another man took his place and Rags was hauled out, protesting.

"She was just goin' after him! Jesus . . . what's the idea?"

His offended tone didn't faze Rusty. "If ya wanted a private show, ya shoulda bought all the tickets!"

Rusty pushed him to one side and called for number four. One of the men detached himself from the waiting shadows and disappeared down into the hole.

Rags went to the edge with the rest of the men and peered in. "Listen, you guys . . . the least ya kin do is tell us what's happening!"

Slim heard a hoarse whisper and Rags, who'd assumed the job of relaying the action, repeated it softly for all to hear. "She's helpin' him take off his clothes. He looks scared!"

Another message was relayed to Rags, whose stage whisper grew louder. Slim looked forward to see if the deck was still clear. Two more men came grumbling out of the narrow opening in the big timbers. Slim recognized Warndahl's voice.

"Why the hell don't ya let some guy in there that knows what to do? She's got him backed up to the wall. Ya can't even see him!"

From the two men who'd taken their places Rags got another round of description. "She's tryin' to kiss him, but he don't wanta play. He looks like he's gonna run outa the place!"

From the shadows came Hammer's voice. No one had seen him come up on deck. "He won't run no place. I got the door propped from the outside!"

A ripple of low laughter ran through the intent little crowd and two more men took their places. Rags was silent for a moment, then he called down into the opening. "Hey . . . what's goin' on? Give us the scoop, will ya?" He waited for another moment, then called again. "All right down there, what's happenin'?"

A voice answered in a growling whisper, "Shut up, will ya! I'll tell ya in a minute!"

Slim went to the edge of the timbers and listened. Several others followed. From down in the shadows came a long, low whistle, followed by a voice filled with wonderment. It sounded like Otto.

"Holy jumpin——" There was a long pause, then the voice resumed, "She's got his boom topped! You should see the salami that kid's got stuck on him! If he ever learns what to do with it, he'll wind up being president!"

The tension mounted noticeably as the men came up and two more scrambled down.

"Take it easy, you guys!" Rusty spoke sharply. "You're gonna tip him off!" It grew quiet again for a moment or two, then Rags whispered urgently, "All right, will ya? Give us a break. What's he doin'?"

Slim thought he recognized Brill's booming whisper. "He ain't doin' nothing . . . but he will be in a minute if she keeps that up! From the look on her face, I think she'da paid us for the job!"

Slim heard the voice again, speaking to the couple in the room, coaching from the shadows. "Whoops . . . whoops! Take it easy, girlie, or the show'll be over!"

Rags nearly shouted into the opening. "Fer Chris' sake, never mind coachin' *her!* Tell *us* what's goin' on!"

Brill and his companion came up and two more spectators dropped down out of sight. Otto joined Rags and both of them urged a running account. "Are they in the bunk yet?"

The answer came from Lintz, the wiper on the third watch. "Naw! He's sittin' on the edge with a real silly smile on his face and she's foolin' around! Boy, he's beautiful, ain't he?"

Rags growled at him. "I don't know, ya goofy bastard —I ain't seen him!"

Rusty leaned over the opening. "Come up outta there! There's more guys waitin'!"

Lintz and his companion climbed out reluctantly and another pair eagerly took their places. It was quiet for a few seconds, then one of the men spoke. It was Gonzales, one of the water tenders. "He looks pretty fonny. Why don' he takin' off hees short?"

Otto's hoarse reply was filled with scornful pity. "He's got his shorts off, ya idiot!"

Gonzales' rich Mexican accent was patient. "Not hees onnerwear, gringo! Hees short . . . an' hees necktie!"

Otto snorted down into the darkness. "He can do it in a high silk hat . . . as long as he *does* sumpthin'! What's going on now?"

350

Down in the cramped quarters Gonzales watched through the porthole for a moment, then raised his head toward the top of the opening. "Eets better now . . . she's takeen off hees short. I tell you somtheen, fellas. She's no' very preety——"

Hammer pushed Rusty to one side. "She ain't in there to win a beauty contest, Mex! Vamoose! Let's go!"

Two more pairs of men took their turns at the porthole and gave vent to their frustration with quiet curses, as Ioway's birthday party was temporarily suspended while the girl had trouble with the necktie.

Spots and Roc, the fireman from Brooklyn, were next at the porthole. The fat little A.B. stayed down for less than the allotted minute and crawled up.

Jack scowled at him. "What's the matter with you?"

Spots shrugged. "I don't like her looks!"

The A.B. sneered at him. "Well, now, that's just too goddamn bad! We'll run right out an' get ya another one!" He ended the sarcasm with a disgusted grunt.

Roc climbed up on the top of the timbers. He was a short, powerfully built Italian-American who was the ship's physical culture faddist. "Hey . . . ya better tell da kid how to clean himself after dat dame!"

He addressed the advice to Hammer, who dismissed it with a laugh. "You tell him, Roc!" The A.B. blocked the opening and held the next pair back. "Hold it a minute. I wanta see what the hell that jerk is doin'!" He put a hand on either side of the opening and dropped easily to the bottom of the eight-foot shaft.

The men whose turn it was hovered impatiently. Otto hung his face over the edge and called down, "What's he doin'?" There was no answer. "Come on, Jack! What's he doin'?"

Hammer's head came up out of the blackness and he pulled himself on top of the timbers. "All right, you guys . . . get down there! I don't think this show's gonna run much longer!"

In the dark Slim could see the broad grin on his face. The next two men dived down. Slim thought he recognized Stokes, but he couldn't be certain until he heard the fireman's unmistakable British accent when he returned to the top of the load. "It must be very frustrating for the poor old beast. That Ioway chap hasn't the foggiest notion of how to go about it!"

Hammer defended his choice. "She ain't a beast! You bastards are just sore 'cause ya ain't in there with her!"

Twenty-two men had been in and out of the narrow confines of the peep show in something less than twenty minutes. Each one had had his turn as a spectator, and it was completely clear to them that for better or worse they were witnessing what was beyond a question or a doubt a premier performance. The girl had followed the flustered boy all over the cabin until she had finally trapped him in a corner and, with practiced hands, began consolidating her gains.

At the moment she was holding him in a somewhat unconventional manner while she coaxed him to the bunk. It was obvious that, once having seen Ioway, this thorough-going pro had every intention of fully discharging her obligation to her employers.

Ioway looked down at her uncertainly, but was in no position to retreat without danger of sustaining a serious injury. She smiled up at him and her voice was filled with promise. "Come on, laddie . . . don't be afraid! We 'aven't 'ad the best of it yet, you know!" She urged him toward her and Ioway, trapped between desire and despair, began what for him was a painfully unfamiliar maneuver.

Outside the porthole, on the edge of the dim glow, Rags was poised to relay the next move to the waiting men above. In the last anguished moment of frustration the skinny little wiper had removed his greasy black engineer's cap and slipped a five-dollar bill from the sweatband. From Hammer he'd purchased exclusive rights to the show for five minutes—at a dollar a minute. There had been much grumbling, but no one had topped the offer. Rags pressed as close as he dared and watched eagerly.

Hammer's loud whisper came down from overhead. "All right, popeyes . . . what's he doin'?"

Rags aimed his answer up into the darkness. "Nothin' yet! He's still tryin' to climb aboard!" The fireman watched Ioway's clumsy efforts to get into the bunk and muttered unhappily, "I thought them country kids learned how to climb!"

Hammer still leaned perilously over the edge of the opening. "Ain't he up there yet?"

"Naw!" Rags spat out the word in disgust. "What kind of a goon is this guy, anyway?" He turned back to the porthole and watched Ioway for a moment and coached him from the shadows. "Go on, ya silly idiot, get the other leg up! That's it—— Naw! Naw! Get 'em *both* inside! Gee —zuz!" He paused for a moment and watched. " 'At's bet-

352

ter . . . 'at's the way. Okay now, kid, close yer eyes an'
lower away—ya can't miss!"

From above he heard Otto's impatient whisper. "What
the hell's goin' on?"

Rags looked up quickly. "Nuthin'—he's on his hands
and knees, and ya wanna know sumpthin'? He can damn
near reach her from there!"

Otto groaned painfully. "Well, fer crap's sake, ain't he
gonna do nuthin'?"

The wiper was disgusted. "If ya ask me, I think he's
gonna lift his leg and pee on the wall!" Rags fell silent
again for a moment, then suddenly he alerted and peered
closer through the porthole. He hardly breathed as he
watched hopefully for another moment, then turned to
call to the men up above him.

"Hey, fellas . . . stand by!" Flattening his back against
the timbers, he tipped his head upward and watched
Ioway out of the corners of his eyes. He spoke softly, en-
couragingly. " 'At's it, kid, now ye're gonna make it!
Steady, boy . . . steady——" The wiper purred the words.

Hammer barked at him gruffly, "Louder, will ya?"

Rags ignored him and stood motionless for a moment.
Then, barely suppressing a triumphal shout, he called up
to the waiting men: "He's *there*, fellas . . . he's home!"

There was a flurry of hushed excitement as the men
crowded around the edge of the hole to hear the results of
the final round. Rags' account of the next few moments
was as fragmentary as it was tantalizing. His voice trembled with repressed excitement.

"Boy! Look at her go—wow! She's gonna break the
kid's back! Hold on, boy . . . hold on . . . stay with her!
Fellas, I gotta tell ya . . . it's beautiful! Bee-*you*-teeful!"
The words were barely out when his tone changed suddenly. He paused a moment. "Hey! Hey! What are ya
doin'? Fer God's sake, what are ya tryin' to do? Don't—
don't leave her now!" His tone was pleading as his coaching switched to the girl. "Hang onto him, honey—don't let
him go! He don't know what's happenin'!" His voice rose
to a wailing crescendo, then cut off abruptly. There was
an awesome silence.

Up on deck the men heard him cursing. "Why, you
miserable bastard . . . you crummy yokel! How could ya
do a thing like that to that poor dame? How could ya do
it—how? Go on! Tell me! How?"

Hammer nearly landed on top of him as he jumped

down into the hole. "Fer Chris' sake, what's the matter with ya? Ya sounded like you was with her too!"

Rags didn't answer; he turned away slowly and began to climb up on deck. Hammer stared through the porthole for a moment, then closed his eyes and rubbed a big hand slowly across his face. He followed Rags up on deck without a word. The two of them stood silently in the darkness for a time, then Hammer said flatly, "Okay, fellas, beat it —the show's over!"

The crew stood a moment in silent speculation, then slowly dispersed to find other amusement. Hammer and Rags stared back down into the hole. Below they could see the dim light of the porthole glowing weakly along the sides of the timbers. They said nothing. They just stood shaking their heads, like two men unable to grasp the truth of an impossible disaster.

An hour passed before the two instigators returned to the messroom and sat down wearily to mugs of black coffee. Hammer looked tired, and Slim smelled the heavy sweetness of alcohol on his breath. Otto and Warndahl were playing half-hearted games of solitaire. Spots had gone ashore. Square John had taken the gangway watch and the Shiek had disappeared as usual.

Otto looked at the ex-fighter. "How'd ya make out?"

Jack's shoulders heaved with a mirthless laugh. "Okay. She was so hung up, I had to finish the kid's job behind the shed!"

Otto looked up and brushed away an imaginary tear. His voice dripped sympathy. "Aw, now, that's a cryin' shame! Why didn't ya call one of yer old buddies? We're only too glad to help a shipmate. At least we coulda held yer pants for ya!"

Hammer glowered. "You didn't miss anything. She was already over the hill!" He pulled a cigarette from his shirt pocket and lit up. Exhaling a huge crowd, he turned to Slim. "Where's that stupid jerk?"

The boy looked toward the fo'c'sle. "In the head."

Hammer grunted. "We oughta cut that thing offa him and give it to somebody who knows what to do with it!"

Rusty shrugged. "Well . . . at least we made a buck out of it!"

They turned as Ioway walked past, carrying a bucket of soapy water.

Otto called to him. "Hey, you . . . come here a minute——"

354

The boy looked at them glumly. "What do you guys want?"

Otto got up and walked over to him. Setting the bucket on the deck, he pushed the reluctant boy down on the bench. "We just wanna know how ya liked yer birthday present?"

Rusty added grimly, "We went to a lot of trouble and money to fix ya up, boy! Whaddaya say? How'd ya like it?"

Ioway stared down at the strip of scuffed red deck visible between the edges of the bench and table. His face was white and drawn and he ran his fingers nervously along the splintered top of the narrow weather board. Rusty watched him for a time, then looked nervously at Hammer and the others.

Slim wished they'd let him go about his business. The party was over. Hammer and Rusty had made their money and the men had had their fun.

They sat in silence for a time before Ioway finally spoke. He seemed embarrassed, a bit apologetic. "I don't want you guys to think I don't appreciate what you did for me. Maybe if there was time to get used to the idea, I'd of been all right . . . but I guess after what you said and all —I was sort of expecting a new harmonica!"

— 30 —

Still short one officer on deck, the *Tropic Trader* had moved, in the following weeks, along the south coast of the Australian continent, swung northwest along the fringe of the Indian Ocean to Fremantle, then up toward the Equator to Darwin on the southern edge of the Timor Sea. For most of the trip she had bobbed like a cork with hardly a ton of cargo to ballast her. On watch with the third mate, Slim had felt the beginnings of terror, as two hundred feet of unburdened bow and foredeck climbed up the face of a mountainous green sea, hung suspended for a dreadful instant, then dropped into the trough with a ringing slam. The sea suddenly spread out in giant wings of white foam which furled before the gale and beat for a frantic moment against the face of the bridge.

Holst, in a sweat-sogged undershirt, had resumed scratching his shaggy back against the door casing, and said, "We hit another milestone! Hope she don't pop her rivets till we get to Singapore."

She didn't, and in due time the crew had made the most of its liberty. Indulgent authorities had regretfully insisted that Hammer and Rusty be confined to the ship. Both men had been docked a month's wages by the captain for organizing a rickshaw race in front of the Raffles Hotel and making book on same. There was no law against such impromptu sport in itself, but the drunken collaborators had overstretched British colonial patience by attempting to use half-naked prostitutes for jockeys. As a result both A.B.s suffered financial setbacks from which they never completely recovered.

Slim had overestimated his capacity just once in an effort to get a prized certificate from the "Gin Sling Club." As a consequence he'd experienced the painless process of "passing out" and its painful counterpart, "coming-to." Holst had watched him at the wheel the following day

356

and, although he'd been secretly amused, delivered the boy a stinging lecture on liquor, women, and tatooing. This latter subject was added, because during the process of cramming for the gin sling exam Slim had acquired a small blue foul anchor with red flukes on the cap of his right shoulder. He'd discovered it the next morning when an ugly scab, hidden beneath an improvised bandage of brown paper, had rubbed off and started to bleed. A new scab formed and in the next two weeks had shed of its own accord, unveiling the mark of the sailor which would go with him to his grave. He wondered what his parents would say . . . what Edye would say? He knew that if his grandfather had been alive he would have smiled his approval. The tradition of the sea had lived strongly in the old man, who always said a bit of "needlework" helped keep it alive.

From Singapore the *Tropic Trader* butted her way up the China Sea to the Portuguese island of Macao. There, much to everyone's relief, the Shiek disappeared. Slim was promoted to ordinary seaman at forty-seven dollars and fifty cents a month. The ensuing celebration cost him nearly half the first month's as yet unearned raise. The chief celebrant was Hammer, as usual. Slim took some comfort from remembering his nest egg. In the ship's safe were seventy-five dollars representing half of his pay held back for six months, plus another one hundred and thirty dollars won at poker. It was a tidy sum and he became all the more determined to add to it.

At Hong Kong the tramp had taken on a few tons of mixed cargo, including cases of tea and crates of teak furniture bound for the Chinese shops along San Francisco's Grant Avenue.

In each port Slim and Sparks, with Stokes who had taken to joining them, made it a point to see the principal places of interest and the young sailor cheerfully tolerated the long humid days at sea for the pleasures of prowling through the exotic shops. Slim particularly enjoyed riding into the outlying districts for a look at the real face of a country no longer hidden behind the mask of grinning, dollar-induced friendliness.

During the days in Singapore, Macao and Hong Kong, there'd been almost no fo'c'sle life. Few meals were served aboard and the colored cooks and Filipino messmen had made the most of their unrestricted acceptance ashore. Morale in the steward's department improved noticeably with all hands, except Mr. Pugh who fluttered and grumbled and poked around ineffectually, looking for the merest reasons to confine his brown brood to quarters.

Leaving Hong Kong, the *Tropic Trader* made her way eastward through the Bashi Channel at the tip of Formosa, passed the Batan Islands, and headed southeast to Manila.

As they passed the fortress of Corregidor, the mess boys were beside themselves with eagerness to get home for those few precious days. Chico had become so exited that he'd planned a whole Cook's tour, as Sparks called it, and the little fellow had even gone so far as to promise, "Eet won' cost you wan penny!" He had slapped his bulging pocket. "Een my ceety you' money ees no good!" Slim had agreed to accompany the Filipino, but had no intention of letting him foot the entire bill. As it was, Chico managed to pay for enough things.

The second night Warndahl had been arrested for committing a "nuisance" on a sampan from the bridge across the Pasig River that separated the old walled city from the new. Again a fine had been imposed: this time by both the police ashore and the mate aboard ship.

Chico's Cook's tour had continued for part of each day and, during those pleasant but very warm hours, they had seen all the sights, including St. Augustine Church, built by the conquistadors in 1606. It was here that Chico had given the men an unexpected insight into his character. He had insisted that Spots come to meet a Father Stefano, whose reputation for successful conversions to the "straight-and-narrow" of Catholic morality had become a legend in the islands. The fat problem drinker had been sufficiently impressed with the gentle little priest to attend daily masses. Some time during those ten days in Manila the miracle had happened. Spots had taken another vow. But this time it had not been the hasty coming to terms with God that preceded and followed each past transgression. Something new had happened to the man and it was recognizable even to the insensate Warndahl.

The Swede had confronted Spots one night in the fo'c'sle. "What the hell's got into you lately? Yer stomach give out? You ain't had a drink for three days, if I'm countin' right!"

Spots had replied quietly, "That's right, Gus. I'm off the stuff for good."

Warndahl had regarded him skeptically. "Wanna bet?"

"Sure. How much?"

The Swede had hesitated, then finally exclaimed, "A month's pay, by God!"

Spots had asked the others to witness the deal. "You heard him, fellas."

Turning back to the A.B. he'd stuck out his hand. "Okay, Vic . . . you're on—by God!" He'd added the last two words with quiet emphasis.

Warndahl had looked at him curiously. "You better save your money, sweetheart! I'm bettin' on a sure thing!" He'd winked knowingly at the men around the table.

Spots had replied simply, "So am I!"

There was a new officer on the bridge and a new seaman in the fo'c'sle. Both had boarded the *Tropic Trader* in Manila. Holst had been moved up to second officer to fill the duties of the late Lars Peterson and the new man, named Banner, had taken over the third watch. Slim had changed watches along with Holst.

The new mate was a dark, quiet person, somewhere in his late forties. He seldom spoke on or off duty, but the fo'c'sle scuttle butt had it that he'd taken the berth to get back home to the States after skippering an interisland steamer for a number of years. Apparently his navigation was not equal to Peterson's, for Slim had heard Holst grumble, "He's no goddamn help with that sextant. He's as bad as I am."

The other new member was also an American—a man called Whitey who had signed on as a workaway at one cent a month. He had no seaman's papers, but was a capable hand and fit easily into the fo'c'sle, all the more so because he played a guitar. The instrument was a welcome addition to the ship's symphony, composed now of Ioway and the new harmonica (Chips had shoved it at him gruffly one night, when no one was watching), Whitey and his guitar, and Chico and Bolo on a pair of small native hand drums. The bosun had taken to hanging around the fringes of the crowd, gathered in the darkness of the poop deck, on the pretext of finding little duties that needed tending to. Second Mate Holst was more open about it. He settled comfortably atop a bollard and frankly enjoyed himself. Even Sparks and Stokes knocked off arguing when the first strains drifted up to the radio shack.

The time ashore had flown too quickly for Slim, but the weeks at sea dragged. The endless procession of days that linked the distant ports were filled with enervating menial labor in the searing heat of the equatorial belt. The sun beat down on the steel deckplates that returned its heat in shimmering waves that distorted both the men and the ship.

After a month Warndahl began to grow uneasy about his bet with Spots. The fines in Manila had cost him two months' pay, and now it looked like a third month was in jeopardy. Spots had shown no inclination to drink anything stronger than coffee. The Swede had tried every possible means to get the reformed A.B. to fall off the wagon. He'd even slipped rum into his coffee to reawaken the urge. But the brew had been spat on the deck. The change in Spots was so profound that after two months he could hardly be recognized as the irresponsible, happy-go-lucky souse who'd staggered aboard nearly a year before. Although he never acquired complete mastery of the tools of his adopted trade, they became less lethal in his hands and he even developed a degree of dexterity with a paint brush. But the biggest surprise of all came, when he joined an impromptu concert under the poop-deck awning one sweltering night while the *Tropic Trader* sailed southeast from Manila through the Solomon Islands, bound for Suva in the Fijis.

Ioway and Whitey had joined Chico and Bolo on the rope table and had fallen into a series of improvisations, which generally amused the musicians themselves more than their audience. Then, with that unspoken communication known only to men who make music together, they had fallen into the opening strains of "Mother Machree." Almost without realizing what he was doing, Spots had begun singing. The rhythm had dropped out and the guitar and harmonica carried the accompaniment, as the fat little A.B. contined to sing with more and more assurance, until at last the crystal clarity of his tenor held everyone spellbound. When the song was over, there was complete silence; then Whitey put into words the thought in everyone's mind: "Spots, you've been holding out on us! Where did you learn to sing like that?"

In the darkness they had not been able to see the man clearly, but from his tone they knew that the reluctant admission had not been easy. "I used to make my living doing this . . . until I loused myself up with booze."

No one questioned the truth of the statement, for Spots had confronted them with what was undeniably a completely trained voice. After that night music was a welcome anesthetic that made the heat bearable, and with each performance Spots grew in assurance until there were times when his voice soared along the familiar melodies with such sweetness that the men were spellbound, and the long moment of deep silence that followed each song was their most eloquent applause.

Whitey's contribution was not altogether limited to the guitar. In his own untrained but pleasant voice, he spun out endless folk songs and sea chanteys to which he and Ioway and the Filipinos faked an accompaniment. The verses were mostly unlaundered limericks followed by a simple chorus in which the crew joined with roaring gusto. Sparks and Stokes delighted the gang unexpectedly with a collaboration of their own which Whitey promptly added to his apparently inexhaustible repertoire.

As the days dragged by, a good part of Slim's free time was spent in reconditioning his clothes and in restitching his heavy work shoes. The moisture and paint had rotted the thread that secured the soles. Chips had given him a sailmaker's awl and had shown him how to replace the thread with thin wire, but even this needed constant attention. Off watch, a part of each day was spent scrubbing paint-stained dungarees. The accepted manner of performing this necessary duty was to make a solution of light soojee, stretch the pants flat on the canvas-hatch tarpaulins, and scrub unmercifully with a stiff brush. The process not only removed most of the paint from the clothing, but also most of the protective oil from the filthy tarpaulin with the result that its dark edges were bordered with the bleached outlines of countless pairs of dungarees.

In the moist heat nothing stayed in condition. The insidious, eroding salt penetrated to every part of the ship from her keel to her topmast and all through her cavernous insides. As the work grew next to impossible in the increasing heat, the food grew steadily worse. Finally the remaining meat was inedible and the men turned to the sea.

Early one morning Chips and Slim streamed an old log line from the taffrail and tied it off to a stanchion. At the extreme end of it they had secured a large barbed hook made from the broken tine of a copra fork. To this they had tied a white rag, after having smeared it in blood from the vile liver that rotted in tubs in the reefer.

Bracing the line away from the side of the ship with a slender lath outrigger that would just hold the strain, they returned to their work and waited.

A sudden crack like a pistol shot sent them running to the poop. Motioning for help, they hauled carefully on the line. Between grunts the carpenter mumbled to himself,

"By God we got sumpthin', all right! Feels like we snagged an island!"

Indeed it did feel as though they'd snagged something bigger than Slim had ever felt on the end of any fish line. Hauling away carefully and keeping a steady tension on the line, they finally brought the fish within sight. The word had been passed, and everyone on deck, including the bosun, stood peering over the rail.

Square John was the first to identify the catch. "Barracuda!" he called without change of expression.

Several other men lent a hand and, after a ten-minute struggle, a fifty pound tiger of the sea lay stunned on deck. Slim had seen them before, caught off the California coast, but never one this size. It was over five feet long, a torpedo-like fish with needle-sharp teeth as long as six-penny nails. The sight of them prompted Warndahl to a gory story about a shipmate who had been swimming over the side and had lost an arm in one slashing attack. No one scoffed at the yarn although it was suggested it must have been a shark. The Swede stuck to his guns and offered as proof the fact that the fish had later been caught and the decomposed limb had been removed from its belly. Those who knew something of the speed and viciousness of the great barracuda conceded it could have happened.

They dined well that night and for several nights after, as the outrigger popped repeatedly and more 'cuda and dolphin were hauled in. Flying fish often came aboard at night, attracted by the ship's lights. The messboys picked them from the deck in big pans, for they were a special delicacy.

Slim learned it was the custom for the spoils to be shared with the officers. Morale improved in direct proportion to the improvement in the ship's cuisine. Only the cooks themselves refused to touch the barracuda, for both of them came from the British West Indies where the fish was deemed poisonous. But they dispatched more than their share of dolphin, tuna, and jack.

Down in the fo'c'sle the heat had become unbearable. Between the sun that poured slanting rays under the edges of the skimpy awning and the now virtually uninsulated steam pipes, the night temperature seldom dropped below one hundred degrees. If the lone wind scoop brought in nothing, it rose higher. Most of the men slept on deck, catching a few restless winks between the showers that seemed to pour down every few hours. During these brief

362

cooling deluges the men would stand naked on the after well deck and lather themselves with fresh-water soap. These celestial baths and the fresh fish were the only meager luxuries on the wallowing freighter. The relief they brought kept sorely strained tempers from snapping.

At dawn on the third day, after passing Kermadeck Ridge, they raised Rarotonga. The silhouette of the breath-taking island rose over two thousand feet above the sea. To Slim it was the most moving experience of the entire trip. The stay was short and none of the men got ashore. Anchored off the reef, the *Tropic Trader* was greeted by New Zealand customs officers who boarded from the trading schooner that lay alongside to transship twenty tons of bagged copra. Slim sat on deck during the late evening, listening to the talk and adding another few pages into the installment letter he was writing to Edye to be mailed in Tahiti, some six hundred miles to the northeast.

"I got your last letter in Manila, or did I tell you that? This letter is getting so thick, I'll have to send it by freight! We arrived off Rarotonga at seven this morning and were promptly told that we could not go ashore, because we'd be here just long enough to take on copra. We've been here ten hours now and they're still hoisting sacks aboard. The only thing that's come aboard so far that interests me is a big bag of native oranges. I had some breadfruit too, but it was sort of disappointing. It will never take the place of your mother's homemade biscuits! The mangoes were good and I bought a papaya for sixpence from one of the natives, but I haven't tried it yet. It looks like a melon but I understand it grows on trees. I guess I won't really find out very much about these islands until I get ashore in Tahiti. I really wanted to get ashore in some of the smaller islands, but it looks like we're not going to make any stops. The trading schooners do all the running between them. I found out something interesting today. All the girls who have boy friends wear blossoms behind their right ears. All the ones who want boy friends wear them behind their left ears. If you ask me, the ones I've seen with blossoms on the right side are just plain lucky! None of these girls can compare with the native girls in Wauna! No kidding!

"When we get to Tahiti I'll try to buy you some cloth. I don't think it's made in the islands, though. The guys tell me that it comes from China and Japan. It's imported by the Chinese merchants. I understand they practically own

363

Tahiti, and the French can't do anything about it. Anyway, I'll do my best.

"I guess I told you some pages ago how much your letters meant to me. No, I didn't make any good friends ashore, because we haven't stayed any place long enough to really get to know the people——"

As the words trailed behind the pencil, Slim's conscience bothered him. He had written the words in complete sincerity. But when he reread them, Marge suddenly welled up in his memory. He thought about erasing the lines, then decided to let them stand. After all, there were many things that he didn't know about Marge, too——

"I'm going to cut this off now and get below for some food. The bosun says we're going to top the booms and shove off in about an hour. I'm sorry to be leaving without a chance to go ashore but I guess it's just as well, because most of the folks are from New Zealand, anyway. I'll write again tomorrow—or maybe after we get to Papeete when there should be more news. If I'm lucky, maybe a letter from you???"

Two hours later the anchor was hoisted and the *Tropic Trader* headed eastward toward Tahiti.

– 31 – Skirting Mitiaro and Mauke, the old tramp worked her way across the southeast trades that seemed at war with the warm currents flowing from the northeast. The sea, embroiled in this elemental conflict, tossed the vessel with corkscrewing motions that made Ioway long for his native Marshalltown and Sparks for another chance at the California bar examinations. To Slim it was a minor annoyance that slowed down his progress toward mail from Edye that he knew would be waiting. The last forlorn hope of hearing from Marge had long since passed. Even as he suffered the hope born of his physical longing for her, he harbored another that no word would come to reopen the conflict.

Those nights in Auckland had taken their place in the dim welter of fading memory. Time had done its healing now and the frequent letters from Edye had given tangible substance to those earlier dreams. Each day he had added a page or so to the running account of his travels and new ones would be added after the fresh impetus of her latest letter. It would be, he knew, the last one until he returned to the States. He would be in San Francisco before his letter could reach Wauna. A year would have passed since their chance meeting—a year in which would be condensed more experiences than most others had in a lifetime. From these days and nights would be distilled the bitter brew of future decisions, but Slim was not quite ready to taste of tomorrow's cup; not when Tahiti's brimming cup was being offered.

Just outside the foaming girdle of reef, the *Tropic Trader* took aboard the pilot. The leathery old mariner squinted an imaginary line between the wheelhouse, the bow, and the gleaming white steeple of Notre Dame Cathedral and ordered the ship to proceed along it, dead slow.

The gold cross glinted atop the dark-roofed spire that

seemed to rise from a rolling sea of green acacia trees which hid the town from view. After a brief medical inspection the ship was warped alongside the greening stones of the Quai du Commerce, and the gangplank was rigged.

This was the last stop before the *Tropic Trader* headed northeast across the Pacific. Here her gaping holds would be partially filled with sacked copra, which already stood waiting in pungent piles in the shelter of the long shed. Mother-of-pearl, vanilla, and arrowroot would be taken aboard also, but none in enough quantity to weight the vessel into the sea to her load line. There was something almost majestic about the old tramp, as she towered over the forest of masts that surrounded her. These were the little schooners which, piecemeal, had brought much of her cargo to the quayside. These were the famed traders whose skippers not only wove the slender threads of commerce between the islands, but also carried the mail, the gossip, and lived the adventures that added daily to Polynesia's living legend.

Slim wanted to get ashore, but the bosun picked Papeete as the first port in which he stood gangway watch. As an ordinary seaman this new duty had fallen to him also. He understood later why the bosun had chosen this particular port. The tides were negligible. There was no necessity for paying close attention to the lines and Slim needed more experience, before he could be trusted to judge their tension and haul in on them or slacken them as the ship's rise and fall demanded.

Ioway headed down the steep gangway first, his eyes popping as he looked at the crowd of natives assembled on the dock. Before he had dressed, the men in the fo'c'sle had taken care to give him all the most lurid facts about this Pacific island paradise. They'd told him in detail about the unconventional friendliness of the local girls and had even quoted from the pilot book some of the facts about widespread veneral disease and elephantiasis. They also had told him that the Chinese kidnaped white boys and turned them into dope fiends, citing the late and unlamented Shiek as an example. Though the boy had ample reason to doubt their stories, enough of what they'd said had stayed with him to make him view each friendly dark face with wide-eyed suspicion. He had promised Slim that he would get the mail and return with it, before taking off on any extended excursions.

He was back in less than an hour with a handful of letters for himself and two for Slim: one from Edye and one from his mother and father—the first he'd received since he left home.

Showing no inclination to go ashore again alone, Ioway settled on the bunker hatch and began reading his mail. Slim sat with him as the boy devoured the contents of each letter, folded it, and shoved it into his shirt pocket. He wanted to read his own mail, but decided to wait until he was off watch. He fingered the letter from home with mixed emotions. He'd been afraid of its arrival for a long time now. Somehow, he felt he wanted to read it first— and in private—before opening the bulky pages from Edye.

After Ioway had raced through the last of his, chuckling to himself as he read, he turned to Slim and held out several American bills. "Boy, I sure got a lot of shopping to do here! The whole family sent money and a list of things to get." He counted out fifty dollars. "Slim, will you go with me tomorrow? Maybe we could look around a little and I can buy some of the stuff. They want all kinds of things . . . like tapa cloth and wooden bowls and perfume and ginger. I'm gonna look like a traveling salesman when I get home!"

Off watch at 8 P.M., he joined Ioway in a short tour of the capital city, in fact the only city of Tahiti. Ever since Suva and Rarotonga the look and smell of these Pacific islands had entranced him. He was ready now to accept this most famous of islands as the model for all tropical paradises; but, as he walked deeper into the business district that paralleled the lagoon, a sense of great disappointment filled and depressed him.

True, the streets were fairly broad and clean and lined with tall shade trees, but where were the stately palms bending under their burdens of ripe cocoanuts? Where were the flaming blossoms that he'd been told fired every tendril of every creeping vine . . . and where were the clean bamboo huts with their ingeniously woven pandanus roofs that stood half hidden under waving fronds on the edges of turquoise lagoons? Looking at the rusting, corrugated iron roofs of the dingy buildings, the barely ambulant pushcarts that lined the streets, the dismal Chinese shops with their ancient displays of five-and-dime trash, the smell of stale beer and grease that came from the open sides of little restaurants, Slim's dream of a South Seas paradise died in the glaring light of reality.

Every second doorway seemed to be a saloon filled with

raucous music and even louder men, staggering under a burden of rum and at least one clinging wahine. Half the ship's company was drunk and the other half was in the process of getting there, Slim saw Hammer and Rusty with four girls, a shabby looking bunch of half-caste teenagers who seemed to be always available. Ioway walked along with a look of displeasure and disgust so obviously displayed that the girls turned to laugh at him. For Slim they presented what they hoped were seductive smiles. As he looked at them, he thought of his travel-poster ideal and then of Marge and how much more she belonged in this setting than the girls he'd seen thus far.

They ran into Chips, ambling along toward the ship, and stopped in a small bar with large open sides protected by wooden shutters that doubled as awnings. Slim had a long rum drink that made him warmer. Ioway had a beer that made him sleepy and the carpenter had a gin that made him unhappy. It had been sold to him as a good Dutch product. Obviously the original contents of the brown crock had been replaced with something cheaper— quite possibly many times—from the appearance of the original label.

Out in the air again, they walked along the quay and looked at the schooners. Away to the west a jagged black silhouette stood propped up in bold relief against the luminescence of the star-bright night. It was Moorea, ten miles from the lagoon, fabled as the most beautiful of all the islands of Oceania.

Coming to a grassy area, they rested a few moments on the muzzles of ancient cannon imbedded butt down in the sand. Mooring lines ran from them to the sterns of small sloops and schooners, lying quietly at rest with sails hung limply between boom and lowered gaff. On nearly all the little craft men and women sat talking and laughing and here and there they heard a voice singing to the accompaniment of a guitar. One of the voices sounded above the others and with unspoken recognition the three of them strained to listen to the lilting rhythm of one of Whitey's original folk ballads:

> Oh, I'll sail once more to Singapore
> To see that slant-eyed belle,
> Oh, I'll live ashore and what is more . . .
> I'll lay that lady well!

The song continued through several more verses and choruses which outlined in some detail the troubadour's ambitious plans. When it ended, they heard a round of appreciative laughter and a girl's voice with an unmistakable French accent urged an encore.

After listening for a time, Chips suggested they make their presence known to Whitey and join the party. Ioway declined, saying he had shopping to complete and Slim made good his promise to accompany the deck boy. It was well into the evening when they returned and Slim reached eagerly for the unopened letters. He took the one from Berkeley first. It was in his mother's handwriting—large, legible and firm. Enclosed were several closely written Spencerian pages from his father.

"Dearest Son," his mother had written. Slim could see her sitting at the Early American maple writing desk in the corner of the den. He could see the confusion of old letters and bills crammed into the bulging pigeonholes; and he could see the crosshatch of upside-down, reversed imprints of her distinctive hand on the big blotter and hear the determined scratch of the broad stub pen that all the women in his family affected. He read on: "Being a mother is just about the hardest job a woman has—especially if she's the mother of two boys who, for better or worse, take after their pioneer forebears. But even that is bearable if they don't suddenly disappear, without a word of warning to their family that they've grown up and want to try their own wings! As you know, your father is able to solve almost every problem in the world with his slide rule—but you gave him one that stumped him completely. I think I can safely say that I've never seen him so worried—not even in those hours in the Fabiola Hospital in Oakland, just before you joined the family. You were so noisy when you arrived that I guess it was difficult for us to understand why you were so quiet about your departure!

"It's hard to keep from being hurt when your oldest boy takes French leave. It's hard to keep from feeling sorry for one's self and saying, 'I tried to be a good and understanding mother. Where have I failed that I should be treated with such thoughtlessness?' And then I have to stop and do some remembering. For instance, I remember when you were a little boy and came to me with some grievance against your brother or one of the boys you played with. I always used to tell you that there were two sides to every story. And then I suddenly felt a little guilty about not letting you tell yours. But after you had gone it was too late—so I had to try to reconstruct it for you and when I did, I discovered that you were out on that terrible-sounding 'tub,' as you call it, because your father and I sent you there—not literally—but quite directly at that!

"When Grams came down for the holidays, we had a family powwow and out of the discussion came some understanding—a sort of Something All Mothers Ought to Know. It seems that what I didn't know—or at least didn't realize—was that from the time you were a little fellow you always had a mind of your own and a certain independence that mothers are apt to resent. Mothers like to be depended upon. As I look back now, it seems quite clear that we didn't always take time to listen to your side of the story. It is more than possible, and your father agrees, that you must have been building up some resentments of your own as we, with our great hopes for both you boys, pursued our determined efforts to 'raise you properly.' I don't think we were entirely mistaken. But I do think now that we may have been lecturing when we should have been listening. We are truly sorry for that, son, and when you return you may be sure that both sides will be heard, now, henceforth and for as long as we're together as a family.

"I don't know what kind of a life you have chosen for yourself. There is something about sailing the seven seas that is beyond a mother's ken. But I think your father understands and is a little jealous and, I'm quite certain, very proud. I hear him talking to Uncle Herm and to the men, when we have our weekly bridge party, and I've caught him reading your letters with a wistful look. Grandfather would have liked him to go to sea, too. In a way, you've fulfilled that wish for both of them. Lately your brother has been staring out the window with those ugly old binoculars! Because I'm a mother, I'm holding my breath, expecting to wake up some morning and find him gone, too, for I'm certain that he'd have to assert his independence in exactly the same way his older brother did. There have been no lectures for him, son. Both your father and I just sit and worry to ourselves. He has that same determination you have and if he decides to go, we'll not try to hold him. I do wish, though, that you'd write to him and tell him exactly what it's like out there. Tell him the truth. You mentioned that you'd had some bad weather and that several of the men were disagreeable. Bad weather and disagreeable people darken our lives, no matter where we live or what we do—and one of the important parts of growing up is to learn how to shelter yourself from both.

"When I say I worry about you I don't mean about what you may do, for I know the stock you come from and I know with all our mistakes, we've given you boys a sound foundation upon which to start your lives. Boys like you don't turn 'bad.' Make mistakes, yes—but I know in my heart that you'll find your way and develop your own sense of values. You've known right from wrong most of your life and your father and I have watched you learn to make decisions. We've seen you waver, we've seen you tempted, we've seen you hurt—and we've wanted to put our arms around you when you took your medicine like a man. I guess we're taking our medicine now, too, and the loneliness and uncertainty has been bitter at times—but we'll try to take it like grownups. You've made it much easier with your letters.

"It took a lot of thinking back for me to be able to write you this letter in all honesty. I had to talk with your father and Grams and together we remembered our own determination to run away and get married. We remembered my own determination to become an opera singer and the sacrifices your father made during those lean years when I was finishing my training. And in remembering we think perhaps we've grown to understand some of the drives that compelled you to turn your back on us and find your own way. It seems to me that I'm pretty old to have just learned some of the things that only recently have been made clear.

"And so, son, we just want to say this to you now: if you've found something out there that you feel is worth dedicating your life to, then—with our blessings—get in there and, as Dad would say, 'Give 'em heck!' But just one thing: make sure it's really worth while. At your age you can't possibly know how quickly your best years fly by. The only real tragedies in this life are those people who make a wrong choice and don't find it out until too late or who lack the courage to change. Life can be a wonderful, soaring adventure—or it can become an endless parade of days filled with hopeless drudgery. If there is a hell, it must be here on earth for those poor souls!

"This is all for now, honey. Your father is writing a page or so which I'll enclose. When you think of us, remember that we love you with all the love that's in us. You two boys have made life 'a wonderful, soaring adventure' for your father and me. You are free, now, to soar

371

on your own. You make your decisions, secure in the knowledge that we hold no strings on you and that our prayers are with you always. I was astonished when I realized not long ago that I, not you, had received the most valuable lesson from these anxious months. For that, my big boy, I thank you! God bless you, Lewis, and bring you home safely. Affectionately, Mom."

Slim sat for a long time with the letter lying open in his lap. It was not the sort of letter he'd expected from his mother. He would have wagered almost anything that the letter would have been filled with reprimands and admonitions born of self-pity and calculated to play on his responsibility as a dutiful son and arouse in him an uncomfortable sense of guilt. Instead, here she was actually thanking him for making her face up to some facts about herself. He wondered if he would have the courage to face up the same way. Suddenly he understood some things about his mother for the first time and, in so doing, struck the first glimmering spark of self-understanding. She had used the word "resentment." Now he wondered how much of his own recent action had been motivated by resentment and how much by an honest desire to follow in his grandfather's footsteps? Seeing the word on paper, seeing his mother admitting it in herself—and surmising its presence in him—brought him face to face with the technique of rationalization. Even though he had not yet learned to apply the correct label to it, he suspected that he'd been motivated by drives that probably were not what he had thought them to be.

There was no denying his love for the sea—its never-changing mystery—its absorbing, ever-changing beauty. The sea had helped make bearable many of his problems. It had clarified a few but had solved none, and he sensed now that peace must lie somewhere in their truthful solution. His thoughts wandered to the outer edge of his own understanding. Then the solid footing of logic began to give way, losing its ability to sustain, and his thoughts soon disappeared in the restless sea of emotion, leaving behind only a ripple of memory where reason had once been.

He folded the several double-sided sheets and set them beside him. Picking up his father's letter, his eyes ran across the first line of the meticulous script:

My dear young Salt:
    As usual the burden of conveying the family

"news" rests with your mother but I want to sneak a little message of my own into the envelope. We've read and reread your letters many times and you can never guess how anxious we are to have you with us again, and to hear firsthand of your adventures.

When you wrote of Mr. Peterson's death we felt a sense of personal loss, for we know how much you admired his devotion to duty and his facility with navigation. When I studied civil engineering, I discovered a few of the mysteries of navigation because the principle of locating a point on land is precisely the same as locating one at sea, when one uses the sun and stars as guides. If I had a sextant, I'm sure we could locate our house here on Santa Barbara Road just as exactly as Mr. Peterson located the *Tropic Trader*. Of course I'm a little rusty now. We might miss it by a few blocks!

Knowing you, I imagine you've taken to ship's work as easily as you've always adapted yourself to everything else—with the possible exception of school? But that's not fair, is it, because you certainly did well in the subjects that interested you. And perhaps that should always be the test of anything one chooses for a life work. Perhaps we should ask, "Do I undertake this with interest?" Then the second question should be, "Does it serve the greatest good of my fellow men?" That in itself carries very special rewards—rewards that are in direct proportion to the pertinence of the service itself. Personally, I have never regretted becoming an engineer but I must confess that being one of hundreds of men who plan a dam or a power plant is serving a bit more remotely than one who peers into a test tube and comes up with a marvelous new medicine or a new understanding of the nature of a disease for which specific medication or surgery could be devised.

Slim let the pages drop a moment and smiled to himself. There it was! He'd expected reproof or at least a reminder of the medical career in his mother's letter. Instead she had turned a reproachful eye upon herself. The prod had come from an unexpected quarter. In the past his father had confined himself briefly, often tacitly, to seconding his mother's motions. There was a small surge of the old resentment as he lifted the pages again.

I guess I used that particular example because last week our good friend, Max Freeman, died. He was one of the wisest and kindest men your mother and I have ever known. He died of peritonitis, following a ruptured appendix. As we sat with his family, I couldn't help asking why, with all our wonderful technical strides—conquering the air and the sea and, to some degree, even human nature with the research of Drs. Freud and Jung—we have not yet found ways to combat infections like that and the pneumonia which nearly took you from us when you were a little fellow. I guess each of us has his place—but how blessed are those whose interests and enthusiasm take them into the sciences where the really great frontiers are waiting for a new kind of pioneer! I remember telling you once, as we stood looking at the family grave markers in old Shasta, that every one of those men and women had given their lives to clear the land, so that their children could live in peace and security. That is the lot of the pioneer—and also his reward. His progeny have what seems to me to be a moral obligation not to let that work be taken for granted or left unextended. I am certain as you read this, Lewis, you will silently accuse me of "grinding an ax" and I'd be less than honest if I didn't admit to the hope that one of my boys would find that his destiny lay in the path of a more direct service to his fellow men than I have chosen. It seems to me, as I write this, that we as a nation are too much occupied with the creation and elaboration of our comforts. I imagine they have their place, too, especially for you after you return from your present humble surroundings! We are obsessed with building the world's largest or gaudiest this or that—and in the meantime some of the research labs at our best colleges are finding it difficult to raise sufficient money to buy basic equipment. Young people who might find great creative satisfaction in science are being encouraged to make a lifework out of glorifying everything from toothpaste to threshing machines. These items are all well and good in their place—but what about the place poor Max was in, with helpless doctors deliberately exuding confidence, so his wife and children wouldn't suspect the truth? I'm sorry, son! I don't know when anything has made me feel so saddened or helpless as his death. I imagine you must have known how I now feel when you stood beside your second mate and waited for expert help that was not forthcoming, because it had too many prior demands on it. By the way, if you could find time to write a letter to Gloria and little Maxie, junior, filled with good old ripsnorting adventure, it might help take their minds off their deep hurt—at least for a time.

I intended this to be one page, but I've turned into quite a chatterbox, haven't I? It will be good to see you, my boy, and to let you be the chatterbox for as long as you care to. Your mother and brother and I can hardly wait to hear all about it in person! Your loving Father.

The news of Max Freeman's passing shocked Slim. Ever since he could remember, "Uncle Max" had been a frequent and welcome visitor, both at the house in Berkeley and, during the duck- and goose-hunting season, on the ranch in northern California. Both he and his wife had been enthusiastic members of the Sierra Club, and the two families had often joined forces to assault the pinnacles of many of California's highest peaks. Together they had scaled Mount Young, Unicorn and Cathedral Spires, Mount Dana and Mount Lyle and, finally, the highest of all peaks in continental United States, Mount Whitney. Joint trout fishing expeditions had been arranged nearly every summer that took them on foot and the youngsters on burro-back into the remote fastness of the upper Tuolumne River.

Slim remembered those wonderful days, when he and his younger brother and Gloria—as good a tomboy and mountain goat as you could find, even if she was a girl—would take off down the meadows by themselves and return, each with a limit of rainbow and eastern brook trout. Somehow, "Uncle Max" seemed as permanent as the mountains he loved so well . . . and now he was gone. It was hard to imagine the kids without their dad and a lump grew in Slim's throat, and with it a rising rage at the injustice of these tragedies. With unuttered words he railed at fate for having taken this gentle man, whose great knowledge and humor made the world around him come alive with happy adventure. Irrationally he asked why it had to be such a man? Again, why not a Warndahl or a Hammer or a Rusty or the bosun—men who renounced beauty for ugliness, humor for salaciousness, and compassion for cruelty?

Putting the letter on the shelf beside the unopened one from Edye, he climbed down from the bunk, vaguely aware of some new discomfort. His back itched and he reached awkwardly behind and tried to scratch between the shoulders blades. He tried unsuccessfully for a moment and the awkward position cramped his arm. Remembering Holst's effective technique, he stepped to the corner of the built-in lockers and rubbed their edge across the irritated area. It was one of the few times he'd been completely alone in the fo'c'sle. Even Russian John was not in his bunk. Spots had gone ashore with him earlier in the evening, one of the infrequent times the strange Russian had consented to company.

Slim went back to the bunk and pulled down the light blanket. The straw-filled ticking was in hopeless shape. Most of the tinder-dry stuffing had been pushed toward the ends by his burrowing back, with the result that the square springs pressed through the thin cloth and dug into his flesh. He pulled the blanket off and threw it over the wire that supported the ragged bedspread screen. Taking the mattress by one corner, he pulled it free of the burlap sacking that overlaid the wire. As he did so, scores of pale brown bugs fell on the deck and scrambled about in a frenzy of indecision. They were cockroaches—hundreds of newly born ones that had hatched in the warmth beneath the bag of straw. Stepping up on the edge of Hammer's bunk, he looked closely at the burlap and found a teeming, scurrying mass still there. Several large roaches, at least two inches long, rushed around in the sudden light.

Slim snatched the burlap from the springs and dropped it on the deck. The vile underdone-looking bugs scurried beneath or behind anything at hand and disappeared within half a minute. Taking the filthy bedding on deck, he shook it vigorously over the side, then hung it on the chain rail. Those roaches were the biggest ones he'd seen. Sharing a bed with even one of them was out of the question. Slim had heard that kerosene drove them away. He resolved to get some in the morning at the little garage directly across the Quai du Commerce. In the meantime, the problem was a bed for the night. Hanging in his locker was the key to the sick bay. He remembered it now and made his decision. Taking along Edye's letter, he climbed to the boatdeck and unlocked the door.

Sparks heard the footsteps and poked his head out of

the radio shack. "What are you doing—confining yourself with a case of the South Sea crud?"

Slim shook his head hopelessly. "No. I'm trying to hide from a million cockroaches that have taken over my bunk!"

Sparks raised his eyebrows. "You think *you've* got cockroaches? Come in here a minute! I'll show you the biggest one in the world." He motioned the boy inside.

As Slim stepped across the coaming, he saw Stokes. His expression was one of patient resignation. "He's referring to me, old chap. It's his puerile way of evening a score. You see I've just proved conclusively that our wireless wizard is, in reality, a Mongoloid idiot." He smiled pleasantly at his opponent and waited for the consequences.

Sparks removed his glasses and wiped them deliberately with a corner of a soiled hand towel. Squinting through them to test the result, he replaced them carefully and turned to Slim. "As an example of how low I've sunk in this ignoble Merchant service, let me tell you that I actually find this bastard's babbling amusing at times!" He indicated Stokes with a sidelong squint. "And as further evidence of my degeneration, I freely admit that I tolerate him purely for the pleasure of being able to drink good coffee from his percolator. It's his only asset!" Reaching for a mug, he poured a third cup.

Slim looked from one to the other and chuckled to himself. "What the devil are you two haggling about now?" He accepted the steaming mug and slumped on the edge of the bunk.

Stokes waited a moment for Sparks to answer, then decided to assume the responsibility himself. "When this discussion began, it related to the aesthetics of the rite of circumcision . . . but in the bungling logic of our myopic mastermind here it has degenerated to a painful pruning of the prick for prophylactic reasons!" The little fireman grimaced with disgust.

Slim shook his head uncertainly and ran long fingers through the shock of sun-bleached hair. "I guess you guys'll have to settle this without me. I don't even know what 'aesthetics' means!"

Stokes shot him a pitying look. "This lamentable ignorance seems to characterize your whole generation! Aesthetics—spelled by the way with an 'A'—may be roughly expressed as an inspection of the relationship between mind and beauty. For example, I probably offend you, for you see only the grubbiness of my exterior. Whereas, if you

377

were to view me through the eyes of an aesthete, you'd perceive my true inner grace, and this shabby body I inhabit would, perforce, become a thing of beauty!"

Sparks slammed his empty cup down on the desk. "Horse shit! Horse shit, I say! In all my days I've never seen such a crock of pure, unadulterated——" He groped for words to express the ultimate indictment and finally gave up with a silent appeal to heaven and a hopelessly frustrated wave of his skinny arms.

Stokes, his eyes twinkling with repressed pleasure, saw a chance to pursue the discussion and pique his friend through the ordinary seaman. "Fredericks, one of the things I find arresting about you, aside from your acknowledged superiority at porcine castration and the stitching up of gaping epidermis, is your willingness to be instructed. Who knows? Perhaps in rough soil like you lie the renascent roots of a lost Anglo-American culture, the sole remaining repository of which, I understand, is your city of Boston. Therefore, on this off chance, I welcome the opportunity to enlighten you! The discussion, then, concerns the probable reason for the ancient ritual of circumcision which your friend here also grossly refers to as 'cock-bobbing!' "

Slim struggled to keep a straight face, as the little English fireman indirectly pressed his barb into the fuming radio operator.

"I don't want you to think that in the midst of plenty, as it were, we are two evil old men who, lacking the means and ability to fornicate, simply sit around and talk about it. However defensive that may sound, it was this extremely available supply of native 'quiff,' as it relates to your friend Hammer, that suggested the topic. That vulgar and pugnacious person was seen by me this afternoon drunk and whimpering in front of an oriental bazaar run by one Joseph Lum. He was being ridiculed by two hybrid native 'blossoms' of a variety more ancient than respected, and the apparent reason was his inability to make good on certain of his usual extravagant claims to masculine prowess. When I remarked to your friend Sparks here that the fellow's ego had been dealt a mortal blow through alcohol and ignorance of the efficacy of the Polynesian technique of circumcision, he challenged me. When I met this challenge in a fair and forthright manner, he denounced me as a liar."

Sparks turned in protest, but Stokes silenced him with an imperious gesture. "Ah! Ah! He didn't use that precise word, mind you . . . but there was no mistaking the implication!"

Sparks resumed the argument from the sudden suspension in which he'd been left. "All right, I'll call you a liar in the plainest language—a liar! And before you start wallowing in your own verbal diarrhea again, let me tell our young friend what you said!"

He turned to Slim. "This moth-eaten Encyclopedia Britannica claims that the Tahitian girls cannot be satisfied by the whites, because their own native men are circumcised full grown, in some haywire manner that makes them end up with a swingin' war club! He says these dames play the white sailors for suckers, but do all their fun-lovin' fornication with those wild-looking, double-jointed Kanakas! I simply asked him to prove his cock-and-bull story—no pun intended!"

The radio operator looked expectantly at Slim in the hope that he would throw the weight of opinion to his side. When support was not forthcoming, he renewed the challenge to Stokes. "Go on, you dilapidated prevaricator! Let's hear about this wonderful circumcision . . . and after you tell us about that you can show us where the aestheticism comes in, too!"

Stokes blinked thoughtfully and extinguished a soggy cigarette butt. "If I may answer the last part first, old chap, I'd say that any native ritual, whose result can reduce to a blubbering slob that homicidal hulk called Hammer, is aesthetically beautiful by right of special interpretation. As for the particulars of the ritual itself, like so many another of its kind, it pertains to the coming of age of the male. It conforms in essence with the Jewish 'bris' which celebrates the commitment made by Abraham to the Lord—also to similar rituals performed by the Mohammedans and also to the rites of many other races and cultures since the early Egyptians.

"While I'm quite prepared to admit a certain logic in the theory that its purpose was bodily sanitation in areas where cleanliness was hard to come by, I nonetheless must stand on its religious and aesthetic significance which seeks to reaffirm the ancient covenant and to celebrate a young man's ascension as a 'giver of the seed.' Since those were also the times of sacrificial appeasement, the practice probably was perverted to that end by most peoples. However, if we can agree that the foreskin is a blasted nuisance, anyway, and that loping off the whole member would have been highly impractical, we can also agree that whatever the purpose, they made a wise decision!"

Sparks puffed angrily on his cigarette. "All right . . . come to the point!"

Slim listened with amazement and amusement, as the fireman continued, "I shall! And in doing so, we come to the wonderfully simple logic of these incredible Polynesians. They managed to turn the whole painful business to a splendid advantage! Using a primitive wooden blade, they substitute for the usual circumferential incision two longitudinal ones—top and bottom. The resulting flaps are folded under and covered with native medicine. In a matter of two weeks or so, this immensely enlarged organ is ready to be pressed into the . . . uh . . . service of the community!"

Watching and listening to the little English fireman's perfectly modulated flow of language, Slim tried again to solve the riddle of the man. Both he and Sparks knew that Stokes had been legally trained and had for a time been a solicitor in London. Sparks had once conjectured that he also might have been a king's counsel and because of some cataclysmic misfortune, had renounced his birthright and profession and fled to the total obscurity of the fireroom. Neither Slim nor Sparks would ever question him.

Stokes leaned forward slightly, as though to impress his final point. "Now then, since my earlier reference to aestheticism was made in what might be called a 'jocular vein,' I would like to impose upon our wireless friend here and connect the loose ends of the discourse by saying that the unaffected simplicity of these people, in their pristine state, their totally unself-conscious attitude toward copulation and procreation—which they accept as naturally as the flowering of the frangipani or hibiscus—is a thing of exceptional beauty in itself, and therefore is aesthetically satisfying! More than that, there is beauty for the aesthete in the wonderful simplicity of this compromise which, in one fell swoop, permits the Polynesian man to fully satisfy the demands of *both* his faith and his females!"

As far as Stokes was concerned, the discussion was at an end. His annoyance at Sparks would be forgotten in the sweet blush of victory and would reappear early in their next discussion, as soon as he could prod the radio operator off balance and goad him into becoming emotional and personal. Sparks knew what was happening and fought against it, but in the end Stokes' complete mastery of his emotions, and consequent ability to absorb the personal attack, baffled and eventually defeated him. He admitted defeat in many ways, this time by presenting Stokes with a roll of toilet tissue. "For your chin, old boy!" The fireman looked archly past the rude offering at the percolator and calmly broke the connection.

The evening was over for Slim, too, and, with the bulky feel of Edye's unread letter in his shirt pocket, he excused himself and retired to the sick bay. Leaving the heavy outside door hooked back against the bulkhead, he locked the hot weather screen from the inside and stripped off his clothes. In the comparative coolness of the cross-ventilated upper bunk, he settled back comfortably and eagerly read what he knew would be his last letter from the girl. When he had finished the pages, he held them for a long time and Edye's presence filled the little room. The night breeze that came down from the mountains bore the faint perfume of jasmine, mingled with copra and ginger, and the sensuous odor heightened the illusion and he felt again the softness of her hand and heard the gentleness of her voice.

He longed to see her—to give her the presents he'd chosen so carefully and to take her in his arms. But even in his longing there was that old undercurrent of fear that they both might discover the dream and its inspiration had become strangers. His reason struggled wearily with rebuttals until, half-reassured, he dropped off to sleep.

– 32 –

Nearly a year had passed since the *Tropic Trader* had left San Pedro and headed southwest out along the Pacific. Now, with her holds and decks unburdened and with barely enough cargo to pay for wages and oil, she had begun her long northeasterly run back across the Pacific from Tahiti to San Francisco. There she would begin again the search along the coast for more cargos, and the men would begin anew the monotonous cycle of foul work and fouler play.

The vessel's hull rode high out of the water. With not more than two hundred tons of copra and a few tons of mixed cargo, she barely "wet her pants," as Holst put it. With the south equatorial current pushing against her starboard plates and the northeast trade winds buffeting her a point or so off the starboard bow, the helm was cranky and difficult to hold.

After clearing the Marquesas Islands there was nothing to obstruct her course. It was unlikely that a single ship would be seen or even spoken to on the radio for the next three weeks. The sense of complete isolation made itself felt throughout the whole ship and it seemed to Slim that the men were more dependent upon each other for diversion and for the small encouragements they exchanged to relieve their own hopeless monotony. He sat on number five hold and listened, as they told of ships they could get that served food as good as one could find in the best hotels, of cooks who had been famous chefs, hiding at sea from alimony-conscious wives or because of addiction to alcohol, which lost them steady shore-side jobs. He listened to tales of captains who deliberately insisted on the finest food for officers and crew to prevent any turnover. On their ships, as on the steam schooners, fewer men did more work and for it received better food and more money. But, unlike the schooners, they also received clean linen daily. On and on they rambled through an imaginary

382

world that satisfied their maximum needs. Most of them had gratified their desires for women—in fact had satiated them—and the conversations veered away from sex for the first few days. Slim knew that after a week or so at sea the talk would start again, building up to its usual filthy crescendo during those days before they re-entered the Golden Gate.

Warndahl was back in form. His arm had completely mended. The deep-rooted ailment that expressed itself in verbal sex orgies was as virulent as ever, and he alone kept the subject alive and impatiently awaited the day when boredom would again dispose his audience to respond to his vile eroticism.

On deck the work routine had settled down to the endless round of chipping, scraping, painting, and soojeeing. But paint was being used sparingly and areas that should have been completely done were being spotted instead. The old tramp had had her brief moment of beauty in New Zealand, when Mr. Samson relayed the captain's orders to have her bright and shipshape. For a short time the change in the ship had been reflected in the men. But as rust eroded the ship, time had eroded morale until it was at its lowest ebb. On the bridge even the officers seemed shabbier and much in need of replacing basic wardrobe that took a constant abuse from the elements.

The evening concerts by Whitey and Ioway were still the most popular events. The messroom was too hot for poker, although Hammer and Rusty seemed not to mind it. Money was scarce and IOUs were plenty. Cigarettes won in poker were offered for a dollar a carton of unbroken packs. Most men smoked on credit from the slop chest against the unpaid wages held back by the steward. Several of the men had bet away all they had coming. At the moment Hammer was trying desperately to recoup some of his losses. The peep show had helped, but that money had long since been shot on drinking and women in the months that had passed. Spots' bet with Warndahl had been won and the fat little A.B. began a metamorphosis that was amazing, even to those who witnessed it day by day. He had promised himself and everyone who would listen that he would quit the sea and go back to singing. No one doubted him when he also added that he'd never drink again if he lived to be a thousand. On Sundays he prayed and counted his prayers on a small rosary that Father Stefano had donated.

The ship was infested with roaches and copra bugs and

383

the men had even tried a homemade fumigation job on the fo'c'sle with a spray called "Black Leaf Forty." It worked for a while but after the can was used, its contents diluted with gallons of water, the bugs reappeared. Slim and some of the others aired their bedding each day. The engineers had made an unsuccessful attempt to reinsulate the steam pipes that ran overhead in the fo'c'sle, but the heat became unbearable as they neared the Equator. Most of the men slept on deck, if at all.

Stokes and his percolator were regular visitors to the radio shack and Slim spent as much time there as possible. He enjoyed listening to the bitter struggles that took place and occasionally joined in them, when the subject was general enough to admit theory that didn't necessarily need proof beyond its own common sense. Most often these discussions took place with Sparks alone and Slim enjoyed them. On more than one occasion he left the radio operator with something to think about.

The days wore on and were recorded on the chart in a series of erratic little lines that sometimes joined and more often didn't as they inched their way across the big sheet in the general direction of San Francisco. The *Tropic Trader* passed into the counter equatorial current and then into the edges of the north equatorial current. The trade winds continued monotonously and at times the sparkling seas piled high enough before them to roll the engine's exhaust out of water. It was then that the ship lost headway and the engineers conferred with the bridge and spoke of regaining vacuum by pumping sea water into the deep tanks.

Slim stood his watches, day and night, and tolerated his deadly hours in the blazing sun. Never once did the bosun assign him to work in the relative cool of the shelter deck, where much remained to be done. But the ordinary seaman went about his duties without complaint and left the Russian-Finn no room to argue. Slim sensed a slight change in the bosun's manner since his fight with Warndahl. But the pressure was kept on him, only now with less sarcasm and abuse. In the months aboard he'd come to expect little relief from the drudgery. His brightest hours were spent aloft where he could look over the sea and, by looking down, change his perspective and reduce the *Tropic Trader* to the dirty little world she really was.

His hours on the bridge were bright, too, and Holst continued his efforts to teach the boy the rudiments of piloting and navigation. He'd suggested several times that Slim try to get into the Merchant Marine Academy, where young men wishing to become career officers could get the best available training. Slim had been enthusiastic at first but noncommittal of late, and he felt sure that the second mate was aware of his changing attitude. He wasn't quite certain what had brought about the change. For that matter he didn't really understand its nature: that it was a slow building up of residual resentment and disgust for the vileness that permeated shipboard life. The feeling was still overbalanced by the occasional sense of real accomplishment that rewarded him after a new challenge had been successfully met. He had not yet learned that the reward is automatic and, as his father had suggested in speaking of service, in direct proportion to the effort given.

The nature of the endeavor was not important. The reward was the effect of an immutable law. The cause was the successfully completed endeavor itself. The result of the law of cause and effect, which Slim understood as it was revealed in his friends Sparks and Stokes, was as yet unrelated to himself. Since unawareness of a law does not preclude its operation, Slim enjoyed the fruits of accomplishment on one hand, and on the other chafed under the effects of an environment in which he was a spiritual alien. He only vaguely sensed that the time would come when he would have to end the growing indecision, renouncing his birthright and surrendering as Stokes had done, or denounce the life openly and reappraise his future course. For Slim the choice was still not clear. For some weeks now he'd been vaguely aware of a growing anxiousness to get home. Though he did not suspect the cause, his mother's revealing pages had removed most of the resentment that had been responsible for his leaving. The simple directness of his father's arguments had reawakened it momentarily, but in rereading the pages some of the obvious truths had taken root against his will and had put out strong new shoots of reason.

Then, of course, there was the last letter from Edye which had brought with it new longing and an urgent desire to see her—to hold her and to reaffirm their love. In the steaming fo'c'sle Slim dug her last letter from the locker and went to the poop deck. There was still enough light to read and enough privacy, too, for the men who were off watch were lounging around on the hatch. Turning his back to the wind to shelter the pages, he went over them for the dozenth time. "My dearest Slim," she had begun.

"It's terrible to want to fill these pages with gooey girlie things about how much at least one of the natives of Wauna misses her guy, but that's the way gooey girls are! I've been wracking my poor aching head to find some news, but I know you're not going to be interested in such trifles as the new wall paper in the hall or the fact that the furniture is all rearranged again. Dad says he's going to bolt it to the floor to keep Mother from changing it around. I've tried to tell him that if he did, he'd deprive us of the only real change possible in this little town. I've told Mom that if she's really smart, she won't ask him to help. See how wise I'm getting? I'm learning how to handle men! I'll be so expert by the time you get back, you'll never be able to get away!

"Oh, Slim, I'm such a shameless little hussy—and such a lonely one, really. I do want to see you again and you've never really told me in your letters when you think you'll get back up here. I know you would if you really knew. It's terrible to know that this is the last letter I can send. I can only hope that it won't be too long before I get another from you. You've been good about writing, my darling sailor of fortune. (I know that's wrong because they're only supposed to be soldiers of fortune, but it doesn't make any sense to call you that! Maybe I should just call you 'my darling?' Would that be all right, please?)"

Slim never read the letter without seeing her at the lumber office or in her room, gnawing on the end of the pen, and sometimes he could see her face and feel her presence so vividly that he longed to reach out and take her in his arms. In the months that had passed the memory of Marge had faded into the tenuous stuff of unreality, and through her pages Edye had transmitted so much of herself that she moved with him through every waking hour. She was with him at night, too, and as he read along he remembered the strange nightmare he'd had, when this letter was brought aboard in Papeete. It had been so real that he'd awakened in a sweat and Hammer had kicked the bottom of his bunk again and cursed him. For a long time it had worried him and its disturbing allegorical riddle still haunted him.

He remembered seeing the smooth, domelike slopes of a volcano. It had seemed like Mount Lassen, the still smouldering cone, east of the ranch at Proberta. He had found himself climbing it alone and, upon reaching the rough, cleft rocks near the top, he had come upon a great vertical crack in the lava. As he pressed his palms against the smooth stone, it had felt warm and a rush of hot air from the opening had struck his face. Peering into the dark recesses, he'd eased his body through and felt his way along the narrow corridor. Before he could see anything he heard a deep rumbling and felt stronger blasts of hot air rushing past him. He'd wanted to turn back but something drove him on, until he found himself inside the mountain standing on a ledge high above the edge of a large round lake of boiling red molten lava. Stretching away from the walls of the black dome that covered this glowing hell was a dangerously narrow path that ended on the opposite side. He could see blue sky through a portal where the path terminated.

And then his mother and father had inexplicably appeared and had beckoned to him to come around to their side. He had stood hesitantly for a moment, wondering if he could edge his way along the precarious foothold without falling into the agonized, vicious sea. Just as he'd been ready to start, he felt someone behind him. Turning, he'd discovered Marge. She was completely nude and her arms were outheld. She had smiled, and the unbearable longing for her welled up in him again. Then he had heard another voice, calling from a great distance. Looking across the glowing lake, he'd seen Edye, standing where his parents had been. He had tried to motion to her, but couldn't raise his arms and he had no voice. He remembered trying to shout. The words were lost in the rumbling crescendo of the volcano. He had turned to Marge again and she was still smiling and waiting. He'd turned back to look at Edye and discovered his mother and father had joined her. They were all imploring him to make his way around to their side.

Then, as he had started to move, a searing blast of hot air struck his face. The smooth rock seared his back as he pressed against the wall. His face dripped with perspiration and the treacherously slick stone burned through his shoes. He could see Marge moving slowly toward him, and across the angry lake he saw Edye again, smiling and waiting. Then, suddenly, Marge was at his side pulling at his arm and he'd been filled with fear, for there was barely enough ledge to stand on. He had tried to shake her off, but she laughed at him. Then, without warning the narrow rock ledge began crumbling at his feet. He heard Marge's mocking laughter and her words: "The name's MacLaine, *please* come again———" Then, in one sickening drop, the rock had broken away. As he felt himself falling, he cried out in horror. The echo of his voice still filled the fo'c'sle as he awakened, drenched with perspiration, his pulse racing and a suffocating weight on his chest. Hammer cursed and struck him from below.

The curtain of his bunk had been snatched open. Otto had looked in. "Fer Chri'sake! What the fuckin' hell's the matter with you? Have you started usin' the needle?"

Slim had blotted the sweat with the dingy towel and stammered in confusion. "Whew! Man———" He'd shaken his head to orient himself again. "I musta had a nightmare!"

Otto had looked at him skeptically. "You musta had somethin', sailor! You was screamin' loud enough to wake the dead!"

Slim had climbed down from the bunk and walked on deck for an hour. The feeling had lingered for days and now it came back again, unaccountably, without reason, but he thought it was curious that the remaining impression was the picture of Edye standing with his family, waving to him to cross over to their side. He could not remember the fall.

Slim shuddered involuntarily, as he relived in a fleeting instant the ordeal of the dream. He lifted Edye's letter from his lap and began to read again:

"I'm writing this page Friday night because I thought maybe there'd be some more news by this evening. The only thing I could scare up is a rumor that Mr. Slater had a big brawl with the new boss. I know they spent a lot of time going over manifests. There have been mistakes showing up and the head office wants a change in bookkeeping. If they change things too much, it might mean the end of little old me and my handy adding machine! Hope not! I suppose I might as well tell you that I'm not mentioning it to bribe you or anything, but I thought that maybe—just maybe—this summer I might take a little trip down to San Francisco or somewhere—just to get out of the city limits of Wauna for a while. I think Mom and Dad would like that too—for me, I mean. They think I work too hard and don't get out enough. Wouldn't it be wonderful if the *Tropic Trader* should decide to be in San Francisco at the same time?"

Slim smiled as he read the lines. He had smiled dozens of times over them and dozens of times the same picture had come to mind: Edye with his family in the big house on Santa Barbara Road. He knew that she would take them over completely with her loveliness, her gaiety and sense of humor. Edye knew nothing of his family, except the rather sketchy outline of his life at home, drawn during the family-style discussion in the Morrison kitchen.

As he thought back over the evening now, he realized a bit remorsefully that the picture had not been accurate, the impression he'd left of his parents had been vaguely unfair. It had not been accomplished by an act of commission, but rather by one of omission for the purpose of justifying his own actions. The possibility of Edye's tentative plans coming about had set him dreaming and, since the family letters had arrived, he was more anxious than ever to bring about a meeting. His eyes turned eagerly to the pages again.

"It's a funny thing and I sort of wonder if other people do it too—but when I read your letters, it's almost as though you are here again. The only thing that worries me is the way I sort of put you together in my mind. The trouble is you don't come out looking like a sailor. Not that you don't—but it doesn't seem to me you feel as much like a sailor as like something else. I don't exactly know what I mean, I guess. Sometimes I see you being a business man or a lawyer or even a lumberjack. Of course, when I see you being that, I know it's wishful thinking because, if you were a lumberjack, you'd probably be working around these here parts and that's just me being selfish. Besides if you were, I'd be worried sick, knowing that you'd probably want to be a topper or something ridiculously dangerous. Why can't you keep your feet on the ground, young man?

"I talked to Mom about it the other day. I asked her what she thought you looked like. Know what she said? She said, 'That young lad looks to me like he can be anything he wants to be and if I'm any judge of men, when he decides what he wants to do he'll do it better than most!' Mom's a pretty wise old girl, Slim. So don't try to hide from your destiny! She's right and I know she is, because I felt the same thing the first time I saw you. End of lecture!

"Oh, what the heck can I write about, anyway? Darn it! I want to say lots of things—and then I get stubborn and say, 'If he wants to find out what I want to say to him, then just let him come back here and find out! And if he doesn't, then it'll serve him right—and I'll be brokenhearted.' If you turn out to be a Lieutenant Pinkerton—well, don't expect me to go moping around my teahouse, singing sad songs! No, sir! I'll just pack my kimono and come after you. Oh, m'gosh! I just remembered! Pinkerton was *really* a louse! I'm sorry, darling, I guess I picked the wrong character. But, anyway, Lewis Fredericks, you've got me so frustrated! First thing you know I'll be like that poor old spinster, Josie Lee, who lives up the street. Every time she's disappointed about something, she starts to eat —candy and cake and all kinds of fattening things. So just watch out or I'll start doing that—and then I'll get like her: three axe handles broad across the you-know-what! So mind your p's and q's and don't make a fat old maid out of me! Can't you just see me, honey keeping cats and saving your letters under a glass, bound in lavender ribbon —and pressing your favorite wild flowers between the pages of Shelley and Keats and Robert Browning? You can't? Well, neither can I! So the best thing for you to do is to skeedaddie back to our side of the world, so I can get another look at what I've been worrying about for nearly a year now!"

Slim grinned to himself. He could see the girl standing before him, looking up with fun twinkling in her lovely eyes and her mouth compressed in mock annoyance. He wanted to reach out and wrap her in his arms and hold her cheek gently in the palm of his hand and tuck her head under his chin. He wanted to take her little face in both hands and bring it close to his and feel again the inexpressible sweetness of her lips and feel the sag of her body against his, as she surrendered to the wonderful pleasure of being close. He'd felt all those things once, that night in Wauna, and now he wanted to know them again and again, and he chafed at the plodding tramp and the endless run for home.

As he looked back over the thousands of miles that had already disappeared in the sluggish wake, it seemed as though his entire life had been spent on this rolling, pitching, rusting ship. All his yesterdays ashore lost their reality beneath the weight of dull work, tedious hours of leisure, and the ever-present filth that overbore all else. Suddenly, as he held the letter, Slim was sickened by the echo of Warndahl's laughter that drifted aft on the wind. He knew that laugh and the other laughs that followed, and he knew the kind of talk that evoked it.

He finished the letter, put it in his pocket and turned to face the wind. He could see the men sprawled on the hatch cover. The corner of Hammer's mouth glistened from the ointment he'd given him to cover an ugly sore that had developed on his lower lip. Holst had mentioned it during the watch. He'd spoken with disgust of "those dirty animals whoring around with anything on two feet" and had told Slim to keep an eye on the man. The second mate had expressed concern over the looks of it and guessed that it might be serious. In the ship's medical book Slim had read of the symptoms of syphilis. He had learned that a crusty lesion often appeared at the point of contact. Hammer dismissed the thing as a "cold sore," but had taken the medication to make it more comfortable. Unbeknownst to the others, Chico had taken to keeping the A.B.'s cup and silverware separated from the rest.

"Hee's seek . . . etts no good!" The little messman had shaken his head seriously. He'd seen these things before. *"Eees muy malo . . . desaseado!"* He'd spit in disgust. "Sleem, you stay away from heem. *Si?"*

Without his knowing it, the scale was leveling for the ordinary seaman. Each bright letter from Edye, each dull moment of disgust brought its comparative revelation. Gone was the old reluctance to view the Merchant Service with eyes other than those conditioned by earlier hopes and plans. Gone were the handy excuses and rationalizations for the behavior and sex preoccupations of his shipmates. Even the word "shipmates" repulsed him. Of all the men he sailed with he took pride in knowing Chips and Square John and some of the men in the black gang. For Holst, Sparks, Stokes, and Chico the feeling was one of affection. For the others, disgust and growing contempt.

The bosun stood apart and, as the months had gone by, Slim had wondered about his earlier impressions of the man. He had first thought him to be dirty, but in reality he was clean. He was rough and inarticulate, but his clothing and his quarters were spotlessly kept. The unnecessary pressure was reserved for him alone, but the brutality was expressed as often in his dealings with others. Slim bore the heaviest load and did not understand why. But he had learned to respect the man's efficiency and unquestioned seamanship. The bosun knew his ships. He could get more service out of gear and more coverage out of a gallon of paint than seemed humanly possible. Samson rewarded him with a permanent berth and also, Slim suspected, little side "bonuses" that kept the man happy and well-supplied with money.

The boy's open hatred of the bosun had by now smoldered to glowing embers, devoid of most of their heat. Instead of hating, he was trying to understand. The lesson learned in the bar fight with Warndahl had borne unsuspected fruit. Slim was learning how to appraise an adversary. One day he would also learn the technique of neutralizing many of them or converting them to friends.

— 33 — As the *Tropic Trader* pushed doggedly against the sea, the air cleared and turned noticeably cooler. The sea was glassily smooth, and spirits were buoyed by a restless anticipation that pervaded every member of the crew. Grumbling subsided and hard work was tempered with more patience and rough good humor. Most of the men were not going home, but back to a starting place to begin anew the monotonous round of tramping through the Pacific. A lucky few might find berths on tankers and steam schooners, and others might go back to the "floatin' hotels" for a trip or two, before the passenger ship formality drove them back to the less disciplined life aboard the freighters. But for most of them there would be no homes—now or ever.

Slim felt certain that Ioway would leave. Spots would go and there was a chance that Sparks might make good his threat to quit at last. The officers who had wives would spend a few comfortable days at home; then the undercurrent of restlessness would tack them around their shoreside anchors and turn their thoughts back to the ships, the uncertain cargoes and still more uncertain ports on the far side of the world. Their wives would try harder to "make things nice," knowing as they did, the futility of their gentle labors. During his hours on the bridge Slim had heard the men speak of their homes. He knew Holst maintained an apartment in San Francisco for his wife, that Samson had a family in Oakland. Banner had a mother and father living in Stockton. If Peterson did have a home, he had returned to it by now as a serial number on a routine notice from the United States Shipping Board and the Naval Reserve District.

As Slim stared into the binnacle and checked the ship's gentle meandering, he thought of these men and of his own home. He thought of Edye's home in Wauna and Marge's in Auckland and of the bekilted old warrior who

393

had glowered at him from the wall and become his conscience each night he'd entered the house. He wondered what really made a home. His own was so comfortable and filled with love and yet he'd conspired to leave it. He'd seen other people with less comfort and less love about them fight to stay and it occurred to him that perhaps a home was nothing in itself; that it's furnishings and size and location were unimportant details; that the real spirit of home abided in its occupants. It had to be that way. Otherwise, how could one explain those who were miserable in palaces and happy in hovels? And how about the bosun whose only home was the dingy stateroom on the starboard main deck? But when Ivan closed the door behind him, he took into those cramped quarters the mysterious ingredients of his own happiness and security and, ergo, transformed it into his home.

The secret of a home, then, must be in what one brings to it . . . and Slim wondered what he'd brought to his own . . . and whether or not it really *was* his home. A father's home, he thought, is a son's home only until passing years and expanding interests transform it into a sort of loving prison. That's the way he had come to feel about his own. His mother and father had become gentle jailers who restrained him with smiles and implied obligations. He wondered why he was thinking these things, and in the midst of his wondering another vagrant thought passed and left its unsettling wake: had his leaving transformed their home into a sort of jail in which his parents were imprisoned with their loneliness and concern for him and with their disappointment? He remembered Edye's lament —expressed so often but always with humor—that Wauna had suddenly become empty, when the *Tropic Trader* disappeared in the fog that morning. He smiled as he remembered her words: "It's so small now, darling, that if I stumbled on Main Street, I'd land outside the city limits!"

He remembered Stokes' simple requisite, expressed to Sparks and himself one evening in Haywire House, the radio operator's not-so-affectionate name for his own home—the radio shack. "Home for me, my dear chaps, is any place where I may plug in my percolator; where I, ex-Englishman, may joyously commit my daily act of treason against Sir Thomas Lipton!" He had poured himself another cup of strong coffee and patted the battered pot affectionately.

For Stokes security and comfort lay in his commanding ability to dominate an argument; in the solace of his English cigarettes and expensive Mocha and Java coffees; and sheer luxury was represented by a carefully concealed bottle of Martel's Cordon Bleu Brandy. The battered pot and the cigarette box were the dexter chief and sinister chief of his blotted escutcheon. The honor point had long since been obscured. He carried with him these symbols of the past, transporting them into a self-made Land of Cockaigne where he privately partook of their delights. Home, then, Slim thought, is less the frame of the house than the frame of mind. The final examination of his own frame of mind could not be deferred much longer.

Later that night, when he stood lookout behind the apron plate, he looked up into the black crystal dome of the sky made so luminous by countless stars that he felt he could see beyond the nearest one out to the next and so on to the outermost reaches of third dimensional space. He remembered having the same feeling before, when he and his father sat on the top of Lambert's Dome in Tuolumne Meadows after a late fishing trip to Dog Lake.

There he'd come to know his first few stars and the constellations that contained them. Polaris, like a sparkling gem in the handle of the Little Dipper, the bright hub around which the universe seemed to revolve, and the Big Dipper, looking like a saddle blanket on the back of the Great Bear, with its two pointer stars inviting the imaginary line to be drawn through them by wayfarers searching for true north. Slim looked for them now, still low on the horizon.

The two hours passed quickly and Whitey came forward to relieve him. He was almost sorry to go aft. Making a bed on the rope table, he slept til dawn.

Night grayed then glowed into day; the day burned white, then dimmed into night, and again Slim stood his lookout and his watch at the wheel. He slept on deck when the weather permitted and suffered below when it didn't and a little rail fence of pencil lines on the chart traced the tramp's crooked northward course. The paint locker was empty and the ship's work was reduced to a minimum. So was the ship's larder. The poker sessions grew more fevered, as men fought to win the games that counted. Otto recovered some of his losses. Chips was even. Warndahl had no credit left and owed three months' wages, one to Spots, which he had no intention of paying. Rusty was ahead in cigarettes and IOUs, and Slim had won and held onto several big pots that he'd put with the rest of his money. He limited his playing to the chips

395

he bought in the bank. When those were gone, he quit. If he won, he observed fo'c'sle etiquette and played until duty took him from the game. Hammer was a heavy loser and on two occasions had growled at the ordinary seaman for not putting more money into the game. Slim had refused to depart from his own planned playing economy and Chips' warning look had deterred the surly ex-fighter from pressing his argument.

The sore on the A.B.'s mouth had disappeared, but the man seemed changed. The rugged vitality seemed lessened, somehow, and he had grown irritable. Most of the crew gave him a wide berth and several times during the past week he'd asked if there was anything in medical stores that would "pick him up." He'd complained of feeling logy. Slim had given him a physic of powdered licorice, but any psychological effects it may have had soon wore off.

The sea had the smell of home now. Great patches of kelp slid by the plates and were sucked into the wake and shredded by the churning blades. Off to the right Slim could make out long sandy beaches and the high, ocherous cliffs of La Jolla. Later in the day he saw Catalina Island and to the east Dana Point and Laguna Beach. Dark green hands of ice plant clutched at the crumbling crests of the eroded escarpment; above the eucalyptus trees reared graceful limbs into gray-green clouds of leaves. In the veiled distance he traced the high outline of the desert barrier.

Slim leaned on the starboard rail and looked with eyes that felt more than they saw. He thought it strange that he could experience at once happiness at being home and loneliness for some of the things that lay scattered along the path of those recent yesterdays. Through the worn sole of his heavy work shoe, propped on the lower pipe, he felt the life pulse of the ship busy living its today, and he wondered what its tomorrow would be—and his own—and the wind whispered in his ears hushed words from yesterday: "Today is the tomorrow you worried about yesterday; tomorrow never comes———" He wondered why he remembered them now . . . and he thought about tomorrow and knew it would come and that every day would have its tomorrow and every tomorrow would hide its truth until the challenge of today had been met. Slim knew the challenge was upon him.

During the night the twin-stacked S.S. *Harvard* slid by, lit up like a sea-going carnival. With her sister ship, the

S.S. *Yale*, she ran an express passenger service between San Francisco and Los Angeles. Slim had seen them often with the double chevrons on their stacks, earned with distinction as troop transports during the World War. For them, the four hundred-mile run was an easy overnight trip. For the *Tropic Trader* the distance would require another forty hours.

When Slim went on wheel watch, at eight the next morning, they were off Point Conception, and twelve hours later Point Piedras Blancas was abeam. The second mate had been unusually quiet during the watches. He spent most of the time on the wing bridge, adding his keen eyes to those of the lookout. The next morning at eight o'clock he was squinting through the pelorus, taking a bearing on the northern end of Monterey Bay. Slim took the wheel from Hammer and steadied the ship on three hundred and ten degrees. The first mate and Holst plotted the bearings for a fix and corrected the course westward a trifle to clear Pigeon Point. Holding her on the new heading as she took the long Pacific swells almost broadside, Slim watched Holst pacing the starboard wing bridge, peering occasionally through the binoculars, puffing incessantly on the wind-frayed butt of a cigarette. Except for a quick check on the compass, the man hardly came into the wheelhouse during the first hour of the watch. At two bells he stepped inside and opened the front of his windbreaker. Firing a fresh smoke, he took his favorite position against the sill of the forward window.

"We ought to pick up the pilot boat about noon. You glad to be back, Slim?"

The boy was startled by the sound of the officer's voice. For an hour he'd heard nothing but the soft click of the tachometer and the wind-muffled clang of the little bell on the forward end of the wheelhouse. "I guess I am, sir."

Holst half turned on his elbow to look at the ordinary seaman. His eyes squinted to concentrated slits, and the base of his nose glistened with an unfelt drop. The cold cigarette was wedged in the corner of his mouth, soggy along half its length. "What are you gonna do now?"

Slim avoided the man's eyes and looked into the binnacle. He checked a slight swing and spoke, his eyes still downcast. "I'm not sure, sir. I guess I haven't given it much thought——"

"The hell you haven't!" Holst turned and looked out the window for a moment. "The day you don't think about things, I'll know it."

The boy looked up quickly. Guilt and embarrassment mixed uncomfortably in him. There was silence again for a while—the sort of silence that worried him. He thought of things to say that might ease the tension without putting him in the position of answering definitely, but before the words were framed the mate spoke again.

"Have you any idea how much you've learned in this last year?"

"Yes, sir."

The mate walked over to the binnacle and glowered across its temple-like brass dome. "No, you haven't! But it's written all over you!"

Slim busied himself with a wheel that barely needed turning.

"What's a sidereal day?"

Here it came again—another of Holst's sudden oral examinations. All through the months Slim had conditioned himself to expect them on any of a dozen subjects that the officer had discussed informally with him. Six months after he'd learned it, the man had still asked him to box the compass—sometimes backwards! Now it was sidereal time, something that had taken weeks for him to visualize but one of the basic elements of celestial navigation.

"It's the time between two transits of the equinox, sir."

"How many hours in a sidereal day?"

"Twenty-four, sir."

"How many hours in a solar day?"

Slim smiled inwardly at the mate's effort to trap him. "Twenty-four, sir."

"Which day is the longest—the solar day or the star day?"

"The solar day, sir."

"How much shorter is the sidereal day?" Holst was baiting another trap.

"Three minutes, fifty-five point ninety-one seconds, sir."

"Are you sure?"

"You told me, sir!"

"How do you know I know?"

"We're here, sir!" Slim nodded toward the coast line.

The mate grinned, then winced as he unstuck the cigarette butt from his upper lip. "That's right. But don't forget: two other guys helped!"

"I know, sir, but since Mr. Peterson . . . since he's gone, I think you've gotten as good as he was!" After the words were out, Slim wished he hadn't put it just that way. He intended a compliment.

The mate squinted at him again. "Wasn't I always?"

"Sir . . . I . . . uh——"

Holst cut him off. "You're right. He was the best I've ever known. But you're also right when you say I've gotten to be a little hotter with a sextant and a pencil. The practice did it. Whatdaya think I keep asking *you* questions for—to hear myself talk?"

"No, sir."

Holst wiped the base of his nose with the side of his hand and, finding moisture, looked at it briefly and wiped it on the side of his trousers. "Why have you learned all the things that Peterson and I have thrown at you for the past year?"

Slim knew he'd have to be wary of his answers now. "Because I was interested, sir."

"Because you *was* interested? Aren't you anymore?"

"Yes, sir . . . I am."

The second mate squeezed his eyebrows together and his lips compressed into a tight line. He seemed to be having difficulty framing a thought. He rubbed his back gently against the edge of the window frame and tugged impatiently at the visor of his cap. Bracing himself as though against some expected impact, he asked the next question quietly. "Are you gonna stay with it?"

This was the question Slim had most dreaded. It was the question he'd most often asked himself during the past several months. When he asked the question of himself, he could postpone the answer as he'd done many times before. But the question was now being asked by another—a man who had taken the time and trouble for some half-understood reason to make a considerable investment in him. He knew Holst and Peterson had both known of his intention to follow the sea and become a Merchant Marine officer. He understood that much of the time they'd given to instructing him had been done because they were responsible men who one day would like to see their ranks filled with new men, just as the generation of officers before them had. What he didn't understand was Holst's seeming dedication to the task; his thoughtfully planned course of instruction, which had moved from the simplest ABCs of piloting on through to the elementary astronomy necessary to celestial navigation.

Slim not only feared the question, now that he faced it, but resented it, too, because of the personal obligation to the mate that was implied. His emotions were curiously like the ones he'd felt when he'd been forced to an unwilling decision at home. There was much about Holst that reminded him of home. The man had become a synthesis of his father, grandfather, and mother, perhaps because he had the same determination and patience. He displayed them now, as he waited quietly but expectantly for an answer.

Slim stared at the compass without seeing, until Holst jarred him with a short order. "Check it!"

The answer was temporarily postponed by the task of bringing the ship back on course. He glanced up at the mate when the lubber line steadied. The man's eyes were drilling into him like gimlets, but the rest of his face betrayed nothing of his thoughts.

"Cat got yer tongue?" There was an edge of sarcasm that the boy hadn't heard before.

"No, sir. I just want to give you a straight answer, that's all."

"You have already! For a guy who claims he hasn't done much thinking, you've made a hell of a lot of decisions, haven't you?"

"No, sir . . . I haven't made any decisions. I've just been thinking——"

"*What* have you been thinking?" The question was a challenge.

"I've been thinking about whether or not I should stay at sea, I guess. Whether it's the best thing to do . . . the best kind of a job."

"And you haven't made any decisions yet, is that right?"

Slim thought he detected a hopeful note in the man's voice. "Not really, I guess, sir."

Holst nodded to himself. "Do you think the life is too tough, is that it?"

"No, sir. I guess lots of things are this tough."

"I'll tell ya something, kid. The toughest thing a man ever has to do in this world is to make up his mind. I don't mean about whether he wants to go to the head or lay some dame. I mean about what he wants to do with the one life he's sure of. When you came aboard, I thought you'd made up your mind about that. So did Pete."

It was the first time Slim had heard the mate refer to Lars Peterson by a nickname and it was the first time the boy had caught a glimpse of the affection that seemed to have existed between them. The fact that he'd used the nickname and the tone of his voice made that clear. It also made clear the tactics Holst intended to use in his persua-

400

sion, just as it indicated something of the urgency he felt about making his point.

"I guess we were wrong, huh?"

For Slim this was the toughest question of them all. "Sir ——" He was sparring for time now, as he had in the fight with Warndahl, only this man was not his enemy. He was probably the best friend he had on the ship and perhaps one of the best he'd ever know. One thing he knew for sure: he didn't want to hurt Holst, but he didn't want to try to spare him that hurt by lying.

"Sir, can I ask you a question?" Instinctively Slim had made the only possible move. He'd put the second mate on the defensive.

Holst reacted by lowering his arms slowly from the window sill and jutting his head forward. "Go ahead!"

Slim rotated his neck to loosen the collar of his watch jacket. "I don't know how to say it, sir . . . and I don't want to sound like a fool——"

"If you're a fool, you'll sound like one!"

He snapped the words out with finality, but the boy would not retreat from the offensive. The question had to come, foolish or not. "Sir . . . I know I told you and Mr. Peterson I thought I wanted to be an officer . . . if I had brains enough . . . and I meant it when I came aboard . . . but now I guess I'm not sure about some things."

Holst snorted and shifted impatiently. "I'll say you're not!"

Slim struggled to put the question into words, but they did not form easily, because the question itself was not entirely clear to him. He tried doggedly. "Oh hell, sir." He blurted out the rest of the words: "I guess I want to know why you think it's so important to teach me . . . I mean, for me to become an officer?" He held his breath for a moment, then lowered his eyes to the compass.

Holst stood perfectly still and the smile on his tight lips was not in his eyes. After a moment he moved directly in front of the binnacle. Slim felt the perspiration breaking out on his body, and his hands grew moist around the spokes. The question had been badly put and he knew it. It hadn't come near encompassing the feeling that had prompted it. Without really understanding the full import of the urge to question, the boy was seeking arguments to counterbalance the persuasions of his family, of Edye, and of his own jumbled and painful attempts to plot a clear course for himself. In his own way he was trying to get a "fix"—to establish a position for himself in the sea of time that lay ahead. He wanted something more dependable to steer by than the beclouded guide stars of his own reason and the arguments of those who loved him, which he'd lately come to suspect were rooted as much in selfishness as in objective concern. He hoped somehow that Holst, this man with no emotional attachment to him, could supply at least one line of position—some impartial point of view based on the simple addition of his demonstrated assets. Life these past months had been piling experience upon experience, often before he'd been able to comfortably shoulder the burden and, suddenly, in the silence that followed his question, the burden had become unbearable. He forced his eyes up from the compass to Holst's face, and he knew the man could see the misery in them.

"All right, kid. I'll answer your goddamn fool question!" The mate extracted a cigarette from a pocket inside his windbreaker and deliberately moistened its end and placed it in the corner of his mouth. The lips clamped tightly around it, and he held the match concealed in his thick hand. Suddenly it snapped into flame and Slim cursed himself as he jumped.

The mate smiled. "Yes, sir . . . I'll answer your goddamn fool question . . . and *I'm* a goddamn fool for doing it!" He leaned his lower arm on the dented brass binnacle. "You want to know why it's important for *you* to become an officer in this lousy stinking Merchant Marine . . . is that it? All right . . . I'll tell you. It isn't!"

He waited for Slim's reaction. There was none. He blinked and squeezed his sea-gray eyes into narrow slits that seemed trapped in a webbing of fine wrinkles. "I don't think it's important to teach *you* at all. But I do think it's important to teach some young punk *like* you who has the brains to do the job and the brains to see how important it can be! As far as you personally are concerned . . . you don't mean a goddamn thing to me!" He straightened up and his eyes bored into Slim's.

The boy had taken the worst the bosun had been able to give him in those early months without feeling anything but anger. There was no anger now and any annoyance he'd felt for so clumsily phrasing his question disappeared in a wave of regret. He suddenly felt he'd destroyed the one relationship that had had meaning for him during the days and nights of doubt, fear, and bleak boredom. He'd turned off his only source of dependable friendliness in his anxiety to be reassured. He heard the biting sarcasm in the mate's voice, but couldn't perceive in what it was rooted.

"You don't count except that you're a name and a number on a piece of paper. When you sign off, your discharge will read: 'Seamanship, Very Good; Character, Very Good.' If they had a place marked 'Brains' . . . I'd mark it 'None!' "

Slim locked his jaw tighter and waited for the next onslaught.

"I know what happened to you! You listened to your grandfather tell you a lot of yarns about the sea and the wonderful life of a sailor. He made it sound like those books, and you began to think you were Milton Sills playing in the 'Sea Hawk' or something. You go ahead screwin' around with your imagination until you finally sell yourself on the idea that you want to be a big brave sailor. And then one day you get up guts enough to run away to sea." He looked at Slim closely. "You know something? I'm beginning to think the bosun was right about you. Yes, sir, by God . . . I think he was!"

Slim recoiled inside, as from a solar-plexus blow, and opened his mouth to protest but the mate cut him off.

"You know, he thinks you American kids don't have guts enough to stand the gaff. That's why he keeps pouring it on . . . to see when you'll crack!" He shook his head ruefully. "By Christ, you almost had us *both* fooled!" Holst inspected the cold cigarette and walked to the milk can. He pinched off its end and lit the remaining half. The whole time he kept his eyes on the boy, and Slim returned the look without wavering.

"I asked Boats how you were making out a few weeks ago. You know what he told me? He said of all the kids that had come aboard in the last three years, you looked like the only one with guts enough to make a sailor. Whatdaya think of that?" He paused a moment, but expected no answer. "It's a godamn good thing for you that you didn't show your hand to *him!*" The second mate looked at the end of the cigarette again. The flat relit taste annoyed him and he pushed it roughly into the can.

Anger was rising in Slim now; anger at the injustice of the mate's arguments; at the unfairness of the man's appraisal of the situation—and anger at himself for the ineptness of his own expression and for not having thought things through for himself. Slim knew that five minutes of unreasoning rage and misunderstanding could cancel out a lifetime of friendship. He didn't want to let the man destroy the one thing he valued most in the whole trip.

"Sir . . . if you'll let me . . . I'd like to——"

Holst wheeled and thrust his face fiercely up at the boy's. "Shut up! I'll let you talk when I've finished . . . and what I'm going to say is more for me than for you! I've got to convince myself that I'm not crazy for trying to add just one decent man to this Godforsaken service." He walked to the wheelhouse window again and looked off to the right. "See that headland up there?" He indicated a point of coast line barely visible off the starboard bow.

"Yes, sir."

"That's a monument to a guy who made a bad mistake and lived to learn a lesson from it. That's Bark's Landing on the other side. That's a place where a guy named Holst took a wrong turn and got into one helluva lot of trouble. This country let me off pretty easy for my mistake. I'd like to pay it back by giving a good officer to my profession! This is the first time I've had a chance to look for one. And I thought my luck had held and I'd found one when you came aboard. I've watched you learn. I tried to help you learn. I talked Pete into helping you, too—without telling him why—and he went along with it. I'll tell you something else, too! I don't have any kids. I always wanted a kid of mine to be an officer. I used to think about that back in the German Navy before you were born. I used to look at you sometimes, and say, 'Ya know sumthin' . . . I'd have settled for a kid like that . . .'"

He rubbed his forehead with the palm of his hand and shook his head sadly. "What a goddamn fool I was!" A sudden thought struck him and he looked quizzically at the boy. "I want to know something. Where did you get the guts to beat the shit out of that Swede? Tell me that!"

Slim could feel the anger in his eyes. There was no apology in them now and no reticence about taking this opportunity for rebuttal. "Sir"—he groaned out the words deliberately—"I've got guts enough to do any goddamned thing I want to do . . . if there's a good enough reason for doing it! I've got guts enough to sail on every bug-filled tub with every rotten-minded bum of a sailor on every piece of water in the world big enough to hold a ship . . . *if* there's good enough reason to do it! There was a good reason for my running away from home. There was a good reason for my going to sea instead of being a . . . a lumberjack or a bindlestiff . . . and there was a good reason for my asking you that question, too . . . even if I didn't say it the way I wanted to!"

Slim heard the words coming from his mouth with a

404

strange detachment, almost as though another were speaking. He saw Holst's eyes staring at him in unblinking concentration. He was conscious of a trace of wonderment, too. The momentum of his speech carried him on and the words came without being summoned, and now they were saying exactly what he wanted them to say.

"You said, sir, that you wanted to give the Merchant Service an officer, because it had done something good for you. At first I didn't understand what you meant, when you said I don't mean a 'goddamn thing.' I do now, and you were right. I don't mean a 'goddamn thing' to you . . . but I do to *me!* And before I make up my mind to do anything, I want to know *all* the reasons for doing it . . . and for *not* doing it! How do I know how important it is for me —not for you, sir, but for me—to spend the rest of my life with the kind of morons I live with in that fo'c'sle? Suppose I stay in the service until I know enough to try for an officer's license . . . and I make it . . . and then find out that I'm on the beach because the Merchant Marine has gone to hell and I'm the youngest and dumbest third mate in the world? It's gonna be too late for me to go back to school and try to be a doctor or a businessman or even a good rancher."

He glanced quickly at the compass and steadied the wheel. "All my life I've needed reasons for things. I was brought up that way. I've got two letters in my locker filled with reasons why I should come ashore. They're from my family. I've got a dozen or so from a—" he hesitated—"from a good friend. But in nearly a year I haven't heard one single reason why I should spend the rest of my life out there, except that I thought I wanted to." Slim lowered his voice and looked down into the shadowy interior of the binnacle. "All I meant by the question, sir, was that I wanted some reasons."

Second Mate Holst had stood without moving a muscle. He had listened to every word and the intonation of every word that came out of the ordinary seaman's mouth and as he listened he had tried to remember the first day he'd seen the kid. He tried to remember whether it was the time he'd happened on deck off the Columbia River bar when the bosun was about to take him apart with his bare hands, or whether he'd noticed him earlier and seen something in the youngster that made him look again. He remembered well the look on the deck boy's face then. It was the look of one angered enough and courageous enough to charge into certain defeat . . . for a good reason. He remembered the look on the face, as it had concentrated on the bewildering task of taking the helm for the first time and later, as it had struggled to unravel the mystery of the compass and its points, and still later the first simple navigational diagrams.

He looked for that face again now . . . and saw, instead, the face of a man. The shy boy was gone. In his place was a lean, hard young seaman with brains enough to find out what he wanted and courage enough to get it. This was the beginning of a man who, one day soon, could and would sail straight to his destination, once he'd fixed it. Holst looked at the face and the unafraid eyes and suddenly felt ashamed—not for what he'd tried and would continue to try to do, but for the manner in which he'd tried to do it. His face relaxed and they stood in silence. Slim looked at the chronometer and rang three bells. The mate returned to the window and for a moment stared across the dancing diamond path of morning sunlight that stretched to the ship from Bark's Landing. Closing his jacket, he walked out to the pelorus on the starboard wing bridge.

It took fifteen minutes for the cross fix to be taken and plotted, then Holst returned to the wheelhouse and put the instrument back in its wooden box. Leaning against the window with his back to the slanting sun, he watched Slim for a time, then cleared his throat noisily. "Fredericks . . . I guess every man has a right to know the reason for everything he's asked to do. Sometimes we try to find out by thinking for ourselves. When it comes to figuring out yourself . . . it's kind of like trying to see the keel from the bridge . . . it ain't easy!"

He looked thoughtfully at the binnacle and twisted a gray hair that protruded from his nostril. He pulled at it tentatively, then poked it up in the nostril impatiently. "I don't know that I'm the best person to give you reasons . . . but I'll sure as hell try." He looked at Slim and the old twinkles twitched at the corners of his eyes for an instant, then spread their crow's feet out from the corners and they both understood that apologies had been made and accepted.

"First of all, the Merchant Marine isn't going to hell. It's there already! It may take a few years to get it out again and maybe I'll never see it . . . but you will . . . and young men like you can make it the kind of service this country deserves. I think I've told you once that this isn't a maritime country anymore. It's too big and has too much . . . but that's all going to change. Right now the shipowners are getting away with murder. When they have to fight with more foreign bottoms and with the railroads and trucks for interstate trade, things aren't going to be so good. Then the government is going to step in and subsidize them, even more than now to keep them from windin' up on the short end of overseas trade. Conditions in the fo'c'sle, as bad as they are, are better than a lot of other countries' ships. But that don't make any difference to Americans. They won't put up with it. That's why so many professional seamen and ex-Navy guys take good shore jobs. A good sailor makes a good rigger, a good construction worker, a good warehouseman, a good stationary engineer, if he's from the black gang . . . and that's the way it goes. That's why our fo'c'sles are full of foreigners and bums of our own who are one jump ahead of the law. And that's gonna change, too!

"Right now the unions are all falling apart. Furuseth's running around like a hog on ice. The IWW's getting nowhere and neither are the others . . . here or on the East Coast. But they're on the right track and one day some guy is going to come along who's strong enough to put the whole shebang together. Then, kid, comes the big change!"

Holst paused and looked at Slim intently for an instant. "That's when bright young officers and good able-bodied seamen are going to come into their own. That's when going to sea is going to be a decent profession again. This country can't afford to be a second-rate maritime power. Ever since 1918 Uncle Sam's been a full-grown man . . . but he doesn't believe it yet! When he does . . . there won't be any more foul tubs like these, carrying the American flag into foreign ports. Every ship and every sailor is a kind of ambassador for a country. If you think that isn't important, look at Norway, Sweden, Denmark, and Holland. Anywhere in the world they'll tell you those are the best and cleanest ships. Even Japan equals them now. To the world those ships mean a strong, clean, respectable country. That's how you always think of the 'squareheads,' isn't it?"

Slim nodded in agreement. The mate jammed a piece of shirt tail down under his belt and hitched at his trousers.

"I have a funny feeling that it's pretty goddamned important for the world to think that way about the Americans too. A clean ship and a smart crew are the best Ambassadors we can have because they are seen by more strangers and can make more friends than the whole fuckin' stuck-up State Department put together! You oughta be one of those ambassadors. You're cut out for it. You could be one of the best!"

The stocky, grizzled-gray little mate wrinkled his brow and squinted again. He stuck his lower lip out a little and stared at the deck for a moment. When he looked back at Slim, there was a trace of concern on his face.

"Well, Fredericks, I'm not a very good speech maker, but I think that about covers it for now." He lowered his head and peered hopefully from under his shaggy brows. "Did I sell you anything?" Holst seemed almost bashful.

A wide smile warmed Slim's face. "I'll tell you one thing, sir. You've given me more to think about in the last five minutes than I've had in some time. And I want you to know something, Mr. Holst"—it was the first time he'd called the officer anything but "sir"—"I really appreciate it. Thanks a lot!"

The second mate scratched the margin of hair between his ear and his cap band. "Shoulda done it a long time ago! You're welcome, Slim." He punctuated his reply with a quick nod and a smiling wink.

34

When Slim came off watch at noon, the *Tropic Trader* had moved twenty miles north of Pacific Grove, and he remembered with sudden regret that he'd forgotten to look off to starboard for a glimpse of his grandfather's old house. He knew that if he'd looked in time, he'd have seen its ornate Victorian cupolas rearing their compound curves above the flat blue-green tops of the Monterey pines. The house was owned by others now, but in memory it would always belong to those days of his childhood.

As he looked at the rocky amphitheaters, rising above sandy crescents of beach, he wished that the old man were still living; that he could have climbed to his lookout and watched the old tramp go by. Slim could almost see the smile of pride on the old captain's face as he squinted through his ancient binoculars, watching Ordinary Seaman Fredericks complete the last leg of his first year-long voyage. Slim harbored another wish, too. He would have given a great deal to have been able to take the train to Salinas, then the bus to the coast for a conference with his grandfather. He felt certain his decisions would have been simpler, if the arguments could have been evaluated by the hard-headed ex-Royal Danish naval officer.

At four o'clock the sea-weary freighter wallowed north past the Farallones, then turned eastward toward the Golden Gate. Along the shore Slim could see San Francisco's old amusement park, "The Chutes at the Beach." To the left of the roller coaster's latticed arches he saw the boxlike structure of the famous Cliff House. He remembered the first time he'd been there with the family. They had seen a matinée performance of "Capital Versus Labor" with Kolb and Dill and had dined next to a big window overlooking the ocean and Seal Rocks. A famous dance team—he thought their names were Fanchon and Marco—had entertained, and for years he'd carried with him the exciting memory of that day. It was one of those cherished first thrills. His first day at sea had been like that, too. He suspected he was now in the midst of another experience that would engender its own unique memory.

He felt the ship quiet beneath his feet and heard the lessening rush of the wash as she lost way; he saw the pilot boat come alongside and watched the topcoated, fedora-topped man hasten up the starboard ladder and join Mr. Samson on the bridge. Slim started as the two vessels exchanged staccato whistles and resumed way. Off to the port were the biscuit-brown hills of Marin County, the earth rich beneath the gossamer veil of pale spring green. To the starboard were the high, rocky walls surrounding the pebbly ramp of China Beach. Down the steep face he could trace the dangerous zigzag trail hacked by hardy bathers who dared the swift tidal race.

As he watched the high cliffs of the channel widen into the bay, he looked for the barracks of the Presidio and tried to locate the red-roofed two-story building that had housed him for thirty days the previous summer, when he'd joined the Citizens' Military Training Corps as a basic trainee with a unit of the Sixth Coast Artillery. He could see the gray concrete battlements of once well-concealed coast defense batteries, commanding the narrow throat of the bay. Most of them had been deactivated long since, but at Fort Baker and Fort Barry he'd served several exciting days as a "powder monkey" on the six-inch disappearing rifles. In a "shoot" with the regulars his gun crew had crowded them so closely with hits on the offshore target that the old timers had taken a ribbing and had been ordered to extra practice. He had enjoyed those days and they, too, had carried their own special brand of excitement. Down in his locker, he remembered, he still carried the sharpshooter's badge won on the rifle range; and he smiled ruefully as he recalled how overconfidence had cost him the coveted Expert Rifleman's Medal and had taught him a good lesson as well. Being ranch-raised and brought up with guns, he thought city boys were a cinch to outshoot. What he'd not reckoned with was the efficiency of the Army's methods of instruction, which the sergeant had told him later could teach his old maid aunt to "shoot the tail off her pet canary at one hundred paces!"

Happy and useful days they'd been, and he realized now that much of what he'd learned in the barracks with Company B had been useful in his present company. It takes a

410

little doing to get along with men in the compressed society of the barracks room or the fo'c'sle. Compression builds explosive internal pressures in men, as well as machines, and he'd learned well the fundamental principle of surviving that precarious relationship: respect the other fellow's right of privacy; if necessary, fight for your own.

As the engine-room telegraph rang for dead slow, the yellow quarantine flag was hoisted and the *Tropic Trader* eased toward her temporary anchorage. From up forward came the roaring rattle of anchor chain and the flukes sent up two fountains of yellow foam. Swinging around the chain, she headed up into the flowing tide and came to rest. The waiting launch transferred personnel from the Health Department, customs, and the Bureau of Immigration. A tug headed out from its pier and secured to starboard, ready to take the tramp to her berth. The crew was assembled midships for the usual cursory medical examination, then the uniformed doctor left quickly to check another ship. The immigration and customs men would stay with her to the pier and customs would assign a permanent watch, until they had satisfied themselves that the ship carried no contraband liquor or narcotics.

Slim walked aft and hooked a heel over the lower rail. He wanted desperately to free his mind, but it was chained to the ship by the past months as surely as the ship was chained to its anchor. He looked out across the white-ruffled crests of the mud-beige water to Alcatraz Island. Those men were chained to a ship too, he thought, for the steel and concrete prison blocks seemed to rise like grim superstructures above a gray stone hull. As he looked out toward the west, he saw the evening fog bank moving in through the Golden Gate. The lowering sun had set aglow a bright border along its top edge and wispy fingers felt around the smooth shoulders of the hills that stood for one last moment in bold relief, then disappeared with unexpected swiftness beneath the moist mantle. Deep within the misting tide, fog horns called hoarse warnings to ships searching through the void.

He was glad the *Tropic Trader* had been early to her anchorage. He'd watched the stealthy inundation many times from the comfortable hilltop home across the bay. For a few moments the city would stand sharp and clear before the moving curtain. Then, suddenly, it would be gone, its outline visible only as rectangular galaxies of incandescent light which in turn would disappear, their bright points diffused to a sourceless glow behind the low, luminous cloud. To the east the slanting rays of the setting sun struck and fired the panes of countless windows along the crests of the hills. Beyond the brown-green hummock of Yerba Buena Island was Thousand Oaks and, at the top of the ridge, Santa Barbara Road.

As his eyes roved over scenes so long familiar, he found the reservoir of old emotion unexpectedly brimming again. With a thousand miles of open sea still separating them he'd even welcomed the prospect of returning to tell his tales to an eager and loving family. But now he was uneasy, and as he looked toward home there echoed in him the familiar rumblings of rebellion and he found himself framing defenses for battles not yet joined. He did not recognize that a good part of the uneasiness could be labeled guilt—guilt for many things, including not having answered Holst directly. He did recognize that a good part of it was his restless longing to see Edye who now seemed so close. To his left, in the gathering mist, he could make out the Admiral Line Piers and the stern of the *Ruth Alexander*. In the *Tropic Trader*'s safe was more than enough to buy his passage to Portland. The bus fare from there to Wauna was negligible. As Slim leaned against the rail and ran his hand lightly along the chilled, chipping metal, he felt also an unsuspected tinge of regret that these were the last hours of a first great adventure. It was beyond reasoning that he should be reluctant to leave his berth on the *Tropic Trader*. He did not know that the rusty old tramp had been the battlefield on which had been fought his war of independence and that in victory he was loath to vacate the newly won ground. Here, all the adversaries had been met and vanquished; to the east and north were other battles and days of decision against unknown odds. And so he leaned against the rail and looked toward home and struggled with indecision until the fog enveloped him and he hunched the sheepskin collar higher around his neck.

He didn't hear Chico until the messboy was beside him. They leaned on the rail a few inches apart and the little Filipino spoke gently. *"Amigo, la cosa es muy dificil.* No? You stay weeth the sheep?"

Slim thought for a moment, weighing an answer; but, as it had been with Holst, so it was with the messboy. The words wouldn't come. He stared down into the dark water thirty feet below and fought to summon up the truth. He felt its presence but its form was obscured. In the name of the friendship they had given, some of these men deserved an answer. For his own sake as well, Slim knew that the answer could be no less than the truth. He wondered why he couldn't make some conventional excuse for not having an answer or why he couldn't use one of those handy, humane little lies designed to spare friends the smart of unpleasant fact. For himself he wanted quick freedom from the torment of indecision, but the way was lost . . . the signs incomplete and confusing.

"Sleem," Chico moved closer and he spoke softly with understanding. "Eet's hard to make op your min'. Eet's not so hard eef you don' hob a fomily . . . then you jus' go." He put a hand lightly on Slim's forearm. "Why don't you go home now an' see your mother an' you' father? You hob a good beezit . . . then you make op your min'. Okay?" He grinned and slapped his friend on the back affectionately.

Slim's smile was warm with appreciation. His fingers closed gently around the back of Chico's neck and he gave it a playful little shake. "Chico, you've got more brains than anyone on the ship!"

The messboy's expression grew serious and he wagged his head in denial. "I don' hob brains! *You* hob brains . . . but I know sometheeng! Eet's berry hard to hob brains! Eef you like me . . . you hoppy, you sod . . . seek, well . . . hot, cold . . . thot's all! Eet's easy!"

He nodded at some silent conclusion, then looked up appraisingly at the young seaman. "You like a tall straight tree, Sleem. You stan' waiteeng to see wot they make from you. One mon could beeld a good house from you. Another mon could make only . . . only . . . what you call heem . . . box for the dead . . . coppins?" He slapped the palms of his hands together to punctuate his final comment. *"Amigo!* I theenk from you they going to beeld a good house!" He left the rail and moved toward the welldeck ladder. *"Hasta Luego!* They goeeng to pay off when we dock. I get ready now. Hob berry pine P'ilippino girl in Son Fronceesco. I go see!"

Chico, like most of his countrymen, had trouble with his *F's* and *V's* and Slim smiled gently, as the little man waved and disappeared down onto the lower deck. For one who professed inability to think, Chico had left considerable food for thought, and Slim's mind began to gnaw at the bitter stalk of truth. He understood that the boy is the raw material of the man, and, until he reaches the time of decision, he is the sum total of the skill and purpose of the hands that shaped him. He had long known that, although a number of skilled hands had shaped him thus far, the final man who'd bear the label "Lewis Fredericks" would be shaped by his own hands, implemented by his own decisions. He thought again of the words Holst had spoken in defense of the sea. He thought of the sudden and understanding release won from his mother and of his father's unexpected moralizing. He thought of Edye and of her subtle, sometimes selfish, persuasions. But most of all he thought of Mike and of Peterson, of the dumb luck and native dexterity that had enabled him to sew up Mike's slashed face and of the impenetrable mystery of anatomy, diagnosis, and internal medicine that may have robbed Peterson of his last chance at life. Slim had no way of knowing that the second mate's spleen had been ruptured; that death would probably have come from undetectable internal hemorrhage, even in the presence of skilled medical aid. He had cursed his inadequacy during a thousand moments of silent self-impugnation. To have been able to diagnose the injury correctly from the symptoms it produced might have insured the one slender thread that for a brief moment held life to the broken body. To have been able to identify that thread, even though it had been hopelessly strained, would have been a useful service of a high order. Slim knew that a physician's analytical insight was partly intuitive, as was an artist's, but the ability to amplify that insight with knowledge —to give it form and meaning—was the result of years of painstaking study.

He had been told many times that the inescapable prelude to knowledge and achievement was hard work. He hadn't really understood the meaning of the words until he'd found himself staring down at Peterson's convulsed body and was trapped in the morass of his own ignorance. With that understanding had come the firm resolve to take the necessary steps to successfully travel the road of his final choice. His dilemma then resulted not from an unwillingness to work, but from his present inability to make a final choice. The voices of reason and conscience clamored for recognition above the well-meant commotion of special pleading and advice from those who loved and from those who respected him. He stood at the main crossroad and around him were those who would influence his course. His grandfather and Holst bid him travel the paths of the sea; his mother and father urged him to travel homeward and from there prepare to explore the ramified roads of medicine; Edye's was at once an expressway and a detour. In each letter she'd made it plainer that he was her man. She'd found him, she loved him, and she wanted him. She had too much honesty to deny that she'd take him as he was now, and too much reason to refute the wisdom of waiting for him to master his profession. Slim's emphatic understanding of her own dilemma added poignancy to his, for he understood also that within reason the decision for both of them lay with him. Before him lay another road marked clearly with the memory of Marge. He could hear again the whisper of acquiescence, the muted echo of her anxious murmur, the breathless sounds of urgency and the fury of fulfillment. And there the road had ended—hard beneath the deadfall of their desire.

For Slim there was still another way, well-loved and familiar, for it followed the furrowed loam through cool, arcaded avenues of orchard; around the mounded shocks and across the stubbled knap of hay fields. It meandered along rivers and creeks and paused beside trout riffles and green-scummed tadpole pools. It dared the furnace blast of barren foothills, innocent of any shade and overlaid with ancient lava, then plunged at last into the fastness of aspen thicket and evergreen. It dipped beside a moss-bound spring, moved through corridors of blue spruce, tamarack and yellow pine, then burst out above the timber line and crunched deeply up the snowy steepness to the towering crystal crests of the High Sierra. He needed no guide along this path; he'd been born to it. In summer he'd felt it warm beneath his bare feet, and in the winter its icy muck sucked at the soles of his boots and burdened them with sticky blobs of black adobe. Very early his grandmother and uncles had taught him the ways of the ranch. He'd learned its chores and the mysteries of the creatures who inhabited its waters and its trees, its burrows and its windfalls. But no one there had urged him to stay; or, for that matter, had they pointed out a better way. How, by reason alone, to choose one of these ways? It was a problem to challenge the wisdom of the gods, for he had become, it seemed, the hero of his own Odyssey and Marge had become his Calypso, Edye, his Circe—or was she Penelope?—Holst, his Cyclops and home, his Ithaca. During his wandering, each had laid upon him a bond made more binding by his own affection. Each marked a crossroad and became at once, by insistence, both a beacon and a barricade.

The flat of a big hand struck him squarely between the shoulder blades and nearly knocked the wind from him.

"What the hell are you doin' here, Buddy? Ya look like ya lost yer last friend!"

Slim turned and faced Hammer. The ex-fighter was displaying what he hoped was an engaging grin. "I was lookin' for ya. I seen your gear was packed and I didn't want to miss sayin' good-by. You've been a great shipmate, kid!" He opened his hand and looked at the white scar in its palm. "Yes, sir, Slim—on the level—I ain't gonna ferget, and if there's anything I can do for ya, you holler and you got it. Look at this hand. If it wasn't for you, I wouldn't have it!" He flexed the thick fingers, then wrapped them into a great fist and punched it resoundingly into the cup of its mate. The force of the blow shook his shoulders. He nodded his head in satisfaction and buffed the knuckles against the calloused left palm. "Yes, sir, boy, it's as good as ever—thanks to you!"

Slim looked at the face: the broad grin that twisted up at one corner and down at the other, the eyes that narrowed to scar-puffed slits beneath the ridgy bone of his brow; the broad, traplike jaws, and the ears, thickened from the buffeting of padded gloves. It was the face of a young brute with strength enough to crush and brains enough to campaign with simple strategy. Slim knew from his manner that Hammer was after something. He suspected the A.B. was going to ask him to wait for payment on the IOUs won in the poker games. He'd already made up his mind to forget them as bad debts. He owed nothing to any man in the crew and, although he'd not said it, no man owed him a thing that had not already been paid. He had six hundred and eighteen dollars in the ship's safe. That was plenty.

He accepted a proffered cigarette and light, before he replied, "I did what I could and I'm glad your mitt healed all right." He smiled. "Be careful next time. They don't make bottles the way they used to!"

The ex-fighter laughed loudly at the little joke, then suddenly grew serious. "Listen, kid . . ." He hesitated uneasily. "Uh . . . I don't mean to be pryin' into your business . . . but are you gonna stay on the ship?"

The sudden resentment flared again. He answered shortly, "I don't know. Why?"

The A.B. shifted nervously and, for the first time since he'd known the man, Slim felt he was really worried. "I'll tell ya, kid . . . I need a favor! It's nothin' much . . . just a loan. I know you got money, so I figgered if you was shippin' out again I could give you another marker and

416

pay ya back later. In the deck gang you and Chips are the only guys who took care of yer dough . . . and that big bastard wouldn't give ya the sweat off his balls!" He spat over the rail and waited.

"How much do you need?"

"Ah, hell . . . I don't know. Not much. I gotta see a doctor. I ain't been feelin' good since I had that cold sore. I guess I got something in my system. I ain't got any cash comin' at all. I had to borrow against it to even get a lousy fuckin' drink . . . after those bastards on the bridge started clippin' me with fines!"

He opened his jacket and unbuttoned the blue denim work shirt. "Looka this——" He indicated a rash that ran down through the coarse hair below his collarbone to a point just above his navel. "I don't know what the hell it is . . . but it started comin' out a couple of days ago. It don't itch or nuthin', but I want to get it looked at just in case I got some sorta crud. I don't want to go to no Marine Hospital. With a rap on me, they'd find out sure as hell. I figger I can get one of them quacks on Mission Street to go over me. In the meantime I could lay low until this tub is ready to sail again. She's goin' in for a bottom job, so they'll only need a standby crew.

"I could keep in touch with ya . . . and sign on again when she's ready for sea. I'll tell ya somethin' else, pal . . . so ya won't worry about the money. I can pick up a couple of club fights in South Frisco. A win's good for twenty-five or fifty bucks . . . six rounds . . . it's easy dough!"

Slim watched the man rebutton his shirt. He didn't like the looks of the rash, just as he hadn't liked the looks of the "cold sore." In the medical manual it had stated that a hard chancre developing at the point of contact was followed by a secondary symptomatic rash, usually four to six months later. Not nearly enough time had passed, but there were other symptoms like the headaches and the raw sore throat of which the man had complained lately.

"What do you say, kid . . . how about it?"

Slim hesitated a long moment before answering. A loan to Hammer was a loan lost and he knew it. Once the money had been given, the A.B. would disappear. If he did keep his word and sail again, assuming he was able, the debt would be deferred with a series of excuses or outright repudiation.

"Look, Jack. I know you're good for it . . . but I'm not sure that I'm going to sign on again for another trip. Let's

417

forget the IOUs . . . maybe that'll help a little, anyway."
He felt uncomfortable as the man's face broke into a slow,
twisted smile. But there was no forced friendliness in the
cold eyes this time and the note of phony camaraderie
changed to purring insincerity.

"Okay, kid. You don't have to tell me yer business. If
ya don't want to lend money to an old shipmate, that's up
to you. No hard feelin's——" He smiled broadly and extended his hand.

Slim took it reluctantly and they shook. It seemed to
him that the A.B. squeezed unnecessarily, but he made no
sign to indicate feeling the pressure and neutralized it in
part with his own.

"No, sir, kiddo. When a guy's done as much for a shipmate as you did fer me . . . a little thing like turnin'
down a loan ain't gonna change a thing." He turned to go
but stopped midway to the ladder. "If ya really think yer
goin' home, pal . . . I'd like to buy ya a drink. How about
it? I still got half a bottle of Black and White."

Slim nodded in agreement. "Thanks . . . I'll see you in
the fo'c'sle when we get alongside."

"Okay . . . don't forget!" He directed an exaggerated
salute to the ordinary seaman and, still grinning, dropped
down the ladder to the after well deck.

Slim felt vaguely uncomfortable at the prospect of having a drink with Hammer; first, because he didn't want to
swig from the same bottle and second, it was not like the
man to give up so easily. He knew that Jack was not lying
about wanting to see a doctor. He knew he was desperately in need of money for that purpose. The man had
mentioned it before, and it was apparent to everyone
aboard that he was not the same rugged, perfectly func-
tioning machine he'd been during the earlier months of the
voyage. Hammer was sick. The crew knew it and he knew
it. Slim was positive the fellow would try to get money
somehow. In Australia he and Rusty had replenished their
coffers by rolling drunks and fags. He would probably try
to roll some of the despicable homosexual "he-whores"
who lurked in the dark doorways along Howard and lower
Mission Street, but they seldom carried more than change.
Slim shrugged at his own unspoken concern. He'd meet
the problem of Hammer when and if he came to it again.
He finished the cigarette and flipped it into the bay.

Heavy steps resounded on the companion ladder and
Chips came out on deck. "Ain't the mate here yet?"

Slim shook his head. "I haven't seen him."

The big carpenter looked forward quizzically. "Wonder what's keepin' them? We shoulda moved into the pier ten minutes ago. I want to draw some money and get ashore. This is my town, sailor!" He grinned at the ordinary seaman and jerked his thumb toward the Ferry Building off to the left. "This is the friendliest city in the world. I got lotsa friends here!" He suddenly remembered something. "Hey! You got a family here, too. You gonna see em?"

Slim smiled. Chips was the only one so far who had not asked him directly whether or not he was going to sign on for the next trip.

"They live in Berkeley. As soon as we pay off, I'm going home for a while."

Chips looked at him closely. "How much money you got?"

"Six hundred dollars . . . or thereabouts."

"You gonna draw it all?"

"I believe so——"

"You gonna draw it tonight?"

Slim wondered about the carpenter's questions. It was unlike him to make any such personal inquiry. "I thought I would——"

Chips glanced at the companionway. "What's your hurry? Why don'tcha stay aboard tonight and shove off in the morning? Unless you're gonna take stand-by and sign on again, you can leave tomorrow as well as tonight."

When Slim didn't answer immediately, he went on. "Ya know, there's a lot of guys gettin' off this ship broke and owin'. They're not too fussy about how they get their hands on a little dough, if you know what I mean."

Slim chuckled mirthlessly. "I know what you mean! I've met one of them already."

Chips frowned. "Wouldn't be a guy name of Hammer?"

The young seaman looked surprised. "Yeah! He wants to borrow some money. He needs to go to a doctor. I think he's on the level about that all right!"

The carpenter looked at him closely. "Ya didn't give him any, did ya?"

"No. I told him I'd cancel the IOUs. That'll save him about thirty bucks."

"That'll save shit!" Chips spat out the words. "That son-uvabitch never had any idea about payin' off them markers. He'll bully or wheedle his way out of every one of 'em. It's a good thing he don't owe me. I'd wring every goddamn dollar out of his hide!"

Slim shook his head uncertainly. "I never counted on

419

the thirty bucks anyway, so it's nothing lost to me. I'll be glad to get clear of him!"

The carpenter glowered at Slim. "Just make damn good and sure you do!" He pulled out a cigarette. "I'll give you a tip. When you go ashore, put all the bills you have and your discharge papers in your shoes. Ordinaries don't make so much that it'll be uncomfortable . . . and it's a helluva lot safer. Just keep a few bills in your pocket. If you leave when I do, I'll walk ya up to the Ferry Building, but it'll be a lot better if you pay off tomorrow!"

The tugboat sounded two shrill blasts on its whistle and the *Tropic Trader* got underway again, angling for the end of the pier. Through the swirling mist Slim could just make out the dark shapes of the long dock sheds jutting out into the bay. Here and there above their roofs he could see the hazy tracery of topmasts and rigging. It took nearly an hour to tie up and set the gangplank, and when at last Slim went below for coffee, he was tired and impatient to get ashore. He had intended to call his father and catch the same ferry home if they'd tied up in time, but it was out of the question now. By the time he paid off, collected his gear and got to the foot of Market Street, it would be past eight. As much as he hated to stop, he'd have a quick bite at the terminal restaurant before catching the ferry home. The trip across the bay and up to Arlington Circle on the connecting S.P. electric train would take over an hour. He'd phone from the other side and have the family drive down to pick him up. At the very earliest it would be nine-thirty or ten before he could make it. He felt a shiver of excitement as he thought of the meeting . . . the comfortable home . . . the first honest-to-goodness tub bath in nearly a year.

Collecting his clothing, which had already been partially packed in the duffle bag, he stuffed it beside his shaving and sewing kits and the packet of letters from home and from Edye. All that remained now was to sign the pay slip and say his good-byes. He stowed the bag for safekeeping and snapped the heavy brass lock. After a final check of the bunk and shelf, he made his way forward to the steward's quarters. Several of the men were hanging around outside the alleyway that led to the petty officers' mess. He saw Mike, Otto, Brill, Square John, and Spots. Of these men, only the latter spoke to him. The others seemed preoccupied—almost strangers. Indeed, all at once, everything about the ship seemed strange. It was a different vessel—suddenly empty and dead, like a disheveled Pullman car at the end of a long run. Slim didn't fully understand that the change was normal to the way of life aboard ships. The men of the crew, strangers at first, became friends of necessity. When the necessity ends, they become strangers again. The past dies with the handful of back pay that represents the meager fruit of its days. For most of them the night would bring rotten booze and roistering women whose favor would diminish with the money. Later some of the men, in strictured pain, would curse all women and the hopeless life from which there could be no escape.

Slim had to wait twenty minutes before his name was called. Ioway joined him. As the lowest ranking member of the deck gang, the deck boy would be the last to receive his pay. As they leaned against the rail, looking aimlessly down into the deep shadows between the ship and the dock, he probed gently into Slim's future.

"I'm sure glad to be home, aren't you?"

"Yeah . . . I guess so."

There was a long silence before the deck boy tried again. "I'm heading for Marshalltown. Boy . . . home's gonna look awful good to me! How about you, Slim?"

. "It'll be all right, I guess."

The boy frowned to himself and tried for a direct answer. "Slim . . . are you gonna stay on this ship?"

"If you mean tonight . . . no. If you mean for another trip . . . I don't know yet."

Ioway pushed himself back from the rail. "I've got exactly one hundred and forty-one dollars and sixty-five cents coming. I'm gonna get me a freight train from Roseville over the mountains and as soon as I get to the Midwest, I'm gonna pay my way home on a bus. You can have your chipping hammers and scrapers. From now on I'll take the hoe and cultivator. And I'll tell you something else, Slim. I'h going to be the biggest man at the Farm Bureau meetings when I tell the guys some of the things we've done!"

Slim's eyes twinkled. "I wouldn't tell them *everything,* if I were you!"

Ioway looked confused for a moment, then remembered the Adelaide episode with an embarrassed smile. "Heck, no!"

Spots emerged from the alleyway and called to Slim. "You're next, pal!" He patted a bulge in his pants pocket. "Wish me luck, you guys. The only thing that's gonna pass my tonsils from now on is plain water and the sweet strains of 'Mother Machree!' "

He headed toward the gangway and paused at the top for a moment. "I'll let you guys know where I'm working. It'll be a pleasure to make you pay to hear me sing!" He laughed at his own joke and disappeared down the side of the ship and into the shadows of the long pier shed.

Slim went into the messroom. The steward, the first mate, the chief engineer and the bosun were seated at the table. With them were two men in civilian dress. Pugh doled out the money in big ten- and twenty-dollar bills and Slim signed the ship's book. The first mate handed him an envelope containing the money that had been locked up for safekeeping together with a discharge paper signed by the captain. He noted that he'd been graded "Very Good" both for character and seamanship and he smiled to himself when he remembered Holst's later regretted comment about "brains."

The mate looked at him sharply. So did the bosun. Slim felt uncomfortable until the officer spoke. "You did a good job, Fredericks. If you want to ship with us again, Boats'll tell you where to go to get your lifeboat ticket. We'll take you back as an A.B."

The ordinary seaman stood straight in the presence of the first mate. He looked at the man and then quickly at the bosun. "Thank you, sir . . . thank you, Boats. I'd like to go home and see the family first."

The mate smiled and nodded his head in dismissal. The bosun's face was impassive. He made no sign that he'd heard. As Slim departed, he could feel the man's eyes boring into his back.

Slim stepped out on deck and motioned the young deck boy inside. "Good luck, Ioway. I enjoyed knowing you!" He held out his hand and they shook warmly.

"Me, too, Slim. If you ever get to Marshalltown . . . look me up. You sure as heck can't forget a name like Horatius!"

"I won't forget the name . . . and I will look you up! Take it easy hoppin' freights, boy. It's easier to walk with two legs!"

Ioway smiled and disappeared into the alleyway. It was the last Slim saw of him. He thought he'd seen the last of Spots, too, when the happy-go-lucky and apparently reformed "dipso" had rattled down the gangway. A half hour later, when he came forward with his sea bag, Slim heard loud voices down on the dock. Descending the gangplank, he approached a knot of men standing over the singer's unconscious form. He was pale and out cold. The front of his coat was damp and he smelled of alcohol.

"I figgered he belonged on this ship. We found him over there between the pier sheds." The stranger indicated the direction of Pier 45 which was a dozen or so yards south toward the Ferry Building. "He don't have no money or papers on him. Looks like he was drunk and got rolled fer his wad!"

Slim kneeled down beside Spots. There were no marks on him and from appearances it certainly did look as if the fellow had at last fallen off the wagon. But Slim knew that he'd left the ship cold sober less than an hour before. It was not likely that he'd been able to get soused unconscious in that time, even if he had foresworn his vows which Slim felt was highly unlikely.

"Looks like Rusty wins his bet . . . if he can find Warndahl and collect, don't it, Doc?"

Slim glanced up into Hammer's grinning face and rose slowly. He looked the A.B. straight in the eye. "Who do you suppose would do this to the poor guy?"

The man shrugged and smiled. "How the hell should I know? Some guy that needs money, I guess. That narrows it down to about a thousand guys right in this neighborhood, don't it, kid?" He pushed the boy playfully in the ribs. "I'll tell ya one thing . . . I'm walkin' on the other side of the tracks when I go uptown tonight. A guy that would do this"—— he indicated the unconscious Spots—— —"would take the clothes off yer back!" He shook his head sadly and stared up the gangplank.

Slim watched him and wondered whether he'd been aboard or on the dock when the stevedores found Spots. As he watched Hammer, he heard the bosun saying, "Ya can't bring him back on da ship. He don't belong here no more. Lay him over dere till he comes around."

Slim moved up the gangplank after the A.B. As he climbed, a sudden thought came to him. At the top he called, "Hey Jack. How about that drink you promised me?"

Hammer turned in surprise. "What——?"

"I said, how about that drink you promised me? I'm ready for it now, if you are!"

Hammer hesitated a moment, then smiled broadly. "Jesus, kid. I didn't think you'd really go fer a drink with me. I finished it all off myself. Why the hell didn't ya ask me earlier?"

Slim smiled back. "Forget it! I don't really want a drink. I just didn't want to hurt your feelings. Like you said, we've been good shipmates. The first day I was on this ship I had a drink with you. Remember?"

The A.B. looked at him. The smile stayed on his face but the eyes grew cold and wary. "Yeah . . . I remember . . . and ya got laid, too, didn't ya?"

"That's right."

A sudden thought struck Hammer. He moved closer and his tone became elaborately confidential. "Listen, kid . . . I got a great idea. How about you and me goin' to that joint again? We'll buy another bottle and get our nuts popped . . . just for old time's sake. Whaddya say . . . okay?"

Slim hesitated. He wanted to confirm his suspicions, but that needed careful strategy. "Geez, Jack . . . I'd like to . . . but that's a lot of dough to lay out for both of us. I'm gonna have to stretch what I got for a long time." He shook his head uncertainly.

Hammer dismissed the problem with a wave of his hand. "Pick up your own share like last time, pal. I borrowed a couple of bucks from an old friend. I'm set. I can't go see a quack until tomorrow, anyway. A little gin and a good hump never made anybody feel bad. Come on . . . let's go!"

Before Slim could reply, Rusty came around the end of the deckhouse. Seeing Hammer, he stopped. "Hey . . . I've been lookin' fer ya. You and I gotta little business to finish, ain't we?" He rubbed his thumb and fingers together in the classic pantomime of one wishing to feel the fineness of coin.

The A.B. looked annoyed. "I'll see ya in the fo'c'sle in a minute." Turning back to Slim, he smiled reassuringly. "I'll get rid of this guy. He wants to borrow from me. Meet ya on the dock in ten minutes."

As he started to move away, Slim called after him, "Listen, Jack, you go on. I gotta see Sparks and the second mate!" He had not really told a lie, because he had never intended to leave the ship without saying his farewells to Sparks and especially to Holst. No matter what the future held, he didn't want to lose track of the man.

Hammer looked at him suspiciously. "What the hell are you doin'? A little while ago you was bustin' yer ass to get offa this tub. Now you want to hang around. Okay . . . I'm in no hurry. Holler when yer ready." He turned and followed Rusty across the well deck and aft to the crew's quarters.

There was not much question in Slim's mind now about Spots' fate. If Hammer had money, it meant only one thing: he and Rusty had done a job on the fat little A.B. and Rusty was taking no chances on not getting his cut. Hammer's liquor was gone because he'd forced it down the seaman's throat and spilled it on his clothes. Slim culdn't prove it . . . but he'd have bet all he had on it. It was not the first time he'd seen that partnership in action. He had no intention of being its next victim. In his heavy work shoes he could feel the uncomfortable but reassuring tightness of the inner soles, comprised of six hundred dollars in bills. He'd kept about eighteen dollars and change in his pocket. Watching the two disappear into the alleyway, he climbed the ladder to the boatdeck for a visit with Sparks. He knew that, if the ex-prizefighter had money in his pocket, he'd not hang around the ship for long. His strategy now was to outwait him, then take his own time about running the gauntlet to the Ferry Building. Chips had gone ashore, so he'd have to make the half-mile walk alone.

Sparks was rummaging around in the drawers beneath his bunk. Stokes was sprawled comfortably in the bolted swivel chair; the unplugged percolator stood on the desk. He looked up in surprise as Slim entered the radio shack. "Well, well now . . . see who's joined us again—the distinguished surgeon general of the Asian-Australian Line!"

Sparks turned around and looked up from the untidy drawer. "I thought you'd sneaked off the ship to avoid the emotional torment of this touching farewell." He looked at Slim owlishly and a smile began to twinkle in the ordinary seaman's eyes.

"I saw you packing, so I came up here to wish you good luck."

"What do you mean 'good luck' . . . good luck at what?"

"Good luck at anything you decide to do . . . like getting on a Matson Line ship."

Sparks blinked at him for a moment, then stood up and leaned thoughtfully against the edge of the bunk. With careful deliberation he selected a cigarette, inspected it, moistened its end, and placed it in his mouth. He held the match poised but unlighted and as he spoke the cigarette bobbed up and down, punctuating his words like the tail of a chirping bird.

"My long drawn-out young friend. I've reached some conclusions about my adopted profession. As a result, I've decided to leave it. First, to escape from the necessity of keeping further company with the likes of this mangy son of Britain . . . whose prime purpose in life is not only to keep himself from thinking . . . but to prevent others from doing so. He thereby insures himself a ready audience of idiots for his constant stream of pseudo-intellectualism. If I may vivify: he titillates his cerebral erection continually, but never to the point of orgasm. Therefore, no new thoughts take seed, gestate, and are born to the world of reason. In short, I've tired of inhabiting this sterile wooden womb into which enters, with certain exceptions, the intellectual sperm of only the most impotent pricks! It is my intention now to force its varnished vagina and emerge into the world, its oldest infant, freed at last from the umbilical cord of this corrupt pot!"

Sparks gestured toward the percolator and its owner with the unrestrained mannerism of a ham actor. Slim waited for the retort which he felt certain from experience would be forthcoming from the English fireman. But none came. Stokes smiled, but it was not the same smile of anticipation that usually preceded his rebuttals. To Slim it seemed almost wistful, as he looked off into space for a moment.

When he spoke his voice was gentle, without sarcasm. "Slim . . . a simple translation of the foregoing might be stated thusly: Our good friend here has at least wearied of his self-imposed exile and now fears its continued boredom more than the fancied oppression that induced it. This is progress. Also, secure in the knowledge that his retreat is guarded, he has saved for me his last and most unjust personal barb. I find it a bit difficult, being bested by one who has not learned his ground rules on the playing fields of Eton. However, if I may pretend clairvoyance for a moment and look into the future, I see a highly intelligent man suddenly smitten with remorse for not having recognized sooner the identity of his deliverer."

Sparks fumbled the match and finally lit the damp cigarette. There was a curious expression on his face, as though his long-time opponent had suddenly stripped off his frowsy jester's guise and revealed beneath it a nobler habit. Slim looked at them both and was discomforted by a growing embarrassment. The clear stamp of truth on the fireman's words suddenly made him wish he had not been present at the revelation. But there was still more to Stokes' prediction.

"In the sodden depths of boredom I've often voiced the gibberish of a fool. From the temperate heights of reason I've occasionally voiced a clearer thought. Until now, I feared it had gone unheard. A life without service is a life without meaning. Once, in an effort to serve what I felt was a worthy cause, I irrevocably forfeited the meaning of my own. Forgive my selfishness, then, if I try at times to give it some small point by fixing the meaning in others."

Sparks pretended to be occupied with a small fragment of tobacco sticking to his tongue. He finally deposited it on his upper lip and wiped it away on the back of his hand. Slim could see his downcast eyes blinking rapidly and watched the prominent Adam's apple travel up and down beneath the thin, prematurely old skin.

Stokes collected his outstretched legs beneath him and looked for a moment as though he were going to rise. He paused on the edge of the chair as another thought struck him. "I'm going to miss you two chaps." He looked at the ordinary seaman. "Slim . . . you're the junior and quite properly the quietest member of this debating society. Occasionally you've been its unofficial referee. For the points you scored on my side, I'm grateful." He nodded his head in emphasis. "It would seem to me that you have the basic equipment to win any game you please. Unfortunately, combat of one sort or another is man's normal state. Just make certain before you go into battle that you've chosen the war worth winning!"

Stokes looked directly at the radio operator. The look was an appraising one tempered with friendliness. There was no trace of hurt. "Sparks . . . I've waited a long time to see you pack and really mean it. In your war you've been battling the drummers and the buglers, not the marshals and the generals. One day you'll learn that your opponents are issues, not people, and when you do . . . you'll begin to serve very effectively some of the causes you've espoused so often during these past three years. For instance the worthy and I fear sometimes lost cause of the downtrodden American seaman. Count your hours, then count your dollars. You'll find they add up to quite an issue. You know the sea and the men who sail it. Go argue for those poor, frustrated, inarticulate bastards. Give voice and reason to their open-throated bellows of rage. Add to their limited vocabularies . . . a few *eight* letter words! Do it with the simple eloquence of reason and conviction!"

The shabby little fireman rose from the chair and

picked up his percolator. Wrapping the worn cord around it carefully, he cradled it in his left arm. He extended his right hand to the radio operator. "So long, old boy . . . I can only hope that your successor has your taste for good conversation and good coffee. Nothing yet devised is more effective for easing the painfully slow passage of time!"

Sparks looked up and took his hand. His manner was subdued. "So long, Frank. I'll watch the shipping news. When you're in, I'll come aboard. It was time well spent!"

Stokes' sudden grin so lighted his nondescript face that Slim was no longer aware of the toothless gap. As he reached the door, he turned to Slim. "In parting, laddie, you might remember this: the sea is a restless mistress. Once clasped to her heaving bosom, man is not long content with another!" He paused reflectively, then looked up again. "I don't recall who wrote that . . . but it's quite possible I did! Cheerio!" He smiled again and disappeared into the night.

Neither of them spoke for a moment. The radio operator stared down into the open drawer, then closed it with a push of his foot. He blinked at Slim, pushed the glasses higher on his nose, and shook his head uncertainly.

"There goes one of the strangest guys I've ever met . . . and one of the smartest. He gives me the creeps sometimes. Ever notice those eyes? They don't belong in that face. They look like they can see everything there is to see . . . all the time!" Sparks shook his head in wonderment.

Slim walked over to the door and held the handle. "I don't know what I'm going to do yet, Sparks. But if you stay ashore . . . we're in the Berkeley phone book on Barbara Road. If I'm there, we'll get together. If not, leave word with the family where I can reach you, and I'll write and let you know what's happening."

The radio operator smiled and for the first time in a long while Slim saw the old gleam in his myopic eyes. They shook hands and Slim patted the door frame.

"I remember the first time I fell through this door and all but puked on your deck. Thanks for what you did then . . . and for everything you've done since."

"Including the Waverly Bar in Aukland?"

Slim laughed. "Especially the Waverly Bar! I'll be seeing you, Sparks. Take care of yourself . . . and good luck!"

"The same to you, Doc . . . and don't stitch up anyone without a license!"

Slim smiled and stepped out on deck. Picking up the duffle bag he'd leaned against the bulkhead, he slung it over his shoulder and descended to the main deck. In the galley he said a quick good-by to Mr. Jones who was finishing up the night's work. Mr. Bones had already gone ashore. So had the Filipino boys, but Chico had left a small package with the steward. Slim picked it up and opened it. It was the rosary that had been the mess boy's constant companion ever since Slim had first met him. Slim felt badly that he could not have seen the little man to thank him in person. He passed Russian John, standing gangway watch, huddled on the port coal bunker. Going to the bridge, Slim knocked on Holst's door. He was about to leave when it opened.

The second mate's face was covered with lather, but Slim could see he was pleased. "Hey . . . I thought you'd gone ashore. What are you doin' around here this late?"

Slim dropped the bag down on the deck. He stuck out his hand awkwardly. "I just wanted to come by and ask you if you and Mrs. Holst would come over to Berkeley and have dinner with us some night soon?"

The mate wiped off the lather and fixed Slim with a thoughtful gaze. Then his mouth widened into a grim smile. "Kid . . . if I came over and saw the kind of a home you come from, I'd probably never try to get you back on this ship . . . so I've got an invitation for you, instead. We'll be in dry dock at the Union Iron Works in Oakland for a week. Why don't you stop by . . . and sign on as an able-bodied seaman?" He wiped his hands on the towel and reached out. "So long now, Fredericks. Let's be seein' you soon!" Stepping back inside his cabin, he closed the door.

Slim made his way to port and stopped at the head of the gangway. Russian John looked up slowly and the boy saw the cluster light reflected for a second in his cavernous eyes. "John . . . did Hammer go ashore yet?"

The old Russian thought for a moment, then nodded slowly. "He go . . . long time."

Slim looked at his watch. He'd stayed aboard a lot longer than he'd expected to. He'd be lucky to get home before midnight. Waving a quick farewell to the cough-wracked but surprisingly durable old man, he rattled down the gangway to the dock and walked under the towering plates toward the Embarcadero. In the dark distance to his right he heard the warning whistle of a switch engine on the Belt Line railroad, and the rumble of freight cars being shunted along the waterfront. As he reached the street, he looked to his left along the curving line of giant dock buildings that stretched south to the Ferry Building. He could see less than a block in the fog. It was a long walk with the heavy duffle bag. He wished the Embarcadero were served by streetcars. He even looked for the identifying light of a taxi, but the waterfront street was deserted. Through the swirling curtain he could make out the high cliff of Telegraph Hill, overhanging the street. At the top lights shone mistily in the windows of unseen houses. Resigned to his task, he lengthened his stride and set out along the glistening pavement of what seemed like the loneliest waterfront in the world.

– 35 – The fog swirled around green-shaded lights over the gaping doors of Pier 43. Inside another tiny light glowed in the empty watchman's booth. Behind him Slim could hear the metallic clank and hollow bumping of a line of boxcars being started again by the blunt little switch engine. From on beyond Fisherman's Wharf and to his left out on the bay he heard the mournful moan of foghorns and the warning hoot of small craft. These harbor sounds were the only ones that reached his ears. The reassuring squeal of steel wheel flanges against the curved trolley rails and the insistent clang of trolley bells were still dampened by distance and the muffling fog. Not even a pale glow marked the position of the Ferry Building's blazing tower.

Slim turned his back to the outer edge of a square of oil drums left standing outside the pier shed and lowered the heavy sea bag to the top of one of them. From their markings he could see they contained tung oil, consigned to the Sherwin-Williams Paint Company whose huge electric sign dominated the foot of Market Street. As a youngster he'd been delighted by its animated bulbs that spilled a bucket of paint over the globe and the slogan, "We Cover The World," which blinked insistently at the hurrying commuters. Slim smiled as a vagrant pun wandered through his mind: "I've covered a bit of the world myself . . . and painted a few towns!" He sat heavily on the flanged edge of the round metal container and twisted his feet uncomfortably in the money-stuffed shoes. As soon as he got on the ferry, he'd get some coffee at the commuters' snack bar and loosen the confining laces. He figured he could put up with the discomfort for another ten minutes or so. Reaching inside his heavy jacket, he took out a cigarette and lit it.

"Hold that match, will you, pal?"

Slim jumped at the shock of hearing the voice behind him. It was Hammer. He'd apparently been waiting in the

431

shadows by the side of the pier shed. Slim fought to steady his voice, but the start had left a knot of fear in his throat. He held the burning match cupped in his hand as the A.B. leaned over it and puffed the smoke to life.

Hammer straightened up slowly and smiled. "What are ya shakin' for, kid! Ya cold?"

Slim didn't answer the question. He tried to hold his hand steady, but he knew Hammer had seen it tremble. "They told me you and Rusty had gone an hour ago. I figured you were tired of waiting."

The ex-fighter twisted the corners of his mouth down and shook his head. "Naw . . . Rusty got tired. But me . . . I never get tired of waitin' . . . not for a pal! I'll tell ya somethin', pal"—he leaned on the word—"I sure want to buy that drink. Yes, sir . . . I want to buy it real bad . . . an' ya know what with?" He smirked at the ordinary seaman. "With the money you're gonna loan me——"

Slim still leaned against the steel drum. In this position, Hammer's face was directly on the level of his, and he looked at it closely in the eerie yellow glow of the dock light. His own face was in shadow. There was no pretense of friendliness in the A.B. now—just that same intent, deadly pale stare and the suggestion of a twisted smile. Slim had seen the expression many times in the past year. He knew full well its implications. As he watched the face now, the edge of fear that had risen in him began to recede before the rising flood of hatred for this man. He'd felt it before . . . for the Swede. With Warndåhl the revulsion had arisen from the sea of filth in which the man wallowed and into which he'd sought to pull Slim. With Hammer the feeling had arisen from a deep hatred for the bullies of the world who take what they need by terrorism.

Suddenly the fear left and, as had happened once before, it was replaced by a cold resolve. He felt his muscles relax as tension was replaced with quiet readiness. This man was no unreasoning bull of a fighter. He was a trained and murderous machine to whom a life that challenged him was something to be disposed of . . . as he'd tried to do with Mike and with the dockworker in the steamy little hole-in-the-wall café on the south side of Market Street. In the instant of silence that preceded his reply, Slim knew that his only chance was to outthink the man. Muscle for muscle, Hammer had the advantage of weight and training. Thought for thought, Slim knew he had the edge. He called quietly on the experience with

Warndahl and made a quick mental note of the surroundings. Behind him was the Ferry Building—a good long quarter-mile down the Embarcadero. To his right and slightly behind was the black maw of the open pier shed and the wide dock that ran around three sides of it. No ship was tied to the north side. A small coastal steamer reared her skinny stack and masts into the haze to the south side. To his left was the broad, dark-cobbled width of the Embarcadero, its western margin butted hard against the towering cliffs of Telegraph Hill. If there was a watchman, Slim thought, he was making his lonely rounds. He also knew from experience that these old pensioners wanted no trouble. He'd seen them turn their backs on dock brawls. Generally they carried only a flashlight. Sometimes there were telephones in their little cubicles. Most of them sat huddled over their kerosene heaters, puffing on pipes and dozing away the time between rounds.

Slim forced a disarming smile. "I thought you said you'd borrowed some money from an old friend. I guess I misunderstood, huh?"

A biting edge of sarcasm crept into Hammer's voice. "Yeah, buddy . . . you misunderstood. I want to borrow the money from *you* . . . on account of us being such good pals. I just hate borrowing from a stranger!"

Slim nodded sympathetically. "I know what you mean. I hate lending to a stranger. I guess poor old Spots did, too . . . only I've got a hunch he thought he was talking to a friend, don't you?"

The smile faded from Hammer's face and the lips curled into a snarl. "You're getting too fuckin' smart for your own good. I told ya I want to 'borrow' some money. Now get it up!"

Slim spoke soothingly. "You don't have to get tough, Jackie boy. I'm your pal, aren't I? You keep telling me I am. How much do you want, old pal?"

Hammer snapped back the answer. "I want every fuckin' penny ya got, kid . . . except yer carfare home! Now get it up! You saw what happens to guys who argue, didn't you?"

Reaching slowly for his pocket, Slim took out a thin roll of bills. There was a ten, a five, and three singles, plus change.

"Did Spots have time to argue?"

Hammer's hand shot out and grabbed the money and a white fury flared in the ordinary seaman, but the moment

433

was not quite right. Turning slightly to his left to take advantage of the dim glow, Hammer fanned out the bills and counted them. "Eighteen bucks! What the hell are you tryin' to get away with? You paid off with four hundred bucks—that I'm sure of—plus the poker money those suckers paid you. Where's the rest of it?"

Slim smiled. "I figured I might run into some 'friends' who'd need it, so I left it in a safe place. I'd hate to have it fall into the hands of strangers . . . wouldn't you?"

The boy's attitude puzzled Hammer slightly. He'd not expected the kid to give him the money quietly, but neither had he expected the calm defiance he was meeting.

Slim felt the momentary hesitancy and moved to take advantage of it. "I've got a proposition for you, Jack——"

The bull-like A.B. glared at him suspiciously.

"Quit the shit and get the dough up!"

"I'll split it with you. How's that? After all, a pal whose hand I saved wouldn't want more than a fair shake, would he?"

Hammer mulled the words for a moment, then smiled. If the kid did get up half of it, he'd know where the rest was hidden.

"Okay, kid. I'll take half. That's gotta be two hundred and fifty bucks at least. Right?"

Slim confirmed the figure. "Right." He turned his head suddenly and listened in the direction of the pier shed. As he did so, Hammer involuntarily turned and looked in the same direction. In that split second, Slim's two feet shot out like a battering ram. The heavy loggers struck the A.B. full in the stomach. The breath exploded from him in a heaving grunt and he sprawled backwards on the paving. As he lay gasping and heaving, Slim abandoned the sea bag and jumped up on top of the drums. Racing diagonally across them in the direction of the shed, he jumped down, squatted in their shadow and listened. He could hear the maddened curses of the ex-fighter as he scrambled to his feet. Slim heard him start around the left side of the pile. Running low, Slim headed across several yards of open street and ducked into the darkened interior of Pier 45. The only light came from the sickly bulb in the watchman's still empty cubicle. Moving quickly down the wide center aisle, he stumbled over a pile of wooden pallets and barked his shins. Turning to his right, he saw the dark mass of a cargo stack. Feeling with his hands, he recognized the burlap-covered bales of manila hemp. There were a few tons of them in the *Tropic Trader*'s holds.

Feeling his way along the face of the stack, he came to a narrow aisle that ran into the pile and dead-ended against the south wall of the building. If Hammer trapped him in this black, cramped alley, it might well become his own slaughterhouse. Slim searched for a foothold. He couldn't tell how high the bales rose above his head, but the aisle was narrow enough so that he could easily force his way up by pressing his hands and feet against the opposite walls. As he worked quietly up the steep sides he heard the running thud of Hammer's shoes and the echo of his voice.

"All right, you lousy prick! This time you're gonna get the works. I know you're in there. I'll get you if I personally have to move every fuckin' case in the joint!"

As the echo of Hammer's outrage subsided, Slim heard the rolling rattle of a heavy door on its overhead tracks and the raspy voice of an elderly watchman. "Who's in there? I heard ya . . . come on outa there before I call the p'lice!"

Slim stopped climbing and, above the pounding of his own heart, tried to listen. There were no sounds, except the distant harbor noises. Then he heard the scraping shuffle of feet, moving slowly along the middle of the building. The eliptical spot of a flashlight swept along the floor beyond the narrow aisle, then disappeared. He thought he heard heavier shoes scraping nearby; then it became deathly still again. He didn't dare try to climb, so he wedged himself halfway up the wall of bales and waited. Unaccountably, Stokes' words came back: "Just make certain . . . war is worth the winning . . ." Again he thought he heard the scrape of heavy shoes and again the watchman called. It was closer now.

"I hear ya, back there! Come on out . . . this ain't no flophouse. Come on out, or I'll call the cops! I'm goin' to phone right now . . . I'm warnin'——"

The sentence was not finished. It ended with a padded thud, a low moan, and the uneven sequence of impacts as a body collapsed to the asphalt.

Again silence, then Hammer's voice. "Awright now, buddy boy . . . that leaves the two of us. I know where ya are now, shit-heel . . . so pretty soon there'll just be one of us . . . worth about eight hundred bucks. That's not bad pay for a few minutes' work . . . is it, wise guy?"

Slim saw the flashlight beam probing again and he knew that Hammer had taken it but was bluffing about the hiding place. The beam traveled along the top of a stack, several aisles from him, and spilled onto the steel rafters high overhead. He knew it was a matter of time before the systematic search revealed his hiding place. He had to climb silently to the top now and stay perfectly still. With every muscle straining to move smoothly, he forced his way up a foot at a time, until his head appeared above the top of the bay formed by the four-foot bales. They were stacked four deep, so he reckoned himself to be sixteen feet above the floor. Hammer continued to betray his location by walking along the center aisle, probing both sides with the beam of light. When he came to the first of the narrow aisles, he ran quickly to it and Slim heard him mumbling to himself. In a moment he hurried to the next one and the next until the beam of light shone into the place Slim had just vacated.

He lay face down atop the dusty bales. They must have been there for months, he thought. The dust choked him and he took the handkerchief from his back pocket and covered his nose and mouth. The stalking seaman kept on moving slowly along the wide aisle. Slim heard him bump into the stack of pallets and curse loudly. He wasn't calling now—just moving relentlessly, searching each aisle of stored cargo as he came to it. Opposite Slim, on the north wall of the building, were stacks of wooden cases. He had seen them briefly, when the watchman's light had fallen on them. Hammer discovered them now and moved closer. Slim watched the light. He couldn't see the man, but started inside when he realized that his assailant was climbing up the stepped front of the stacks. From the top Hammer would be able to see across the building to the top of the bales that sheltered him. Slim worked his way back from the edge until his feet touched the south wall and flattened himself into the mounded tops. He lay there breathing lightly and the dust tickled his throat. As the ray of the light swept toward him, he buried his face and waited. Hammer was slightly lower and the beam would not strike him directly. He waited and listened and felt a moment of panic, as the dust stirred the tingling start of a sneeze. In anguish he pressed his finger hard against the base of his nose. The act short-circuited the nerves that caused the spasm and he waited for a long anxious moment for the sensation to subside.

Meanwhile Hammer had come down from his lookout and had crossed again to Slim's side of the pier shed. He heard the heavy footsteps move slowly along the main aisle that extended to the extreme end of the building. The steps retraced themselves until they were directly below again. Then they stopped. He could hear the man breathing. In a moment the steps resumed the slow, patient cadence of a hunter stalking game. They stopped again—this time at the head of the narrow aisle just below him. Slim held his breath and waited. The steps quickened and entered the aisle and suddenly the beam of the flashlight stabbed straight up, within inches of his face. Then he heard a low, satisfied growl.

Hammer's voice was directed to the top of the stack. "Oh-ho! So that's where you are! Ya left some tracks down here, kid . . . and they don't come back out. All right . . . now that we know where we are . . . let's get this over with. Only you ain't gonna lie on the deck like the nosey old bastard. No, sir . . . you're gonna go splashin' right inta the bay. That's where you're goin' . . . and when ya get there . . . you're goin' ta hell, ya sneaky, doublecrossin' *gentleman!*"

Slim knew the heavy layer of dust had trapped him. If Hammer hadn't taken the light, he could have stayed concealed until daybreak, if necessary. But the light had made it just a matter of time. He'd known it all along. What he hadn't been able to figure out was just what to do, but a decision had to be made quickly now—in the next few seconds—and it had to be the right one. Without the light following him he could have traveled over the tops of the stacks and let himself quietly down to the floor, as soon as Hammer had started to climb. But he gave up the idea immediately. If the man got to the top, he might still get a lead, but, as soon as he jumped to the floor, Hammer would do the same and the whole gut-wracking chase would begin again. If he could, he'd have to find a way to end it now.

The possibilities raced through his brain as he strained to make out Hammer's next move. He could hear the A.B. directly below him. He felt the uneven stack rock slightly as the man's weight pressed against its sides. Hammer's arms and legs were shorter than Slim's and the climb was more difficult for him. As the stack rocked, an idea suddenly struck. It would be a desperate gamble, but it was his best chance . . . his *only* chance! He decided to take it. Quickly his hands felt for the inside edge of the first tier of bales that formed the wall up which Hammer was now trying to climb. He pushed against it cautiously and it rocked. Swinging around quickly, he sat up, faced the narrow alley, dug his heels into the crack between the bales,

437

and heaved with all his strength. He felt it start, then gain momentum. Below in the darkness, Hammer didn't see the two-hundred pound missile until it whished past him and bounced dully on the floor. Slim heard the man's startled yell. He began prying feverishly to topple the others. The second one plummeted down into the narrow space . . . then the third. His muscles blazed in protest. Two more went together and he could hear Hammer's muffled shouts. The man's voice was filled with fear and rage. The big bales had trapped him in the passageway and the trap shut tighter as several more tumbled down on top of him. Leaping across to the adjoining stack, Slim kicked the top bales loose and sent them crashing down atop their mates. As he labored furiously, he barely heard the cries of the man buried now under more than a ton of rough hemp. He was alive and probably not seriously hurt, judging from the sound of his voice.

When the last bale tumbled into the void, Slim stood up. Gasping, dizzy, and sick from the dust, he was unable to move for a moment. He stood panting, trying desperately to catch his breath. His eyes, accustomed to the darkness, could make out the still form of the watchman sprawled against the black floor. He looked down into the narrow bale-filled canyon in which Hammer was trapped. He could see the beam of the flashlight still shining faintly through the angular openings in the helter-skelter heap of confusion. Moving carefully, he climbed down the broken face of the avalanche until his feet touched the paving. He stood quietly and listened. From deep beneath the heaped bales Hammer appealed to him.

"Get me outa here, kid! Come on . . . get me outa here, before I smother. Come on . . . I was only kiddin'. I just wanted to scare ya. I didn't want a dime of your money . . . just a little loan. I don't even need that now . . . so come on . . . get me outa this! My legs are caught——"

Slim walked up on the bales and leaned his face over one of the cracks outlined by the glowing torch.

"Can you hear me, pal?"

The answer came back immediately, eagerly. "Yeah! I hear ya, Slim. Come on . . . start shovin' these things offa me. Be a pal! Come on, kiddo . . . we're all straight now. You won! Get me outta here, and we'll go to that joint on Van Ness Avenue. I'll blow us to the bottle and the dames. Come on . . . start shovin'——" he waited hopefully for the boy to answer.

Slim looked down into the tumbled pile. A smile spread slowly across his face and he began to laugh quietly to himself. He called down to Hammer. "Did you say you wanted me to start shoving, pal?" He gave the last word bitter emphasis.

The trapped man hesitated, then answered quietly. His voice sounded surprisingly close and urgent. "Yeah . . . hurry up, will ya?"

Slim deliberately rocked one of the bales with his foot. "Okay, pal . . . I'll start shoving. I'm shoving off, right now! I think the cops'll be able to get you out of here faster than I can. You can buy *them* a drink . . . and while you're at it, take them up to Van Ness Avenue, too. If you don't, it's going to be a long time before you get laid again! So long, wise guy! Next time louse up your enemies . . . not your friends! Or are you too dumb to know the difference?"

He waited a moment, but the man was quiet. "Did you hear me, Hammer?" He waited again, but still no answer.

Slim turned and stepped down off the bales. Walking to the watchman, he knelt beside the man and felt his pulse. There was none. Slowly he made his way through the dark to the little cubicle. Taking down the receiver from the wall box, he called the operator and asked for the police. He gave a false name to the desk sergeant, directed him to Pier 45, and told him what he'd find. Then he replaced the phone, walked outside to the oil drums, and retrieved his sea bag. Before he reached the Ferry Building he heard the scream of sirens and saw two police cars speed north along the Embarcadero. He heard the switch engine puffing in the distance and the long blast of a ferry pulling out of the slip. Directly ahead the lights of the Ferry Building began to glow brighter through the fog. He heard the edgy squeal of steel wheels and the warning clang, as a Market Street trolley swung around the loop in front of the terminal; in another moment yellow thistles of light glowed through the fog and then he was beneath the familiar arches, headed toward the change booth.

Inside the waiting room he dropped onto one of the long, smooth, slatted benches. His shoulders sagged and he suddenly felt overcome with weariness. He looked at his clothes. He was covered from head to toe with fine brown dust. It was smeared on his jacket—on his arms and on his face—as fine as the gray-green alfalfa dust that had covered him in the barn during haying season. He slipped off the heavy sheepskin jacket and beat it with his hands.

439

Curious people turned to look as the noise intruded upon the sepulchral silence, then returned to their dozing. It would be thirty minutes before the next boat to Berkeley.

In the men's room Slim washed, then dropped a nickel in the pay toilet. In the privacy of the stall he put his boot up and unlaced it. He did the same with the other, then seated himself and slipped them off. From the inside of each he removed the sweat-soaked bills. They bore the imprints of the balls of his feet. He smoothed them quickly and put them in his pants pocket. After a time he came out into the waiting room and walked restlessly around, watching the exhibits. On the wall above the entrance to the boats, an animated picture machine presented advertisements. He watched it for a while, then thought about coffee, but the shop was outside the waiting area and he'd have to sacrifice his fare. He decided to wait until he got on the boat. Then he remembered he'd forgotten to call home. That would have to wait now, until he got to Oakland Terminal.

He heard the arriving boat press its rounded bow against the planked pilings and he heard the short whistle and the rattle of the chain over the ratchets, as the gangplank was lowered. He heard the drum of many feet outside the waiting room . . . and in another moment an attendant rolled open the huge door and the little knot of late commuters, hurrying from habit, made their way along the corridor that led to the lower level.

Once aboard, Slim went topside and ordered coffee and a doughnut. He was famished and the woman who ran the concession looked at him curiously as he wolfed the first one and ordered another. Brushing the powdered sugar from his hands, he walked forward, slid the sticking door open, and let himself out on the open upper deck. He could see nothing but the wall of glowing fog. Here and there a formless light passed behind the thick veil and from out on the bay an incoming Key Route ferry blew noisily. In another moment the whistle above his head released its ear-splitting blast and he felt the hull shudder and heard the railings and windows vibrate, as the giant side wheels began to turn. He heard the churning rush of the water foaming against the sides of the slip. The force increased and the vessel began to move. Clear of the slip, it poked its way cautiously out into the night. Slim bundled himself against the sudden damp breeze. After a few minutes, in which he tried vainly to force his mind to think clearly, he turned his back to the wind and lit a cigarette. Walking to one of the sheltered side benches, he sat down and stared blankly out into the night. Another S.P. ferry loomed, eerie and white, as it passed close to port. Lights ablaze along its double decks, it looked like a ghostly palace recently emptied of its revelers. Slim marveled at the skill of those captains who so competently guided their unwieldy craft across the fog-enshrouded bay. To strangers who worried about the crossing, he was always ready to repeat the story that these legendary boats were the world's safest transportation.

Slim didn't know what made him look up. Perhaps he caught its gleam in the corner of his eye . . . but there it was: through a ragged rent in the low blanket of fog, he saw Polaris; diagonally down from it he found the two pointer stars and, in the middle of the handle, Mizar. The fog was breaking as it often did, running halfway across the water; thinning, then dissipating itself against the invisible barrier of air that protected the east bay.

He watched the stars until suddenly they were blacked out by the dark shape of Yerba Buena Island. Once past, they were there again—more of them now—glistening like random diamonds flung high into a void. And then, through the rising curtain, he saw the dull gleam of lights strung along the shore from Oakland on the right to El Cerrito and beyond on the left. In another moment the lights gleamed higher along the skirt of the hills and then, suddenly, the veil was lifted and the dazzling lights of tens of thousands of homes shone glitter-bright against the deep black backdrop of hills which themselves stood in bold relief against the translucent blue-black of the night.

Slim rose and walked to the guard chain, blocking the fore part of the upper deck. Looking back over his shoulder, he could see the captain and mate in the ornate pilothouse, dimly silhouetted in the soft glow of the compass light. The sight sent a curious pang of loneliness through him for that other wheelhouse. Ten more minutes and he'd be climbing aboard the high red electric trains with their diamond trolleys pressing overhead against the humming copper wires. He could almost see the shower and hear the crackle of electric blue sparks as the rollers crossed intersecting wires, and he could hear again the hiss of air brakes and the conductor's mannered call: "Fourteen' Street . . . Fourteen' Street . . . this way out, please!" There would be other stops, then University Avenue . . . Arlington Circle; next the long stairs up to the fountain . . . the winding drive in the family Chrysler

. . . the sharp turn into the garage . . . the short steps to the porch shelter . . . the big oak door and home.

All this would happen within the next half hour. Slim leaned on the rail and the sulphurous odor of the tidal flats assailed his nose; then a change of wind sweetened the air and he could smell the scent of blossoms and the faint pungence of pine. The look . . . the feel . . . the smell of home . . . and suddenly the last year fell away and he was on his way back again, after another evening in San Francisco. He could feel the tug of familiar emotions: the restlessness . . . the uncertainty . . . the gnawing fear of facing up to his own desires . . . the obligation to listen . . . the old discouragement with school . . . the old friends walking and talking in the same old patterns . . . the same look . . . the same feel . . . the same smell.

He looked around again. Nothing had changed, but even as he struggled against the unwanted tide of recollection he knew that something had changed—nothing he could see, nothing he could smell; but he could feel it, inside. And then the past year came back: the *Tropic Trader* . . . the men and the ports . . . Edye . . . Marge . . . letters . . . Warndahl . . . Chips . . . Peterson . . . Holst . . . Hammer. Suddenly he wondered about Hammer and a mirthless chuckle rose behind clamped jaws. Then he wondered again about home and about his mother and father and brother. They would be leaving the house the moment he phoned . . . to drive down and park in the circular space beside the fountain. His father would look at his gold "railroad watch" and, at precisely the right moment, they would get out of the car and walk down the steep flight of stairs to the mouth of the tunnel; there the train would disappear with a shrill hoot of its air whistle and the rising whine of its electric drivers, after releasing its scattered passengers. His mother would hug him, then say, "My goodness, honey . . . it's wonderful to have you back . . . but what made you so late?" His father would hug him, too, and the stiff bristles of his whiskers would make a pleasant scratch on his face. His greeting would be, "Welcome home, big boy! We thought for a while you'd shipped out again!" His brother would wear an embarrassed smile, hitch at the belt of the fashionably soiled corduroys that seemed always about to slip below his skinny rump, and say, "Hi—— "And Slim knew what he'd say, too. There would be no need to practice the words . . . either words of greeting . . . words of explanation for being late . . . or the words of the interrupted narrative that would follow episodically, coinciding with mealtime and with the two hours of after-dinner leisure. Then his mother would pull her shawl closer, give the dog an annoyed order to move from the hearth and, lifting aside the brass firescreen, would poke another five minutes' worth of heat from the dying embers.

As his eyes searched along the diagonal line of lights that marked Arlington Avenue and followed them up topmost the hill to the cluster of bright pinpoints, one of which was his house, he knew that nothing had changed for them. They were a year older, perhaps a year grayer . . . and a year closer to the end of their dreams. In spite of the letters he knew they would be the same . . . but *he* was not! For the first time in his life he could stand aside and look at them and at himself. For the first time in his life, Slim saw them not in conscious conspiracy, but as individuals following habit patterns of their own choosing —confident, at first, and later afraid and unable to free themselves from the deep rut of their own grinding. He saw them harboring a secret hope that their boys, beginning to trace a new periphery, would expand the concentric circle of family experience and one day help them up out of their rut to view the enlarged domain and receive the well-earned rewards of their "unselfish nobility."

He could hear his mother's voice, a mixture of pride and self-pity, saying, "Your father and I may not have accomplished all we wished for ourselves, but we never stinted when it came to giving you boys a better chance." He could see her assured smile and the envisaging eyes that seemed to look beyond the two of them to the fading outline of some earlier dream, and he could hear her quietly add, "Your father and I know that both you boys are going to make us proud of you!"

Slim found himself wondering and worrying, too, that into at least one of the receptacles of family tradition and culture, perhaps, would be poured an alien admixture which would appear to increase its fullness, but would not blend with the rest. He felt through his jacket at the bright new tattoo on his right shoulder. No badge of pride, this! He thought of the rooming house on Van Ness Avenue and again he could hear his mother's voice: "If a boy of mine ever had anything to do with a girl like that, I'd disown him!" These were no conjured words. He'd heard them many times in recent years . . . and they had carried with them an increasing burden of guilt. He thought of Marge and the boy who went to her willing arms . . .

and the man who so unwillingly left them. For a while he thought of Edye, and then the stars disappeared and the edge of the great black-roofed pier shed slid over his head and the boat back-paddled a roaring maelstrom. Then the gentle bump, the tortured creaking, the rattling chains . . . and the waiting trains.

Slim was home.

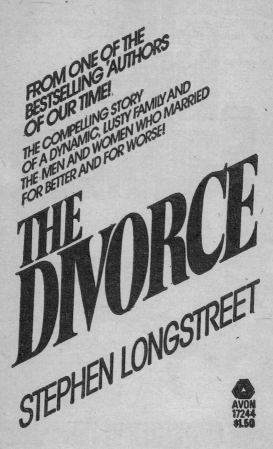

The Eiger Sanction

AVON
15404
$1.75

THE BESTSELLER BY TREVANIAN

THE BIG BESTSELLERS
ARE AVON BOOKS!

I'm OK—You're OK
  Thomas A. Harris, M.D.   14662 $1.95

Jonathan Livingston Seagull
  Richard Bach   14316 $1.50

Open Marriage
  George and Nena O'Neill   14084 $1.95

You & I
  Leonard Nimoy   17615 $1.50

Maria
  Maria Von Trapp   17921 $1.50

The Divorce
  Stephen Longstreet   17244 $1.50

Nothing By Chance
  Richard Bach   14704 $1.50

California
  Leland Frederick Cooley   15941 $1.75

Memo from David O. Selznick
  Rudy Behlmer   15412 $1.95

The Eiger Sanction
  Trevanian   15404 $1.75

The Brothers System for Liberated
Love and Marriage
  Dr. Joyce Brothers   15834 $1.50

Island Paradise
  P. R. Pickney   15388 $1.50

I Come as a Thief
  Louis Auchincloss   15438 $1.50

Where better paperbacks are sold, or directly from the publisher, include 15¢ per copy for mailing; allow three weeks for delivery.

Avon Books, Mail Order Dept.
250 West 55th Street, New York, N. Y. 10019